THE THUNDERBIRD CONSPIRACY
OSWALD'S FRIEND ROBERT KAYE

R. K. Price

Based on Actual Events

Quiet Owl Books

The Thunderbird Conspiracy
Oswald's Friend Robert Kaye

Cover Design by Jennifer Welker

Set in 11-point Garamond Pro

ISBN-13: 978-0615658353
ISBN-10: 0615658350

Published by Quiet Owl Books

Quiet Owl Books
P.O. Box 58
Montrose, PA 18001
www.quietowl.com

Printed in the United States of America

Quiet Owl Books are available for bulk purchases in the US at special discounts. For more information please contact the Special Markets Department at sales@quietowl.com.

Preface

W.H. "Bud" Carlson was a fine man, handsome, clever and enormously funny. He was always the life of the party. A happy-go-lucky kind of guy. Sensitive and caring. But unknown to most Bud carried a heavy burden, a painful episode that may have contributed to his early, untimely death at age forty-seven. Yet there was joy in Bud's life. His daughters. His ranch outside of Denver, which became a refuge from his many fears and sorrows. Bud was a romantic. Tales of the Old West were his favorites. Yet when it came to the hard knocks of life he was a rigid pragmatist.

There was no flimflam with Bud Carlson. He hated liars. Regardless of how painful it was the truth was paramount. That's why when he shed the burden he carried for many years and told me the fascinating story of Robert Kaye, a Hungarian immigrant who claimed he knew, and allegedly collaborated with the Kennedy assassin Lee Harvey Oswald, I had no reason to doubt even a word.

Bud befriended this mysterious enigma of a man and in doing so became entangled in the most notorious crime of the 20th century. Bud's account of Kaye, who portrayed himself as a freedom fighter wounded in the great Hungarian uprising against the Soviets in 1956, was revealed to me on a wintry Colorado day about three weeks before Bud's ravaged heart gave out on him. Yet I did nothing about it. I stashed the story away in a reporter's notebook letting it lay dormant in a folder for nearly forty years.

Bud knew he was dying when he finally spoke to me. He had kept his secret locked up inside all that time. Bud was a patriot and an avid admirer of President Kennedy. He desperately wanted to believe his government's hurried conclusion that Oswald had no accomplice. For a long time I had the same conviction. But no more.

Bud's harrowing experience at the hands of U.S. law enforcement brought on by this phantom created profound doubt in his mind, and it haunted Bud to his death. He chose me to be the one to hear it all. Though honored, I carry Bud's heavy burden. I regret to have waited so long to retell it. In his weakened state, it took Bud an entire day to tell me all he knew. It was one of his final days. In the end he was exhausted, yet free, and he said, "Do with this what you will."

Okay, Bud, I will do my best. Here is more fact than fiction.

To Bud's Memory

Part I

Grand Island, Nebraska
February 1940

1

Bud Carlson, son of Henry and Vera, brother of Dorothy and Genevieve, was driving far too fast. Riding in the front seat of his new 1940 Ford coupe which Bud's father bought for him for his seventeenth birthday, was Norman "Scooter" Barnes, his best friend. Bud was pushing sixty-five miles an hour. It was as fast as the coupe could go. He had buried the speedometer out of sight. Bud shrieked with delight.

Scooter had scored two pints of corn liquor from the Taylor brothers, Randy and Ronnie, whose farm was about three miles from the Carlson spread, which was about five miles east of Aurora, Nebraska. In two or three swallows Bud and Scooter had gulped down a pint each, and the one hundred and twenty proof moonshine, distilled with precision in a remote corner of the Taylor's twelve hundred acre plot of hard, dry, western Cornhusker land, hit their guts with the force of a sledgehammer.

Both the driver's side and passenger windows of the coupe were rolled down, and the cold, biting February wind blasted through the cockpit to rustle Bud's long, wavy black hair and redden his cheeks. His eyes watered from the force of the frigid gale. Scooter had his head out the passenger's side window, catching the full rush. He began to scream in mimicking harmony with his friend.

Suddenly their shouts of joy turned to terrifying cries of anguish as two plains antelope, a horned male and his mate, darted from the shadows in front of the careening coupe as it barely maneuvered around a tight corner on the loose gravel country road. Bud jerked the wheel to the left, but the panicked animals unexpectedly lurched and leaped simultaneously in the same direction.

Bud spun the wheel hard to the right. He cleared the doe, which had jumped higher and farther than her mate, but caught the buck at midsection. The impact slung the male's big body skyward, slamming it into and partially through the car's windshield. The coupe lifted on two wheels as Bud fought for control. The animal's deeply cut, bloody rump pierced through the fissure in the broken glass. Its normally stubby white tail was twitching and stained red. Bud could not see. Warm liquid rushed down his forehead to temporarily blind him. The buck, acting only on nerve impulses, convulsed grotesquely with all four legs flailing to escape the razor sharp glass hole that trapped it. The vehicle veered again to the left and started to roll.

First, Bud's birthday present went side over side until it reached the ditch to the left and then the coupe was airborne completing one and a half end over end flips before landing on its roof crushing it so thoroughly as to leave a space even with the lower window casings. Neither of its human passengers had remained inside the vehicle to ride out the acrobatic spectacle.

As the car spun and flipped Scooter flew to the right through the open window, landing on his back thirty feet away from the wheels up Ford now resting on the bare, frozen wheat field. Bud was ejected to the left as the car made its last side over side rotation. He too landed on his back, but before he rested, the back of his head came down first and at a bad angle to catch the upslope of a tiny trench in the uneven plowed field, which had the consistency of hardened cement. His awkward landing snapped his number three and four cervical vertebrae, instantly paralyzing him as his bruised spinal cord went into spasm. Meanwhile the creature, quiet and missing one horn, had replaced the two boys in the front seat of the demolished vehicle. Its eyes were glassy in death.

Nancy and Tom Clark were on their way home from a square dance in Grand Island and witnessed the spectacular crash. Bud had sped past their lumbering along Dodge pickup truck on a straightaway about a quarter of a mile before he had lost control. Their fortuitous presence near the scene would spare the lives of both teenagers.

Tom shifted the old Dodge into second gear and rammed his foot to the floorboard when he saw the coupe's headlights flash their beams toward the night sky. They sped toward the scene. As they approached Nancy gasped at the sight of the careening car, and in disbelief, screamed, "Oh, my God." The rickety truck slid to a stop in the middle of the road. Tom leapt from the cab and ran into the darkened field. He found Scooter first. The boy lay on his back in a torn T-shirt and soiled long johns. He reeked of alcohol and his own waste. At some point in the bedlam Scooter had lost his trousers, shoes and his bowels. His bloodied head lay motionless, but his arms and legs moved freely as if he were carving a snow angel in the dirt. Then he began to laugh hysterically. His face and neck were streaked with blood. Tom used his handkerchief to wipe Scooter's skin in search of cuts. He found none, and guessed the blood was that of the dead animal's. After a brief examination, it appeared to Tom that Scooter was not hurt badly probably because he was too drunk to realize the predicament he was in. Tom let him lay and laugh, afraid to move him for fear of unseen injuries. Considering how few people travel along this road at this time of night, Tom was sure if he hadn't found the lad he could have laid there and frozen to death. Tom knew there were two people in the car when it sped around him a few minutes before the crash. By the time Tom left Scooter to search for the other boy, Nancy had swung the pick up truck around in the road and was gunning its ancient engine as hard as she could back toward Aurora to beckon help.

Before running into the darkness, Tom had had the presence of mind to retrieve a flashlight out from under the seat of his truck. Tom scanned the pitch-black field with the sharp beam of his flashlight. He moved away from Scooter sweeping in an arc to cover as much ground as quickly as he could. After what seemed like an eternity but in less than five minutes Tom found Bud about thirty yards away from where Scooter laid and could now be heard crying. He shined his flashlight in Bud's face. Bud's eyes were open and he lay stone still, not moving, not sensing the bitter cold around him or anything else. Tom knelt beside him. Bud's eyes blinked and he gazed into Tom's face. In a daze he did not speak. Trying to bring comfort Tom said to him, "We've gone for help."

Tom removed his heavy winter coat and covered Bud's upper torso. He remained there for a few minutes before pulling it off Bud to begin his quick shuttle between the two boys using his coat to bring warmth to each. He waited and prayed for Nancy's success and quick return. Nearly an hour later, help arrived. By then, Toms' bare fingers were numb and red with on-setting frostbite.

Before they placed Bud in the ambulance the attendant had instructed Tom to grasp either side of the boy's head and hold it tightly just in case he might have suffered a neck injury. Tom held Bud's head in his hands for the long, washboard bumpy ride to the hospital, later being told by a nurse that he probably kept Bud out of a wheel chair for the rest of his life. At the hospital x-rays confirmed the neck fractures and spinal cord swelling. Heavy sedatives kept the teenager from tremors and traveling bone shards, which might have severed the spinal cord to kill him instantly.

The doctors at Grand Island Memorial Hospital had little experience in dealing with fractured necks, so they called in an orthopedic surgeon from Lincoln to fuse the cracked bones in a fashion to allow Bud's deeply bruised spinal cord to heal. Driving as fast as he could across the Nebraska tundra, it still took the surgeon several hours to arrive. In the meantime Bud lay unconscious on a gurney, neck stabilized, inexperienced doctors wary of moving him, awaiting the surgeon's arrival.

Less than twenty-four hours after the moonshine, antelopes and tumbling Ford, Bud was patched back together, rigid in forty pounds of white plaster, extremely fortunate to have survived, and beginning to feel a tingle in his toes. Bud was in the hospital for four months; three of which sheathed in a body cast that extended from his pelvis to the base of his skull, around his jaw line and under his chin. A metal rod was implanted in the plaster from beneath his chin to the top of his sternum region to assure his head and neck did not move.

Scooter suffered a broken pinky finger on his left hand and a huge black and midnight blue bruise that covered both cheeks of his butt. Scooter's worst injury from the crash was the roaring two-day hangover. He visited Bud on the third day of his extended confinement and tried to make him laugh, but all Bud could do was roll his eyes and attempt cracking a smile.

Continuing their lavish attention on the boy who could do no wrong in their eyes, his mother and sisters wailed at his bedside for nearly a week, taking turns feeding him, reading to him, rubbing his feet, massaging his legs and arms; anything they could do to make their baby son and brother feel more comfortable during his ordeal. Henry, on the other hand, stood back and grumbled, waiting for the chance to remind his son of the consequences of irresponsible behavior. Silently, he thanked the Lord for sparing his son's life, but as any good father would he would not forgive the transgression without some form of punishment. At one point, thinking he was out of earshot of Vera, Henry said to Bud, "If I have anything to say about it, the only thing you'll be driving anytime soon will be the tractor."

With his jaw clamped shut by the cast around his chin Bud couldn't offer a protest, but Vera did, saying, "Henry, shame on you. How could you scold this boy in his present state? You should do nothing but kneel in prayer to God for giving him back to us."

To that Bud managed a genuine smile

Uncle Bud after the car crash.

2

The Carlson children were an exact fifty-fifty purebred mix of Swedish and French. They were also Methodists. Devout and devoted, so at least Vera thought. She contributed the French lineage tracing her family back to the southern regions of France and a great, great grandfather who joined the legion of ambitious, thrill seeking recruits of the legendary Marquis de Lafayette to fight the British alongside the colonists in the American Revolution. A "proud heritage for sure" was Vera's fond description. After victory at Yorktown, Vera would boast, a young and dashing Henri de Scoville charmed the beautiful daughter of a colonist, married her and settled in the Catskill Mountains region of New York. Soon thereafter, along came their first born son, Amasa, who just like his father, hated the Tory invaders and went off to fight in the War of 1812 serving under Old Hickory himself, Andrew Jackson. Amasa's son, Daniel, Vera's beloved pappy, left the homestead at a young age, found himself a bride by the name of Julia and settled in Illinois. Not long thereafter the Civil War broke out. Daniel joined the Union forces, was eventually placed under the command of Ulysses S. Grant, and fought with him in nearly every battle along the southern tier from Vicksburg to Shiloh and from Fort Donelson all the way to Appomattox.

After General Lee's surrender Daniel went home, packed up his wife and sons and headed west to Nebraska. There he took his Army pension and his land grant plot of bone-dry soil. He toiled rather unsuccessfully as a farmer, became the local sheriff, a lawyer, then a representative of his precinct in the new Nebraska State Legislature. Daniel tragically died of pneumonia when Vera, his youngest, was only nine.

Henry liked to be called Hank. He was third generation Swedish. His father simplified the spelling of the family surname adopting Carlson rather than one of the other many variations such as Carlssen, Karlsoon, or Carllsseen. Legend had it that some families misdirected their line of ancestry with confusing surname spellings to confound the authorities that were chasing them across the globe for infractions committed on an international scale. Hank's father was a simple man. He wanted a simple name. He would take his chances if someone was looking for him.

The Carlsons were outstanding farmers. Central Nebraska's harsh, God forsaken, wind swept plain proved arid and lacked natural nutritional quality dirt. Despite those obstacles, Hank could seemingly irrigate and fertilize a field with a couple of gallons of water, and a shovel full of manure. His reputation preceded him and his neighbors would jealously extol his virtues, claiming he could grow "damn near anything he put his mind to." Didn't matter what. Wheat, corn, soybeans, alfalfa, even radishes, carrots, and onions. Some people thought if old Hank had wanted to grow pistachio trees in his back yard in the middle of winter, he could.

So when Hank's daddy died when he was twenty-three, Hank came to preside over the twenty-four hundred acre Carlson agricultural empire. At its peak, two years after he married Vera and Genevieve was six months old, Hank had fifteen full time farm hands, ten gas engine tractors, three combines, two hay bailers and thirty-seven pigs, not to mention a two acre vegetable garden and twenty-two Jersey milk cows.

Hank was tall and lean. His face was angular and prematurely wrinkled. A wisp of grey hair was all he could display by the time he reached thirty. In contrast Vera was short and stout. Strong as a bull just like Hank, but she was hefty as the farmhands used to say behind her back, especially after she had Bud. The Carlson farm prosperity during the 1920s did not come easy. It was backbreaking work. The summers were scorchers; the winters capable of creating icebergs, and in between, there were about three weeks of cool, balmy days and clear starry nights. Despite it all Hank produced bumper crop after bumper crop and banked away the profits for an infrequent rainy day.

Then came the end of the 20s and the beginning of the 1930s and so much like the vast majority of America's family farmers at the time, the Carlson place began its decline. Hank was one of the first in the Aurora and Grand Island farming community to notice that the weather had changed. Less rain. More dry, hot days and windy nights. Colder temperatures. It was even colder than the typical piercing blasts of January through March. The soil was more difficult to plow and clumped together in bigger clods that were harder to separate, moisten and fertilize. One planting season while cutting a row in his corn silage field he broke the blade on a new plow. At first he blamed a field hand for failing to tighten the bolts but then he discovered the ground had simply refused to give way, instead surfacing a rock the size of a basketball to produce an unbreakable obstacle.

The harvest of 1931 produced break-even returns on the Carlson investment. A year later, they lost ten thousand dollars. By 1933, the losses rose to twenty-five thousand, and the next year they topped a total loss of fifty thousand dollars. At that point Hank was broke. Always protective, he told no one, particularly Vera. Except for two skilled machine operators who doubled as mechanics Hank by then had lain off his entire crew.

He sold off, at a loss against his note to the bank, all but two tractors, one combine, and a hay bailer. He kept the pigs and milk cows to provide protein for his family but traded two of his prized, quick as lightning quarter horses, for two dozen chickens and a mean as hell red rooster. He built a hen house and painted it red like the rooster and hunkered down to weather the economic storm.

By the time Hank had run through his literal nest egg his daughters were in their early twenties and the Great Depression was winding down as the war years loomed on the horizon. Genevieve and Dorothy began to dream about their futures away from the farm. Hank couldn't blame them and Vera encouraged their goals apart from the business of agriculture. While still in high school Genevieve found a job at the bus depot in Grand Island. She joined the Greyhound Bus Company after graduation so she could travel far and wide free of charge on their luxury over the road diesel powered liners. Every vacation that came about found her on the first bus out of town.

Her sister Dorothy wanted to be a nurse. She was a whiz kid in math and science, particularly biology and even during her middle school years she yearned to wear the nurses' cloaks and caps and white rubber soled shoes. She was a healer who brought her mother warm broth when she was sick and in bed, which was often. At the age of thirty-seven Vera was diagnosed with an acute form of Type One diabetes. Vera was a demanding patient when she confined herself to her upstairs bedroom, so Dorothy learned quickly how to handle tough cases. Vera also hated needles but she needed twice daily doses of insulin to regulate her wildly fluctuating blood sugar levels, so injecting her mother before and after school also became one of Dorothy's duties. She loved it and felt important carrying out her tasks with precision and compassion. Dorothy also kept a well stocked first aid kit in her bedroom ready and willing to patch up cuts, pad blisters, pluck splinters and sling up sprained arms and wrists of the short hand, overworked field crew and members of her family. Her high school grades were so good that she had little trouble gaining admission and a partial scholarship to the nursing school at Creighton University in Omaha.

Bud was a different story. He was the baby of the family and being so, he soon realized as early as the age of six or seven that his needs could be met by simple yet obstinate demands of those around him. His strategy worked most of the time. If it didn't, tantrums were in order when all else failed. He wanted no part of the life of a farmer. For one thing he despised getting dirty. His only concession to that personal edict was his unending war games carried out on the floor of the main house living room involving his huge collection of hard carved wooden toy soldiers which had been passed down to him through generations of military enthusiasts on his mother's side of the family.

For the most part Hank left Bud alone to his games. Occasionally, just to indoctrinate the child to the hard realities of life, Hank would bring his son, generally kicking and screaming, into the fields with him, placing the boy in his lap for a ride on his John Deere. Often it wasn't worth the effort and soon Hank would head back to the house with Bud under his arm squirming and whining all the way until he was released to run back inside to return to his play. Hank got little support from his wife on the matter of Bud's rebellion against life on the farm. She too saw her son escaping the oppression she often felt as she stared out her kitchen window at the vast, desolate countryside longing only for their next trip to Lincoln or Omaha and a night in a hotel with Egyptian cotton sheets and soft feather pillows on which to lay her head.

After Bud's hospital confinement he was gingerly transported to his upstairs bedroom, made over as a crude but functional hospital suite. He spent another two months there before the doctors began to cut away at the cast that encased him. At month seven all that remained was a steel strapped reinforced rubber padded neck collar, which immobilized his healing upper vertebrae preventing even the slightest movement of his neck in any direction.

Bud missed his senior high school prom and had to receive his diploma directly from Charles Cameron, the Aurora High School principal, at a ceremony in the Carlson living room. Bud was propped up in his father's favorite easy chair to take his certificate. Bud felt terribly sorry for himself missing what he often described as "the best year of my life," and more often than not he made life miserable for the ones who cared for him most. Both Genevieve and Dorothy had rushed home when informed of his accident to help care for him fearing their mother might not be capable if she was brought down by an insulin imbalance. Yet no matter how hard they all tried to make things better for Bud nothing was right. It was either too hot or too cold in his room. His food never tasted right. The bed was too hard or too soft. No one came to see him, but when they did he was mean and surly.

He lost twenty pounds while convalescing; weight that he never seemed to gain back and hold for very long. His nearly six-foot frame was slender at best and rail thin at worst from that point on. He was frail, susceptible to colds and flu which he irritated with a heavy smoking habit that he picked up while languishing away the hours in his makeshift second floor infirmary. He read every Zane Grey novel published at the time, loving each Wild West yarn spun by the grand master cowboy storyteller. Bud wanted to own his own ranch someday running plenty of cattle and breeding plentiful palominos. He just had to figure out how to have someone else do the work.

Slowly he healed both in mind and body. In the late summer of that year he was able to venture out on his own, his neck still in its brace, yet capable of walking without help. His strength began to return and his attitude began to change. He had finally realized how fortunate he was to be alive and that he had been given a chance to make something of himself even though he knew, and so did Hank, that whatever it was, it wouldn't involve farming.

Bud's first real job was as a daytime soda jerk at Monte Jessup's Drug Store in Grand Island. It was the perfect job for him at the time. The work was easy, pouring Cokes, making sundaes and malts and milk shakes. He didn't have to move around too fast, and he could keep from turning his head from side to side most of the time. His neck still hurt when he would turn too fast. He kept his neck brace handy and wasn't ashamed to put it back on when the pain got too great. He began to enjoy his customers. Scooter came by every day after work at this job as a clerk in Johnson's Feed Store. He always ordered a cup of coffee and a bowl of strawberry ice cream and never failed to try to coax Bud for a night out on the town.

Bud repeatedly declined Scooter's offer. For the time being he was content with working a normal eight-hour shift from ten in the morning until six at night. Vera drove him to work in Hank's pickup truck and picked him up each evening. They were usually home by six-thirty. After dinner Bud would read and listen to the radio until he went to bed around ten. This humdrum routine continued day after day, week after week until December came and went and 1941 began. Genevieve returned to her job with Greyhound, taking a post at the bus depot in Salt Lake City and Dorothy returned to begin her second year of nurse's training in Omaha.

Gradually Bud started to mature as well. He discovered new, simple pleasures like tableside conversations with his parents. He took joy in reading his books and laughing at Jack Benny on the radio. He even began to help around the house with light chores for his mother. She couldn't believe her ears the first time he offered to help her with the supper dishes. Then life again tumbled for Bud, just like his prized birthday gift did on that frozen night.

It happened the moment Connie Blakely walked into the drug store one brisk, blustery March afternoon to buy a tube of bright red lipstick and relax with a cup of hot chocolate at Bud's soda fountain. The lipstick was intended to match or at least accentuate her fiery shoulder length red hair.

Connie was the only child of James and Charlotte Blakely, natives of Kearney, which is about forty miles southwest of Grand Island. Bud later discovered that the Blakely family had moved to town after James opened a branch office of the law firm of Thomas, Dixon, and Davis at which he was a senior partner. James Blakely was what was known as a water lawyer. Water was precious in Nebraska and the rights to use it were in constant dispute, which made those who made their livings litigating those disagreements very happy and often very rich.

It was no coincidence that James Blakely, esteemed barrister of TD&D, uprooted his wife and daughter out of their lifelong mini estate on the best avenue Kearney had to offer to take up residence in nearby, less than fashionable Grand Island.

It so happens that five largest farms in Grand Island, excluding the Carlson's, were about to declare war on each other over an eighty-year-old irrigation rights contract executed a generation ago by their respective ancestors. Each family head now claimed the other coerced their forefather into signing the contract. The matter came down to inches. That is inches in the depth of the water flowing in the irrigation trenches that snaked their way through the fields at any particular time on any particular day.

All sides wanted more inches and each alleged the other side was stealing their inches absent right or payment. Two coalitions among the five families were formed to oppose the others. When James came to town, three families had ganged up on two, and all had pooled their money to fight for their respective causes. James gleefully placed himself and his courtroom expertise square in the middle of the warring factions. Both sides approached him for representation. After he weighed the evidence and the heft of their retainer checks he chose the family alliance of two and buried himself in the case in preparation for trial set for December 1941.

Hank knew each of the litigants like he knew the sound of his chugging John Deere. Luckily he was able to stay out of the fray because the Carlson land's water supply was wrapped tightly in a rock solid contract for a portion of the County's stream rights to a tributary off the North Platte River. Hank's daddy had deftly negotiated the agreement some forty years prior.

So, the lovely Connie Blakely strolled into Jessup's Drug, shimmied herself up on one of Bud's stools and promptly stole the soda jerk's heart. The first thing she did was apply her new shade of lipstick and dab the excess by seductively kissing the napkin Bud had given her when she was seated and had ordered her steaming sweet brown drink. Bud, working at the other end of the counter, tried not to watch her actions but couldn't help it, and overfilled Scooter's coffee cup, creating a puddle big enough to drip onto Scooter's new dungarees. He had replaced the soiled ones lost from the accident.

"Damn it Bud. Look what you did," Scooter exclaimed before spinning his head to see what Bud was painfully straining his stiff neck to glimpse.

"My God," Scooter said just loud enough for Connie to hear, "that's the most gorgeous thing I ever seen in this town, or anywhere for that matter."

Connie coyly pretended not to hear him, having practiced her shrouded ignorance of the countless accolades, which came her way from the young and sometimes old male population. Her ability to hide behind a veil of modesty came largely from her mother's stern instructions on how to handle the whistles and catcalls that cascaded around her nearly everywhere she went.

While wiping up the spilled coffee Bud fired back at Scooter in a disgusted whisper, "Keep your voice down you fool. She can probably hear you."

"Who cares, man? She's a goddamn knockout," was Scooter's response, but this time most assuredly loud enough so it was impossible for her to ignore.

She did, or at least appeared to pay no heed by turning away and grinning at the jar of jawbreakers placed next to her.

Bud left his friend with a soaked bar rag in his hand and walked to the sink to rinse it out. Two noisy grade school kids came in just about that time and ordered a banana split to share. As a result Bud's intention to see if Connie needed a refill was diverted while he fixed up the gooey concoction for the boisterous pair. By the time he was done, she was gone.

Crestfallen, he ambled over to her place at the counter to retrieve the cup and saucer and when he got there, he noticed the napkin tucked under her empty cup. The perfect bright red imprint of her lips jumped off the white paper cloth. He picked it up, resigned to toss it in the trash but then he saw the handwriting running at an angle across the bottom corner. It read:

Tell your friend he doesn't impress me. I like the quiet type. Loved your hot chocolate. See you soon, Connie.

Bud smiled broadly. He felt a warm rush rise up his relentlessly sore, tender neck. He folded and placed the napkin in his pocket and picked up her twenty-five cent tip.

Connie returned to Bud's counter three more times before he got up the nerve to ask her for a date. After she accepted he panicked. He hadn't driven since the crash and even if he decided to, all he had to drive was Hank's old pickup truck. His father's 1938 Cadillac sedan was in the shop with a blown clutch. It had been there about six weeks. Hank had said at dinner a night or two before Connie's acceptance that he expected to have the money to pay for the parts and labor to have it fixed in about another two weeks. Things were still very tight around the Carlson household so there was no chance that the Cadillac would be ready for the Friday night affair. The Cadillac was the only acceptable vehicle with which to squire a lady of Connie's stature around the Nebraska countrywide. Hank's pickup was out of the question.

On the Wednesday before their first official date Bud was betting it would be their last. Scooter's ancient clunker, a 1931 Chevrolet, was unavailable. He claimed to have "a hot one on the hook" for Friday night. He and Amy Goodnight were heading for a dance over at the pavilion in North Platte and there was no possible way that anyone, even his best friend, would threaten "a sure thing with Amy."

Certainly, Bud's expectations were not that high. Not even close. All he was planning was a movie at the Grand Theatre in Grand Island. It was playing *Adam Had Four Sons*, starring Ingrid Bergman. Bergman was Bud's all-time favorite actress.

Near the end of a truly miserable shift that Wednesday (his neck hurt and his anxiety grew hour by hour over his lack of Friday night transportation) Bud was doing his best to avoid complete despondency. Scooter, however, was unremittingly rubbing it in on how he should take a few lessons from his friend on "scoring" when Connie happened to stroll in. She didn't come straight to the counter; instead diverting her path to the cosmetics section apparently in search of more beauty items. As he watched her disappear behind the shelves, Bud had three immediate thoughts. The first was to tell Scooter to get the hell out of there, which he did and Scooter scampered away on command. The second thought was that she didn't need makeup to make her more beautiful, and the third; he concluded Friday night was going to be a disaster.

He was washing glasses in his pall of gloom when a few minutes later he heard, "What's wrong with you? You look so sad. Are you sick?"

Connie was seated on her favorite stool. Her elbows were on the counter leaning forward to catch his response. He rose from the sink too quickly, somewhat startled by the sound of her voice. In the same motion he turned his head and the pain nearly knocked him to his knees. He tried to hide his grimace. He didn't do a very good job.

"Are you all right?" she asked in a tone of genuine concern.

He instinctively grasped his neck and strained to say, "I'm okay. Just a little sore today. That's all."

"You look terrible. Should I get my own hot chocolate?"

"No, no. I'm okay. Really," he said, the pain beginning to subside somewhat.

"Don't try to be such a he-man. Put your neck brace on if it makes you more comfortable," she instructed.

Bud ignored her directive, poured her hot chocolate, and placed it in front of her.

"I'm glad you came in. I was hoping to see you before Friday night," he said.

"What's the matter? Are you backing out?" she asked, becoming more indignant with each word.

"No! Are you kidding? I wouldn't miss it for the world. It's just that I don't have a car. I can't tell you how embarrassed I am to say that. But I don't; I mean, have a car. I haven't driven since I wrecked mine. Scooter won't lend me his and I won't even mention the only other alternative I have," he said.

"What's that; the other alternative?"

"My Dad's pickup truck," he responded sheepishly.

"Oh. Look Bud. I wouldn't care if you picked me up on a mule. You and I are going out together Friday night. We're going to see that movie at the Grand, and you can swoon over Ingrid Bergman all you want. Then we are going over to Nan's Café for a late night snack before we decide what to do after that," she again instructed.

"By the way, I will pick you up. My Dad's letting me have his car for the night. You'll like it. It's a new Lincoln," she added.

"Are you sure? Now I really feel like a fool," he admitted.

"Stop it. I can imagine how difficult it might be for you to start driving again, especially after what happened to you. Not to mention how painful it might be to turn your neck from side to side, watching out for kids in the street, dogs and cats, pretty ladies, and old farmers with their hay wagons," she said, trying to lighten up the conversation.

She concluded with, "You be ready at six-thirty. You don't have to wear a tie if you don't want to. Please bring along your brace. I want you to be comfortable all night long."

With that she slurped down the last of her drink, put a dollar on the table and slid off her seat with a smile and a pat on his hand, which was resting on the counter.

"See you Friday. Be ready. I won't be late."

3

Connie Blakely and Bud Carlson were the talk of the town from that first Friday night on. They made the most handsome couple. They were seen together in all the right places at all the right times. They attended the First Methodist Church together every Sunday. They were prominent at the Future Farmers of America annual banquet in spite of Bud's vow never to go near the organization as a full-fledged member. They were at nearly every dance at the pavilions in towns stretching from Grand Island to Minden; Oxnard, to McCook; from Aurora all the way to Ogallala; of course, stopping in Kearney on many occasions along the way. They even made it to the annual statewide Rotary Club dinner dance in Lincoln that year. Connie's father was secretary treasurer, so they joined her parents for the festivities.

Bud was not Connie's only admirer. From the moment he met her, Hank was squarely in the palm of Connie's hand. She charmed him to no end. In Hank's mind, she was absolutely ideal as a potential mate for his only son. Vera, on the other hand, wasn't so sure. She wasn't quite taken in by the girl's effervescence and her carefree demeanor. Vera was skeptical of Connie's outward, unbridled embrace and silently objected to the way she flaunted her hourglass figure and the seemingly endless supply of the latest fashions with which she clothed herself.

Vera strongly adhered to the theory that women should work just as hard as men to make a positive contribution to their families and society as a whole. Anyone who "had it all handed to them" was not worthy and should be approached with caution was Vera's take on things. Connie's "silver spoon" as she called it made her unworthy of her son's affection. For once, Vera kept her thoughts and her suspicions to herself. Her son had changed. He had become a man, carrying himself with a certain swagger, not haughty or conceited, rather bold and gentlemanly humble. Vera did admit that Connie's style was rubbing off on her son and since she had long encouraged him to find his way off the farm she grew to accept that Connie just might be his ticket, despite her lingering doubts.

Genevieve and Dorothy met Connie at Thanksgiving dinner that year of 1941. Connie had insisted that she and Bud would join her parents for an early feast around two o'clock at their house in town, so the Carlsons had to delay their dinner at the farm to around six so the glamorous couple could be in their presence.

Connie was under a microscope the whole time. Bud's sisters would not endorse their baby brother's romance without their full screening of the candidate. The dinner table talk that day was like a severe cross examination Connie found almost as passionate as ones she often watched her father deliver to hostile witnesses in a crowded courtroom.

In the end though, Connie prevailed. She had them both giggling like schoolgirls with her tales of adolescent exploits while traveling with her parents on shopping sprees to New York, San Francisco and Chicago. The third bottle of a very fine Chablis that she had brought along for the festivities helped ease the tension and smooth her way into their confidence.

While Bud's courting of the most eligible bachelorette in town continued, the town's attention was riveted on the upcoming water trial scheduled to start on Monday, December 8 in Hall County Court, Room 2 before the Honorable Wilbur Hastings presiding.

James Blakely, Esquire prepared for trial like never before. In his research he convinced himself and his clients that he could shred the so-called binding-in-perpetuity agreement among the parties. The voiding of these agreements would therefore legally negate the position of opposing counsel and the arrogant bunch they represented. Real delight came in billable hours, including numerous depositions and trips to Lincoln for records research. The total hours far exceeded five hundred. At a whopping twenty-five dollars an hour, he soon saw another move for his family. He envisioned Omaha as their new homestead and hanging a shingle for his own firm. If he won the case, the monetary damages based on decades of lost benefit from diminished allocation would probably top four hundred thousand dollars. James would secretly smile to himself thinking of the forty percent on damages he would earn based on the retainer agreement.

James was loaded for bear. The town was ready and anxious. Factions among the citizenry were formed in support of or opposition to the contentious families. Headlines were written. Bets were made. Odds were given as to the outcome. It was a circus atmosphere that in most other communities in America would have garnered little or no attention, but in Grand Island it was better than if Joe Louis was fighting Max Schmeling again in Center City Square.

The court bailiff, Ronald Harper, was immediately the most popular man in town since he would decide who among the general populace would be admitted to the courtroom to occupy the limited public seating space. On the day before that fateful Sunday, Ronald had decided to issue tickets on a first come first served basis but allow those admitted first to remain only through the first half day's proceedings. At the lunch break Ronald was determined to collect the tickets from the morning group and reissue them to the afternoon attendees so no one would feel slighted.

Of course, Ronald's plans were abandoned that Sunday afternoon. Across town James slammed his briefcase shut and closed his file for the time being after Judge Hastings called to indefinitely postpone opening arguments. As the horrifying news of the Japanese attack in Hawaii screamed over the radio everything and everyone stopped. The world had changed in that instant. A contentious fight over ownership of theoretical inches of irrigation water no longer seemed important; trivial, inconsequential and meaningless. Suddenly, without warning, other things mattered.

The war careened into Central Nebraska as it did everywhere in America. Grand Island sent three hundred and fifty-five of its young men to serve in the first two months after Pearl Harbor. Another two hundred seventy would embark in the next four months and after that, in total, well over two thousand, nearly twenty percent of the region's population, would leave home for the battlefront. Scooter joined the Navy. He took his training in San Diego and was assigned as a heavy gunner on the battleship Missouri. Sadly, Bud didn't go. He couldn't. His neck injury kept him out of the service and in the arms of Connie Blakely. He wasn't happy about it, however. He would have gone to fight, but one look at the x-rays of his upper vertebra was all it took for the Army doctor to stamp his papers unfit for duty and send him home.

Grand Island and Aurora also sent their women to serve as well. Nearly one hundred became WAVES or WAC's while well over fifteen hundred went to the front lines of the factories to make the materials needed for war. Genevieve quit the bus line and went to work at a munitions factory in Omaha. Dorothy remained in nurses training until she graduated and went to Denver for advanced trauma instruction awaiting her appointment to the Army Nurse Corps. To her great disappointment her name never came up for recruitment. She remained at the bottom of the list because her eyesight was poor and she was handicapped to some degree by her thick glasses. She fought her status throughout the war, but failed to overcome the physical standards set by the Army so she remained stateside, frustrated, and angry at the system that denied her the privilege to serve.

Like all of their neighbors, the Carlsons were fiercely patriotic. By the time spring planting came around that year of 1942 a keen, overriding sense of duty had gripped the citizens of Hall County. They put aside their differences to make the maximum contribution to the war effort. At City Hall on the night of April 12, 1942, Hank chaired a unification meeting of the farm families including those on both sides of the water dispute. All five families in the squabble over the ownership of mere inches of water attended along with sixty others representing the vast majority of landowners in the region. Before the night was over, James Blakely's future took a plunge deeper in depth than Hank's main water well.

Over his vehement protest, right there before his eyes his clients settled the heated controversy on a handshake, and asked James for his final bill. No trial, no share of a potential settlement, and no new bright and shiny Omaha law firm with his name as principal partner engraved on a brass plaque next to the front door. James was furious, devastated, heartbroken, and shattered. He had lost before he could begin, and to top it off he had looming debts with no potential source of income to apply to them. Charlotte Blakely had no idea the extent to which her husband had plunged them into the financial abyss. When he revealed the depths of their straits a week later she cried and stormed off to her mother's house in McCook, taking Connie with her.

Bud knew nothing about the reasons for the Blakely family uproar. All he knew was his girlfriend had given him a vague excuse for leaving town with her mother for a few days to visit with her grandmother. Bud found her explanation very odd but did not at first question her any further. His anxiety grew and he demanded more information when after her third week away and another strange telephone conversation ended without a date certain for her return. She refused to talk further and abruptly hung up the receiver.

Bud occasionally would see James Blakely entering or leaving his office. One evening after finishing his shift he waited for Connie's father outside the West North Front Street office building and approached him as he walked to his car parked in a nearby parking lot. At first they were cordial and shook hands when they met.

"Mr. Blakely," Bud said cautiously, "this is probably none of my business, but can you tell me; would it be possible for me to know, why your wife and Connie have been gone so long? Are they coming back?"

"Bud," James responded with a painful look of resignation, "they may not be back for some time. I cannot tell you why, and I strongly advise you not to go looking for them. It has nothing to do with you, son. These are private matters, and until Connie comes of age to make her own decisions, I'm afraid she will not be permitted to visit or associate with folks in this fine community. Connie will be going off to college soon. Her choices are numerous as you can imagine. So frankly you should not expect to hear from her, perhaps ever again. For your information, I will be leaving soon myself."

"You have to be joking!" Bud exclaimed, his voice rising higher than he intended.

"That's enough, Bud. Now if you will excuse me. I have been courteous to you. You need to accept and respect what I have said. My advice son; move on with your life."

James turned, got in his car, and drove off without another word. Bud was stupefied; shocked and at the same time livid. He didn't deserve to be treated like some second-class, starry eyed, smitten teenager who could be kicked aside with a disrespectful brush off.

"You son-of-a-bitch," Bud shouted at the fleeing vehicle.

That night over dinner Bud told his parents of his tale of woe. Hank advised him somewhat in the same way as James Blakely had, but with a little more sympathy. "Don't cry over spilled milk," was Hank's ultimate advice. Vera, as usual in matters about Bud, would not be cast off so easily. Her anger rose as her son's story unfolded, and while reassuring Bud that his life with the ladies certainly was not over, she offered a full range of hypotheses about the Blakely's mysterious disappearance ranging from divorce, to deathly sickness; even going so far as to suggest an unexpected and unwanted child.

"Mother, for God's sake, I never touched her," Bud bellowed indignantly.

"I'm not accusing you," she reassured him, but then added, patting his hand as she spoke, "there may have been others."

At that point Hank interjected his own theory, which in a matter of a week's time had become widely accepted around town.

"He's broke. He gambled on winning the water case and when the families settled on their own, his world collapsed around his ears. Mark my words; what he told Bud has been rumored for some time. I know it's true. He's packing up and will be gone before the week is out. Word has it he's got bill collectors hounding him night and day. He bought that fancy car of his on credit and the bank's ready to go after it. I'd say they better hurry before he high tails it out of town first."

"Well, I declare Henry, (she called him that when she was not pleased) why didn't you tell me that before? I'm your wife, you know. You should tell me those things." Vera's anger was now directed at her husband.

"Don't like rumors. Don't like talkin' behind people's backs. But these are the facts. Wasn't about to say anything until the facts were out," Hank responded calmly.

"Wow Dad, you think it's true. They have so many nice things. Always had money; seemed to be carefree. Happy all the time," Bud offered.

"I know it's true, son. All of it borrowed. Sad to say, maybe even their happiness."

Part II

Esztergom to New Orleans
July 1958

4

Many people argue that it was that flying fragment of granite sent flinging from the cornerstone of the Bazillika in Esztergom, Hungary, and not changing his first name from Roman to the Americanized Robert that rendered him susceptible and doubtful. They believe abandoning his Hungarian heritage and becoming Robert had very little to do with his unsteady view of himself and his purpose. In truth, they say, it was the sixteen-inch scar trailing from his right hip nearly to his right knee that fashioned his handicap, a condition that later in his life propelled him to overcome it with fierce verve. Others believe it was simply a woman who should be blamed, or credited for his dependency depending on one's point of view.

The Red Army of the Soviet Union is responsible for the shrapnel that ripped into Roman Sokolowski's leg and unalterably changed the course of his life. Roman's father also played a major part in his transformation. Roman was the brunt of his father's jokes. His ridicule and unjustified scorn were always present even when he didn't speak. When Roman was old enough to care his father took great pleasure in unceasingly questioning his son's manliness. Roman wouldn't admit that about his father. He refused to point to his father's culpability. Roman kept things like that bottled up inside. He loved his father one minute and despised him the next or at least he thought he did.

Roman also would not admit to himself or anyone else that he was in the wrong place at the wrong time when the tank-fired artillery shell slammed into the building's edifice, slightly missing its intended target. It was that wayward missile unexpectedly veering to the left of the two thousand kilo, double iron doors heavily adorned with gold and silver icons of the Christian deities beckoning the faithful to worship therein that took Roman down. No, Roman was supposed to be at the Bazillika that day to defend it. He was ordered to remain at this duty station at all costs, at the head of the line, leading his ragtag platoon against the armored Soviet throng. It was his obligation, above all. His father said so. He loved his father. Yes, he thought so on that day.

On another day, not too many years into the future, Roman wasn't thinking about his father or taking his orders. Instead he stood nervously at the head of another long line of humanity. This time, though, he was not their leader.

"What is this? How am I supposed to pronounce this one? Jesus Christ, you people; why don't you come up with better names? Sam-bu-ski? San-lo-ski? Lo-min-ski? God, this is impossible," declared the portly, overwrought Immigration Officer as he scanned through another stack of papers for another occupant from an endless procession of bedraggled urchins whose feet had not been on solid ground for two weeks. All of them, men, women, and children alike looked to Conrad like they'd missed every meal on every day since boarding their ocean-crossing vessel for their fourteen miserable days at sea.

"Sir, it is Sokolowski; Roman, Sokolowski; S-o-k-o-l-o-w-s-k-i," Roman politely interjected.

Conrad Jenkins, formally known as Cornelius Estaban Giguere, an odd amalgamation of Spanish and French blood resulting from a patrician's late night frolic with a Cajun housemaid, looked up and into the face of his latest emaciated applicant for entry into his beloved adopted homeland. "Son, let me give you some advice. You ain't never gonna get along in Na'lins or anywhere else in this U.S. of A. with a name like Roman Spuminski, or whatever. Christ, with a name like Roman, people'll think you're a smart ass or something."

The room spun as Roman looked into Conrad's eyes, a smile crossing the officer's face and a bead of sweat dripping smack onto the middle of the paper which Conrad held in his ink-stained fingers. Roman had never felt heat like this before. Never in Esztergom nor Budapest nor southern France. Stagnant oppressive air hung heavy over the shut tight anteroom where Conrad sat and waited for Roman's response. Roman's stomach growled and whined and his head reeled again. There was no chair on which to sit. The overhead fan anchored above Conrad's head spun so slowly Roman could count the blades as they rotated.

A string of humanity stood outside Conrad's cubicle. It stretched the length of the fifty-yard corridor and around the corner and out of sight. Suddenly someone in line shouted in broken English, "Move it you bastard. We been here for four hours!"

"How about Robert?" Roman stammered.

"Robert's good," said Conrad.

"Okay. Now the last. The last name Robert," Conrad ordered.

"Okay," Robert replied.

"Okay what?" Conrad questioned, his frustration beginning to grow.

"Okay, Robert Okay," Roman offered.

Christ in heaven; dumb Polacks, Conrad thought, "No, Robert, not okay. That's stupid as shit. Okay?" Conrad proclaimed. When he spoke he suppressed a hack from deep in his throat prompted by his thirtieth Camel cigarette of the day.

Robert had misunderstood, but ventured a mimic of Conrad anyway. "Kay, Robert Kay," Roman responded hesitantly.

"That's it... Robert Kay. But I'm gonna put an 'e' on the end of it so it don't look sissified when you write it. Got it? Robert Kaye, with an 'e' on the end. Now take this and get out of there." He handed Robert his papers after scribbling his signature to the bottom of one. "You'll be a citizen in six months if you keep your nose clean and report to the Immigration office regularly as to your whereabouts. If not they'll send your ass back to Poland," Conrad declared.

"That's Hungary," Robert Kaye corrected.

"What? Yea, I'll bet you're probably hungry," Conrad allowed, as Robert stepped around the officer's desk to exit through the back door of his office.

"Next," Conrad shouted, and as both doors simultaneously opened in front and back of his tiny office it brought the slightest puff of fresh air to strike the back of Conrad's neck and forehead, bringing momentary relief, but failing miserably to dry even a portion of his sweat soaked uniform blouse.

Robert passed through the doors sensing no change in the oven-like atmosphere that squeezed his head and girdled his chest, making his breathing painful. And his leg, it always hurt. He refused to be controlled by the throbbing that came with every step. He dragged it along when the pain became severe, and today, a new day, a great day, his first American day, his leg lagged behind him scuffing the inside sole of his shoe. His leg refused to keep up with his body, holding him back, refusing to march evenly up St. Charles Avenue toward the address of the boarding house on the paper tucked in his shirt pocket.

Robert thought to himself as he shuffled along, his attention momentarily shifting to the passing bright green trolley car traversing the median strip of the boulevard, that he would keep his name, his real name, just in case he needed it some time for an alias. Maybe he would have more than one alias and use several names in America. The first one he got was easy to get so getting new ones could be easy as well. America seemed to hand out names with as little effort as passing gas and certainly less discreetly, Robert surmised, suppressing a grin.

Robert's stomach made noise just then, again trying to reconcile itself with accepting the meal Robert had just consumed from a street vendor near the Port of Orleans pier. For seventy-five cents Robert got his first taste of crayfish gumbo yet he had no idea what it was. It looked to him like chunky soup. It burnt his mouth like a hot iron, but the big bowl full of the crispy shells shed by the little bright red creatures accompanied by a giant piece of cornbread filled his belly to an incomparable satisfaction. With his strength temporarily restored he had set off two hours before with directions to his new home from the first black human being he had ever seen in his life. He spotted him propping up a street lamp with one hand and sipping from the contents of a brown paper bag with the other.

Robert showed this black human oddity the paper from his pocket, and in the best English he could muster, asked the strange looking creature, "Which way to here?"

"Damn, you a funny lookin' fella. Betcha just got off da boat. Dat hat of yours sho is strange. Well, welcome to America friend. Wanna sip? Don take too much," the street lamp anchor offered.

"Thank you, no," Robert replied after sniffing the top of the bag and realizing his stomach had completed another back flip.

"Soot yo self. Lemme see cheer what you got. Oh, yea, ain't too far. Easy walk. Maybe just a mile yonder," offered Robert's new found guide.

"You see cheer you jest head on up Julia Street here to Saint Charles; take a left and keep walkin' till you hit Franklin Court, then ya take a right till ya find Harmony which is right next, maybe a block or so from Toledano Street. Got that young fella?" His guide asked.

"Yes, Sir, I think so; well maybe," Robert replied.

"Damn, I'll tell ya 'gain, but I ain't gonna tell ya a third time. No Sir," he warned. So he did tell Robert again, and Robert set off but after generously presenting his guide two bright silver dollars he had acquired from a passenger on board his transatlantic New Orleans-bound passenger ship. They had been in exchange for a fine pair of a calfskin gloves he'd taken off a dead Soviet solider on the outskirts of Visegrad the winter before. His guide was dumbfounded by the payment. He could not utter a word as Robert hobbled off toward Harmony Street.

Finally, two hours later, his duffel bag feeling like ten thousand kilos still strapped to his back and his leg firing arrows of agony through every fiber of his being, Robert stopped on the sidewalk in front of Twenty-four zero seven Harmony Street, New Orleans, Louisiana. Wiping the sweat from his brow he gazed up upon the wraparound porch of the three-story four gabled roof colonial antebellum and nearly cried with relief. His new home. God, it's huge, he thought to himself, dropping the duffel to the ground and collapsing down upon it to rest and wipe the salty perspiration from his brow. It was August and the temperature on the thermometer beneath the bank clock what seemed like ten kilometers back on Saint Charles Avenue had read ninety-eight degrees. Robert didn't know the difference between Fahrenheit degrees and Celsius as a means of measurement but that didn't matter. All he knew as he passed under that clock all those kilometers back was that he was about to suffocate.

Now as his heart rate lessened and with his breathing under control, he looked up from his perch on the sidewalk directly into the stark white-hot sunrays. He had to squint to make out three obscure figures seated in rocking chairs on the porch, fans in their hands waving frantically and wide eyes staring back at him. No one was saying a word. The trio was just watching Robert Kaye lying there in a bedraggled heap. They waited and fanned until finally one of them shouted, "Move along boy. We don't allow no loiterers around here. Now git!"

5

Robert lay naked on his bed. The moisture that once drenched his body had long since dried to form a crusty salty layer. Cool air was blowing mercifully across him courtesy of a grill encased rotating fan sitting on top of the pine chest of drawers angled in the corner of the room. The fan squeaked loudly with each full sweep. Three hours had passed since being ordered off the property by the rocking chair bound guards stationed at the front entrance of his enchanting new dwellings. Robert had stood from his seated position on the ground when hearing the command to depart, and boldly declared his right to occupy the premises. He limped through the yard and up the stairs to hand the second black man he had ever seen in his life the papers announcing his arrival and the receipt for his first three month's rent.

This was not before hearing two more threats from one of the three front door fanning and rocking sentinels to "shoot ya dead in yore tracks," and "call da law to remove yore stone cold carcass." He ignored both attempts at deadly intimidation and kept on hobbling toward his protagonists to present his credentials.

"Mrs. Dionne, better come here," yelled the second black man ever to enter his life. "We got here a boy says he paid da rent and wants to come in." While they awaited Mrs. Dionne, Robert and the others on the porch eyed each other warily. Joining the bib overall clad black man's fellow guardians was a silver haired, bespectacled prim and proper looking white lady dressed in a flowery gingham dress, white sandals covering her petite feet and a pearl necklace dangling from around her withered bony neck. She was the first to smile and say, "Clarence, this here boy doesn't look like an intruder. He just needs a bath. Besides he just might be the one we've been expecting."

"Na," said her other porch mate, a white man whose skin was nearly as dark as Clarence's, but his from the sun. "He c'aint be the one we been lookin' fo. He suppose ta be a big strappin' feller, come here from Europe or somethin'. Been fightin' in some war over dare against them Commie bastards. Not some scrawny, half starved lookin' crippled up kid, look like da skin fallin off his bones."

"Now, see here Boudreaux. You hush up," instructed Miss Hattie, "you and Clarence just sit here until Mrs. Dionne arrives and we'll see if this young man is to be welcomed into our home."

"What's your name son?" she asked.

"Robert, Madam,"

"Ooooh, listen to that! He called me madam. Sure haven't heard that in many years," gushed Miss Hattie.

"Well, glad to meet you Robert. They call me Miss Hattie and here next to me is Clarence, and over there sits Boudreaux."

Clarence and Boudreaux both let out a harsh "harrumph" in return. Robert tipped his sweat soaked hat to one and all just at the moment a woman, tall and stout, stark angular features, dressed in tan slacks, a bright orange linen blouse and salt and pepper hair pulled back tight in a bun pushed open the screen door and stepped upon the porch. Her look was quizzical but not threatening.

"What did you say your name was?" Mrs. Dionne asked.

"Robert, Madam" he replied, "Robert Kaye."

"I have no record of a Robert Kaye seeking lodging here. I have a notice and payment from an agent in France to expect a young man with few English skills, but of fine reputation. The funds received are adequate. Robert Kaye is not a French name. Are you an imposter?"

"See, Hattie, I tole you, he's nothin' but a bum. Git him off this here porch, 'fo I take my cane to 'im." Clarence warned.

Robert's head twirled again. He sought his balance, leaning his back against the pillar supporting the roof above the porch. He caught his breath and composure just enough to respond in halting English.

"Mrs. Dionne. I am the man sent to you by Mr. Francois. He used my money to book my passage here and pay my lodging for three weeks. I am not French. I am Hungarian. I flee my country after fighting the Soviets to seek better life in America. I come through France since French people offer help to those like me. I take new name to become American. Good name. I hope. Here are my papers. Good papers. You see," Robert said, beseeching her as best he could.

Another "harrumph" came from Clarence and Boudreaux, and another "hush" from Miss Hattie.

Bianca Dionne took the papers from Robert and scanned them carefully. After a moment she raised her eyes and looked deeply into Robert's.

"I see Mr. Francois's signature. It appears valid, the same as affixed to his correspondence with me about you or the person I assume is you," she acknowledged.

"I am that person. Please believe me," Robert said, now pleading openly.

After a few moments of silence, broken only by the sound of the three rocking chairs creaking on the wooden planks of the porch, she spoke again, "Robert, I see sincerity in your eyes. You may gather your things and follow me to your quarters."

An empty plate of corned beef and cabbage sat on Robert's nightstand. He swatted a fly away from the remnants of his second meal of the day as he rose from bed to realize a strong shiver passing through his body from a sudden swish of air thrust toward him by the circulating fan. He hadn't slept, but had just dozed off to the sounds of the twirling fan and the crickets outside beginning their evening songs. At that moment his leg did not hurt. He wondered why as he looked down at the angry red jagged scar. He touched it, running his fingertips along its wandering path down to his knee. Then it spoke to him, reminding him of its forever presence with a familiar twinge like a needle piercing his flesh followed by a dark moaning ache deep from inside.

He stood, putting weight on the limb testing whether the ache would become acute. It didn't take long. He winced as he moved to his right to search for his only other set of clothes he had neatly stored in the top drawer of the dresser on which the fan continued on its rotating side-to-side motion. He pulled back the white lace curtains shrouding the window beside the dresser and looked down upon the bandana-topped head of an apron clad black woman, the first he'd ever seen, hanging clothes on the back yard clothesline. Mrs. Dionne was standing with hands on hips in the foreground observing. Robert recognized the clothes on the line and those remaining crumpled in the wicker basket on the ground next to the laundress as his own.

Mrs. Dionne collected his filthy garments after delivering his food and suggesting he rest for a while before coming downstairs to join the others for afternoon tea. It was not a request, rather an order Robert sensed, so even though fatigue consumed every muscle and fiber in his body he knew he must obey. That's why he had desperately fought beckoning sleep and now dressed to meet his fellow boarders.

Much to his delight the daily gathering in Mrs. Dionne's main floor parlor was cut short when Miss Hattie had a slight seizure and dumped her dainty tea cup and saucer on the floor, splashing its contents on Boudreaux's freshly pressed cotton slacks. Before Miss Hattie begun to quiver and spill, Robert had met and politely paid his respects to Miss Deborah Henley, Mr. Anthony Dominique and Mrs. Margeaux Claire, all residents of Mrs. Dionne's fabled gabled house on Harmony Street. He failed to learn the surnames of either Clarence or Boudreaux and couldn't determine whether Miss Hattie was her first or last name by the time Mrs. Dionne had dismissed the others and requested; no ordered, Robert to remain behind for a second cup.

"Robert, you have tonight to relax and rest some more. We begin serving breakfast promptly at six thirty in the morning, but after seven will not you be allowed to eat. You will be expected to leave the house by seven thirty to look for work. You will find work despite your infirmities because if you don't you will not remain in my house for more than a week," Mrs. Dionne lectured.

A week, Robert thought. He'd paid from the silver coins and currency given to Mr. Francois for three weeks, not one, including passage. How can she say one week? He chose not to object or correct her mistake just then. He let it pass for now. She was not to be interrupted.

"You will notice in my house most of the people are older than you. You are young. Some of them cannot work, but you can and you must. Idleness will not be tolerated," she added. Then she asked, "Do you have a trade, a skill you may ply?"

"Yes, Madam," Robert replied, "I have skill in how you say, electronics? I know about machines that work from electronics. I learn before the war. My father's friend was an electronics. He taught me."

"Good. Excellent. Much need in New Orleans for skilled electricians. That is what you are - an electrician," she corrected.

"Yes, Madam. Electrician. I be an electrician," Robert declared.

"Now off you go. You will have clean clothes awaiting you when you return tomorrow night after a hard day's work, Robert. Remember that. A hard day's work, Robert," she pronounced again.

"Yes, Madam, a hard day's work ahead," Robert acknowledged.

In bed now, naked again but this time with the cool, crisp, detergent smelling sheets covering him Robert lay, content, comfortable for the first time in many weeks. He sucked in the air in his room since it was rid of the humid pall that had hung about him since limping down the gangplank and stepping ashore those many hours before. The wind had swept the stifling, wet atmospheric blanket away. The rustle of the leaves of the huge magnolia outside his window provided ample evidence. Sleep will come to Robert quickly and he knew his dreams would return. However, he was not afraid this night. Thankfully his fear had temporarily deserted him.

6

When Robert's dreams came they were mostly about his father, a man demanding respect but a man consumed with denial and frothing with betrayal. Robert's most vivid dreams of his father were recounting his nightly lectures to his sons, Roman and Rudolf, as he sat sipping cheap port and expounding on the day's latest social and political events.

Roman would nocturnally relive the stories of his father's escapades as the first of this century's self declared Hungarian Freedom Fighters. Fodor Meszaros Sokolowski was Roman's father. His father liked his name just as much as Robert had liked Roman. Fodor's name translated into the curly haired wolf. Fodor's hair was a tightly wrapped mop of blonde curls and when he was a boy growing up in Esztergom he learned to fight early in his life as his rowdy, sniveling classmates, boys and girls alike, delighted in tugging and twisting his golden locks and calling him "l'any" loosely meaning little girl. This particular night as Robert slept deeply in his mind's tunnel of darkness his dream was about the war, his father's war against the Soviets, one that Roman would fight again some twelve years later.

Fodor was a Jew, a fact he hid with a strident obsession. Roman knew about his father's heritage, not from him but from his mother who revealed this intimacy as she lay dying, a victim of a ravaging flu epidemic that had swept their beautiful city by the Danube.

Roman was just nine and Rudolf but seven when their mother's angelic face grew cold in her bed and the undertaker came to cart her away. She would laugh and sing no more and her stories of gardens, and flowers and birds and blackberries and swimming in the river only blocks from their home fell silent forever to be replaced by tales of radical politics and war by the man who hung a swastika on the wall above their front door.

Fodor stood apart from his sons at the gravesite preferring the awning of a giant oak on the day she was buried. From a distance away from the mourners he listened to the priest utter his final prayers over the closed casket of his Catholic wife. The words of the priest meant nothing to him, like water gushing through the puncture holes of a caldron and soaking the ground at his feet. He loved her once but she rejected all that drove him. All that made him what he was on that day. She didn't understand or appreciate him because she was ignorant. He could never make her revel in his achievements, so he gave up long ago and found his pleasure, his reason for occupying his place on this earth, in his beloved Hungary and in his undying allegiance to the Arrow Cross Party.

In his dream that night, in Mrs. Claire's New Orleans boarding house, Roman stared intensively into his father's eyes, concentrating on every word he spoke. Rudolph was beside him at the table, both sipping goat's milk, a delicacy made available only to those whose fathers wore the patch of the crossed arrows on their brown shirtsleeves. Rudolph's eyes blinked heavily. His head bobbing up and down.

Roman kicked his brother's ankle under the table. Their father would be incensed if either fell asleep during one of his sacred lectures. If exposed, Fodor's wide leather barber's strap would be plucked from the hook on the wall and briskly applied to their backsides.

This night Fodor was speaking of their country's history and its hatred of the Jews in their midst, a topic drilled into the skulls of his sons on many of such nights.

"My sons," he began, "you must never forget that the Jews of Hungry account for only five percent of our population of eighteen million. Yet the Jews live in the biggest houses with the most rooms. Jews control all the money. Ninety-one percent of the currency brokers are Jews. Eighty-eight percent are members of the stock exchange, and ninety percent own all the factories. They have the most children in university, the most doctors, lawyers, engineers and chemists, and they control the newspapers."

"Our country was founded in revolution. Religion has failed it throughout our history. The Christians, the Catholics, your mother's church have been the scourge of our country. The church has failed to challenge the Jews, which is a race, not a religion just like the blacks of Africa. Today I heard our leader, our regent Miklos Horthy openly declare his anti-Semite views. He finally said to one and all that he considers it intolerable that here in Hungary everything, every factory, bank, large fortune, business, theatre, press and commerce is in Jewish hands, and that the Jew is the image reflected of Hungary, especially abroad."

"Our national Army, our Hungarian National Socialist Party and the Arrow Cross are the answer my sons," he continued after gulping another glass of port from the bottle on the table before him, "Admiral Horthy's policies of eradication will not fail. Hungary will regain the territories lost in the disastrous treaty of Trianon. This is 1939, dear ones, and at long last our Regent has passed the laws restricting the hated Jews from commerce, from our schools, and banks. No longer can Jews work in government, and the number of Jews in any undertaking of consequence will be limited to twelve percent which is the number of them representing of our entire population."

Fodor drew a deep breath and a wry smile crossed his lips. His eyes, Roman noticed from his nocturnal outpost, no longer seemed focused, gazing instead at the emblem fixed above the door.

"Today, my sons, I found glory. I performed my duty with honor. It was the first of many to come. We began on the long road toward restoring our country to its once perfect state, a state without the Jews. We took back from them what they had held from us for so many years. The place was near Maria Valeria Bridge. A jewelry store owned by the Kocsis, a family of six. The head of the family was Ambrus, a name in our language meaning immortal. He offered no resistance when we smashed his display cases and beat his sons with our clubs. He stood by when we dragged his wife and daughters to the back room behind the curtains and had our way with them, many times. The youngest of them was very sweet, a maiden for sure. She was my favorite. Ambrus is surely mortal now as his blood spilled in great gushes when his throat was opened by my blade."

"I am free. Our glorious city of Esztergom is free. Our country is free of these mongrels. Their bodies will never be found. The Arrow Cross has struck!"

With that, Fodor's raised an outstretched arm. Before long it fell to his side and his head thumped the table toppling over the empty bottle of sweet liquor. He began to snore in steady waves. Roman gently eased back his chair and that of his brother and they stepped quietly to their beds.

Robert awoke, his body drenched in sweat despite the waves of cool air running its length every few seconds with each rotation of the fan. The clock on his bedside stand read five a.m. He knew he could not return to slumber although weariness consumed him still. He would wait for the sun to rise before his second day in America would begin. He would struggle this day to rid himself of another of his father's tirades. Yet he feared, Fodor's messages from long ago that haunted his dreams had taken deep root in his soul.

7

Robert was the first at Mrs. Dionne's communal breakfast table and his landlady signified her pleasure at his promptness with a quick smile and a pleasant, "Good morning."

"Robert, where do your plans take you on this fine day?" she was quick to inquire moments before Anthony, Mrs. Claire and Miss Deborah Henley entered the dining area of the big house and found their seats around the huge fourteen foot rectangular oak dining table that dominated the room.

Robert's senses were awakened by the intoxicating sounds and smells of fresh bacon sizzling somewhere on a stove nearby, coupled with the delightful aroma of brewing coffee and biscuits baking to what he hoped would be a golden brown. He was surrounded by opulent but worn and frayed blue velvet curtains hanging listlessly from tarnished brass rods above the four elongated windows that brought sparse but welcomed natural light into the room. The Persian rug under his feet displayed large nearly worn through sections of its original weaving, having long ago lost many of the intricate patterns adorned by the colorful dyes that once brought a sparkling sheen to the silk. The dark, almost black mahogany sideboard, mismatching the dining table, was absent some of its hardware and dull white rings from left-too-long water glasses or seeping cocktail decanters were now permanent in the topside veneer. Nevertheless, Robert was captivated. The cracked coffee cup put before him by the bandana lady, this time wearing a blue instead of the red one, did not bother him and it didn't leak when he put the steaming liquid to his lips for a cautious taste. For a moment he was lost in this heaven of earthly delights but shook himself conscious again with a prompt response to Mrs. Dionne's line of questioning.

"Madam, my search for the employment begins back at the places where the boats arrive. Piers, I believe you say, Madam…at the piers."

"Wrong, you little cuss. Wrong," broke in Clarence being wheeled in to the dining chamber by Boudreaux who pushed his friend's chair up to the table and took a seat to Clarence's right. By this time all the table settings were occupied with Miss Hattie arriving last, dainty and bright in a pale pink sundress, smelling vaguely of lilac perfume.

"You know nothing. There ain't no jobs at the docks for people in your condition. You got a bum leg in case you didn't notice," declared Clarence looking over the outstretched arm of the bandana lady now pouring his coffee in the cup she'd placed in front of him.

"They'd run ya over in the first hour. Crush ya like a bug. You got to be quick and nimble to git around them docks and them boys ain't takin' kindly to no gimps. How'd you think I got in this here chair, boy? Didn't land here 'cause its nice and comfortable. Them dockworkers, them stevedore sons-a-bitches put me here 'cause I weren't quick enough to git out of da way of a swingin' crate of tractor parts comin' off a diesel powered merchant ship from South America. Broke me back when I tried to jump aside, but me busted ankle from trippin' over a curb down on Bourbon Street hobbled me just enough, so WHAM, it got me square in the back. Broke it in three places," Clarence added almost as an afterthought.

By this time those around the table were staring at him wide eyed with mouths gaping open. All except Robert who was entranced by Clarence's telling and yearning for more.

"Why Clarence," Miss Hattie exclaimed, "I never knew that about you. I'm so sorry, my dear, I had no idea."

"Indeed, Clarence that is a tragic tale. You should have told us about your accident. All of us would have been much more sympathetic, I am sure. Perhaps more willing to help you accomplish your daily activities," Mrs. Dionne chimed in. "By the way, Clarence, please watch your language from now on."

"Shore enough. Ain't no problem Mrs. Dionne. I'm jest tryin' to help the kid out. He got no business down at the docks. He needs to go find some cushy job. Like stockin' food for the grocer or maybe runnin' the trolley or somethin'. Somethin' he don't have to move around too quick at," Clarence offered.

"That's awfully sage advice dear Clarence," proclaimed Miss Claire with a pound of sarcasm dripping from each word.

"I am the electrician," Robert injected not really understanding Miss Claire's tone or meaning. "I have skill. Know electric machines. Can fix. Find a job with electrician. But not at the piers?"

"Damn, hear that?" Clarence asked, turning to Bourdeaux who was paying more attention to the sunny yellow scrambled eggs and crispy brown bacon heaped high on his plate and at his fingertips courtesy of Miss Bandana.

"The kid here say he's an electrician. Can fix machines. He don't look like he's smart enough to tie his very own shoe laces," Clarence speculated with his mean streak returning in full force.

"Now see here Clarence," Miss Hattie scolded, "You leave this young man alone. We should take him at his word. If he says he possesses those worthy attributes we should encourage him, not be critical."

"Yea, Clarence, shut your trap or I'll smack you over the head with that pitcher of orange juice, sitting right there in front of you," sternly warned Miss Deborah Henley.

Robert turned to Miss Henley with surprise not having heard her speak before and sensing by the tenor of her voice that she was serious in her rebuke of Clarence. Then as he turned back to eye the target of her warning, he could detect the old man had abruptly adopted a new found meekness. Clarence spoke no more during the meal except when Mrs. Dionne asked him and the others gathered to eat that morning about their plans for the day. In response all Clarence would do was mumble something about a game of checkers in the park; that is if Bourdeaux would push him over there.

Between hearty bites of the succulent food Robert repeatedly glanced over at Miss Henley and on two occasions he caught her eyes affixed on him as she dabbed the corners of her mouth with the once lily white but now slightly grayish lace napkin retrieved from her lap.

He didn't find Mrs. Claire quite as interesting as Miss Henley for some reason so his attention remained on the one with the throaty, husky voice that had presented the most severe reprimand to his latest critic.

Robert had never considered himself fancy with the ladies, but before the uprising and the mangling of his leg he had some reputation in his neighborhood surrounding Vorosmarty Utca, the street on which he and Fodor and Rudolph lived. He was one who could charm the damsels and occasionally he found pleasure with a woman companion on an outstretched blanket covering the ground along the west bank of the Danube.

Even before those memorable encounters, while in his middle teenage years Fodor would allow Roman to accompany him to the weekly society meetings. It was there that more than one lovely radical believer in the Arrow Cross Cause would allow the dashing son of the post commander free will while hiding in the meeting hall's basement storage closet, all for the "glorious good of the Motherland."

Although his injury was confined to his leg Roman's mind saw it differently. The shrapnel also had severed that part of him; that vital inner fortification every man must have. Fodor, speaking to him in his dreams, never ceased to remind him of his handicap. "Why do you think women will flock to you now? What do you have to offer? She will have to do all the work," he would cackle and heckle spewing his port across the room. "All you can do is just lie there."

So Roman's shell solidified, resisting those who offered soothing comfort to reassure him that his leg didn't matter. He could not trust them. They were playing with him, tossing him about for their own entertainment. Placating him with their phony sympathy. Fodor said they would. He told him so in his dreams. A sound prediction. Roman's anger rose. He dismissed them all and they all quit coming, all except Fodor.

Moments passed in silence until Mrs. Dionne pushed back her chair signaling mealtime had ended. Robert scanned the faces of the others as Mrs. Dionne stood and he realized all had put down their forks and were reaching to gulp the last of their coffee or juice before rising from their places themselves.

Robert took the not too subtle hint and did the same. He again caught Miss Henley's look but this time it followed with a quick smile and an ever so slight nod of her head. She was dressed in a dark blue jacket and skirt. Her freshly pressed pale blue blouse was buttoned to her slender neck. A tiny gold chain fell to the base of her throat. She was tall, Robert realized, maybe taller than him even when he stood erect and painfully placed equal weight on his right leg. Her angular face, long sharp nose and high forehead may have added to the allure of her height or maybe it was the three inch patent leather black heels she was wearing that made her seem to tower over him and the others.

Robert could only imagine the shape of her body, mostly hidden by the jacket that looked like it had been made for a man. He had never seen a woman dressed like her before. It vaguely reminded him of a nightclub in Budapest he'd once visited that featured dancers on stage in men's clothing who would shed each garment, down to their lingerie which also came off with one easy tug when enough coins would pile at their feet.

Her blonde hair was worn long and flowing over her shoulders. Two gold loop rings poked through each ear lobe. Robert noticed her hands when she placed them on the back of her chair to push it in.

Long and sleek like the rest of her. Her nails extending beyond the tips of each finger by a slight margin, not like a man's at all. They had a bright sheen to them but were colorless.

Robert's attention was broken with, "Good luck to you today," Mrs. Dionne said from across the table. "When you return this evening, please come to my room to report on your day's activities."

"Yes, indeed Robert, good luck to you today," added Miss Hattie as she scurried toward the staircase presumably to return to her room.

"Yes, Madam," Robert responded, before quickly turning back to search for the fascinating lady in the man's suit. Then she was gone, or nearly, walking briskly through the living room toward the front door. Robert's gaze fell upon her movement toward the exit, and despite the length of her jacket it did not hide the swaying motion of her hips.

"Hurry along now Robert. You have a busy day ahead of you," Mrs. Dionne said, again breaking into his thoughts and providing him the clear instructions that he needed to get moving at once.

Robert hurried out of the dining room as best he could on a leg that momentarily refused to cooperate with the other. On the entry hall table laid his leather satchel given to him by Mr. Francois on the day he boarded the ship at the harbor in Marseilles. He snatched it on his way out the front door. He left his hat in his room thinking perhaps Clarence had been right about it not fitting in to the New Orleans fashion scene. In his case was one piece of paper; a carefully written two paragraph letter in English from Master Electrician Gergely Kovacs of the Kozpontban district of Esztergom which was only about a one kilometer walk from the only house Roman ever lived in, except, that is, for Mrs. Dionne's.

Robert made his way down the stairs and on to the all too familiar sidewalk in front of the house. He had no idea where he was going. Should he turn left or turn right? He knew if he turned right and retraced his labored steps to St. Charles Avenue and turned left, eventually he would make his way back to the docks and pier, now a forbidden place if he were to take the second piece of advice from Clarence. So he decided to turn left into the unknown. Choosing that route was certainly better than risking a broken back and landing in a wheelchair for the rest of his life.

As Robert plodded along he came to South Liberty Street. He turned right this time. Liberty Street sounded like a good street to be on, on this particular day. Yes, liberty was what he was looking for.

Liberty Street would bring him good luck. So he stayed on it past Seventh Street, then Sixth Street, toward Fifth. He was surprised that his leg seemed better this bright Monday morning. Less pain always gave him a sense of greater strength and mobility. For a moment he thought he could run, but abruptly dismissed that notion when he stepped too heavily off the sidewalk curb into the intersection with Fourth Street and nearly buckled and fell when the pain struck him like a lightening bolt. He slowed his pace after that, ambling along until reaching First Street where upon at impulse he turned right again.

By then the rows of houses neatly kept lawns white picket fences and countless magnolia trees, and cats and dogs and kids on tricycles and mothers hanging clothes and fathers with their own leather satchels, but wearing suits like Miss Henley gave way to a corner grocery, a barber shop, an auto repair shop, a pawn shop and a consignment store for women's clothing. Robert stopped briefly in front of the grocery store and again recalled what Clarence had said. But I am electrician, he reminded himself, so instead of seeking out the manager for a job interview, he went inside and bought himself an ice cold Hires Root Beer responding to the temptation irresistibly brought on by the gleaming orange and white sign affixed to the red brick wall next to the front entrance. The drink cost him a nickel. It was beyond delicious. He drank down the bottle in massive gulps and produced a loud belch that caused a disgusted glare from a woman passing by on the sidewalk. He smiled sheepishly in return. He had exactly one dollar and twenty cents in his pocket after his splurge for the refreshment, more than enough, he thought, to buy lunch and maybe have some left over for another bottle on his way home. The rest of his money, one hundred and fifteen dollars, was sewed into the lining of his duffel bag, laid flat and tucked under the mattress in his room on Harmony Street.

Why was he so carefree, almost whimsical on this day when he should be in a terrible frenzy over Mrs. Dionne's warning to evict him unless gainful employment came his way by week's end? Robert had no answer. He could not fathom an explanation. He just knew, somehow, finding Liberty Street a while back would bring him luck.

Two blocks away near the corner of South Rampart and Thalia Streets he saw the sign:

Roblinski's Appliance and Radio Repair Shop:
We Fix It Or You Don't Pay

8

"What do you vant? I am busy. I see you carry noting for me to fix so vhy are you here?"

The words came fast from the quivering jowls of Sigmund Roblinski who barely looked up from his work station located behind the counter of his tiny shop. He was addressing the first person to step inside that day and alert him to their presence by the tinkling bell suspended over the front door.

Robert gulped and tried to provide a cogent response to the rude greeting but before he could speak Sigmund was at him again.

"I have no money for hand out. You go somewhere else. If you vant to rob me, you can, but there is no money. I warn you so you vill go to jail for noting," Sigmund warned.

Robert finally mustered up a response. "Sir, I am no robber. I am honest man, looking for honest work. I come to your shop today to seek employment. I am electrician. You need electrician? I am good electrician. You see here."

Robert deftly retrieved the single page letter from his satchel and placed it on the glass countertop behind which Sigmund continued to sit, now appearing to hide from view, hunched over his workbench.

From somewhere back there Robert heard: "Are you stupid, boy? I say to you I have no money. I fix the radios, the televisions, the appliances for people in this neighborhood and sometimes they pay, sometimes they don't. If they don't pay, I keep. You look around, stupid boy. See all these radios, and toasters, and irons, and hand mixers and all of those televisions? You think I vant them? No. I fix and people no pay. So I keep. I try to sell, but nobody buy. That's why I have no money. So you go now. Leave me be. This customer who owns this electric fryer pan may pay. I fix. I think she vill pay," Sigmund declared.

From a place Robert could not tell Sigmund suddenly emerged and stood to his side, wiping his hands on a dirty red cloth. "Please leave my store or I vill have you arrested," Sigmund advised as he approached.

Robert stood his ground looking down on Sigmund who was looking up at him with a stern, threatening expression. The top of his head was devoid of even a single follicle, yet thick, long waves of steel grey hair at the sides swept back over his ears into a curly tangle at the back of his neck. His arms were muscular. The fingers of his hands were little more than stubbles. A red ruby ring encased in shiny gold was displayed on the middle finger of his right hand. His white shirtsleeves were rolled up past his forearms to his biceps. On his left appendage a brilliant tattoo appeared to Robert to be a delicately carved family crest.

"Please read letter, Sir. I am fine apprentice in my country. I come to New Orleans to find job. My master was Gergely Kovacs. The best electrician in my country. My father's friend. He train me at everything. I can fix. Let me show you. You no have to pay," Robert offered.

Sigmund stood silent, eyeing Robert up and down. Robert pushed the letter toward him. Sigmund stepped back.

"Where you from boy?" He asked.

"Hungary, Sir," Robert replied.

"Romania. My home," Sigmund pronounced. He took the letter from Robert's outstretched hand. Sigmund turned and disappeared behind the counter in a quick stealth movement. Robert could hear the ruffling paper and then a sigh as he presumed Sigmund had found his workbench chair. He saw a hand reach up and adjust the green shade lamp secured over the table to shed better lighting for him to read.

Minutes passed. Robert shifted his weight from his good leg to his bad and back again. His eyes scanned the tiny, cluttered shop. He noticed a heavy blue brocade curtain to the left of Sigmund's position. Light shown outward through the crack in the drapes. They were not tightly drawn. Beyond them he could faintly make out what appeared to be another workbench standing in an anteroom. No one occupied that space. The bench was clear of objects. Robert began to pace back and forth in front of the counter. His bad leg hurt.

Finally when finishing one of his short marches in one direction, he turned and Sigmund was there. Letter in hand. Robert nearly bumped into him.

"Boy, I may have work for you. You come back tomorrow or next day if you vish and I see then. I make no promises. And I have no money, but maybe some work for you. Maybe a test first to see if you are good like Mr. Kovacs say here. Maybe then I find some money. No promises. What name you have?"

"Robert, Sir. Robert Kaye."

"That is no Hungarian name. Why already you have American name already? How long you been in New Orleans, boy?" Sigmund asked.

"Just two days, Sir," Robert said.

"You get American name at checkpoint immigration? You get name from Conrad, Immigration Officer, Jenkins?"

"Yes, Sir, Officer Jenkins, Sir."

"You ashamed of Hungarian name boy?" Sigmund's voice grew harsh. "What's your real name?"

"Roman, Sir, Roman Sokolowski. I need new name to fit into America, Sir."

"Bullshit. In my shop you are Roman." Jenkins gave me name of Reynolds, Sam Reynolds. I told him okay, but I have not use it. Name is on my papers, but Roblinski is my name, noting else. Maybe I see you tomorrow Roman."

Robert sensed it was time for him to go. He wouldn't press his luck with the shopkeeper any further so without another word he went to the door and exited to the sound of the tinkling bell overhead.

9

Robert in America, except in Roblinski's shop on Rampart Street where he will always be known as Roman, spent the rest of the day aimlessly wandering the streets of what he heard a fellow pedestrian tell the woman companion at his side, "This is the famous French Quarter." It immediately brought to mind Mr. Francois's instructions of a place not to miss visiting. "What I hear it is a delightful section of New Orleans where you will find many of life's pleasures if you so desire and if there's money still jingling in your pocket," Francois had said with a mischievous grin.

While limping along Robert became conscious of several conversations in French and when he did he would momentarily stop his monotonous meanderings to listen and try to interpret what was being said. He had vowed to maintain his fluency in French while at the same time perfect his growing command of English, ridding himself of his accent as quickly as humanly possible. However, in doing so he feared losing sway over his harmonious Hungarian dialect. Fitting in America was much more important, so good English speaking would be his main goal. If that meant sacrificing his native tongue, so be it.

As Robert haltingly walked along he recalled that Mr. Francois only spoke to him in French at each of their meetings, which took place in his spacious teak paneled office overlooking Pierre Puget Park which was not far from The Abbey of Saint-Victor. According to Robert's human trafficking agent, the Abbey was one of the oldest places of Christian worship in all of France if not all of Europe. During his two-week stay in Marseille awaiting his expedited and likely forged travel documents, Roman grew to love the idyllic Mediterranean seaport city even though nine of those fourteen nights were spent under a bench in the beautiful Pierre Puget Park. The other five nights he slept in a run-down fifteen franc a night hostel situated on a narrow winding street in the Panier District, also not far geographically but light years away economically from Mr. Francois's posh palace of business. Roman had saved only enough for five nights of lodging because he hadn't been told he'd be in France longer than that. Each morning at sunrise Roman would rise and walk to take in the breathtaking view of the "Petit Nice" on the Corniche with Frioul and Chateau d'if .

He would wash up in one of the dozens of public fountains; find an early-to-open pastry shop for a croissant and piping hot cup full of thick black coffee before rushing to be the first in line to see Mr. Francois. Despite rising earlier each morning not once was he first in line. Not even close. Each time he arrived at Mr. Francois's reception area it would already be occupied by a dozen or so would-be immigrants just like him. All were eagerly waiting and willing to pay Mr. Francois's processing fee of two thousand American dollars a head for all the credentials needed including passable passports to gain entry into the United States. That was two thousand dollars, not francs; Mr. Francois would always say, not including transport.

Depending on your preferred means of travel, either in the hull of a merchant freighter or as a stowaway on a cruise liner confined to sleeping areas in the engine room or galleys Mr. Francois's special ticket cost an additional five hundred dollars; also in dollars not francs. Roman chose the galley of the passenger ship and on his second day at sea he discovered a spare waiter's uniform behind the galley's nonperishable food section. This is where he and three others had cots and blankets awaiting them when they were smuggled on board at two o'clock in the morning of the day scheduled for the ocean liner's departure.

With his sparse but adequate English language skills he convinced a befuddled and often drunk head chef that he was one of twenty servers who worked for him. During the crossing Roman made one hundred and seventy-five dollars, not francs, in tips working double shifts.

At around two o'clock on his second day in America, Robert found a street-side diner aptly named Abe's Hot House known for its Hot Spicy Barbeque Pulled Pork Sandwiches according to the hand painted sign in the window. When he entered it truly was hot inside. Maybe the hottest he'd ever been in his life. At least by ten degrees hotter than on the sidewalk outside because of the lack of ventilation and the full force flame of the cooking pots filled to capacity with bubbling sauce soaked reddish brown pig's meat.

Robert took a stool at the counter next to another black man. He had by now quit counting them and didn't think much more about it. He ordered another Hires Root Beer and one of the specials. All totaled seventy-five cents, the same as the cost of the gumbo from the day before. He was glad. He had money left in his pocket. When he bit into the sandwich his mouth was immediately set aflame worse than from yesterday's crayfish concoction, but he quickly got used to the piercing spices and devoured the meat and bread with relish. He lingered at the counter of the diner for nearly an hour swallowing two tall glasses of ice water besides the root beer to ease down the meal before resuming his labored walk through the renowned neighborhood.

Another thing Mrs. Dionne told him that morning was that she would be unhappy to see him return before six o'clock in the evening. That's how long people worked in New Orleans, she said, from seven in the morning until six at night so she expected that's how long Robert should be out looking for a job on his first day.

Dinner at the boardinghouse was served promptly at six forty-five so he would have forty-five minutes to clean up preferably to bathe before joining the others for their suppers. Robert had another hour to kill before he should begin his walk home judging from the time it took for this morning's trek to Rampart Street and right smack dab into his future with the old and cantankerous Mr. Sigmund Roblinski.

He heard that expression from Clarence as part of his harangue at being "right smack dab in the presence of this flea-bitten vagabond" – meaning Robert. Robert understood the implications of Clarence's reference. Now he adapted the phrase to place himself square in the middle of Mr. Roblinski's life from now on. At least he hoped so.

What should Robert tell Mrs. Dionne upon his return to the boarding house? Did he have employment or not? Would Sigmund accept him that next day when he planned to arrive bright and early at eight o'clock, even though the hours posted on the glass pane of his front door read, "Shop Hours 9 to 5". He wouldn't care if he was early by an hour before Mr. Roblinski was to open for business on that Tuesday. He would be waiting for him. Right then he decided to lie to Mrs. Dionne and declare himself fully employed after only one day's search.

He did just that. He lied. Mrs. Dionne was delighted, but Robert was thunderstruck when she told her tenant she would be verifying his story with a telephone call to Mr. Roblinski that next morning "just to be sure."

Even though the moist tender pot roast, potatoes, carrots and brown gravy and ice tea served for dinner at precisely six forty-five was stunningly delicious, Robert's stomach was churning from what he faced that next day. He was silent through the meal, and would excuse himself before the others, failing to notice the sideward glances from Miss Henley seated to his right. His fellow tenants were talking in rapid succession, but Robert's mind raced along with his ailing stomach paying little to the chatter about everything from the furnace like heat outside, to the breakdown of the St. Charles Avenue trolley, to the dandelions infiltrating the front yard, and finally to Miss Henley's promotion from receptionist to personal assistant to the junior partner of the law firm of Walker, Walker & Schmidt.

Clarence had asked her, "What da hell is a personal assistant in da first place. What do ya do, shine his shoes?"

"No, you silly," Miss Hattie broke in, "she will become more important each day, helping her boss address legal matters and such for so many of our fine New Orleans citizens."

"Isn't that right, Miss Henley," Miss Hattie asked seeking confirmation of her theory.

"That is correct Miss Hattie," Miss Henley affirmed.

"Shit, dat's beyond me. Should come up wit a new name, like junior vice pardner, if yo ask me," Clarence offered. "Git me otta here Boudreaux. This here talk is makin' me crazy. Need some peace and quiet and a long smoke after a supper like dat."

"Congratulations to you, Miss Henley. I am sure you deserved it after all the countless hours you've given to that firm," Mrs. Claire offered.

"Well, thank you, Margeaux," responded Miss Henley. Even in his distracted state Robert sensed a chill in the exchange between the two female dinner companions. He wondered why.

At that point Robert excused himself and hobbled from the room. Shortly thereafter Boudreaux wheeled Clarence away. Miss Henley remained, wondering why Robert seemed to ignore her overtures. She missed most of Miss Hattie's description of the wonderful lilies blooming in the backyard, and Mr. Dominique's complaint that the broken trolley made him late for work at DeSalle's Antique Emporium conveniently located at the corner of Dauphine and Iberville. She did find it interesting when Mrs. Dionne proclaimed, not without skepticism in her tone, that Robert had secured a position at Roblinski's Appliance Store. She couldn't remember the official name of the establishment.

"I know that place," announced Mr. Dominique. "It's on Rampart Street. Didn't know he was still in business.

"We will find out tomorrow," Mrs. Dionne assured herself and the others.

10

When Robert arrived at Sigmund's storefront at his self-appointed morning hour of eight he found the yellowed stained roll up paper curtain hanging behind the windowpane of the front door tightly drawn. The "Closed" sign was flipped into position unmistakably declaring the status of current operations inside. To give his leg a rest after his nearly mile walk, Robert eased his way down to sit on the protruding section of brick windowsill. He would wait where he was for the hour to pass. However, the time didn't elapse so quickly, for Robert's mind was filled with his dream from the night before. Haunting it was as never before.

Again it was another journey back to Fodor and Rudolph and his father's ranting. As before he was with his father and brother seated at their kitchen table smelling of smoke and sweat and burnt sausage and pungent port spilled by his father's careless pour into his now empty glass. Cups of untouched goat's milk sat in front of Roman and his brother.

Robert's dream this night took on a new, eerie twist. The scene was fixed in his mind. He replayed every second of it sitting there on the windowsill awaiting Mr. Roblinski's arrival. This time Robert's dream of Fodor and Rudolph and Roman placed him in an audience of one, sitting alone in a vast empty theatre that reminded him of the Vigado Concert Hall in Budapest. It was there a year before the uprising that he saw the American play Gypsy about America's most famous burlesque queen. Performed in his native tongue by local thespians Roman loved every minute of it. Tonight in his dream love would not abound.

Robert's dream found him in that vacant vastness of the theatre patiently waiting for something, not knowing why he was there or what to expect. The darkness was broken by the red glow of the exit signs on each side auditorium. The Hungarian Gypsy Rose was nowhere to be found. Then it began. Curtains opened and under the glare of a bright spotlight were the three familiar characters seated at their respective tableside positions in the exact center of the stage. From his chair on stage Roman turned to stare down at Robert seated in Row 7, Seat Number 13, the seat his mother took for every performance she managed to attend away from the watchful eye of Fodor. An anguished look fell upon Roman's face. His father and brother sat motionless in their places. The one-man monologue punctuated by Fodor's frequent slurring did not start until Roman brought his gaze from Robert to his father in a nodding motion signaling him to begin.

Act 1 of this night's evocative one act play was particularly intense as his father's invective soon grew to a high pitch. Fodor's message that night was to remind his sons of the tragic destruction of their country by the Treaty of Trianon of 1920 perpetrated by the heartless Jews and their greed for money and power.

"The peace treaties signed after the First World War redefined the national borders of Europe and punished our country mercilessly after our tragic defeat," Fodor began.

"The forced dissolution of our glorious Austria-Hungarian Empire at the hands of the blood thirsty Jews spelled disaster as new multiethnic kingdoms and republics were formed comprising of all manner of scurrilous races. To the north the Slovak bastards, all traitors beyond a doubt, formed the new state of Czechoslovakia. Transylvania was ripped from us to become part of Romania, while the southern areas of our homeland were devastated when Croats and other rebel Slavs formed the illegal state of Yugoslavia.

"My sons, our mission must be to reunite our nation state. To slaughter those responsible for our dismemberment and triumphantly return our country to its rightful dominance in Eastern Europe."

As Fodor took a breath and spilled more port into his glass, Roman again peered down at Robert with a somber look of sympathy. Robert was puzzled at Roman's animated stare wondering who should be sympathetic of whom. In his dream he gawked back at his alter ego and squirmed in his seat, suddenly becoming extremely uncomfortable. Robert then took his eyes away to scan the empty seats around him peering through the vast hall as far as his eyes could see. All other seats in the empty auditorium were cushioned and covered in soft, supple red leather. His seat, number 13 in Row 7, had no cushion, nor red leather covering. His seat offered only bare splintered wood. Nail heads protruded around the edges holding the wood in place. They scratched and tore at his skin in places where his body rested. He squirmed again, seeking comfort but found none.

Fodor's voice shattered his thoughts. "In the end the Jews found a way to influence the capture of nearly two-thirds of our nation's land area. Imperial Germany was and remains our friend, my sons. Never forget that. Always trust our German brethren. We went down to defeat together, but we will rise again in victory to recapture what is ours and eliminate the vermin that brought on our disgrace." Fodor blurted out in force.

"We were not defeated by England, or the invaders from America. We were corrupted from inside by the disease plague of the rat infested souls of the Hebrew. Now we have begun to heal. The Arrow Cross will sever the blood supply nourishing their cancer on our society," his voice now cracking and echoing through the otherwise stillness of the theatre. "Our savior is the strong will of our hearts in a united cause. Look our across our borders my sons. Look to Germany and their rarified Chancellor for the support we need to defeat our enemies. We are joining his fascists' crusade in numbers growing daily by the thousands."

Robert felt himself recoil at the latest of Fodor's outbursts, but he didn't know why. Then Act 1 was complete. There would be no Act 2 in this night's performance. The curtain was closing at the moment Robert's mind had been jerked from its slumber by the sudden clanging of his alarm clock.

Reliving his startling awakening that morning while sitting there in front of Mr. Roblinski's shop brought on another upright jerk and cold shiver to Robert's body even though the morning sun had warmed the pavement at his feet and its rays had heated the glass window at his back to bring moisture to his clean shirt.

11

Robert squinted into the brutal sunshine just as it peaked above the rooftops of the buildings across the street from Roblinski's shop. He rose from his seat on the windowsill and began a slow lumbering pace in front of the store. He didn't have a watch so he wasn't quite sure of the time but he felt it was nearing the appointed nine o'clock hour. He looked for a clock but found none. He was disturbed and shaken still. He couldn't discard the hurtful physical effects of his dream from the night before. When the dreams came they always left him drained and lethargic as if he were there again in the kitchen, his ears ringing from Fodor's uproar, desperately awaiting his father's final hateful spew before succumbing to the liquor and his own frantic exuberance. When his stupor overcame him, Roman and Rudolph could finally go to bed.

Right then Robert felt that fatigue, the same as he experienced on those many horrific nights. His anxious walk past the threshold of Roblinski's hoped-for haven of employment was unsteady.

He tried to concentrate on the speech he planned for Mr. Roblinski. He would further attempt to justify his desired position by volunteering free labor at the spare workbench, and if that was not compelling enough he would fall back to accept any task, however menial it might be. All he wanted on this warm and humid Tuesday morning was to have the shopkeeper confirm for Mrs. Dionne his status among the gainfully employed. However, his mind kept racing back to the night before, to his hard nail head-puncturing seat stationed in the empty concert hall devoid of cushion and upholstery and love. The deafening sound of his father's adoration for the German Dictator. His own revulsion of that pronouncement left him curious and perplexed.

Was he just remembering how frightened, how repulsed he was as a child by his father's odious actions or was he just now beginning to consider that his father was wrong? After all these years of acceptance and embracing the man's ideals, maybe Fodor was mistaken after all. Was that why Robert shuttered and withdrew so suddenly at hearing, seeing and reliving last night's scene? Had he mellowed in coming to America? Had his beliefs suddenly abandoned him in deference to the freedoms he had already begun to enjoy? Maybe these were just fleeting moments of childish nostalgia, a weakness to overcome like the weakness in his leg and the weakness brought on by his new name?

He sat again on the sill, tired of walking, and suddenly had an overwhelming craving for a Hires Root Beer. His mind thankfully leaving its introspective examination. He fought with himself over whether to leave his post and embark on a search for the drink or remain loyal to his self-imposed undertaking to be the first to arrive and hopefully the last to leave. A few more minutes passed. The heat intensified. Robert stayed put, overcoming the temptation to move. Then finally out of the corner of his eye Robert saw the closed sign rotate and the paper curtain rise.

Robert waited a few seconds before opening the door to enter the shop. He barely caught sight of the back of Sigmund's grey mane before he swept around to disappear behind a jagged row of old RCA and Motorola black and white console models. Robert stepped toward the counter in cautious pursuit of the shopkeeper.

"Stupid boy. I have no money. I lost everything yesterday," Sigmund proclaimed from his mysterious perch. "The woman with the hand mixer paid me two dollars. I ask but that old bastard Markowitz to pay. He owes me fifty for fixing that Curtis Mathis at the end of the row there. But he says he can't pay 'til Thursday. I collect maybe twenty dollars for fixing three Hoovers, but no more. How do you expect me to pay, stupid boy? I have to eat you know, pay for lights. I see you dare sitting like a bum on my vindow sill. Over an hour. What you vant from me?"

"Mr. Roblinski. I want a job. I need a job. I am not a stupid boy. I am a man. A good man who can work. I can help you make money. I can help you collect from those who owe you money. Please don't call me a stupid boy again," Roman asked without reservation.

There was a long silence.

"Are you there, Mr. Roblinski?" Roman searched to his right. Suddenly Sigmund appeared to his left, startling him again. "Is this man a phantom? Roman playfully thought to himself.

"Roman. Maybe you are not stupid as electrician but you are stupid coming to me for job. Why you not look at place like Sears or Monty Ward? They have big appliance shops, but maybe they don't repair, just sell new. I don't know. My son is dead only six month. He was my helper, my apprentice, soon to take over my shop. He was kilt when fast car ran red light and struck him on his bicycle delivering fixed Sunbeam iron to nice lady Mrs. Mitchell on Friday. She always pay on time. His bench is empty in back. He was seventeen. His mother die of tuberculosis year before. I like to be alone now," Sigmund said. But not in a way Roman sensed was sincere.

"No Roman, you are not stupid," Sigmund allowed before stepping away.

Sigmund scurried around the counter again leaving Roman to himself. Just then the tiny bell over the front door tinkled to announce the first customer of the day. Roman did not hesitate. He walked up to the man carrying a table top radio, one of those new ones, bright sun flower yellow in color and made of that new plastic compound called Bakelite which was all the rage at the time.

"May I help you, Sir," Roman asked.

"Damn thing. I buy it two weeks ago and now it quits. Turned it on last night and it works, maybe thirty minutes. I'm listening to fine show tunes over WSHO when I smell something like burning garbage. Then I see smoke rising from the top and it sparked and went dead. Can you believe this? Cost me thirty dollars for thirty minutes. Can you fix?" The man inquired.

"Yes, Sir we can fix," Roman responded with assurance.

"Thank you. I will come back tomorrow to pick up. You fix it and I will come back tomorrow."

"No sir," Roman said, "I can't do that." He handed the radio back to the man.

"What? You said just a minute ago, you can fix. Now you tell me you can't. You didn't even look at it. How do you know you cannot fix?"

"I didn't mean that, Sir. What I meant is you will give me a deposit, money down for me to try to fix. With that money, I will work to fix. Without it I cannot. If I fix your radio you will owe me more money. If I cannot fix, you come back tomorrow and I give you back your money and your radio," Roman patiently explained.

"Wait a minute. Where is Roblinski? He never makes me or anyone else in the neighborhood pay before he fixes things. Where is he?"

"He is not here just now. I am Roman. Roman Sokolowski. I am his new assistant. I will do the job of fixing the radio, but first you must pay five dollars. If I fix I will charge you fifteen dollars total, so when you come to the shop tomorrow and the radio is working you pay another ten dollars. If I don't fix I give you back your five dollars and the radio. Also if I fix and you pay me fifteen dollars and radio breaks again one year from tomorrow, I fix again but that time for free. If I can't fix second time, I give you all your money back. But if radio is broken and you did it, like it falls on the floor, that is your fault and not mine so I would not give your money back. It is fair deal. No?" Roman offered.

The man stood quietly for a moment looking first at Roman, then at the radio placed back under his arm, then to Roman and then back to his radio, not quite sure what to say even though he opened his mouth once or twice while exercising his eyes.

Silence from behind the counter. Not even the sound of lamp shades being adjusted or paper shuffling or screws turning. Not even an audible breath.

After a few more moments Roman broke the silence in an attempt to break the stalemate. "What is your name, Sir?"

The man appeared to remain somewhat in shock. He didn't answer right away. He just kept looking at the radio he held and around the shop presumably searching for Mr. Roblinski. He seemed to avoid Roman, so Roman started to ask again.

"What..."

"My name is Janos, Jozsef, Janos. I know Roblinski for many years. You say he is not here?"

"Yes, Sir, he is not here at the moment. Everything is all right. He is not sick, just taking a brief rest to think things over about his shop and all these televisions and appliances here he fixed and no one paid for," Robert explained.

"I see," Jozsef acknowledged.

Jozsef then slowly and cautiously presented the faulty receiver back to Roman as if it were a delicate, rare piece of priceless china. Robert accepted it reverently. Jozsef then reached into his back pocket and retrieved his wallet. He plucked from it a five-dollar bill and handed it to Roman.

"You fix it and I bring you more money tomorrow," promised Jozsef, still looking a little befuddled but graciously bending in a half bow of politeness before pivoting and walking out the door, the bell signaling his departure.

Roman turned and walked to the counter, placing the radio and the currency on the glass top. He was startled slightly when he heard a muffled sniffle and the honk from the mystery man behind the counter when he blew his nose.

"I have cold. You are a bold, pretentious young man, Roman," he heard him declare. "I am surprised at your actions, taking over my shop as if you own it. Then you offend my friend and neighbor. What am I to do? I should throw you out."

Again Roman was looking one way toward the direction from which the voice came and when he looked the other way, there stood Sigmund seemingly appearing from thin air.

"But you know that son of a bitch Janos screw me five, maybe seven time having fix his tings and he never pay. Always tell me he have no money or he tell me to keep and sell. Tink I'm a pawnshop or someting. I'm glad. First money I ever see from that son of a bitch. You did good, Roman. You fix?"

"Yes, Sir. It is probably just a blown tube or condenser. These models, made by Philco, bad for blowing tubes. I see these kind in Hungary and practice on them to fix. If you have tube from Philco television or another radio maybe same part number will work," Roman suggested.

"I have similar model I tear apart in back room. Television, no radio. If you like you can look to see. You have permission," Sigmund allowed.

Roman took his leave, going behind the sacred counter for the first time, pulling back the curtains to enter the sanctuary behind. He heard Sigmund return to his station, saying no more. Roman walked past the empty, clean workbench of the shopkeeper's son, its chair pushed in under.

The back room was as cluttered and as unkempt as the outer room with all manner of electronic paraphernalia scattered about in heaps and piles. Empty wooden shells of console televisions were stacked three to four high from the floor up. Beside them were at least a dozen cathode ray tubes, all with very black glass screens. One whole table perhaps twelve to fifteen feet long displayed every make and model of gutted out radios imaginable. Another table across an aisle barely wide enough to squeeze through held hand mixers, toasters, clothes irons, electric heaters, fans, and even what Roman thought oddly looked like a man's penis from which a power chord was attached. Some devices were dismantled. Some remained assembled and looked functional. All were strewn about and looked like they had rested in their places for some time. In another corner as many as twenty upright vacuum cleaners stood erect in a strange 'v' shape suggesting that by arranging them this way Sigmund was signifying something but at that moment it was too baffling for Roman to decipher.

Placed beneath the table full of crippled, dysfunctional electronic mishmash Roman found a cardboard box heaping with glass tubes. He pulled the box from its place and gently pushed aside the debris to find room on the tabletop. It didn't take him long to find the Philco emblem and a clear bulb indicating its ability to conduct electricity in proper voltage. Roman snatched the tube quickly and walked back through the curtains to find Jozsef's radio. It remained where he had placed it before. Without another thought he grabbed it with the intention of beginning his work at the empty bench just behind him but was stopped abruptedly with…

"No one works at Isaac's bench. No one!"

Roman froze.

"Where then shall I work Sir?"

"Work at the counter for now."

Within twenty minutes Roman had disassembled the Philco, but discovered the first tube he had found was one model number off, meaning if he would have installed it, it would have potentially overheated and blown itself or the others in short order. So he searched again in the cardboard box until he found another tube with another model number, which he knew was slightly less powerful and would reduce the risks of overheating. He installed that one and soon the sweet sounds of WSHO, presenting New Orleans finest tunes from Broadway, came drifting from the tiny plastic encased speaker to fill Sigmund Roblinski's outer showroom. Roman immediately recognized one of the tunes as the classic "Let Me Entertain You", the headliner song from the only good play he'd ever seen. He smiled, remembering on that night in Budapest Gypsy prancing about in her red gown blocking Fodor from entering the stage.

Over the music, Roman heard, "Take the five dollars. Put it in your pocket. That is all I have to pay you this day. You may stay if you like. Make yourself busy if you like. There is a Sylvania fourteen inch in the back that belongs to Petrovitch. If you fix he may pay."

Roman's day was heaven. He got sound but no picture on the Sylvania by lunchtime. Before he left on a thirty minute break in search of a Hires Root Beer and a corned beef sandwich he spotted a picture tube that was compatible and knew by the time the afternoon was over he would have Petrovitch's entertainment center ready for viewing The Jack Benny Show was on at eight o'clock that evening. Of course

Roman had no idea who Jack Benny was but he pretended to know when Sigmund said it was Petrovitch's favorite show and might pay more if he had it fixed in time.

At three o'clock Sigmund gave Roman Petrovitch's telephone number to announce that his television was ready for pick up and was "in perfect working order." The voice on the other end of the line sounded stunned at the news and said, "I vill be right over."

At three thirty the telephone rang. It was the first time it had rung all day. Sigmund rose from his workbench where he was applying his skills to another Sunbeam iron to answer.

Roman had a feeling who was calling.

"Yes, this is Mr. Roblinski. Yes, I know the boy, err, man. Yes, he is here."

Then a long pause. Robert waited. His hand shook. He had to put down the wire cutters he was using to trim the excess off the single speaker hookup in the front of the Sylvania before he reattached the back panel. He was working at the table in the back room but could hear the one-way conversation. His leg suddenly began to ache.

"Yes, I am here," was Roblinski's next acknowledgement.

Then finally, thankfully he heard, "Yes, Mrs. Dionne, the young man work for me. He has job in my shop. Be assured. He is good boy, err, man. Thank you, Mrs. Dionne."

At four o'clock Peter Petrovitch, who could have been Roblinski's brother, if not his first cousin since they looked so much alike except Peter was absent Sigmund's gray mane, tinkled his way into the shop. Sigmund was nowhere to be found, having disappeared without a trace. From behind the curtains Roman came to the front to greet the customer.

"Here to pick up television," said Peter. "Where is Roblinski? Who are you?"

"Roman, Sir. Mr. Roblinski's assistant. He is out on errand just now. Like I said over telephone, your television is in fine working order in time for Mr. Bunny. You may come to back room to see. I have adjusted rabbit ears for good reception."

"Don't try to be funny kid. I have to see this," said Peter admonishing with rising skepticism.

They both disappeared behind the curtains. A few moments later…

"Good. Very good," said Peter when they both reemerged. "I vill take it vith me now and return with money, maybe next week when I am paid at job."

"No, Sir. You will pay now or you will not take with you. Work is done. You must pay now or Mr. Roblinski will sell. That was your bargain," Roman patiently observed.

Peter adopted nearly the same look as Jozsef had only hours before when hearing similar words.

The staring began and the silence fell just like they had that morning.

Finally, almost pleading, "But I tell my wife, we have television to vatch tonight. Jack Benny is on. What am I to do?"

"Simple, Sir. Pay me thirty dollars and you please your wife," was Roman's advice.

Five minutes later with thirty dollars in the previously empty cash drawer, Roman returned to his makeshift worktable to dismantle a King Oscillator electric shaver. In his examination he soon discovered the twirling blades were mangled beyond repair. Replacement parts would be difficult to find but he vowed to search every cluttered corner until he found them.

At six o'clock, Roman heard Sigmund walking across the front shop floor. He stepped through the curtains and watched as Sigmund flipped around the sign and pulled down the paper curtain.

"It is six o'clock. We close."

Roman realized he had only forty-five minutes to return to Harmony Street and arrive at Mrs. Dionne's dinner table on time. Robert resisted a sense of urgency to get moving. He had to wait no matter how long it took for confirmation from the shopkeeper. Was he to return?

In the center of the aisle between the rows of mostly broken electronic gadgets, Roman came from behind the counter while Sigmund headed toward it. They both stopped, meeting face to face. Sigmund looked Roman up and down as he did the first time they met just the day before. Roman only stared down at him.

Silence. Observing. Contemplating. Waiting.

"You may arrive at eight o'clock as you did today, but I arrive at nine. You decide," Sigmund finally said.

"Yes, Sir, eight o'clock. "As you wish."

Part III

Grand Island, Nebraska
August 1942

12

Monte Jessup received his draft notice in August of that first year of the war. A week later before boarding the Union Pacific passenger train for basic training in California he asked Bud to take over managing the drug store in his absence.

Bud accepted the job, gladly hanging up his apron, vowing never again to wash another used chocolate-crusted sundae dish. He took to reading pharmacy books in recognition of his new, broader responsibilities, thinking at the time his career might head in that direction. Homer Bradford had been Monte Jessup's pharmacist for seven years and he wanted to remain in that job indefinitely. He also had been exempted from military duty with flat feet and an exceptionally pronounced heart murmur. Homer wasn't happy when Monte told him that Bud would be his boss, but he accepted his fate and returned to his pharmacy to fill Mrs. Norton's prescription to treat a spastic bowel condition.

After a month of agonizing, gut wrenching study, particularly the chemistry sections of his primer guide for the state pharmaceutical board examination, Bud grew tired of the prospect of becoming a pharmacist. He closed the book on that chapter of his life after becoming completely and forever baffled over the chemical compound of aspirin. One day while waiting on a friendly couple shopping for a pair of crutches to aid their son who suffered a broken leg from leaping from a combine platform, he realized he loved to sell. He relished the thought, in fact embraced the challenge and found a giant thrill out of "closing the deal," no matter how small it might be.

On that particular day he not only sold the boy's parents the best and most expensive set of crutches in the store, they also bought rolls of Ace bandages to wrap the leg when the cast came off, and to add to it, several bottles of lotion to sooth and moisturize his skin. Bud also sold them three jigsaw puzzles to occupy their son's time while he convalesced, a basket full of toiletries to make him feel and smell like a man plus cover up the stench from the sweat soaked gauze wrapping the cast on his leg and finally a case of Nesbit Orange, his favorite drink. All total; thirty-five dollars as opposed to their original plan to spend only seven dollars and seventy-five cents on the crutches.

That's the way it went with Bud. He was the ultimate Super Salesman. He would spot a customer, watch them wander through the aisles for a few minutes, determine what they appeared to be searching for or conclude they were just browsing, and then he would pounce.

"Yes, ma'am, may I help you find that tube of toothpaste? Oh, you know we have a special on toothbrushes this week. Oh, you don't? Well, let me show you. My goodness, I almost forgot tissues and cotton balls and foot powder are also all on sale. Remember, as the war drags on these basic products that make our lives just a little easier are going to diminish, so I suggest you stock up on them while our supplies last." That became his favorite refrain.

With one customer a dollar twenty-five cent sale turned into a twenty-five dollar take and Bud had to make three trips to her car to deposit all the goods she had purchased.

He used the war and the rationing of America's commodities to support it as a way to boost sales, instilling fear, playing on greed, and when given the chance the common human tendency to hoard. This strategy sent his store revenues through the roof and his profit margins expanding like the width of his Aunt Mildred's behind.

After only three months on the job, Jessup's Drug realized unprecedented income and a four thousand two hundred thirty-seven dollar net gain. By that time Monte was on his way to join the Allied invasion of North Africa and had no time, let alone the opportunity to read Bud's glowing reports. Monte's mother was in the Sunny Side old folk's home unable to comprehend the figures or even that night's dinner menu so she had no way of interpreting Bud's progress. Monte's father had died three years past, so all Bud could do was pile up the money in the bank and barter with more suppliers, sometimes paying premium prices particularly for "watch list" items such as nylon stockings and petroleum based skin creams to fill his shelves and keep his patrons coming back for more. Bud never went over the government's declared quota system for the scarce items; he just found abundant reliable sources to fill his orders when his stock ran low.

On the sixth month after his managerial appointment Bud gave himself a raise to thirty dollars a week. He moved out of Hank and Vera's house and into an apartment across the street from the store, took out a loan at the bank and bought himself a 1939 Buick four door, two new suits, five shirts, seven ties and three pairs of shoes. Then he took Nancy McKinney out for dinner. Then he took Cynthia Jones out for dinner and then Bonnie Buford. He asked Bonnie out a second time but cancelled the date after he found out she was married and her husband was training to be a fighter pilot somewhere in the Nevada desert. So instead he went on a date with Vicki Pierce. He was discreet in his skirt chasing and was extremely careful not to reveal to anyone, particularly his companion at the moment, about the person or events that had captured and may have enraptured him a night or two before. There were but three decent restaurants in Grand Island and Aurora at the time, so he made sure each of those establishments became the single select spot for only one of his favorite female cohorts. As his circle of would-be conquests grew he was forced to expand his culinary options outside the community to assure that each of his lady friends concluded they were the extra special one occupying his time and spending his money.

On many nights after the meals were concluded and after proper courting got out of the way, he became active in other ways with more than a few of his willing dates. He always used the privacy of his inviting, well-decorated apartment with its separate side entrance for intimate entertainment, sometimes lasting well towards sun up. Bud was discreet, plus he had to avoid being spotted by jealous female friends left at home that night.

Connie Blakely managed to creep back into his brain more often than he wished, but as the months rolled by she began to fade from his consciousness and his dreams, especially those dreams which were often interrupted by a caress and coaxing from the person lying at his side.

Despite Bud's prowess and success both at work and off duty, he soon grew restless and bored. He wanted something better, something for himself. He needed bigger sales, more interesting products and greater challenges. That opportunity arose on the second anniversary of Pearl Harbor. He found out about it while attending a memorial service with Vera and Hank at the First Methodist Church for those killed in the Japanese attack. Tim Ryan, who was serving in the South Pacific on the aircraft carrier Ticonderoga, told his sister Martha and Martha told Bud that they were interested in selling their small furniture store which was only two doors down from Jessup's Drug. Martha said Tim had written to her to say he was no longer interested in the family business and if he survived the war he planned to move to Oregon to begin a new life. Martha said she had no desire to run the business alone and all they wanted for their inventory was five thousand dollars and for someone to take over their storefront lease.

Bud was fascinated at the prospect. He'd never thought about selling furniture but it was sure as hell better and more rewarding than selling hair dye. In spite of his rather lavish spending habits on expanding his collection of feminine trophies, he had saved around seventeen hundred dollars. He talked to Hank that afternoon and Hank was surprisingly enthusiastic about selling furniture, saying he could scrape together around two thousand, but for that he wanted a twenty-five percent interest in the store. Bud agreed with no hesitation. That left only thirteen hundred and he was sure he could borrow that much from the bank. His only real problem was figuring out how to run the drug store and his furniture store both at the same time.

He was not about to abandon Monte who was now deep in the desolate desert of Egypt helping the British drive back the Axis forces which fought fiercely under the command of the wily Nazi Field Marshall Erwin Rommel. In addition, he had given himself a second raise to seventy dollars a week, money he richly deserved in his mind and by the time Ryan's Furniture became a real possibility for Bud he made sure Monte already had nearly forty-thousand dollars nestled away, awaiting his return from the battlefront.

Except for Homer, who remained permanently implanted behind his drug counter, Bud replaced most of Monte's clerks and stockers with his own crew of loyal personnel on whom he had grown to rely for day-to-day operations. His conclusion was that he could run both businesses, with equal success, by simply shuttling between stores keeping an eye on everything while applying his salesmanship skills with balanced proficiency.

The bank came through with the loan with few conditions but Bud was unhappy when the final interest rate went above three and a half percentage points. Nonetheless, a month later he closed the sale with Martha who exercised power of attorney for her brother and on the same day he took down the Ryan Furniture sign and replaced it with his own that read B.C. & H Fine Furnishings.

On close inspection Bud found the store's stock of merchandise sorely lacking. The first thing he did was launch a full-blown liquidation sale to give him room to resupply with much higher quality pieces. With discounts as much as sixty percent, Ryan's old stock scurried out the door permitting Bud to purchase his selections from better-known manufacturers. He especially liked Stickley and Duncan Phyfe styles and the designs and quality being produced in the High Point area of North Carolina. It didn't take him long but it did take another two thousand dollar loan from the bank, this time at five percent interest, to fill his showroom with the fashions befitting his taste and those in his market area.

The agriculture business in Central Nebraska was thriving at this time with government subsidies helping farmers mass-produce for the war effort. There was some disposable income available from these households and Bud's instincts were telling him to take advantage of a tendency in people to spend for things of comfort to help sooth the frayed nerves of a community and country at war. He struck while the iron was hot, working eighteen-hour days hustling between stores and racking up strong sales in both locations. During his stepped-up, almost frantic pace, he was forced to curtail his romantic endeavors, which at times left him lonely and frustrated. Sleeping alone was not to his liking and contrary to his newly adopted nature.

On balance though, Bud was happy and gratified with his accomplishments. He had escaped the powerful grip of farm life and was making his way in the business world on his own, plus as the months passed he was building an adequate nest egg for himself.

Meanwhile the war was grinding on slowly but inevitably toward its successful conclusion. Bud's acumen for selfish exploits kicked in again in early 1945 when Dirk McDaniel put out the word that he wished to sell his Texaco gasoline station at the corner of West South Front Street and West Lincoln Highway. Old Dirk was nearing seventy. He had only one mechanic left. The other two had been gone for two years after being drafted. Dirk was tired of changing tires and pumping gas, plus he had barely broken even the year before due to gasoline rationing and shortages of replacement parts and tires. He hadn't sold a quart of oil to a motorist in more than two weeks. It was time for him to retire. Ten thousand dollars was all it would take for the corner lot, two pump stations, two repair bays, an adequate stockroom of second hand tires, and a fairly good display case of parts, mostly for Ford and Chrysler products with an emphasis on truck components.

Bud couldn't pass up the chance. He offered Dirk seven thousand cash and a note for three thousand payable over five years. Bud was in the gasoline retail business before he knew it. This initiative however cost him all his savings, plus he had to help guarantee the loan from the bank with cash flowing from the furniture store. Yet he was willing to take the chance.

Bud figured that when the war ended, gasoline rationing would end, cars and trucks, instead of tanks and troop carriers would be made and people and products would be on the move again. Dirk's location was excellent, right at the intersection of the main state highway, yet still positioned to conveniently serve local traffic from the neighborhoods.

Tommy Banks had just been discharged from the Marines as a result of a fairly severe ankle injury suffered when a Jeep slipped off a jack at the motor pool at a base camp in New Zealand. Tommy had been a Sergeant in charge of repairing fleets of every type of vehicle the U.S. government claimed it needed to defeat the Japanese, and now that he had returned home and married Alice Randall he needed a job and fast. Bud hired him the day after settling with Dirk and made Tommy a partner a week later when he produced three thousand dollars from accumulated back pay and savings to buy into the business. Bud took that money and, to Dirk's astonishment, paid off his note four years and eleven months early.

Now Bud found himself scampering among three locations during the day. He hired a full time manager for the furniture store. Tommy immediately assumed responsibility for running the gas station, and soon thereafter Bud promoted Martha Billingsley as assistant manager of the drug store. With the news Homer was furious about not being considered yet again soon got over the latest snub, quietly returning to his rightful place with only a whimpering protest.

What would have been a bucolic Sunday morning of church going turned raucous as celebrations spilled onto the streets. It was September 2, 1945. The war was finally over. Even the farm wives were strutting and twirling in front of Jessup's Drug and B.C. & H's Fine Furnishings waving champagne bottles and singing "Onward, Christian Soldiers." Bud got drunk on VJ Day. It was the first time since the accident. Life couldn't be better. In his happy haze he had a brief thought that the only thing missing in his life was Connie.

Little did he know.

13

It was the unmistakable red hair that got his attention. It didn't hurt that his next acknowledgement was her bouncing breasts descending the steps of the three o'clock Greyhound parked at curbside outside the bus depot. Bud happened to be driving by at the time on his way to meet with Tommy to go over the prior month's receipts. He pulled into the depot parking lot and watched her step heavily onto the sidewalk. The bus driver following close behind. He opened the baggage compartment beneath the passenger section and retrieved her luggage, placing it on the sidewalk in front of her and climbed back into the bus. There were four enormous suitcases. She looked bewildered at first, livid moments later, and then collapsed on to one of the bags, putting her face in her hands as if she had begun to cry.

Bud debated what to do next. Should he run to help or should he simply drive on? Tommy was waiting. They were thinking about buying a new set of Craftsmen tools, costing two hundred dollars, and hiring another mechanic to keep up with their expanding repair business. He had no time for women right then and particularly no time or tolerance for Connie, especially Connie. He simply could not resist and was transfixed at the sight of her. Hypnotized nearly, unable to move. He just stared. For her part, she just sat there. People walking by had to alter their paths to avoid her. She and her belongings were blocking two-thirds of the sidewalk.

Finally as if in a trance, Bud shut off the engine, got out of the car and walked over to where she sat. He tapped her on the shoulder and asked, "Need some help?"

Bud missed his appointment with Tommy that afternoon and later called him to apologize. He could never figure out why or how so quickly he found himself in her clutches. That afternoon lugging her luggage to his car and helping her find the apartment she had rented over on Cottage Street was just the beginning of never ending tasks for Bud, linked to her every whim, wish or at any particular moment, another neurotic demand. From the second he tapped her shoulder Bud was sunk, deep and desperate. First it was consoling her over her parent's divorce. Then it was sympathy for her father's drunken binges following his bankruptcy. Then, he heard how the world turned completely against her when she was forced to withdraw from Colorado College in her senior year, just five semester credits short of graduating with a teaching degree in English literature. She had no friends. They shunned her now. She had no place to go. She knew Bud would help her. He still loved her, right?

Yes, he supposed he did love her, if that's what it was. He wasn't sure about anything other than the fact that he was more miserable without her than with her.

She settled into her apartment and permanently ensconced herself in his brain. Bud helped her find a job at the County Library and with her near college degree she proved to be a good, thoughtful, helpful librarian.

Bud did his best to balance his daily business obligations with her incessant needs. He began having trouble concentrating. Sales in all three locations slipped just a bit during the first six months after Connie's humble but dramatic return. The declines were barely noticeable but were enough to set off an alarm with Bud and his accountants.

Monte was unaware of these details as they affected his store. After the war he decided to reenlist and was stateside now at Officer's Candidate School in North Carolina. Thanks to Bud, Monte's cash reserves had continued to grow now hovering around sixty-thousand dollars. In his latest letter Monte announced that he had no immediate inclination to return home and was seriously thinking about the Army as a career.

Bud asked him if he wanted to sell the store, but Monte politely declined. In subsequent correspondence the tension between the two grew a bit with Bud pressing the point and Monte resisting until Bud threatened to resign. That's all it took for Monte to reach a compromise. Bud would cut his weekly salary to seventy-five dollars a week (he was now making one hundred and ten) and in return he would get a twenty percent ownership stake in the business with options to buy more at the end of each year if profits continued to grow. They didn't settle on a purchase price for a higher ownership percentage but Bud was sure within five years he would own the place outright without having to incur large sums of debt.

Sales volume at the furniture store dropped off the most as Bud was forced to miss many of the better high ticket buyers since he showed little or no resistance to Connie's insistence to be at her side at every spare moment. He was in a heated frenzy. A Ferris wheel ride that wouldn't stop. He loved it and hated it at the same time. The only thing he wouldn't do was pay her rent and when he said no to that, she told him she wanted to move in with him. That too was out of the question. Not that he didn't want to sleep with her every night; it was Vera who put her foot down.

"No son of mine is going to live in the same house with a woman unless they are married," was her fervent declaration.

Connie rejoiced at that pronouncement. It was wedding bell music to her ears.

Bud finally concluded that if he married her he just might be able to return to work as before. He had enough money stashed away and was taking enough home from the three stores that they could live rather comfortably as long as he could control her spending habits.

"Sure, you bet I can change her," he emphatically told Scooter who had come home for a month after being discharged but was only stopping off on his way to San Francisco to join a merchant marine company.

"Once I marry her, she'll understand how important it is to live within a budget. She buys things because she's insecure. It fulfills a need in her. She strives for attention. When we're married all of that will be different. She won't need the world falling all over her," Bud said, reassuring himself much more so than his friend.

"Bullshit," Scooter said, "no man can change a woman like that. She's got something deep inside her gut that's like a gnawing hunger. She's got to feed it and no matter how good a lover you are, or how big a house you buy her or the tons of clothes you put on her back, she will never be satisfied."

Bud gazed at his friend. His eyes were fraught with desperation. He reached inside for a defense or any means of retaliation. No one should speak that way about the woman he loved so uncontrollably. Oddly, nothing came. He found no words. He drained his shot glass full of scotch.

"Look friend," Scooter said, realizing advice was better than condemnation, "I know I'm not gonna change your mind. I'm just tryin' to warn you that in my humble opinion the only way to influence that woman's actions is to stand up to her straight on. She has to know that you're her equal, at least, and that you're not gonna accept anything less than that. You've got to lay out the ground rules and stick to them."

"How much is she into you for?" Scooter asked after gulping down his own glass and motioning the bartender for refills.

Hesitant to answer at first Bud finally responded. "About fifteen hundred. Mostly clothes. Now she's buyin' things for the house, and she wants a car. She won't live in the apartment after we're married, so I've already put a down payment on a house over on North Sycamore Street. Not an expensive one, but it has three bedrooms, a basement and a great front porch. You know a brick bungalow. Just painted it yellow. Nice place."

"Jesus Christ, man," Scooter exclaimed, "you're farther gone than I thought. Good seein' ya buddy. Don't wait 'til your last dime to call me. I promise I'll come get you before then."

Scooter didn't attend the wedding. His excuse was that he was needed on the job in California. Bud didn't believe him, but he had no choice so he asked Monte and Monte agreed to be his best man. He traveled for three days from North Carolina on a special Army pass and barely made it in time for the rehearsal dinner.

Connie wouldn't wait until spring for the ceremony so every pew in the First Methodist Church was filled to capacity on a frigid Saturday in February 1947. The noontime temperature on the Prairie National Bank building read minus three degrees. The wind was clocked at twenty-seven miles an hour. A light snow was swirling on top of foot high drifts from a heavy fall the night before. The heat in the church sanctuary was on high but it was not enough to keep cold breaths from being visible from the mouths of most celebrants.

Hank bought Connie a billowing floor length red fox coat for her wedding. Vera was furious at his extravagance but he ignored his wife and gave it to his new daughter-in-law that morning. She wrapped it around her bare shoulders to ward off the chill until stepping gracefully into the aisle on the arm of her father who marched her unsteadily to the altar. James Blakely was living somewhere in Arizona where his daughter found him to plea for his attendance. Charlotte had moved to St. Louis. She brought her new boyfriend along to the wedding and after the rehearsal dinner James, having consumed a fifth of vodka, took a weak swing at him as the wedding party was leaving the restaurant. The real scuttlebutt would come later. Coffee klatches around town were fueled by the extravagant gift Hank bestowed on his new daughter-in-law. Many wondered aloud. Hank would never say.

Connie loved it. Bud thought she looked beautiful. To hell with what people thought.

James told Hank and Bud that he had only a hundred dollars to contribute to his daughter's wedding costs. They told him to keep it for his bus ticket home. Bud shelled out three hundred for the festivities and Hank was good for the rest. He didn't tell his son what the final tab was. Vera wasn't aware of any of this. She was still fuming over Connie's profligate coat. In all, Bud and Connie's nuptials were a momentous event. The loving couple was picture perfect. Mr. and Mrs. America. They motored off in Hank's new black Cadillac for their three-day honeymoon at the Brown Palace Hotel in Denver. It took them fourteen hours to get there, driving no more than forty miles an hour through a blizzard. They later surmised that Connie got pregnant on their second night behind the closed doors of the bridal suite.

14

Nine months and fourteen days later Connie gave birth to a strapping, beautiful blonde haired baby girl. She weighed in at just under nine pounds. They named her Christina and they swaddled her in the most expensive infant clothes, blankets, caps, and shoes that money could buy at the time in Nebraska. Connie would accept nothing less for her precious offspring. Yet after only six weeks of attending to her new born at home in their newly painted yellow three-bedroom two-story Connie decided she would return to work at the library. So she hired a full time nanny. Before her first day back on the job she gave away all of her pre-maternity clothes because they no longer fit her slightly expanded pelvic region. She also made a deposit at Goodwill of all of her maternity clothes since she knew she would never need them again. Then she went out to purchase a new wardrobe. It took her all day to complete her shopping but that was okay since the nanny was home fulfilling her duties.

Bud objected, complained, griped, and moaned but it did no good. He drowned his anxieties in work and when Bud decided to work there were few who were better at it. Sales receipts at the furniture store shot back up to surpass previous highs. He now seldom missed a major buyer. He handled them personally. In March he became the exclusive dealer for General Electric appliances and stocked all of its lines.

He and Tommy hired that extra mechanic who was an engine overhaul specialist and soon he was bringing in twice his wages per hour. They were also getting away with marking up parts by more than thirty percent against Bud's cost. Bud negotiated an exclusive parts distributorship for Chevrolets. Since he already was the only source for parts for Fords and Chryslers in the area he successfully locked up the market for components for the Big Three car companies. This mini-monopoly resulted in the construction of a small freestanding auto parts store next to the main office of the service station. He hired a clerk to run that business and kept Tommy overseeing the mechanics and pump jockeys.

With a twelve thousand dollar payment to Army First Lieutenant Monte Jessup from Bud's share of net profit receipts that year Bud took down another ownership piece of Jessup's Drug. By cashing the check Monte realized he had a fifty-one, forty-nine percent partner and he no longer controlled the enterprise that had been in his family for forty years.

After gaining majority control Bud emptied the shelves in one section of the drug store, which for years had been stocked with cheap toys and nonsense gadgets and started stocking can goods, cereal, potato chips and candy. Next to those aisles he installed coolers displaying bottled soft drinks and milk. While waiting for Homer to fill their prescriptions shoppers also could fill a grocery basket. The strategy worked like a charm and sales continued to climb.

At home Bud kept up as best he could. No matter how much went into the bank every week there never seemed to be enough to cover her spending. Connie had lay away and charge accounts at every clothing, jewelry, and shoe store in town. The bills came due every month and had to be paid on time. She pilfered the furniture store of nearly every new style in the showroom, no matter what it was, and by the second year of their marriage she had refurnished their house twice. Bud came home one evening and found a new 1948 Super Six Hudson Hornet coupe in his driveway. She said she bought it at a "real good price" since it was last year's model.

In spite of it all Bud remained deeply, forever enshrined in love. Not only with Connie, but with Christina as well. He adored them both.

Christina was a happy but sickly baby. She was slow in gaining weight after entering the world topping the scales. Her mop of curly blonde hair, present at birth, thinned out drastically and by her eighth month she was bald as a typical newborn. To Bud and Connie she seemed to vomit frequently, more than normal. She had little appetite to begin with. Her diapers were wet all the time. Vera had her suspicions about the child's ailments but kept them to herself. She told Hank what they were but refused to share them with her son and daughter-in-law. She prayed she was wrong. She would not be the one to frighten them that way. Later she desperately wished that she had.

Then came the seizure. Bud was awakened one night by the sound of his daughter's thrashing in her crib. When he switched on the light he gasped and staggered at what he saw. Laying on her back his precious baby girl was convulsing uncontrollably. Her eyes were open but rolled back in her head. She was frothing at the mouth. Instinctively he screamed for Connie and gathered the child up in his arms to try to stop her shaking. Connie was on the telephone to the hospital but it was difficult for the night nurse to understand her between her sobs.

Finally Bud heard his wife's frantic screech, "Karo Syrup! Pour it in her mouth!" Unconsciously Connie was repeating instructions she was hearing from the nurse. Then Bud remembered. Vera would always say if his mother ever went into a "fit," as she called it, anyone near her should pour Karo Syrup down her throat to shock her insulin-dominant blood sugar levels back in balance. Then they were to rush her to the hospital because she was having a potentially deadly insulin overdose.

Bud dashed into the kitchen still cradling his baby. Connie slammed down the receiver and was plowing through the cupboards in search of that life saving bottle. She found it on the top shelf over the new GE refrigerator. Bud took a spoon from the utensil drawer to administer the dose, but to his horror Christina's jaw was locked. He couldn't force it open. He was afraid of breaking her fragile bone so he parted her bright blue lips and literally drenched her face with the sticky liquid. Some, an ever so tiny amount, found its way past her lips and down her constricting throat. Bud and Connie were both sitting cross-legged on the kitchen floor weeping and rocking their child, at any moment expecting her to die right there in their arms. Miraculously Christina's violent spasms began to subside. The rigidity in her limbs lessened and she unclenched her baby fists. Bud and Connie began to laugh hysterically as if they had just heard an uproarious joke. Syrup dripping from their fingers onto their nightclothes. They licked some of it off.

Regaining their senses, they jumped to their feet and ran with their child to the awaiting Hudson Hornet for their race to the hospital. The attending emergency room physician told them Christina's life was spared by just two minutes, maybe less. If they had not found that bottle of syrup and splashed it into the child's mouth she would have died most assuredly.

Insulin reaction. Too much in her bloodstream. Hypoglycemia. Unusual since diabetes in children is more common. Diabetes is too little insulin. She had too much insulin that night. Her pancreas knows not what to do. Finally after weeks of tests and terrifying episodes such as the one in the kitchen, Christina's vital organ finally decided to stop making insulin all together. Then the onset of an acute form of childhood type I Diabetes. She will be afflicted for the rest of her life, the doctor said. Most likely hereditary. Most likely Vera. She will blame herself. It's not her fault. At least their baby is alive. God saved her. They will have a case of Karo syrup in the house at all times. Bottles of insulin and sterilized needles would stock their refrigerator. To live, their baby will need painful insulin shots every day. They hope her pancreas doesn't change its mind again, but if it does, they will be prepared either way.

15

After Christina came home from the hospital and her mother and father learned to administer those daily injections in their daughter's rump, each time making her wail, Connie told Bud she would never do it again. Never have another child. At that moment Bud didn't blame her, although he was disheartened with her declaration.

The months rolled by. Business was good but home life turned sour. A gulf between them emerged. Bud was worried and tried to bridge it. Connie on the other hand accepted it. Christina began to thrive. Her medications were agreeing with her. They controlled her blood sugar levels and were keeping her metabolism in check. She gained weight. She seemed normal. Happy go lucky. She loved her dolls.

The holidays approached. Dorothy who had married a man from the Scottsbluff area and had two children by that time, a girl older than Christina and a boy about her same age, were planning to spend the entire week with them in the yellow bungalow. It would be crowded but they would cope. Dorothy had named her daughter after Connie. Genevieve also had married but had no children. She was coming for the holidays as well but they would spend the week on the farm with Hank and Vera. It would be the first time the entire family would gather around Christmas since the ending of the war. Bud was wary of the coming events. He hoped Connie would at least be congenial. To his amazement and delight she adopted the spirit of the upcoming festivities. For the first time in many months she grew warm and cheerful. Such a welcomed change. Even Vera noticed it and rejoiced.

Christmas Eve and the snow began to fall. A white Christmas was coming and Bing Crosby's dream was coming true. Bud scared the children half to death when he climbed on the roof and stomped around ringing sleigh bells confiscated from Hank's tackle shed. Vera cooked a hearty mulligan stew and Bud and his new brothers-in-law toasted Hank with too much whiskey. Hank reciprocated with a few toasts of his own. Vera wouldn't serve her stew until they all sobered up. Around midnight the snow was eighteen inches deep with no signs of letting up. There weren't enough beds in the house for everyone so they slept where they could. Bud and Connie gave up their room to Vera and Hank and retired to a fold out couch in the basement. They made love that night for the first time in six months. On February 5th, she announced she was pregnant.

It came as a shock to them all, but the news seemed to bring the couple closer together. Connie grew docile, even appearing somewhat content. She quit her job at the library and even pulled back spending on herself, instead concentrating in some moderation on new clothes for Christina and an assortment of boy's and girl's infant outfits with the caveat that one or the other wardrobe would be returned for a refund when she gave birth.

Bud was presented opportunities to either buy in or purchase outright other businesses in town including two restaurants. He declined all offers deciding to pour his energies into those enterprises he already had. The month before his second daughter was born he bought another one-quarter interest in Jessup's Drug, leaving Monte with less than a quarter share and literally nothing left to say about how things were being run. Monte was a captain by then and stationed in West Germany.

They named this baby Tonya. She was smaller than Christina at birth. They tested her for any signs of blood sugar abnormalities and found nothing. However, they were warned that diabetic symptoms sometimes delayed manifesting themselves until the child gets older. They would have to watch her and wait. Connie's motherhood mannerisms took over. She fired the nanny and housekeeper assuming those roles with some measure of enthusiasm. She even asked Vera to teach her how to cook. Until she took her mother-in-law's instructions to heart, Bud and his children suffered through many either burnt or raw but always awfully unappetizing nighttime meals.

Their quaint little bungalow soon became too small so they sold it for a healthy profit and bought a white two story colonial with four bedrooms and a colonnade enhanced entrance near Ashley Park. Vera thought it was pretentious but secretly loved the marble floor in the foyer and the fact they had a private guest room for her and Hank when they came to spend the night. Hank was overwhelmed by the two-car garage. Bud let him park his pick up truck inside during their overnight visits.

By then both Dorothy and Genevieve had moved to Colorado. Genevieve went back to work for Greyhound and was an assistant manager at the big bus terminal in Denver. Her husband had been trained as a radioman in the Army during the war and was working at KOA radio and its new television station serving the capital city. Dorothy and her family lived north in Greeley. Her husband was an insurance salesman and she was on regular shifts at the community hospital. The families were together often, rotating their meeting places between the three cities in which they lived.

As commodity prices continued to rise Hank had again regained his farming prowess and by the mid 1950s he was back to full capacity with three, if not four seasonal crops which were bringing in handsome profits.

Bud was a happy man, loving every minute of his existence. Then Connie grew restless. After their girls had gone to bed one evening she told him that she needed to do something outside the home. She was anxious and bored. What could she do?

"You can have your old job back at the library," he suggested.

"No. That's not enough. I need to put my talents to work, to help expand our businesses. I was thinking of something like a brokerage."

"What kind of brokerage? Like a real estate broker or stock broker?" he asked, growing more concerned with each of her words.

"No, no, a commodities broker. I've been reading up on it. The Commodity Exchange, you silly. Agricultural futures, they call it. You play the market. Investing in corn, wheat, barley, even cattle and hogs. Speculating whether prices will go up or down into the future. You do the research and make your choice," she explained enthusiastically.

"What are you talking about? All that is, is high stakes gambling. Like playing a roulette wheel. That's all it is. You have absolutely no experience with it. You have to be kidding," he responded in disgust and abject fear.

"Don't you patronize me," she warned. "I've been talking with Hank about it and he likes the idea."

"What! My father is encouraging you? Is that what you said?" His anger taking over.

"Yes. He and I met with Sam Kincaid the other day," she proclaimed defensively.

"You and my father met behind my back with Sam Kincaid, the local stock jockey for the Merrill Company? This is unbelievable," he exclaimed.

"Bud, now come on," she pleaded in an attempt to calm him down. "We did it to impress you. We wanted to show you that we're doing our homework. Studying the system. The procedures. How to get into the business. What it costs. How to recruit customers. To understand the history of agricultural prices. How to buy and sell at the right time. It's a good business. It can make us rich. There are few women in the game, and I'm just as smart as any man. I want to do it. Hank is willing to put up ten thousand dollars to help us get started," she declared.

"Christ, I think I'm going to be sick," was Bud's response.

16

Bud remembers avoiding the loss of his dinner that night, but that next morning he did lose twenty dollars paying two ten dollar fines for running consecutive stop signs through town during his torrid race to the Carlson farmhouse for an enraged confrontation with his father.

"God damn it, Dad! How could you encourage her like that? What are you thinking? She was doing fine. Better than ever. At least pretending to be a real mother. Doing what she should be doing. Now, thanks to you, apparently she thinks she's going to become some hotshot commodities trader. Do you have any idea what these people even do?" Bud ranted.

"Don't you speak to your father that way," Vera scolded.

"It's okay, my dear. Let him blow off steam. I probably had this coming," Hank said calmly.

"You bet you had this coming. Tell me please how this all came about. Why did you put your money out there for her to grab?" Bud pleaded.

"Okay son. I admit that I should have told you myself, but we wanted to work out the details in advance and then come to you with a business plan. She has spent some time studying the business. She is smart and a quick learner. You didn't know this, but for the past two years or so I have been buying wheat futures and speculating a little on where hog prices might be going. I've done pretty well if I might say so myself. But I'm tired of paying those big commissions to the brokers in Omaha so when she came up with this idea, and it was out of the blue, it sounded like something we should pursue," Hank replied.

Bud had settled himself down somewhat and was listening carefully to his father's remarks.

"Well, I'll be damned. Why didn't you let me in on it?" Bud asked, his curiosity now rising. But then he had to question. "You're telling me her interest in this was just by coincidence. Come on."

"Well, I do admit I told her a little about it one evening after dinner at your house a while back. I was helping her with the dishes and you and mother were out in the yard with the kids. I didn't think she was all that interested, but a month or so ago she came to me with an impressive outline for a start up company. I took it to our lawyer, David Hudgins. He thinks it might work. There isn't a trading specialist in this whole county. When we met with Kincaid, you could tell he immediately felt threatened by it. He doesn't sell commodities, just stocks, so this is way out of his league."

By the time Hank was finished, Bud's fury had subsided to be replaced by cautious reflection. Yet, he still had to take another jab. "You sure it's out of Kincaid's league, or is he smarter than both of you think. Smart enough to stay out of the game."

"Maybe you're right. We'll never know unless we try," was his father's response.

Bud drove the speed limit on the way back to town and he stopped at all the stop signs. By the time the evening was over he had read Connie's plan, discussed it with her further and spent most of the night lying awake thinking of the possibilities.

Like most of Bud's business ventures considering the options and all the angles usually resulted in the evolution of a fairly definitive action plan. By morning, although bleary eyed for lack of sleep, he took the first hesitate steps toward his next venture. First, he reread Connie's outline and came away with an even greater appreciation of her logic, tactics and strategy. Neither one of them had any advanced mathematics education but they both knew the principles behind budgeting, cash flow projections and the management of money. Connie's minor course of study while in college was accounting and business administration.

Early on they concluded that recruiting customers would probably be the easy part. The hard part, the real unknown and somewhat frightening part, was turning other people's money into a profit for their attainable gaggle of clients and most importantly for themselves. Bud was fantastic at selling cosmetics, tires and rocking chairs. Those are tangible things. He can touch and feel them. They are products everyone needs and wants. Here he had to sell faith and trust and capitalize on the need for greed. He thought he could make that transition and the challenge thrilled him immensely.

They would look to Hank to capitalize on his agricultural experience and product pricing knowledge. Then it was up to them to start generating a steady stream of investors offering a torrent of cash.

Were there risks? Certainly. Were the risks too great? No, not if their investment decisions were sound and conservative. They would take the next steps with growing confidence.

With their children safely in Vera's care Hank, Bud and Connie motored off to Omaha for a concentrated sabbatical on the brokerage business. They spent three weeks there visiting every trading house, large or small, gathering more information and establishing business ties that might come in handy in the future. Hank forked over another ten thousand for start up cash matching his son's stake in the venture. They hired Lawyer Hudgins to set up a new corporation and to obtain all the necessary licenses. They hired accountant Benjamin Dunkle to establish the accounting system. They secured a bank advance for another twenty-five thousand to cover initial trading activity.

Connie was beside herself with a joy neither Bud nor Hank had ever witnessed. Having her children was no comparison. It was apparent to Bud that she liked this life so much better. Connie brought back into their employment the nurses and the nannies to stand in for her at home. Bud delegated authority and day-to-day responsibilities to his managers and partners in his other three businesses. Hank hired a top hand to run the farm in his absence.

They opened their office two doors down from the main branch of Prairie National Bank. Their sign out front was not the least bit fancy. In simple block letters it read: Carlson & Company, Investment Advisors & Traders.

Within four weeks they opened twenty-seven individual investment accounts and were entrusted with the savings, in some cases the life savings, of a good number of their friends and neighbors. Their funds under management soon topped two hundred thousand dollars. Bud proclaimed one night that it was a staggering number. Hank threw himself into the unpredictable, highly volatile, and totally abstract world of "futures pricing." Hank would go home to Vera each night churning these thoughts in his razor sharp but inexperienced mind. He explained his new life to her this way:

"Commodity futures contracts are written in two simple ways. Either the contract says on a certain date in the future, usually sixty or ninety days out, the price of a bushel of wheat will either be higher or lower than it is on the day the contract was signed. The contract says you will buy that bushel of wheat, no matter what it is on that future date at the price you predicted it would be. On the day the contract comes due, you must buy the wheat from the farmer or his broker, at the market price on that date. If the trading price is lower than you predicted you've made money. If you guessed wrong and the market price is higher on that day, the contract makes you come up with the difference. The reason you've either made money or lost it is there is someone else out there who predicted the price would be exactly the opposite."

The money was piling up in those investment accounts and Bud and Connie were eager to put it to work. So were their customers. There were fortunes to be made. There were huge commissions to be booked along the way. Three to four percent of the size of each contract was the pricing they applied to each trade. However, they only earned those commissions and made those fortunes if those contracts flew out the door and landed on the trading floor of the Chicago Board of Trade.

Still Hank wanted to study more and to take his time. He did not want to make a mistake. He had to watch pricing trends. Would there be a surplus of wheat or rice or soybeans at harvest time ninety days into the future? This would tend to drive down the price on the contract delivery date. Would weather, pest infestations, lack of fertilizer or some other circumstance result in a shortage prompting increases in prices? It could go either way. Roll the dice and hope, or load the dice with research and common sense. Hank liked the latter approach.

Eventually the pressure to move money became too great. Hank ordered the execution of contracts for all of their investors betting that the unusually hot and dry summer throughout the farm belt would wither enough corn on the stalk to drive prices up by thirty cents a bushel upon delivery in October. The bet was thirty-three thousand. The contracts were due in sixty days. They waited, dabbling in the meantime, on spot trading or short duration contracts of three or four days on hog price fluctuations. Hank was speculating that prices would generally rise since he had a sense that the slaughter houses were exceeding capacity after a new inoculation against a strain of ungodly intestinal worms had been discovered. He was right. Healthy pigs flooded the market that season.

Hank's wheat bet was better than right on the money as well. Big money. At delivery that October wheat prices rose nearly fifty cents a bushel and Carlson & Company cashed in their tickets at numbers more than doubling their client's original investment. Less commissions, their investors pocketed thirty-seven thousand dollars all evenly and happily distributed. They were geniuses about town. Hank especially. Word of their magical touch spread through the countryside. More money flowed in. Soon their client roster climbed past fifty. They couldn't lose, was Connie's view. Bud had a difficult time disagreeing.

As the months came and went the business continued to flourish. Gains outpaced losses. Occasionally, but not often, Hank picked losers like his bet on soybeans, a crop and its history he didn't know that much about. Nevertheless at the end of their first year, they showed returns to their investors of an average of fourteen percent and a profit to the firm of nearly sixty thousand dollars.

Hank hated to admit it, but one day he told Vera that he liked being behind a desk better than on the seat of his tractor.

Then came the winter of 1957. The Farmer's Almanac and nearly every one of its tens of thousands of readers predicted it to be one of the coldest, most severe on record. Arctic cold was supposed to settle over the Midwest and remain there from November through March, freezing the ground eighteen inches below the surface and permanently debilitating the fertile components of the carefully nurtured first layer of soil. Crop prices were set to skyrocket as shortages were expected at every new "supermarket" in every new suburb across the land. Hank jumped on the speculation bandwagon with both feet. Bud supported his decision. Connie was giddy with excitement.

Winter never really arrived in 1957, at least as it was predicted. Summer never left as far as anyone could tell. Shirtsleeves were abundant in January. Cotton dresses were fashionable in February. Corn was knee high by the Fourth of June, not the Fourth of July. Green was everywhere from the beginning of March. The market was flooded with food. There was simply too much for the American consumer to consume. Prices plummeted. By the beginning of September Hank's high price predictions were off the mark by twenty percent and as contracts came due in the weeks that followed, it got even worse. Farmers were dumping their bounties at any price they could get. Client losses mounted. Profits evaporated. Account balances disappeared. Geniuses one day, idiots the next and then the next they were labeled thieves. Clients wanted their losses covered. It was Hank's fault. Bud was a crook. Connie, a no good slut. A rock crashed through their office picture window one night. By mid October when all the contracts were due and payable Carlson & Company was broke. Every dime was being drained from their personal and corporate accounts. It was the first time Bud ever saw his father cry.

That was on a Monday. By Thursday an unbearably thick pall settled over them, dulling their senses and blinding their perspective. Connie lashed out first. The blame would not be hers.

"Hank, how could you be so stupid," she railed as he and Bud were nailing plywood over the broken window frame after the second rock had crashed through during the night before. "You could have broken the contracts when prices started falling. Why didn't you? I trusted you! You're a fool."

Hank was quiet. Bud noticed his father was visibly shaken by her attack but pretended to ignore her outburst. Bud was the one to snap. "Shut up, Connie. You have no idea what you're talking about. Contracts can never be broken. You know that. We are all in this together. If we don't face it head on, there's..." He could not finish before she screamed in response.

"Not me. Oh no, not me. I'm not taking the fall here. You, you two are responsible. I was only taking orders from you. See I'm just a clerk. A secretary. You told me what to do. No mistake. Not me. No!"

By the time she paused for a breath Bud saw her nearly incoherent. Her hands lifted to cup over her ears. Tears swelled in her eyes. Then with a jerk she began rustling through her hair, digging at her scalp. Her eyes went glassy. She picked at her clothing then began rummaging through her desk, finding a pencil and a steno pad. She rose from her seat, saying to no one, rather staring at the wall, "I'm ready to take dictation, sir. How should I address this letter?" Bud went to her. Hank stood in shock, horrified, then crestfallen at the scene.

"Connie, calm down. We'll get through this. You'll see. Think about our daughters. Think about us. Our family is what's important. This is just business. We have each other," he pleaded, choking on his words.

She turned and threw the pad and pencil. He ducked as they flew by his head. A demonic look came over her. He reached for her arm. She pulled it away with a surprising strength. He backed away to let her pass. She was suddenly docile. Smiling but devoid of feeling, she strolled toward the door, retrieving Hank's full-length wedding present as she moved past her desk.

"Let her go, Bud," Hank advised.

They watched her meander toward the door, hearing her high heels clicking in rhythm on the hardwood floor.

"She'll be okay," Hank added uncertainly.

The door swung open and she stepped through it.

"Not this time, Dad," Bud said, "not this time."

She was gone. By the time Bud got home that evening, her closet was bare. His daughters were left alone, playing with their dolls on the living room floor.

"Mommy said she would be back soon," Christina told her father when he arrived.

Bud knew that was a lie.

To help cover losses Bud sold his interests in all three of his other businesses at less than half their value. Hank took a mortgage out on the farm but he couldn't pay the payments on the note since he, among many, dumped his crops beside full-to-the-brim silos or never bothered to harvest at all.

The weeks went by. Bud and Hank were paying everyone what they could. In some cases they asked for more time, promising to do their best when they could. Some people understood, appreciated their sincerity and accepted their plight. They waited for payment without further protest. Others did not and stepped up their demands. It was relentless pressure. Nerves were raw, tensions always at their peak.

On Hank's advice, the morning after Connie disappeared Bud froze all of her accounts, just in case. So when she abandoned her life, Bud knew she had very little money. Her car was still in the driveway. Bud sold it to pay the bills. She must have left with someone he feared.

17

It wasn't a few days but several months before Bud heard from his wife. She called him on a Thursday night and told him to expect to receive a court order that next morning granting her sole custody of their daughters. By the way, she said, the package also would contain divorce papers.

During Connie's exile after they had closed the doors a final time on Carlson's financial empire Bud had gone back to work, but this time as a clerk at Tommy Bank's auto parts store. He also would take late shifts or weekends at Billingsley's Drug, the new name on the storefront after Martha and her husband bought out Monte Jessup who was now a major in the Army stationed in Korea. Humbling didn't come close to what Bud felt every day as he stood behind the counters of both establishments. He was grateful to Tommy and Martha for giving him a chance to scratch out a living while trying desperately to restore some semblance of a reputation in the town. The threats and harassment finally stopped but not until Bud and Hank told the bank officers at Prairie National to display their personal and company financial records to anyone who asked to see them. No doubt, the numbers confirmed they were destitute. They used every cent they had trying to cover the losses until all the money had run out.

Rumors swirled around town for weeks that Connie had run off with a mildly handsome, reputed to be ex-Navy commander whom she had met at a weekend business conference in Davenport; one which Bud was too busy to attend. Bud had little doubt that the whispers among the town folk were true. In fact, Bud thought ahead. He already had his and his children's bags packed when the telephone rang that evening and he heard Connie's shrill voice.

No way in hell would she get his children, Bud swore at her. Even if he had to run away with them himself. He had saved just enough money to get across the state line into Colorado. Connie had no idea to where Dorothy and her family had moved and he would place his daughters in his sister's care while he did his best to legally counter Connie's moves to take them away. It was a good plan, he thought. It would give him time to get on his feet before she got wind of their whereabouts. By that time he would have built his case against her for abandonment and child neglect. He couldn't lose. He just needed time and distance.

Bud sped off into the darkness that night, his beloved babies fast asleep in the back seat of his '54 Mercury coupe in which Tommy's mechanics had replaced the transmission the day before, for free – their gesture of support for a good guy surely down on his luck.

Strangely as he headed west toward Colorado Springs Bud was relieved, cheerful, finally realizing he was free. Free of the yoke of depression and despair that had hung around his permanently damaged neck for nearly two years. Placed there by horrible business decisions and a woman who could torture him no longer. He turned up the radio just a little and sang softly to Bobby Darin's great rendition of Mack the Knife.

Eight months went by before he knew it. His daughters were in school with their cousins. Loving their new lives. Bud knew they still missed their mother but he sensed their wanting seemed to wane by the day. Bud was selling truckloads of furniture for his brother-in-law who had just opened his own store on the east side of town. He and his girls had moved into quaint two-bedroom cottage off Tejon Street just blocks from the store and their school. During the preceding months he met with three different lawyers all of whom promised him a stellar defense of his paternal rights but none was willing to sign on without hefty retainer fees. Bud was short of the money needed to marshal his legal forces but it was okay. He had time. He'd earn enough to put up a good fight. She had no idea where they were. At least that's what he prayed.

Then came Friday, April 13th, a day he will never forget. Leaving Leroy's Furniture for the short walk to his car he didn't spot the Sheriff's cruiser parked across the street. Nor did he notice the couple in the red Pontiac convertible sitting close by, its top down on this balmy spring day, its engine idling faintly. As he dug into his pocket for his keys, a booming voice interrupted the singing of the birds and the contentment in his heart.

"Are you Wendell 'Bud' Carlson?" the burly deputy from El Paso County queried as he slammed his driver's side door and took a quick step across the gravel lot toward him. At that instant Bud knew. His world came tumbling down again.

The deputy handed Bud the papers, and politely but firmly spoke. "I don't want any trouble, sir. I realize this is probably real difficult for you, but I have to do my job. This is a court order signed by the judge this morning requiring you to immediately relinquish custody of your daughters Christina and Tonya to their mother, who by now you probably realize is sitting in that car right over there," the officer said, pointing to the Pontiac and its occupants.

Bud glanced in that direction and immediately recognized her despite a bright red scarf matching the color of the Pontiac that covered her now plainly dyed platinum shoulder length hair. Her eyes were shaded with white-framed sunglasses. She turned her head away when Bud looked toward her.

Bud staggered back, nearly falling. He wanted to run. Run again. With his girls. Away from her. She is unfit. She abandoned us, me and her kids. Don't you understand?

"Sir, I also must tell you that if you don't comply your wife is prepared to press kidnapping charges against you and I'm afraid she might have a case. You apparently took your children across state lines. That is a federal offense. Again, these papers show that...."

"But I'm their father. I have that right," he cried, pleading with the officer but knowing to no avail.

Then fury overtook him. He allusively quick stepped around the massive cop and sprinted toward the pair who was startled by his agility, speed and unmistakable rage.

"You miserable bitch!" he screamed.

The driver, sporting a crew cut, pale, almost sun bleached skin, black sunglasses and a cigarette dangling from his lip, ripped the ragtop into reverse, spinning gravel clanging against the wheel wells and undercarriage. Bud could see the fear on their faces and it gave him a moment's satisfaction before the deputy was on him with a bear hug that lifted him off his feet.

Connie's companion nearly crashed into a telephone pole before gaining control of the Pontiac to speed from the scene. Then Bud was alone with his captor.

"God damn I am sorry about this," the deputy sighed as he relaxed his hold around Bud's shoulders.

Out of breath and now bereft of spirit Bud slowly walked back toward his car. He quietly and methodically picked up the papers strewn on the gravel. The deputy watched from a distance unable or unwilling to insult him further at that moment. With anguished reluctance he had to say one more thing, hammer one more spike in his poor bastard's brain.

"Mr. Carlson. The judge's order clearly states that you have one hour from the point of service, meaning now, to have your children ready to leave with their mother. I suppose she is on her way over to your house now to wait for you. I will follow you there myself just to make sure it all goes smoothly. If you don't comply I am ordered to arrest you and kidnapping charges will be drawn up."

Part IV

New Orleans, Louisiana
September 1956

18

At the appointed six o'clock closing time one week following Roman's appointment as chief repairman the cash drawer at Roblinski's Appliance and Radio Repair Shop contained exactly two hundred and eighty-three dollars. While preparing for closing Roman strongly suggested that Sigmund make a bank deposit on his way home. After some debate over the topic with Sigmund giving his assistant strong assurance that the money was safe right where it was and Roman arguing equally hard for simple common sense, Sigmund finally gave in and made out a deposit slip and filled the plastic bank pouch with most of the cash.

"This veek I pay you thirty-five dollars for you my helper. Is that okay?" Sigmund asked as he handed Roman the money.

"That is fine, Sir," Roman responded accepting the bills. "You pay me what you think you can. If I need more I ask, but thirty-five will be enough. I will stand out there in front of the store to watch you cross the street and make the deposit in the overnight slot. You know where that is? Right on the wall near the front entrance of the bank."

"I know Roman. I have my bank there many years. Have been some time since I make deposit though. You watch and see I don't be robbed. That's a fine ting to do," Sigmund said. Then he added, "I vish you to have key to my shop. You come here every day at eight o'clock sharp, on the dime as they say, and I come at nine. You wait outside. That is silliness. I think I trust you now to have the key. You could have taken money from me many time but you don't. You can come in and work early if you like. I vill not mind."

"Thank you, Sir. I am very much pleased," Roman humbly acknowledged as he took the key and placed it in his pocket.

To have that much money for the bank to receive working as a team Sigmund and Roman repaired three television sets, two RCA's and one Motorola, three radios, one in an old oak cabinet with a lighted circular dial on front, circa 1931, that took them two days to find and match the parts from Sigmund's cluttered and chaotic supply inventory, three vacuum cleaners, one Electrolux, six hand mixers and four irons. The final item, the strange looking phallic shaped device, also was made operative. At least it began humming and vibrating with a new chord properly attached and plugged in. It sat with the rest of the good working order merchandise until one morning when Roman called the woman who had brought it in more than a year before. At first she denied having done so, claiming she had no idea what Roman was talking about. She became highly indignant at even the suggestion. After she calmed down she asked him how much she owed and then hung up the telephone without another word.

An hour later just before closing time that day the lady, The Honorable Marion McMichaels known throughout the French Quarter as the only female judge to occupy the municipal bench in the parish of Orleans tinkled her way in through the front door, her head wrapped tightly in a black scarf despite the blistering heat outside and her face more than half covered with enormous sunglasses. She walked briskly to the counter and without revealing her identity sheepishly told Roman she was responding to his earlier telephone inquiry and said she was there to retrieve her property. He charged her two dollars and fifty cents but she handed him three dollars and told him to keep the change. He placed the instrument in a heavy brown paper bag. She placed the bag and its contents in her purse and stepped lightly back out the door, but not before Roman received a quick smile and a deep throated thank you.

Most of the other items gaining new life at the hands of Sigmund and Roman had been collected by the owners and with each, Roman had to make the same series of demands about payment then or not being allowed to leave the premises with their possessions in hand. The one thing Sigmund had done properly was keep records of which item belonged to which customer so it was fairly easy for Roman to look up respective customer telephone numbers and make the calls. He faced down some resistance when the owners arrived, each expecting to be generously greeted with Sigmund's old way of doing business, but without exception Roman was given the funds due before the merchandise was handed over.

On Thursday of that week, without permission, Roman found a step ladder, went outside, climbed the ladder with a wet paint brush in hand and painted over part of Sigmund's sign forever changing the proprietor's business philosophy that had nearly rendered him broke. From then on people would pay for Roblinski's services and the whole world now knew it.

That night at dinner around Mrs. Dionne's scratched and chipped but highly polished dining table Robert sat next to Miss Henley and while hungrily devouring the mashed potatoes and brown gravy felt her foot caressing the calf of his damaged right leg.

He was startled at the realization of the sensation she prompted and jumped slightly from his seat. No one else at the table noticed his sudden motion. At dinner for the past three nights Robert found sensual pleasure from the quick glances and fluttering eyes directed at him by Miss Henley who had previously been seated either across from him or two or three seats away on his left or to his right. However, tonight he arrived just a minute or two late, and there finding no other empty seat chose the one immediately at her side. At first he was disappointed, sensing that it would be more difficult if not impossible to carry on their tableside flirting without detection but this was so much better than their recent amorous encounters over long distance.

There were risks in their actions, to be sure. On the third night of his residency at Mrs. Dionne's boardinghouse, while he lay in his bed reading that morning's copy of the *Times Picayune*, he heard a faint rapping on his door. When he opened it, there she stood. Immediately he thought she was in his doorway to acknowledge if not perhaps congratulate him on confirming his employment, but he soon realized nothing of the sort was on her mind. Instead she was there to establish for him an additional house rule.

"Mr. Kaye," she began without entering his room and in a quiet, subdued voice said, "It is my omission in not instructing you earlier as to certain rules of conduct while you are occupying your place in my household. Please understand that any violation of these rules will result in your immediate eviction and forfeiture of your rent. I am unyielding on these policies foremost of which is the fraternization with your fellow tenants."

She paused for a moment giving Robert time to respond.

"Yes, Madam. But I am unclear on the meaning of the word you use."

"Fraternization, Robert, means physical contact with the other tenants. It is perfectly fine for my guests to engage in polite, meaningful, and dignified conversation while dining, during tea, or other organized or happenstance occasions. However, it is prohibited under any circumstances for tenants to cohabitate in their private rooms at any time, no matter how short that time may be. In other words, if you are caught in any sort of compromising position with a woman, or for that matter a man in your room, you and that person will be out on the street. Is that clear?"

"Yes, Madam. I understand."

"I am glad of that Robert."

"Is there more?" he asked. "Madam, are there other rules I need to become knowledge of?"

She seemed flustered at his inquiry and stammered momentarily appearing to search for the proper response.

"Well, let's see, Robert. More rules? Oh, yes, your laundry. Yes, your laundry. It must be placed in the wicker basket outside your door each morning. Do you have your wicker basket?"

"Yes, Madam. You tell me that before about the laundry."

"Oh yes, well that must be all then. House rules. Strict house rules. Please remember them. Always obey."

"Yes, Madam. Thank you. I will."

Her uneasiness was still apparent as she turned to descend the stairway off the second floor landing. Robert quietly closed his door thinking the encounter was strange, but taking her admonition to heart.

Now as Miss Henley's bare foot found its way inside his pant leg and her toes curled to gently scratch his hairy shin with her nails, he recalled Mrs. Dionne's words. However, he did not move his leg away in deference to the pleasure of her touch. He felt arousal in his crotch, the first time in many months, and was glad for the sensation, once fearing, as a result of his dreams of his father's unrelenting hazing on the subject of his son's post injury decent from manliness, that he might have lost those feelings forever.

Robert finished his helping of mashed potatoes and asked Mr. Dominique, who was nearest to the bowl containing more, to "Please, pass." Seated next to Anthony who reached for the bowl at Robert's request was Mrs. Claire. Her eyes were narrowed almost in a squint and her glare at him was intense. Frightfully so. She had stopped eating at that moment to hold her knife and fork in a death grip over her plate. Her eyes shifted to cast them upon Miss Henley. Suddenly Mrs. Claire dropped her utensils to create a loud obtrusive clang when they struck her plate. Since the room was otherwise quiet just then the sound startled the other diners including Miss Henley who abruptly jerked her foot from beneath Robert's pant leg.

Even Miss Hattie, who was busy announcing to the group that the annual Garden District flower show was to be held this coming Friday and Saturday, abruptly suspended her pronouncement to investigate the source and cause of the racket. She and the others immediately directed their attention at Mrs. Claire.

"Oh, excuse me. I didn't mean to interrupt. Tonight's dinner was absolutely fabulous Mrs. Dionne. I certainly hope everyone enjoyed it as much as I did. It is unfortunate that distractions sometimes have the effect of diverting one's attention from the wonderful food we are all privileged to enjoy night after night," she proclaimed.

"Well, thank you, Margeaux. I certainly cannot take all the credit for our fine dining. I must also share those compliments with Betsey. She is so special. She does the work of five people. We love her so," Mrs. Dionne responded.

At that moment Betsey the bandana lady was nowhere to be found. Robert looked around the room for her, but since dinner was nearly over he suspected she would not reappear until all the tenants had been dispatched to their respective rooms or to their front porch rocking chairs for an evening smoke. When they were all gone she would be there to pick up the dirty dishes and spend the next two hours washing, drying and putting them away. He had seen her in the process of doing just that the night before when he came back down stairs from his room for a glass of water.

Robert needed some time alone to consider the recent series of events, so he left the table soon after Mrs. Dionne slid back her chair and declared the meal's end. He went to his room instead of joining Clarence, Boudreaux, Miss Hattie and Anthony for their now regular after dinner smoke mixed in with a little idle chatter. Over the past two nights he had enjoyed the time out on the porch watching the sun dip toward the Mississippi, or maybe Lake Pontchartrain, he didn't know which, and mainly listening to Clarence rattle on about one irritant or another arising out of his day's span of time.

When he left the table, Miss Henley and Mrs. Claire were locked in a fiery hateful glare. They were the only two who had remained seated. Bourdreaux had already wheeled Clarence away. Miss Hattie was on her way to her rocking chair toting a short black Cuban cigar she would soon light up. Clarence would have his pipe and Boudreaux would roll his own. Anthony liked Camels and Robert was fond of Pall Malls. On his way home on the night of Sigmund's favorable decision, in celebration he purchased his first American pack of cigarettes and still had ten left. He was a light smoker, only four or five a day and only at lunch or breaks from work at the shop. Yet the after dinner puffs were special and that night he would miss them. Another of Mrs. Dionne's house rules was no smoking in the house or in their rooms.

What was that all about? Robert quizzed himself. Did Mrs. Claire realize what was going on under the table and was she angry about it? Was she warning me and perhaps Miss Henley about the fraternization rule or was she angry about something else? Angry at me? Miss Henley? She had never paid the least bit of attention to Robert up to that point.

Mrs. Claire was as mysterious to Robert as she was to the rest of Mrs. Dionne's tenants. She was not particularly pretty, but could one say was she homely? Just plain, Robert thought. Milky skin. Medium height. Always heavy red lipstick. Not too hefty but not skinny either. Decent figure. Probably around thirty-five or maybe forty years old. She had brownish hair she wore to her shoulders, always with a headband pulling it away from her forehead and causing a dip in the wave beyond in the center of her crown. She dressed nicely. Traditional. Simple dresses. No pants like Mrs. Dionne and not manly suits like Miss Henley. She worked in the French Quarter at a bakery. Robert didn't know which one. There were probably dozens. He had seen her at breakfast only once on her day off, since according to Miss Hattie, she had to be at work at five a.m. "to get the French rolls baking and the croissants flaking before the morning rush."

"She was married once, ya know," Clarence proclaimed during their after dinner smoking conclave the night before. "She had a bunch o' money, that one she did. Hitched to some feller who sold fertilizer to them Cajun rice farmers around Evangeline Parish. He died. Some think he was kilt by a gang o' 'em when day say he cheat dem by sellin' dem sheep shit instead of pig shit. Guess pig shit's better dan sheep shit for growin' rice but not shore it's wort killin' o'er," he added.

"Now Clarence," Miss Hattie scolded in her now familiar fashion, "we don't know that for a fact. All we know is Mrs. Claire had a hard time before coming here and that she is a widow. She keeps to herself. Minds her own business. The only time I've ever seen her out and about is with Miss Henley. Occasionally they skip dinner and most probably eat elsewhere. Could be down as far as Bourbon Street where they go. Just don't know. Very friendly though. Nice lady but moody at times. Keeps to herself mostly."

At the time Robert dismissed most of Miss Hattie's commentary but some of it was coming back to him now as he sat in his reading chair, the one he found in his room the evening after his first official work day and probably evidence of Mrs. Dionne's acknowledgement of his employment. The chair's existence and the floor lamp behind it fit comfortably in the corner of his room opposite his bed. It is there where Robert was enjoying his newspaper and where he decided that night he would start reading Call of the Wild by Jack London.

Next to the dining room is Mrs. Dionne's sitting room where tea is served. In that room are floor to ceiling bookshelves containing what Mrs. Dionne would often remind her tenants is "a fine library of proper reading material."

"Please feel free to borrow any of the books on these shelves. We have an honor system here and expect they will be returned in the same condition they were in when borrowed. I have read them all, some more than once. Please limit your time with each book to two weeks to allow the others to cherish the wonderful literature each contains," she had said.

Robert couldn't concentrate either on the news of the day or Jack London's famous opening paragraphs. His eyes couldn't focus on the words rather he was enraptured by Miss Henley's enticing overture but on the other hand distressed over Mrs. Claire's interruption and apparent rebuke. He soon grew tired in his comfortable reading chair yet remained confounded and confused. When his mind raced helter-skelter with emotions such as these, in his sleep, he often dreamed of his father Fodor. Unfortunately for Robert he would not escape his father's grasp during the night to come.

The opening scene came to Robert moments after he fell into a restless slumber. Again he was squirming for comfort in his hard barren seat, Row 7, Seat 13, protruding nail heads holding the wooden slats in place digging, puncturing the flesh on his back and legs. This night as he awaited the parting curtains, he saw he was not alone. A woman sat directly in front of him, Row 4, Seat 13. Her back was to him. Her posture pine board straight. Her head held erect. Her flowing dark hair attractively styled in the fashion of the day. Her shoulders covered in billowing white sleeves encircling each of her upper arms and shoulders. Robert's view of her was limited from his seat in the theatre positioned higher on the angled floor line. He waited, desperately curious about the only other audience member in the otherwise vast, empty, opulent hall. Yet he sensed he knew her. A faint distant cognitive recognition of someone familiar, someone he cared for. Then she turned in her seat to face him.

His mother. Young, glamorous, breathtaking, breathing without hacking in pain. No sign of blood oozing from the corner of her mouth for him to dab with his wet clothe. The spotlight hanging from the balcony above suddenly switched on to bring her face to life and shine on her striking beauty. Instinctively Robert rose from his seat to run to her but she held up her hand and shook her head no, signaling his approach was forbidden. Her expression in denial was not harsh. At the rebuff Robert settled back in his seat to study her further. He felt a sharp pain from a nail head jabbing at his spine. Love and compassion were there for him to feel and he sensed from her a longing for the embrace of her son. But then the curtains behind her parted and her sweet look suddenly vanished. Disappointment, a feeling of loss and hopelessness then radiated from her. Her eyes dropped from his in appearance of defeat. Had she failed her son, losing him to the central character about to take center stage to expel his stream of vitriol?

In the instant Robert's attention was diverted from the vision of his mother to the scene on stage she vanished from Row 4 Seat 13 leaving him alone once more. Had she already lost him in the struggle for his mind and conscience? Or was there hope for him after all? Was she there to warn him that her loss was imminent unless Fodor's intoxicating rhetoric could be substituted for tolerance, understanding, and even the slightest hint of compassion? He did not know but he hoped. He prayed she would return to his dream to filter the hatred so prevalent in his father's poison idiom.

He was given little time to contemplate thoughts of sensibility, for Fodor already had begun this night's performance and Robert was drawn to his message like iron filings to a magnet.

"My sons, those whose manlike prowess remains, again I take you back to the founding of our movement. You must come to understand why our nation is poised again for greatness. The lessons taught to us by Regent Horthy through his most brilliant appointment of Gyula Gombos as Prime Minister are beyond fantastic. It is because of Gombos's advocacy of social reforms, one-party government, the repudiation and repeal of the Treaty of Trianon, plus our withdrawal from the corrupt League of Nations that our armed forces are no longer restricted and we have linked our military might with that of the Fuehrer of Germany to create an insurmountable force. I still mourn the untimely death of the great Gombos but his successor, the super human Arian Ferenc Szalasi, is proving to be a gift from our heavenly war gods. Szalasi, our leader, is the savior of our Arrow Cross movement," Fodor exclaimed.

"My sons," addressing Roman and Rudolph, and Roman turning to stare at Robert to demand his attention, "do you realize Hungary has now regained parts of Southern Slovakia and Carpathian and the re-patronization of nearly one million loyal Hungarians? A wondrous event. And soon the renegade state of Czechoslovakia will be dissolved and our borders again will be reshaped to encompass the land mass of our empire before the tragic events of World War I. Next, perhaps only months into the future, our sights will be set on Romania to crush its government and bring our citizens back to the warm, gorged bosom of mother Hungary!" Fodor declared in rising crescendo.

At that moment his father paused his bellowing to guzzle nearly the full bottle of port from the table before him. From his position on stage, Roman again turned to Robert. This time all compassion left his face, replaced by a blank expression void of feeling. A look of stoicism. A commander ordering obedient troops. Then Roman stood, beckoning Robert to follow. Roman clicked the heels of his shiny new black; knee high leather boots and raised his arm in a fascist salute to his father. Fodor responded in kind. Rudolph remained in his seat appearing bewildered before shrugging his shoulders and taking a sip of goat's milk from his cup. Robert considered the call but did not move.

Seconds later Fodor began again. Roman returned to his seat. Disgusted. Rudolph appeared to have finished his drink. His eyes drooping, fighting sleep.

"Today, my sons, your father was chosen again to perform a sacred task. My assignment came from Ferenc Szalasi himself. He plucked me from the crowd. Why? Because of my loyalty," Fodor thundered in response to his own question, "and I am proud again. Fulfilled as never before."

"What was my task today, my sons? I will tell you. It was to find a traitor swine Romanian. Someone, anyone in our midst who professes allegiance to that counterfeit nation while having denounced our beloved country. I was to make that person and all around him pay for his transgressions. I knew who to pursue and where to go even before the assignment was mine. My target occupied his rat infested lair only blocks from our home. His name was Fekete, Hector Fekete. In our tongue Fekete means black, black like a Schwarz, black like the lepers of Africa. Hector Fekete lived with his mother. Just the two of them in their hole. I knew that Hector Fekete was a dedicated servant of the gutless Romanian regime. Our intelligence traced his wicked steps across our borders only to return with arms full of hateful propaganda designed to create turmoil, even rebellion within our country. My sons, Hector Fekete will spread the shit from his hands no more."

"After I entered his house from a carelessly unlocked rear door, I surprised Hector and his mother as they slurped their afternoon tea. He was weak. He provided me little resistance. Soon he was tied to his chair and soon his mother was strapped to the table from which their teacups had fallen and shattered on the floor. He watched and cried like a child as I cut the clothing from her with scissors from her sewing kit. She squirmed and squealed like the pig she was. My blade began to peel away her skin, beginning with her sagging breasts and ending at the top of her unsightly pubic patch. Then I moved to her face. I removed her mask of deceit, layer-by-layer of skin until it was gone, stripped away to expose her for what she was. Only blood and bone remained when I finished.

"Then I set her free of her misery, placing what was left in the kitchen corner so her bulging eyes in their sockets without lids could witness my next act of vengeance on her dear son. Her death came before I could begin. A blunder on my part. With Hector it took longer. I used a more precise technique, first removing his ball sack and then his tiny prick before his fingernails and ears, and finally his heart."

Robert woke from the sound of his own terrifying scream.

19

Robert's appointed time in the men's bathroom of Mrs. Dionne's boardinghouse was from 6:10 to 6:30 am and from 7:45 to 8:05 pm each day except on weekends when it was first come first served. The men's facility was at the north end of the second floor hallway while the women's restroom was on the south end. The water closets were identical in design and amenities except for the sanitary napkin dispenser in the lady's room from which Mrs. Dionne charged twenty-five cents per item. At that price Mrs. Dionne pocketed around twelve cents profit on each pad. She supplied fresh clean towels each day at no extra charge.

Robert almost missed his appointed bathroom time the morning after his latest night attending Fodor's ghastly play. Subsequent to his frightful awakening he fell back into an undisturbed dreamless deep ocean sleep. When he finally awoke for good, still exhausted from Fodor's inspired trauma of the night before, it was exactly 6:09 am. He leaped from bed and hobbled to the door in his stark nakedness. He nearly exhibited himself in full to the others occupying the hallway before remembering to wrap his body in his bathrobe left hanging from the hook on the inside of his door.

Even in a normal state of mind supported by a long night of uninterrupted rest, twenty minutes was hardly enough time to properly clean and groom one's self for the day ahead. On this morning Robert rushed through his routine but when shaving, his Gillette double edge razor slipped and drew a deep gash on the right side of his chin spewing blood in horrifying quantities into the sink and on to the floor. When he inspected the wound in the mirror he recoiled at the sight and the similarities in gore to Fodor's retelling of his successful mission during last night's performance.

Roman suffered through the day with fatigue and haunting flashbacks of the nightmare. While repairing an early model Zenith black and white tabletop on a swivel wrought iron stand he chose the wrong voltage vacuum tube, inserted it and blew out the rest with a spark and puff of grey smoke. Normally he would not have made mistakes like that. Sigmund smelled the burning electrical parts and inquired as to its cause. Roman fumbled for an excuse, which seemed to satisfy the shopkeeper who returned to his workbench with no more than a grunt of acceptance.

The day's hours crept by with Roman struggling through each of his assigned tasks. Most of his undertakings took longer than they should have as everything from finding the right switch to connecting wires to positive and ground posts, to soldering circuit boards seemed daunting and unnecessarily complicated. Yet he finished the day with gross receipts for repairs of forty dollars, still besting his boss's intake by three dollars and twenty-five cents. From a financial standpoint it was a reasonably profitable day. From a mental and physical perspective it was debilitating for Roman, until the final customer in the final hour of the workday announced her arrival by the tinkling of the miniature front door bell.

Miss Henley, dressed this time in a grey suit, her skirt at mid calf length, her blonde hair appearing almost platinum slicked back in a tight bun and a bright salmon color blouse accenting it all strutted through the door and down the aisle between the stacked high consoles. She displayed a sweet smile but offered an acerbic greeting for Roman who had been rounding the counter corner on his way to the front door to lock up when she made her startling entrance.

"Well, well my Robert, you look simply awful," she proclaimed as Roman abruptly halted his stride toward the door at the moment seeing her burst in.

"Well, thank you, Miss Henley. I appreciate the compliment," Roman answered with a bit of his own bite, but that quickly turned to a glowing grin in response.

"What may I do for you at this late hour," he asked, and then…

"He is Roman in my shop Miss. We use his proper name," lectured Sigmund who, as always, simply appeared out of nowhere.

"Roman you say, Sir?" she responded curiously to the unexpected interruption.

"Yea, yea dear lady. My assistant known here by God-given name while in my establishment, not name forced on him unvillingly by reprehensative of our government," Sigmund explained and then added, "And you are? How do you know this young man by his American name?"

"Sigmund, this is Miss Henley. She is a resident of the boardinghouse in which I currently reside. Miss Henley, Sigmund Roblinski, owner of this fine establishment," Roman wedged the introduction into the conversation.

"How do you do, Mr. Roblinski? I am Deborah Henley. Glad to make you acquaintance," she said, presenting her hand, receiving his and giving it a vice grip shake that made Sigmund grimace.

Then she added, "Very well. In your shop he is Roman." Then directing her attention toward her fellow tenant, "What is your last name Roman, may I ask?"

"Sokolowski, Miss Henley," Roman answered.

"What nationality, Mr. Sokolowski?" she probed.

"Hungarian, Miss Henley."

"I be Romanian," offered Sigmund without prompting.

Sigmund's declaration of heritage for Miss Henley's benefit brought Roman back with a shock to the night before and Fodor's sadistic account of his maiming and killing of his Romanian neighbors. As his mind instantly recounted the horrifically appalling scene he felt dizzy and placed his hand on the counter to brace himself.

Miss Henley noticed his sudden unsteadiness.

"Are you all right, Roman?"

Recovering quickly, he said, "Certainly. You were saying?"

Looking him over carefully before accepting his assurance she continued, "Oh, yes gentlemen, I am German by birth," she announced in a voice rising with a certain pride.

"Ah, yes, I see," seemingly ignoring her announcement, Sigmund went on, "Now lady do you come to my shop to see Roman or is dare someting we can be of assistance?"

"As a matter of fact, there is. I have this." From her purse she produced a very new looking Schick electric razor.

"I purchased this device less than a month ago. I know it is a man's razor but I find that when it is working properly it does a fine job on the underarms and legs of a woman. You know we German women; well, our tradition has not been to shave in those places, but in America hair on one's legs is considered unsightly and tends to snag delicate nylon hosiery which is so popular."

Roman looked at Sigmund and Sigmund looked back before both simultaneously snapped their eyes downward to gaze upon Miss Henley's shapely legs, which were exposed below the hem of her skirt. At their motion she hiked up her hemline ever so slightly to give them a better view and to confirm her statement.

"Also shaving under one's arms is considered good grooming practice particularly when so many of today's styles emphasize sleeveless designs."

Roman's and Sigmund's glare rose to now take in Miss Henley from waist up realizing she had removed her outer jacket to reveal the sleeveless salmon blouse she was wearing underneath.

"But just this morning my razor went kapuuut. Perhaps you can look at it for me to determine if it can be repaired."

"Yes, yes Miss. We vill fix for you. I vill see to it personally," Sigmund said, snatching the razor from her hand and sprinting away.

Over his shoulder after his phantom like movement back to his workstation Roman heard Sigmund say, "No deposit for her Roman."

"Well, I must admit I did go out of my way somewhat in hopes that you might still be working," she said directing her attention back to Roman after Sigmund's sudden exit.

"I am closing for the night, Miss Henley. I am walking home. Are you also heading in that direction this evening?" Roman inquired after the moisture returned to his mouth.

"Why yes I am, Roman. Indeed you may accompany me."

Miss Henley set an easy pace to their walk toward their home that evening. She was careful not to step too quickly in deference to Robert's slower gait. They didn't touch each other along the way. She resisted the temptation of linking her arm through his, instead keeping a respectable distance between them. A welcomed breeze rustled through Robert's hair but not hers, which in the beginning remained pressed to her head secured by the restrictive knot-like bun. When the cool air blew directly in her face she stopped in mid-block to undo the mundane hairstyle. Robert watched with a certain fascination when her hair cascaded in waves to her shoulders. She shook her head and ran her fingers through her flowing curls to relieve it of any remaining tangles.

"Feels much better," she announced.

"I like it better that way," he volunteered.

"You do now. I'll have to remember that."

"May I call you Robert now?" she asked.

"Please do, Miss Henley," he allowed.

"Only if you call me Deborah," was her response.

"If you wish, Deborah" he accepted.

The air grew cooler as the breeze was persistent in bringing more gratifying relief.

"Unusual for an August evening in South Louisiana," she commented a few minutes later.

Their conversation was uncomfortably labored for much of their stroll, enhanced by two or three declarations of how lovely the evening was, followed by agreement from one or the other.

When they reached the intersection of South Liberty and Sixth Street she stopped again to say, "I think both of us would be well advised not to reveal too much about our friendship just now. You are my friend aren't you, Robert?"

"Yes, I am," he declared.

"Yes, so I'm sure you've had the lecture from Mrs. Dionne about fraternization with fellow tenants as if she is above all that herself," Deborah said with a profound sarcasm.

Robert was taken aback by the last part of her statement, but didn't react and only said, "Yes, I have been told," but he couldn't resist in saying, "I would like to get better acquainted with you, Deborah. I am not sure why you take an interest in me, assuming of course you have. I am but a poor man at the moment. My time in this country as you know is short. My English remains inadequate, but I am working hard on it. I have basic learning while in Hungary but the uprising cut short my studies. I have many things to learn and accomplish and I know I must struggle to achieve. You are such a beautiful woman. It seems silly to me that you are here with me now. And I have my leg. That I will never rid myself of. You understand, yes?"

"Robert, look sweet man," she began rising her hand to touch his cheek, "I have many things in my past that I also bring to our friendship. My struggle here is big like yours. I come here only two years ago with nothing. My German heritage is a burden to carry as memories of the war linger in the minds of many. Yet I work hard and make progress every day I think. I must show people that I am capable of doing a good job and not just show them more of my shaved legs," she added with a chuckle.

Robert smiled at her comment and responded, "I suspect Mr. Roblinski will have your razor running in perfect order in little time."

"I certainly hope so," she smiled, followed by a few moments of silence.

"So now we should part. You go that way on Sixth Street and I will continue along here on Liberty and soon we will meet again on Harmony Street," she suggested with gaiety.

"A good plan, Miss Henley."

"Thank you, Mr. Kaye."

That night during dinner the glaring from Mrs. Claire continued in earnest and was divided nearly equally between them even though Deborah and Robert were sitting on opposite ends of the table.

Robert did his best to ignore her hateful stares, all the while trying to understand their cause. He had barely spoken to Mrs. Claire since his arrival and certainly hadn't done anything that might have offended her, at least that which he could remember.

Is her apparent anger directed at me because of her sense of my friendship with Miss Henley? Why would a woman do that? He questioned himself. Why should she care if Deborah and I became friends, even lovers? It makes little sense he pondered, but then grew weary of his speculations and instead concentrated on the dinner conversations which were underway. His last thought before leaving those worries was a pledge to himself to simply stay out of her way. Mrs. Claire is trouble, he concluded.

When he tuned in to the discussion he heard Mrs. Dionne addressing Anthony with a tone of disdain.

"So let me understand Mr. Dominique. You believe that those black children in Little Rock, a city so dangerously close to our beloved state, should be allowed to attend high school classes with white children? Is that what you are advocating?"

"Yes, Madam," he responded, "I do believe so. It is their right. It is everyone's right to a good education and there should not be separate schools for Negroes and whites."

"Well, I declare," she exclaimed. "I am amazed, utterly amazed at you. Not for a minute do I believe that such a thing is just and appropriate in today's society. I pray to God that President Eisenhower keeps his trap shut and lets the people of Arkansas deal with their Negroes in the way they see fit."

Just then Miss Hattie seemed to come awake and chime in with her question. "Mrs. Dionne, what on earth are you saying? Why would our President have any interest at all in some high school in Arkansas when those ornery Russians are firing missiles in the air and threatening to blow us up any second now? It just frightens me to death. That's what our President should be worrying about if you ask me."

"Very well put, Miss Hattie," complimented Mrs. Dionne.

Turning her attention to Clarence who had previously sat quietly chomping on a delightful meal of meat loaf, potatoes and cooked carrots, she asked, "As the only Negro in our house Clarence, how do you feel about your kind attending the same schools as white children? Do you not believe there should be a clear separation for the good of both races?'

"Well, shit, Mrs. Dionne, I ain't never give it much thought till you just brought it up. I will say I'd sure bet them colored kids gonna get a much betta education if day go to dat dare white school. I made it through fifth grade. Learnt to read and write a little. Give me a leg up on others at the docks and give me just enough sense to read them books in your library and understand most of 'em. If I was goin' to a white school I might justa wrote some." But he didn't give his landlady a chance to answer right then. "Lemme ask you, Mrs. Dionne. If colored folk ain't supposed to school wif white folks or live wif white folk, how's come I be livin' cheer?"

A long pause followed. Deborah broke it.

"Indeed Bianca. Clarence asks a great question. Let me see if I can answer it for you. It seems to me that the only Negro in our house is here because he is a novelty. A spectacle for us to behold." She spoke as if Clarence was miles away. Robert took in her comments curiously. They were making him uncomfortable. He couldn't imagine what Clarence was feeling. She went on. Undaunted.

"He is harmless you see. Other than using a profanity here and there Clarence is entertainment for us, unique in many ways I believe. One who brings another dimension to our lives. Humor mainly. An oddity for some like the organ grinder and his monkey. He gives us pleasure and often a little wisdom. Yet we marvel at how far they've come. How can that monkey do that? We ask ourselves. I for one am pleased with Clarence in our presence." She didn't stop there, adding. "Is that not why you allow him to live here, or is it the direct rent payments you receive from his longshoreman's pension fund?

The others at the table sat in stunned silence.

Without being prompted and absent Mrs. Dionne's signal that the meal had ended, Boudreaux stood and stepped behind Clarence's chair to move him away from the table. Clarence surprised them all with a smile and a timely observation. "Well, ain't you become some sorta philosopher all a sudden. Bitch like you like to find dat dare monkey you talkin' 'bout on your back someday. Scratchin' and bitin' away. Take care now. Goin' for a smoke. Be on wit it, Boudreaux."

When Robert searched Deborah's face for a reaction or even a hint of regret he found none. Blank as a new schoolroom blackboard or a busted television screen. What possessed her, he wondered. A night and day contrast to the sweet delicate flower of a girl whom he escorted home, or close to it, only an hour or so before. Clarence meant nothing to Robert, other than perhaps an irritant. He is harmless and he did warn me off from seeking work on the docks, he said to himself. Why does Deborah care? What the hell? It is not my problem. All I care about is seeing how far I can get with her, he affirmed quite consciously.

Mrs. Dionne's chair remained against the table. She had not looked up from her stare at the iced tea glass grasp in her hand since Deborah's haranguing began.

Mrs. Claire was the one who spoke first. "Truly a remarkable speech. So unlike you, Deborah. Appears lately that you are on edge about something, my dear. I hope you are not ill. I believe you are just confused. Torn between that which you know and that which is foreign to you. You should relax. Don't take out your frustration on poor Clarence. You are not one to perceive and comment on the intricacies of our complex society. Far from it. You are least qualified in that regard." Turning her attention away from Deborah she asked, "Now Mrs. Dionne, are we adjourned?"

"If you ever speak to me that way again, Miss Henley," ignoring Mrs. Claire's question, Mrs. Dionne warned, "I will...." she paused. Deborah ignored her, quickly moving her chair away from the table, standing and walking briskly from the room without another word to anyone. Mrs. Dionne did not complete her halfhearted threat.

When Robert was alone in his room he recounted the day's events with radical swings in emotion. At one extreme he was elated over Deborah's outward gestures of interest in him or perhaps even affection. On the other end of his psychic spectrum he saw a side of her he found quite disturbing. Why was he concerned? Why did it matter to him if she characterized Clarence and all black people for that matter as monkeys? Weren't Negroes just like Jews? His father would have said so. They should remain segregated, apart from their masters. They should be treated as a second class to serve those who are superior. Isn't that the way he was taught? Deborah was only speaking his mind for him, so was it just his tolerance of Clarence that made him question her toxic tongue or were his feelings softening, changing. and was he becoming less of what his father expected of him?

Then there was Mrs. Claire. What was her point? She was really getting on his nerves. First the nasty stares and then her hostility toward Deborah. What did she mean by suggesting that Deborah was confused? Confused about what? It seemed to him that Deborah's views about things were fairly well defined. Surprising, but well defined. What could she be frustrated about? Yes, he concluded, I will stay away from Mrs. Claire but I need to find out what her obsession is over my advancing relationship with Deborah. Why does she care?

Mrs. Dionne seemed to take Deborah's ridicule without so much as a minimal rebuttal. Except at the end, he recalled, when she made that oblique warning which was promptly ignored. God what a strange day, he reflected.

Robert had trouble sleeping that night so he avoided buying his next ticket to Fodor's nocturnal play. In the morning, although exhausted, he was grateful for his restlessness.

20

Robert and Roman settled into a fairly normal routine over the next several weeks. Summer turned into fall and fall into winter with the heat and humidity subsiding to be replaced by the rains and winds and temperatures in the fifties. Occasionally Robert would find the need to wear the light wool-lined jacket he had purchased from Johnson's Fine Men's Clothier on Loyola Avenue. He never found the need to dress more warmly than that for his walks back and forth to work each day, or the halting strolls he often took at noontime on the surrounding streets.

On many of the avenues in the French Quarter, Robert found quaint shops, small restaurants, and specialty stores like Mr. Johnson's men's emporium interspersed with houses large and small, some of which reminded him of his neighborhood in Esztergom that surrounded Vorosmartz Utca, the street on which he and Rudolph grew into men and endured those many years of his father's wrath.

As a youth, Roman found solace away from his house and on the streets of his Hungarian hometown. He found comfort in his wanderings passed the Ancient Stairs, Maria Valeria Bridge, and into the square and the site of the Bazillika. All major boulevards in Esztergom would take one to the steps of the Bazillika. Even those like Petofi Sandor Utca or Kossuth Lajos Uta or Tancsics Mihany Uta would get you there as well, and if you wanted to wander further you could stay on Tanscics Mihany Uta and eventually find the bridge to cross the lovely Danube River.

Roman rarely ventured as far as the blue Danube since most often he stopped his meandering at the steps of the ancient Catholic Cathedral to sit and ponder about going inside. Once, after he had suffered through another of his father's ranting over the diabolical Jew, he found it paradoxical that all the busy lanes in Esztergom led to the Synagogue as easily as they did to the Bazillika. Roman reached that startling conclusion while he rested on those marble steps and waited patiently for Father Krisztian Konrad to come down to the bottom where he sat to again coax him to the sanctity of the sanctuary inside and the cleansing awaiting from a long over due confession.

Regardless of the priest's most fervent and persuasive Christian message specifically designed to capture his heart, Roman resisted. Beyond the massive doors, later in his life the target of that Soviet cannon, Robert found the Bazillika's interior haunting, not healing. As a child he and Rudolph, he clasping her hand and his brother in her arms, would dutifully occupy a pew with their mother every Sunday for Mass. When things were particularly volatile in their home they also would attend on Wednesdays or Fridays or sometimes even Wednesdays and Fridays. From his first memory on, the massive consecrated hall lit by streaking sunrays radiating through the expansive stained glass dome frightened him. The stone statues, the somber icons, the music, the chanting, the echoes of sound brought fear, not peace. The smells of incense. The priest's cold and clammy hands on his forehead. The charcoal he couldn't rub off. There was no escape. His mother clutching her beads, telling him as they walked back to their flat on Vorosmartz Utca that, "This time my dear Roman, God has heard my prayer. All will be right with your father. No more yelling and cursing. Only quiet in our house." A false comfort.

After so many pronounced reassurances Roman knew God did not hear. No matter how many beads she counted and how often the priest's blessing flowed over them, Roman knew nothing would change. There was no God big or powerful enough to stop him. Yet long after she breathed her last tortured breath and the priest laid her beads on her stilled chest Roman returned to those cathedral steps week after week tempting the priest, enticing him repeatedly only to reject his pious and faltering message of hope.

Robert would now wander the streets of the French Quarter often lost as he was in Esztergom. He found he could rest on the steps of St. Jude Shrine on Rampart Street not far from Mr. Roblinski's shop. He would never go inside. He waited for a priest to beckon him but none ever did.

Many nights later during dinner the roundtable debate was intense.

"I am terrified. Aren't you, Mrs. Dionne?" Miss Hattie exclaimed. "Those Communists have shot up that rocket aimed right at us. I can't sleep at night thinking about our grand city and all of us in it being burnt to a crisp just like we did to those Japanese."

"What in Sam Hell you talkin' 'bout woman?" chimed in Clarence. "You jabberin' on o'er dare about them Soviets and that Sputnik? Is dat what you speakin' on?"

"Well, yes Clarence, dear. I am concerned that the…what did you call them…Sav-its…are now in outer space with their spacemen and soon they will be coming out of the sky with missiles and bombs aimed at our destruction. It frightens me to death, I declare. Do we have a bomb shelter in our house here, Mrs. Dionne?" She inquired as an afterthought.

"Geez, crazy woman, she be," Clarence proclaimed.

However, before Mrs. Dionne could utter a sound, Mrs. Claire broke in. "No, Miss Hattie. We don't have a bomb shelter here in Mrs. Dionne's home and I agree with her that we really don't need one. You see the Soviets (she spoke the word very slowly) have launched an unmanned spacecraft into outer space. There are no Soviet, or Russian spacemen up there, only a piece of scrap metal junk circling around the earth. It is a major accomplishment for them, the Communists, but our leaders, President Eisenhower in particular, have assured us that no harm will come from it and our armed forces are prepared to defend our country from any threats that may come our way. Please don't worry, Miss Hattie, everything will be all right," were Mrs. Claire's calming words of assurance.

"There you go again, Margeaux. Spreading the good gospel about Ike. All the things he's doin' for us, keepin' us safe from the Communists while you stubbornly ignore how he has endangered us worse than if he allowed those Reds to come knockin' on our doors right now," chastised Mrs. Dionne.

"What on earth are you talking about, Bianca? As if I didn't know," Mrs. Claire asked ever so condescending in return.

"You know darn good and well what he's done. He ordered our brave soldiers to march against their own in Little Rock. To force those fine patriots in our neighborin' state to integrate their schools. Now just two months after that tragedy, we see pictures of white children being forced to sit and co-mingle with the coloreds. Pretty soon he will order them to drink out of the same water fountains, swim in the same swimmin' pools and eat together at the same lunch counters. Shameful, it is. Disgraceful on all counts. Soon they will be copulatin' with our white girls against their will and our country will be full o' mixed mulattos."

"Doubt that. Suspect some of those white girls may want it," Miss Henley proclaimed.

"How could you say such a thing?" Mrs. Dionne questioned indignantly.

"Saw that new Edsel today on the street for the first time," Anthony interjected in a desperate attempt to change the subject for fear he would be dragged, once again, into Mrs. Dionne's ugly world.

Robert seldom spoke at dinner. He had two reasons for that. First, he didn't want to embarrass himself in case he used the wrong English noun or verb tense or conjugation or whatever unintentional language faux pas might come out of his mouth. Second, he was learning from the others while he sat and ate contently. By listening closely to the dinner table topics, which were mostly current events when Margeaux or Deborah or Bianca weren't at each other's throats, he was able to gobble up the happenings around him, albeit distorted, tainted by opinion and bias and often void of pure fact. Nonetheless he liked to glean a hot topic or two from the conversation and spend his lunch hour the next day combing through the *Times Picayune* for clarification and further enlightenment.

This night Robert was distracted. He couldn't concentrate on the matters of the day. He had barely heard the lively current event exchanges among his fellow diners. All he could think about at that moment was Miss Henley's hair. It was damn near all gone. She had cut most of it off, leaving what he thought was poorly sculptured clumps that looked as if she had slicked them down with hair oil before parting what remained on the side. Christ, if I didn't know better, I'd say she was a man! He exclaimed to himself.

He sat, picking at his food, totally baffled at what he saw. He frequently looked up from his plate to gaze upon her in continuing disbelief. Her gorgeous golden mane that once cascaded down her sumptuous neck, past her shoulders to the middle of her back was lying on some beauty shop floor, severed, shriveled and dying. No one had said anything about her new startling hairstyle since she had pranced into the dining room and plopped down beside Mrs. Claire. That also was astonishing to Robert. Was he the only one to notice that she had violated herself so brutally? He wasn't going to say anything. It wasn't his place. At one point he caught Mrs. Claire stroking the nape of Deborah's neck in a motion that appeared to be smoothing down a wayward strand. Mrs. Claire's smile broadened with each loving stroke.

Miss Henley was not smiling back. She seemed to shutter at the touch of her friend. As a result of the Henley hair catastrophe Robert was missing further commentary, now reignited by Mrs.

Dionne, who could not leave the subject of school integration and the "devil incarnate, Eisenhower" alone.

"His actions may touch off another Civil War," she observed. "He is a scoundrel. To think we revered the man naught a decade ago for his heroism during the war," she declared.

The room was silent. She failed to tempt the offering of a counter viewpoint. Her guests seemingly weary of the subject and wanting to move on to other matters.

Yet Robert had captured just enough of the clamoring to spur him on toward further research on the topics. The next day he would learn that Eisenhower's decision to send in Federal Troops to desegregate Little Rock schools had touched off a firestorm of protest, particularly in the South. Robert would find himself delving deeply into the story when his lunch break began. Also he would search for much more about Sputnik. He sensed a creeping, nagging uneasiness that came with each reference to the growing Soviet menace much like he shared with Fodor at the first threats of a Russian invasion of his homeland those few short years before.

Thankfully it was the normally self-muted Anthony who introduced a new subject, which broke the gloom and ignited vigorous chatter. He spoke of his sighting of a brand spanking new Edsel automobile.

"I saw one too. A red and white two tone," Robert said, directing his remarks to Anthony and momentarily forgetting about the once lovely she-man across the table from him.

"Mine was solid robin's egg blue," Anthony came back with a hint of remarkable pride as if he had just bought one.

"Don't think they'll last very long though. The front grill's funny lookin'. Like it's goin' down da street wif its mouth open catchin' bugs," offered Clarence.

Then even Boudreaux piped up. "Yea, but I like the curves to it. Them slanted tail light wings on the back and the chrome panels on the side. Like somethin' from out o' space."

As if no one else was in the room, the four men kept at it. The ladies said nothing as the gentlemen continued on.

"Where'd you see yours Clarence?" asked Anthony.

"Well, didn't quite see a real one. Seen it in a magazine," he clarified somewhat sheepishly.

"And you Boudreaux?" Robert inquired.

"Down on Canal Street. Mine was a damn convertible! Pretty as a picture. Parked right in front of that whore house, think they call it Clementine's," he speculated.

"That will be enough, gentlemen," Mrs. Dionne sternly ordered.

Before she could say anymore, Clarence spoke words unexpectedly charged with emotion. "God damn it, Boudreaux. How could you leave me cheer alone like dis in dis here chair and you go off lollygaggin' down dare in da Quota getting' ta see a god damn Edsel mobile sittin' in font of a god damn ho house? Thought you was ma friend."

For a moment Robert thought he saw tears begin to well in Clarence's eyes, perhaps Boudreaux's as well.

Right then Boudreaux rose from his chair, again not waiting for Mrs. Dionne's dismissal, and pulled Clarence's chair away from the table. He said with a soothing tone, "Don't you worry none, Clarence, I'll tell you all about it o'er a smoke."

"Well, if this wasn't an enjoyable evening. Quite intellectually stimulating," proclaimed the nearly bald Miss Henley as she too rose from her chair to leave the room. Mrs. Claire remained alone looking somewhat forlorn. The others soon followed leaving her and Mrs. Dionne stationary in their seats.

When Robert entered his room about an hour later after two Chesterfields and more light hearted discourse over the merits of Ford's concept car of the future, he found a note on the floor inside the threshold. He unfolded the plain white paper to read:

I Have to See You. Tomorrow. Please.
I will come by the Shop at 6.
Deborah.

21

Robert had lost track of the days and weeks since the last time Miss Henley paid him the least bit of attention. He had all but abandoned the fantasy of an imminent romantic relationship after their first intimate stroll together on that cool August evening. During their ensuing nightly dinners together he made several attempts to make eye contact going so far as to deliberately occupying empty seats next to her. When successful he tried in vain to prompt another secret caress of his leg by her sensuous toes wiggling beneath the table. It was all for naught. She simply ignored him. During this cold, stark hiatus he noticed that she and Mrs. Claire seemed to have patched up any differences they once might have had. Oddly, the previous evening they appeared overtly affable, sharing smiles, chatter, and even girlish giggles while carrying on one-on-one conversations to the exclusion of him and all the rest of Mrs. Dionne's diners.

Witnessing the two women embrace each other in this way stirred his curiosity even more. Robert was yet to draw any conclusions on the matter but he was increasingly convinced that he had, at least for a brief time, somehow come between Miss Henley and Mrs. Claire causing them considerable friction. That time was now long past, he would moan to himself. It was if she were gloating over the current state of affairs. There was even one occasion during his forced exile when Mrs. Claire offered him a sardonic, "Good evening, nice to see you, Robert" when he arrived at the table for his evening supper.

Nevertheless in spite of her hideous hair he was overjoyed in reading the cryptic note Deborah had slipped under his door. Its discovery and the anticipation of seeing her privately to again possibly ignite a quixotic bond spurred his imagination. Lying in his bed fighting off sleep by rereading the words she had written gave him notable pleasure which he accented by bringing on his own self gratification, an act he seldom performed on himself, but on this night he felt fully justified.

When he completed his task his sleep came fast and all consuming. Moments into the deepest darkness of his repose, he again occupied his place in Row 7 Seat 13 of the otherwise vacant cavernous theatre. When Robert's dream began and he realized where he was the stage was already occupied by the three regular cast members. The theatre hall was empty but for one. In one of his typical tirades he caught Fodor in mid-sentence

"… And my sons, those not nurtured by careless acts, your father has just returned from the service in our elite military where he was posted on our border with the rogue Romanian State. Our month's long standoff with those criminals has ended. I am proud to announce that the Second Vienna Award has been signed re-annexing the entire northern half of Transylvania and a population of greater than one million seven hundred thousand back to our motherland where they belong. This historic victory, resulting in the return of our people and the resources of our land was promulgated by our masterful savior, Adolph Hitler."

"Not a shot was fired, my beloved offspring! Not a shot!" Fodor exclaimed.

Roman looked down from the stage. His eyes scanning the audience as if he was unsure that anyone at all occupied the seats. He smiled when he saw Seat 7 filled with personage of his own image.

Rudolph nodded and his heavy eyelids drooped until his father banged his huge hand flat on the table, spilling his son's glass of goat's milk. Roman ignored the mess. Fodor caught his breath and continued.

"With this remarkable triumph our weakened and disgraced Prime Minister Teleki had no choice but to sign the Tripartite Pact, and at last our nation is forever allied with Germany, Italy and Japan in their Axis struggle for world supremacy. The evil British and Americans will be annihilated without mercy!" Again his voice rising and his arm thrusting upward and outward.

Roman jumped from his seat, goat's milk spilling on his pants. He appeared to have wet himself. Looking childish with the embarrassing stain he stood to emulate his father's salute. Fodor brought down his outstretched arm and leaned on the table, lowering his voice in a husky, menacing snarl. Roman returned to his seat.

"Victory, my sons, will not come without sacrifice and we must always be mindful of traitors in our ranks, some of whom are at the very pinnacle of power. Our pact with the Kingdom of Yugoslavia, a nation of less strategic importance, but one which provides a buffer to our borders and solidifies the geographical integrity of our region was signed by Teleki and the gutless inbred Prince Paul, signifying a bond of eternal friendship."

"What a farce! The height of treachery! Hypocrisy!"

"Within weeks our faithful spies have uncovered how this monstrous monarch has betrayed his own people by secretly aligning with another in his incestuous family. This one is called King Peter and I am sure he has none. I will call him King no Prick." With that Fodor howled at his own joke, throwing back his head in a gesture reflecting on his self-proclaimed comedic prowess.

Roman responded in kind with a handclap and loud guffaw. He looked out to find Robert, motioning for him to rise in recognition of his father's achievement. Obediently Robert stood, a nail head deeply scratching his flesh as he did so. While on his feet he was confused why he was there so he sat back down and rubbed the back of his injured thigh.

By then Roman's attention had returned to his father who had begun again. "...Ahh, but justice will prevail for those righteous in their ways. When King Prick's betrayal became known Hitler's master plan for the conquest of the Soviets may have been threatened since Yugoslavia could be a pathway to the heartland of the Russian rats' nest. Leaving nothing to chance, the Fuehrer turned to his ally Hungary. Who stood in his way, I ask?" he shouted again.

Answering his own question, "Our own traitor, Teleki! He was the mastermind behind denying his countrymen their destiny in joining Germany in its march toward world domination. But, my dear ones, as I have said before, those who are deceitful will pay, and Teleki has paid the ultimate price. The world believes he used his own pistol to remove his own skull and scatter his brains about the wall of his palace. I tell you. No! His miserable life was snuffed out after hours of torture at the hands of the Iron Cross. Oh, what pleasure this has brought to our loyal followers. Now we are free. We have elevated one of our own, Laszlo Bardossy, who will take office tomorrow as our new Prime Minister. Rejoice, my sons," he commanded, "Rejoice."

Then he sat, as if he had exhausted himself with his prolonged harangue. He folded his arms on the table. This night the bottle of port remained untouched. Fodor's glass was empty; no residual stain could be seen on the inside. After several moments of silence he leaned forward, lowering his voice when he spoke. Roman leaned closer to hear. Rudolph was awake, attentive now, seeming to respond more to his father's subdued manner as opposed to his normal agitated state. Instinctively, Robert followed the motion of Roman and his brother, a nail head scratching his back this time when he arched in his seat toward the stage.

"I will be leaving you soon, my sons. I must go to the fight against the Soviet dogs. My duty calls. Our nation will join Germany now that Bardossy is in power. I will carry the Hungarian flag but my heart is with the Nazi regime and particularly with their faithful servants embodied in the Secret Service. They are the fabled "SS" corps, upon which our own Iron Cross was formed. How can I not become part of this glorious movement? I am proud to carry the mantle and I will be proud to kill at every opportunity," he declared.

With that the curtains began to close. Robert was not prepared for that night's performance to end and for his dream to be over. He wanted more, but more of what? His subconscious told him or perhaps reminded him of the time before when his father went to war and he and Rudolph lived life on their own, or more accurately, existed, barely surviving starvation in Fodor's absence. Was the bile of hatred Fodor vomited worth the comfort that came with his presence or did Robert inwardly, callously embrace his father and find solace in his words of wrath? As long as the curtains remained open, that dreaded time apart would not come, that state of abandonment forestalled forever. Yet, this night he could not stop the curtain's inevitable slide to hide center stage. When both sides of the fabric touched and his view completely obscured, he woke, sobbing uncontrollably into his pillow, while curiously messaging a deep bloody scratch on his inner thigh.

22

Miss Deborah Jane Henley entered Mr. Sigmund Roblinski's shop the next day at the appointed six o'clock hour. Up to that time Roman spent a good portion of his day hoping beyond hope that his vision of her closely cropped hair had been another bad dream accompanying the likes he had the night before. His wish was not to be granted. Her cascading blonde tresses were truly gone, replaced by the style more akin to his own. The only shocking difference was she had parted her hair on the opposite side of her head. He couldn't help expressing a look of disbelief and dismay when she walked up and gently pecked him on the cheek.

"Do you like it?" was her first remark. Roman was struck by her question. It was as if no time at all had lapsed between their first and he feared their last encounter in August and the nine weeks that proceeded this November night. She was now seeking his approval of her hairdo when only the night before and so many nights before that he was made to feel no more than dirt under her feet. This is crazy, he thought, too crazy for me. All he could muster was, "It's different."

"You don't like it. I'm crushed, dear Roman, deeply and forever crushed," she responded with a tone that grew more serious as she spoke.

When not thinking about her hair Roman's day was spent on tenterhooks, crying out for validation of her written promise. He was no use to anyone, especially Mr. Roblinski and the five Philco stand up radio and record combination players Sigmund had left for Roman to fix before the day's end. Sigmund promised Harvey Cameron who owned a small chain of Texaco gasoline stations located on strategic street corners throughout Orleans Parish that he would have them in fine working order by closing time. The assignment, of course, went to Roman but Roman had only three of them done by six o'clock. Thankfully Mr. Cameron failed to appear as the late hour approached.

From the moment he began work that morning Roman found his task for the day a curious one. It was not because his labors were difficult, rather he was wondering why all five of the units were identical. They were all the same make and model, however he discovered the model numbers usually engraved on a tiny metal strip on the inside back panels of all the sets were missing. Roman heard Mr. Cameron tell Sigmund that he had purchased the combination entertainment centers from a "special discount distributor, but when he plugged them in, none, "even lit up for Christ's sake, let alone played music," Mr. Cameron complained.

"I promised each of my mechanics at each of my stations that I was buyin' 'em new, high fidelity radios and record players for their work bays. You know, as a present for their hard work. I'm a good boss. Damn right I am. Here I got these goddamn things and they don't play a lick. You wait 'till I find that little bastard who sold 'em to me. I'll wring his goddamn neck," Mr. Cameron assured the repair shop proprietor.

Sigmund in turn assured his customer that the units, once repaired, would never disappoint his men, and when Roman "applied his magic touch," they would, "spark to life with da sweet sounds flowing from dose speakers to sooth your hard-edged mechanics as dey go about changing da oil, packin' da rear axel grease and measuring da break fluid."

That was Roman's first shock of the day. Hearing Sigmund wax almost poetic brought him out of his stupor over Deborah's hair. He sent his customer away in good cheer and with confidence about the outcome of his repair request. Sigmund collected ten dollars as a deposit and promised results by day's end.

Later in the morning Roman gingerly probed around the subject of Sigmund's new command of English prose asking if he was continuing to practice the language arts. In response Sigmund said proudly, "Well, yes my boy, I am reading many books, and each night I stand before the mirror to practice the speech making. Getting better, no?"

"Yes, you are Mr. Roblinski. I must continue my practice as well so you don't leave me behind in our learning."

From then on Roman fumbled and mumbled through the day. Twice in the afternoon Sigmund inquired about the Philcos, only to be told repairs were still underway and progress was slow since he had to replace all the condensers and volume control switches. He added he didn't believe the radios were new since many of the parts showed considerable wear and tear and one or two might need complete overhauls.

Sigmund had left the shop by the time Deborah arrived. He told Roman he had an appointment with his podiatrist to cut off the overgrown calluses on the balls of his feet. That was Roman's second shock of the day, not quite believing that a man like Sigmund, who move about at sound-breaking speed to appear instantaneously out of thin air whenever Roman least expected it, would have an infirmity of the feet. Apparently Sigmund did, so at five-thirty off he went to seek treatment.

The third shock came when shortly before Sigmund left for his appointment he abruptly announced that, "Tomorrow you shall begin work at Isaac's bench."

Isaac's bench had been off limits since the first day of Roman's employment. Roman never mentioned it again after being told in certain terms that it was to remain vacant, bare, unused, even untouched. It was Isaac's shrine, Roman concluded, so he had all but dismissed any notion of ever having the luxury of applying his craft from that lofty location. Roman reverently respected Sigmund's wishes, considering the workstation a monument to his dead son. He even made a habit of walking in wide strides around it, avoiding stepping near, like one carefully strides over a grave.

He rejoiced in thinking about moving his tools to the bench first thing in the morning.

"Robert, I mean Roman, would you be so kind to accompany me home this evening?" Deborah inquired, running her fingers through the strands of her closely cropped hair as if she might be having second thoughts about her rash beauty parlor decision.

"No, not yet," Roman shot back with unexpected furor. "Not until you tell me, right here and now, why you've ignored me for all this time, these last nine or ten weeks as if I don't exist or become mud clods under your feet."

"You mean dirt, I think darling, dirt under my feet," she smiled.

"Now you make fun of me!" he exclaimed, abandoning his self-pledge not to raise his voice.

She stood at eye-level staring at him, their heights nearly equal since she was wearing low heels on this particular day. An expression of satisfaction seemed to appear on her face as she considered Roman's rebuke. He has balls. I like that, she thought to herself. And I can tell he hates my hair.

"Let me explain," she began, "It has been a difficult time for me. I received a promotion, which brought with it added responsibility and I have entered paralegal training with the support of the senior partners at the firm. All of this has kept me so busy, literally consumed with work. Please understand," she pleaded, but in a halfhearted manner.

"How does Clarence put it?" Roman asked, "I think he says it like this…Bullshit!"

"I see you every night. You laugh and smile and joke, but with no one besides Mrs. Claire. Now she is good to you and you are nice to her, while I sit wondering what I have done. I do nothing to you to be treated like you say, dirt. I think we became friends, maybe more than friends. Maybe I am wrong. Now you tease me with your note and then you appear, poof, out of thin air, like magician," he sneered with growing irritation.

Roman's boldness was awkward for him but he sensed a growing satisfaction with his performance so far. Since discovering the note the night before, through the day he pleaded and prayed that she would appear. Now that she had, he was challenging her, demanding answers, standing up for himself. Like a man. Proving Fodor wrong. Maybe it was Sigmund's gift of Isaac's workbench and the recognition that it brought that triggered his newfound swagger. He was beginning to like the results.

"Please, Roman, please try to understand. I want to be friends. I want to be more than friends, I think, but right now I'm confused. I can't tell you why, only that I am. What can I say… in turmoil." Her beseeching appearing more genuine.

"Please, take me out of here. Let's walk. It's stuffy in here, and it's cool and crisp outside. Lovely Louisiana fall weather. Please, let's go. I want to call you Robert. I know Robert better than Roman. Roman seems meaner than Robert. Robert is sweeter, so can we go outside?"

His doubt about her sincerity was beginning to wane.

23

Roman became Robert when he stepped through the front door of the shop. He turned to insert his key and lock it. However, he wasn't sure how sweet he was going to be, yet while still fuming inside he felt the flames in his gut subsiding as Deborah encircled her arm through his and began to lead him away.

"Let's not go back to Mrs. Dionne's just yet," she suggested. "Why don't we stop for some refreshment along the way?"

"You mean possibly missing dinner?" Robert asked somewhat bewildered.

"Yes, Robert. We are adults, you know. It's not like our parents are calling us home for supper and if we are late we will be punished and sent to bed with a blistering," she teased in response.

"I don't know. Where should we go?" he asked.

"Just come with me. I know a quiet place. I'll show you the way," she said, tightening her grip at his elbow.

After covering a three-block distance, but because of their slow pace, taking more than fifteen minutes to get there, Deborah and Robert arrived at the Metropole, a small establishment at the corner of Clio Street and Baronne. Robert sensed they were walking in the opposite direction of Mrs. Dionne's but his concern diminished with each city block they covered. His walk was enhanced by the sensation of her touch and the closeness of her flesh from which he could detect the sweet smell of a faint citrus perfume.

The Metropole was classic New Orleans motif. Dark oak wall paneling, heavy drapes of red and purple, twirling ceiling fans suspended overhead from a fine heavily embossed copper ceiling. There were well-worn booths made of solid walnut with benches for only one, seated across from the other. The dark stained tabletops were gouged with hand carvings of the names of dozens of friends and lovers and possible enemies. Soft, gentle Dixieland music drifted from the brightly rainbow lit chrome Wurlitzer jukebox standing proudly in the corner. A framed mural of caricatures of a seven piece jazz combo graced the wall behind the bar. Gaudy Mardi Gras beads hung from sconces, which shed dim light for the tabletop defacing patrons cavorting in their intimate booths. Strategically placed for all to see and from which to partake at fifty cents each, was a huge ice filled glass encased Oyster Bar, offering grey or off white spiny shelled specimens piled fifteen deep. A boy of about sixteen stood ready in his once white now grey oily stained apron. His hands were sheathed in heavy meshed gloves. In a blink of an eye and a swirl of his oyster knife he opened as many of the tasty Louisiana delicacies as a plate could hold.

Deborah and Robert stepped across the barroom floor and squeezed into an empty booth near the back. Robert scanned the evening crowd noting a cross section of New Orleans populace. It ranged from the business suit salesmen to the dockworker in overalls to the barfly in pink polyester. The clientele, who Deborah said were mostly regulars, filled the twenty or so bar stools that lined the front of the massive polished mahogany slab, adorned by hand carved cherubs at each end. Behind the bar stood the smiling, bearded, potbellied owner. Deborah said they call him Lucas the King. He stood proudly, arms crossed over his midsection, tending to the needs of his cherished customers like a benevolent monarch doling out bounty to his subjects.

Soon after they were seated an all too thin, purplish red haired, teeth stained waitress whose name they would learn later in the evening was Millie, asked for their order. She interrupted Deborah who had leaned across the table to declare for Robert's benefit, "that sometimes Al Hirt himself comes in here with two or three of his buddies and he jams that wonderful trumpet of his 'till all hours of the morning."

"What will it be folks?" asked Millie with a forced grin that was rather disturbing since it exposed her jagged display of a dentist's dream.

"Do you want a tray of oysters," Deborah asked Robert who was still staring at the toothy exhibit.

"Sure, I guess so. Never had them," Robert responded.

"You've never had oysters? My God man you haven't lived!" Deborah cried out.

Turning her attention to the impatient Millie, Deborah said, "Okay, a dozen, please, with horseradish and cocktail sauce on the side, and a lemon, cut in half. Also bring us two Dixie Beers, ice cold.

"We don't serve warm beer, lady. Sure it's gonna be cold," said Millie with a huff.

"Bitch," Deborah proclaimed after Millie strutted away. Then she continued, "Anyway, once I was in here with some friends, and sure enough, Al Hirt came in with Pete Fountain with his clarinet and the place went wild. They played for two hours. Brought the house down. The Metropole was jammed."

"Who is Al Hirt, and the other fellow you mentioned?" Robert asked, now embarrassed at his admission of ignorance over the names. And what about her turn of phrase about bringing down the house? Literally? He thought.

Her eyes went wide in surprise, but she caught herself before exposing another exclamation over his naiveté. "Robert, I'm sorry. I just assumed you knew these people. They are famous musicians in New Orleans and throughout the country, but there is probably no way you could have known about them with so little time in America. I apologize," she said sincerely.

"No matter. I am trying to learn more about America as fast as I can. I do like music. I like the music here. Are they playing Mr. Al Fountain on the music box?" he inquired.

"That's Al Hirt and Pete Fountain, Robert. No, that's Louis Armstrong on the jukebox. He's another trumpeter. He's a Negro, you know, and maybe even more famous than both Al Hirt and Pete Fountain put together. It's strange that that could be the case, you know a Negro and all, but it's true I think," she mused somewhat to herself.

"I have one of those, what you say.... jukeboxes, in the shop now. Mr. Roblinski took one in a week ago from owner of a diner on South Saratoga Street. He told the man I could fix. But I never work on one before. The records whirling around inside and buttons to push to bring them out to place on the turntable. The coin slot that makes it all happen. Very complicated. I hope I can fix. The name on that one in the shop is Seeburg. It is different from the one over there," he said with a slight hint of anguish.

"Oh, I'm sure you can fix it. Hold on. I will go find a tune by Al Hirt and maybe they have one by Pete Fountain as well," she said, rising from the cramped booth to prance toward the sparkling box producing the sweet sounds.

Just as Deborah stepped away, Millie returned with their beers and food. When she placed the pile before him Robert was caught by the peculiar odor and the slimy substance of the grey globs that shimmered in the spread-eagle shells. He suppressed a gag. After succeeding, he took a long pull from the chilled, as promised, mug of southern brew.

Over the speakers hung from each corner of the room came the intoxicating opening bars of *"The Blues My Naughty Sweetie Gives to Me."* Robert wasn't paying much attention to the music just then, instead trying to envision himself, or anyone for that matter, eating the slippery clumps of matter patiently levitating in their juices on the plate at his fingertips.

Deborah returned to the table. "God, those look delicious. You know they say you are only supposed to eat oysters in months with names ending in "R". They say, but Jesus I don't know if it's true, that it has to do with something like their best breeding time and when they mature. It's November, so it's a good time for oysters. Did you also know that oysters can change their sex?" Her enlightening continued.

Her earlier incantations failed to capture his attention, but her latest one did. "Is that right?" he asked with genuine interest, still eyeing the platter as she grabbed a gaping shell from it, spooned a little horseradish on top, squeezed out a drop of lemon, opened her mouth in an odd oval shape, and in one disgusting motion, sucked it in. Down her throat it went. His stomach heaved and he took another swig of Dixie's best.

When his stomach settled he pursued the subject. "Is that true? I've never heard of an animal, or is that a fish, having the changing of its own sex," he said with certain inquisitiveness.

"Oh yes," she assured him. "Oysters are fish and all of them, no matter the species, or if they are male or female, have gonads. So, when they get the urge, they screw themselves!" Unintentionally, she blurted out the last few words and unintentionally launched a chunk of the grey slime airborne across the tabletop, to land square in the middle of Robert's chin.

"Oh, Christ, I am so sorry," she yelped while grabbing a napkin to wipe the wet dripping litter from his face.

Recovering quickly from the fourth shock of his day, while she dabbed frantically at his lower jaw, Robert burst out laughing uncontrollably. She did the same and for minutes they chortled and giggled at each other like flirtatious teenagers at a soda fountain sharing a milk shake on their first date. Only when she observed that, "To top it all off, the gonads are the tastiest part of the oyster," did his sniggering stop. His fifth shock of the day came when she claimed to have found a pair of oyster testicles in the third full shell she retrieved from the platter. "Look," she instructed, shoving the shell toward

Robert's reeling nose. She retreated when he turned away and instead, with relish, vacuumed them down herself.

After Millie shuffled over with their fourth round of iced glazed mugs full of the golden suds she urged, "Come on Robert, please try one." Robert's resistance had ebbed somewhat. Besides, he was hungry. He looked up at the Dixie Beer wall clock suspended over the front entrance and saw it was nearly seven-thirty. Darkness had fallen.

"We've missed dinner, you know," he pointed out with a slight slur and a boyish grin. "Mrs. Dionne will be angry, and I suspect so will Mrs. Claire."

Deborah looked up from staring at the foam in her mug to declare, "I don't give a shit about either one of them. Now are you gonna eat this stuff with me or are you gonna just sit there watching me eat 'em all until I throw up all over this table?" Her voice had a hard edge for the first time since she arrived at the shop. As she spoke Robert also noticed she was pulling at the short clumps of the remaining hair on her head as if by doing so, it might stretch each strand to appear longer.

"All right. Here goes," Robert suddenly proclaimed. She shrieked and clapped her hands in anticipation. Holding his breath for fear of ingesting the noxious smell, he plucked a shell from the platter and started it toward his mouth. She stopped him in mid motion.

"Try the cocktail sauce and a dash of lemon juice. That will help you on your oyster inaugural," she advised. She grabbed his hand holding the shell, full and glistening, to apply the sauce and lemon and then pushed it back toward his gaping yawn. He took it like the man he had become. Sending it slithering down his throat without a bite and with only a lingering after taste. He took a Dixie drink and waited for the regurgitation. It didn't come. Instead, he only hiccupped and asked for another.

She was overjoyed. She rose slightly out of her seat, stretched across the table and with open mouth and tongue ready to plunge, kissed him uninhibitedly. It was then that the combination of her taste, the incongruous creature now inhabiting his body and the beer in which it was swimming in a pool in his stomach, all came together to explode in a belch that even caught Millie's attention standing four booths away. Robert's expulsion prompted another round of hysterical laughter, followed by another round of their now favorite beverage. Before the night was over Robert ingested seven of the slimy masses, plus a steaming bowl of clam chowder and a heaping plate of hush puppies.

They remained in their booth in the back of the bar until midnight. Their talk was scattered, rather meaningless most of the time and lacked substance. At intervals their chatter was almost childish like those milk shake slurping teenagers. Yet there were certain things Deborah revealed that stuck in Robert's brain to be brought forth from the crevasse of his memory in the days that followed. Foremost among those alcohol clouded remembrances was her lamenting over her latest job assignment under the tutelage of an up and coming brash barrister by the name of Earling Carothers "Jim" Garrison.

There were also vague references to weekly meetings she said she loved attending. Those meetings of meaning to her, those meetings that grounded her in reality and brought her senses to their peak. She didn't mention Mrs. Claire again however. Robert had a difficult time following her string of verbal consciousness during her tabletop revelations, mostly because of the booze buzz he was enjoying, yet he somehow took a mental note to ask her more, to probe deeper to the depths of the subjects of her passion. He wanted to do that because he sensed the iconic Jim Garrison, as she described him, and the meetings she regularly attended had become gut level important to her and he wanted to know why. In addition, he was extremely curious about her shunning of the subject of Mrs. Claire.

Near the twelve o'clock hour, interrupting her incessant repartee on these and other topics, Robert reached out to touch her hair and said, "You are beautiful either way, but I hope it grows back fast." With those words, she stopped in mid-sentence and proceeded to cry. Not wailing, just whimpering. A sad resignation, he sensed. It broke the mood and they seemed to simultaneously sober up with each subdued sob. Millie, by then warming up to them, even bringing the couple a free round a half hour before, called a taxi to take them to Mrs. Dionne's.

They rode in silence in the back of the green and yellow cab. Once he reached for her hand, but she pulled it away saying, "It's too soon. Give me time."

Robert, again confused but too tired to question or object, let her latest rejection pass. They arrived at the boardinghouse in minutes. The porch light was on. Robert had his key out and was inserting it in the door when it swung open exposing Mrs. Dionne, standing with hands on hips like an angry grade school matron. Before she could utter a word, Deborah presented a waving finger in her face and warned, "Don't say a fucking word."

Although she was blocking the doorway they both eased passed a silent and stunned Mrs. Dionne to climb the stairs and retire to their separate rooms for the remainder of the night.

24

Robert had forgotten what a hangover felt like. He was miserable the next day. For endless hours his stomach reminded him that it had been cruelly invaded the night before by numerous foreign substances of unrecognizable form, all which proved to be extremely difficult to wind their way through his digestive track and out his over exercised bowels.

At Mrs. Dionne's table that next morning Robert didn't touch his breakfast, opting only for hot tea, a slice of dry toast and four Bayer aspirin. Literally there was no conversation during the morning meal, with each of the participants, including Mrs. Dionne, consumed with their private thoughts, their private infirmities, or their private demons. Deborah was absent from breakfast and Mrs. Claire's glare at Robert was fiendish in its intensity.

His limited diet in the early morning hours only made it worse and he limped off to work at Mr. Roblinski's with a strain greater than normal. His leg and his head hurt with equal intensity. His pace was slow and each step grew more painful.

Roman plunged into his work at the moment of his late arrival. It was the only way he could rid himself of the nausea and his pounding cranium. He took solace, comfort, and joy in moving his tools to Isaac's bench. He did so without further instruction from Sigmund who spoke to him from behind his counter only with a pleasant, "Good Morning Roman," ignoring the fact that Roman had arrived at eight-forty five, exactly forty-five minutes late.

By noon all five of the Philco stand up combination radio-record players, each with their dials fixed on the soft symphonic melodies of station WSHO, were emitting sensuous sounds through their dual speaker systems. Roman stood in the middle of the back room to feel the full effect of the music having moved each of the units into positions around the shop to maximize the stereo effect. Even Sigmund emerged from his workstation to capture the auditory delight.

He said to Roman, "It is like I am one of the orchestra performing a symphony from my first violin chair, hearing the others play with all their hearts."

Roman took his normal break time around one o'clock and by then his appetite had returned. He bought a cup of chicken noodle soup from the Crescent City Diner located down the block and ate it from its paper cup container on the steps of St. Jude Shrine, waiting again for the priest who never came.

When he returned to work with a faint feeling of disappointment that no one from the church had fetched him to partake in the rituals inside, he attacked the broken Seeburg jukebox with a fierce determination. Within minutes he removed the protective glass shield and dismantled the guts of the machine's mechanical and electrical systems. Soon parts were strewn across Isaac's bench and on the floor beneath his feet. He soon discovered that, like so many of the modern electrical marvels of that time, this one also had fairly fundamental and predictable operating characteristics. Wires should be connected in a certain way, grounded when needed, power output when appropriate. The current had to be current, ever present to drive the wheels and gears and levers. Screws had to be tight but in some cases not so tight as to inhibit movements of the wheels and gears and levers. Basic stuff for Roman. The tubes should light up but not glow too brightly. If they did, it might signal an impending overload. He just had to get his arms around it, or better yet his mind into the peculiar herky-jerky movement of the record changer since he quickly discovered that it was this device within the device that was causing the trouble. When he had most of the parts reassembled, oiled, re-soldered, screwed down tight but not too tight and he plugged in and fired up the magical music box he saw that the herky-jerky motion of the stubborn record changer remained.

"Shit. Goddamn shit," he muttered and set about dismantling again. At nearly five-forty five with the sun now gone and dusk taking hold, Roman stood back and listened to the Seeburg sing. Before the music started Roman had to strike "A-7" on the brightly lit red push button keyboard. With that action the semicircle sickle shaped record retriever came up from its stationary holding dock and in a smooth motion snatched a 45-rpm from the spinning rack full of records. Marvelous how it knew "A-7" was Roman's choice. The no longer herky-jerky Seeburg did and within an instant the 45 was spinning on the turntable soon to blast from its speakers RCA Victor Records' latest hit by the sensation from Memphis, Tennessee, Elvis Presley. *Jailhouse*

Rock, number one on the charts for twenty-seven weeks, brought a smile to Roman's lips and a sway to his hips.

He walked home alone that night and arrived just in time for dinner.

The evening began somber and stale but soon livened up. When Deborah arrived she gave Robert a pleasant but not warm smile, like she might even give to a stranger on the street corner. She sat across from him and politely greeted her fellow diners including Mrs. Dionne in the very same manner. They exchanged pleasantries as if Deborah's crude warning the night before had never taken place. All the others were seated and salads were being served when Mrs. Claire made her grand entrance. She was dressed in a sleek and shimmering lime green cocktail dress, cut low in the front and back. Robert couldn't help but stare at her fleshy cleavage. Her perfume was strong. Her hair perfectly coiffed in the latest French twist style. Clarence let out a "whoop" as she took her seat and declared, "holy-moly mama, ain't you somethin' ta look at tonight!"

"Well, thank you, Clarence. I will take that as a compliment," she gushed, and then announced to the group that, "I won't be having dinner with y'all tonight. I expect my date will be here at any moment. We're going to a fund raising ball at the Le Pavilion. I believe it is for the new wing at New Orleans Charity Hospital. Oh, I believe I hear him now, just pulling into the driveway."

At that instant Deborah slammed her napkin onto her salad plate hard enough to scatter her lettuce and utensils about. Her fork bounced onto the floor. She jumped from her seat and stomped away without a word.

Mrs. Claire simply said, "Oh my," and sneered at Deborah's back as she left the room. Robert watched Deborah race away, baffled and bewildered again but less so this time. Her actions, Mrs. Claire's actions and the strange dynamics between the two women were all well beyond his comprehension, so that night he chalked it up to just another bizarre occurrence in a long and contentious series. No longer would he allow himself to be entangled in whatever web they spun. All he wanted was her flesh when time and opportunity presented themselves. He was looking for companionship and sex, not necessarily in that order, and he would put up with her erratic behavior for as long as it took to achieve those goals. Right then he vowed to look elsewhere for the same results. A certain confidence was driving him in that direction and he liked the feeling.

Miss Hattie, seeming to have missed all the commotion said, "I declare, Mrs. Claire you do look marvelous this evening. I remember fondly, my dear, that the annual Charity Hospital ball at the Le Pavilion was indeed a favorite event of my Henry and me. We attended faithfully for many years, of course, until his death. It was always a wonderful evening but I do recall a few times, perhaps more than a few, when Henry was unable to motor us home. One time I found him in the ladies room. He couldn't recall how he got there. That was a particularly bad night. And another time…"

"Yes, yes thank you, Miss Hattie. I must go now. Please have a pleasant evening," Mrs. Claire interrupted as she hurried out of the room, her legs straining in their movement, hampered by the skin tightness of the gown. This only proved to accentuate the sway of her posterior much to the delight of Robert, Clarence, Boudreaux and Anthony who all craned their necks for a last look.

"As I was saying," Miss Hattie began again.

"We don't want ta hear no more from you, you crazy old bat," Clarence scolded.

"Clarence, you behave yourself," demanded Mrs. Dionne who had kept quiet up to that point but apparently felt she had to step in to referee.

It was Anthony's turn again to change the subject, bringing to the forefront a story most men in America were talking about on that fall night. "Isn't that Floyd Patterson somethin'," he remarked. Fightin' and knockin' out Hurricane Jackson in July and then fightin' again less than a month later and knockin' out Pete Rademacher."

"Damn right he somethin'," chimed in Clarence, "Floyd's da best goddamn heavyweight dare is, maybe dare ever was."

"Come on," responded Anthony, "how could you forget about Joe Lewis? Nobody could come close to matchin' up with the Brown Bomber."

"Floyd might be skinnier but he faster dan Joe ever was. All he had ta do was bob and weave, jab and jam, and ole Joe woulda gone down in a heap," Clarence declared with authority.

Robert listened to the exchange intently knowing how he would be spending his lunch break the next day buried in the sports section of the *Times Picayune*.

Mrs. Dionne then spoke. "I assume you are referring to that Negro boxer. I find it disgusting that our country has come to idolize people like him. His kind is nothing more than an animal on two legs trained for violence. Their actions only breed violence among their own kind and worse yet when men not of color stoop to that level of barbarism it can only promote conflict among the races."

All four of the men turned to stare at her in silence, expecting more of her feeble attempt to explain a warped perspective on the timeless art of pugilism. She remained quiet, finishing her main course while the others gawked, with the exception of Miss Hattie who realized the stillness might be her cue to launch into another wacky tale.

"You know, my Henry really didn't have a drinking problem. He was quite strong in that regard. He was just full of merriment everywhere we went in those days. He was so good to me when he was home. It was just those times when I couldn't find him, sometimes for days on end. But he always came home...in the end," she sighed wistfully.

"Dat's enough woman. Cain't stand hearin' no more about dat drunken bastard you was married to," Clarence yelped and then turned to address Mrs. Dionne's remark.

"Well, well dare ain't much mo you can say about dem black boys and dem white boys when day mix it up. Is dare? Spose you'd rather have dem mixin' it up on da streets instead of in da ring, Huh? Ya might not see it dis way madam but da way I figure it, it's better ta have dem punchin' at each other dare wif all da white boys bettin' and da black boys bettin' on whose gonna win, and whoopin' and hollerin' and each of dem in de audience thinkin' day wish day were big and strong like dem dare in da ring, just blowin' off steam so day go home tired an broke, but peaceful like.

"And da ya happen ta remember when, back in '38, when da black boy Joe fought da rematch wif da white boy Max and da whole damn world knew about it? Huh? Seems ta me our boy Joe, our American colored boy Joe, beat da shit outa dat white Nazi boy Max and when he did it was no matter what his skin color was. Very interestin' da ya think, Mrs. Dionne?"

By the time Clarence was through, Mrs. Dionne had stopped eating to listen. Her mouth was open and Robert could see remnants of partially chewed peas scattered about inside. She finished chewing when he was done. She swallowed and spoke.

"A lovely dinner. We should all remember to give a special thanks to Betsey. She worked especially hard on the chicken cordon bleu." Then she was up from her chair and quickly exited the dining room without another word.

Bourdreaux pulled Clarence away from the table and bent down close to his ear, speaking softly, "That was one of your better ones, Clarence. You stopped that old bitch dead in her tracks."

Robert limited his Chesterfields on the porch that night to only one after fatigue overtook him and he shuffled back inside to climb the stairs. As he passed through the front door, Clarence, sitting near, reached up to pull him down by tugging on his shirtsleeve.

"You was sorely missed last night, boy. So was dat strange bitch wit da man's hair. Be careful is my advice. She just might be as dangerous as if I'da let ya go back ta them docks ta work when ya first got cheer." Clarence looked deep into Robert's eyes as he spoke. Robert slowly and gently pulled away to ascend the steps to his bed.

With utter exhaustion overwhelming him deep sleep was minutes away. Shortly thereafter the dreams came with Fodor prancing and pounding the table at center stage.

"My sons as you know I have just returned from the Soviet front. I will enjoy my brief time with you here in Esztergom where we can spend long hours together as I relive for you my many heroic acts while fighting side by side with our German brethren.

"You are aware I am sure that Hungary's declaration of war against the Communist swine at long last allowed patriots such as myself to openly pledge our allegiance to the glorious Fascist cause. Oh what glory we have already achieved! As you know I am a captain in the Hungarian Karpat Group. Just three months ago, my sons, my regiment took the frontal charge in the attack on the 12th Soviet Army. We were attached to the German 17th Army and we advanced far into southern Russia. We fought in the historic battle we now call Uman and my mechanized corps acted as a pincer...Well one-half of a pincer...to encircle both the 6th and the 12th Soviet Armies. In the end our forces captured or destroyed twenty...believe it sons, twenty Soviet divisions!

"The fighting was fierce. I will tell you about a single incident, although there were many, but this one illustrates my courage under fire."

Fodor finally caught a breath, circling the table where Roman and Rudolph sat, to retrieve his bottle of port resting on its surface. He filled his glass. He took a long pull, wiped his lips on his thick brown wool Hungarian Army tunic sleeve and again brought his voice to high pitch. Roman kicked his brother's shin under the table to startle him to attention.

Robert shifted in his bare nail prickly seat, alone again. His father's voice echoing through the rafters of the empty hall.

"On a warm August evening, toward twilight, I ordered patrols out into the field to establish a perimeter for defense before nightfall. My tent was being erected by field servants and our cooks had just stoked a good fire, although our weather reports indicated the temperatures would remain well into the sixties through the night. Perhaps I had fifteen, no more than twenty men with me at the time. Not fighting men, you see, just clerks, radio technicians, cooks and supply personnel. My combat teams were out in the field. YOU UNDERSTAND," he shouted. I WAS VULNERABLE TO ATTACK. The worst possible time. Even I had let my guard down, if just for a moment.

"Outside the tent stakes I had removed my shirt and was preparing to wash my face and hands when the whistle came. Not a whistle one would give to summon your dog, but THE DEADLY WHISTLE OF A MORTAR…A FUCKING SOVIET MORTAR.

"The explosion knocked me off my feet, but I was quick, oh so quick, to bounce up and retrieve my weapon, ready for the battle to come. I looked across the campsite and soon realized our evening meal had been ruined. The shell hit where our cooks were working, leaving human body parts splattered about on the ground to mix with the lovely lamb stew they were preparing. Just then another whistle and another explosion. By then I had gathered my meager defense forces of those men left alive and placed them in line, rifles and machine guns at the ready, to repel the oncoming charge.

"Soon it came. They were like crazed animals appearing on the horizon then charging head long into our wall of fire. My men would fight bravely under my command. Our fingers steady on the triggers. Our aims were perfect. We took down wave after wave of the hideous, snarling throng and delighted in seeing them fall, maimed and dying before our eyes. Soon our ammunition ran low. The Red bastards, although ignorant in so many ways, finally realized their banzai tactics were fruitless, so they dug into their positions to lay siege. Yes, they had the high ground. They took the advantage. The few marksmen among them were lucky to find their targets and some of my heroic defenders began to fall. I alone took no wounds, although with my rank and position sniper after sniper leveled their sights and fired, hoping desperately to rid their forces of the strongest and most cunning of their enemy."

"But I stood alone, their bullets coming near but to no affect. I kept firing, fielding the weapons of those dead around me. It was as if I had an invisible impenetrable shield and only I was protected by the gods to live and fight again."

By this time Fodor was in a state of near exhaustion. He finished his bottle of port, having drunk straight from the bottle. Roman kept glancing out into the audience for assurance that Robert was with him, paying attention, no, paying homage to the GREAT ONE in their midst. Fodor, seated for a short rest, suddenly leaped to his feet to continue his prancing and frenzied oratory.

"Then my sons, they were on me, ignoring the danger I posed. A few in their ranks crept up on my flank to surround me on three sides to pounce in a pack like on an abandoned fawn. But no baby fawn was I to their great surprise! Rather I stood as a huge buck with a rack of sharp horns, slashing and slicing and tearing at their soft, flabby bellies, inflicting terrible wounds. Soon they weakened while I grew stronger and they retreated to lick and patch their devastating injuries. I was invincible and they finally knew it.

"Having heard the gunfire my patrols hurried back to my aid. They found me amongst the rubble and blood. Their base camp in ruins. All was quiet by then. The Soviet menace had retreated, knowing they were defeated by a single super human. Only the blood of others was on my hands."

Fodor finally sat again at the table, looking skyward and raising his arms as if to accept heavenly gifts of gratitude from whatever false god might care. Roman turned to Robert, raising an arm to sweep across the table as if presenting the star performer for one last curtain call. Robert obediently stood to begin a muted, slow, lonely applause. Rudolph, not to be left out, stood to join.

On this night Robert was glad when his dream was over. He awoke to recall many of its details wondering how fantastic a tale it had been. The one thing that kept coming back to him during the days that followed was the peculiar way Roman appeared up on the stage. It was his hair, Robert finally realized, short, blonde, parted on the side, strangely looking exactly like Deborah's.

25

Two weeks passed before Robert and Deborah met again. During that interval she returned to her previous ways, greeting him at dinner with distant politeness, never with a hint of intimacy. Yet as she walled herself off from Robert especially at each meal setting, there also was an obvious barrier between her and Mrs. Claire. They never spoke or acted as if they even acknowledged the existence of one another.

Consequently the women at Mrs. Dionne's table settled into an uneasy gulf of cordiality. However, the men each night filled the void with banter fit for a private clubroom bereft only of cigars, cognac and near naked cocktail waitresses.

Their topics scanned the issues of the day. They speculated on how long star pitcher Herb Score of the Cleveland Indians would be out of the line up after being hit in the face by Yankee Gil McDougald's line drive. They talked about the big mouth tinny, halting voice of a new sportscaster named Howard Cosell. They were amazed with the Dodgers moving from Brooklyn to Los Angeles and they bet each other a dollar that it might or might not take Elizabeth Taylor another six months to divorce Mike Todd and find her fourth sucker husband.

Only when Clarence described Miss Taylor as a "big titted wench who'd bite off your balls rather than cut them off so she could taste your blood," did Mrs. Dionne scold him for "intolerable vulgarity," but she said or did nothing more.

On Thanksgiving night Miss Hattie became so distraught she wept at dinner over the news of President Eisenhower's stroke and the reports speculating that it would disable him with a major speech impediment. It was only then that Mrs. Dionne, while Betsey prepared to serve the turkey, giblets, gravy and dressing, offered an opinion on that topic.

"I sincerely hope the bastard never speaks again so our races can remain separate and peace will be restored to the South." That contribution was followed by a Thanksgiving prayer, which she led. In her missive she beseeched her Lord to "bring us all good health, wisdom, purity and prosperity," but somehow forgot to praise her Maker for even one of His blessings bestowed upon the company she kept.

"None of us is here, dear lady, but for the goodness of da Lord," Clarence said when the heads of the worshipers rose to eye their food, "so next time ya might give dat some thought befo askin' fo his attention."

Mrs. Dionne preferred to ignore Clarence's advice.

It was Boudreaux who further stunned the holiday gathering with his recommendation that all should read the Pulitzer Prize winning *Profiles in Courage* authored by the obscure but up-and-coming Senator from Massachusetts, John F. Kennedy. To their amazement he said he purchased a copy and would be glad to share it with anyone who might be interested.

Clarence was the most astonished, saying, "Shit man, I didn't know ya could read," followed by Robert's request to borrow Boudreaux's copy.

On the Saturday following Thanksgiving, after Robert returned to his room from a brief walk to the hardware store to buy a new pair of wire cutters, he found another neatly folded note under his door. It read:

> *I would be so pleased if you would join me tonight. I want to introduce you to some friends. We meet on Saturday nights for an hour or so to share our thoughts and ideas. If you can I will meet you at 7 o'clock at the corner of Harmony and Fourth Street. The meeting hall is close by at Phillip Street and South Saratoga. Dinner after. No Oysters, I promise."*
>
> *Deborah*

He was there at six fifty-five, watching her approach the corner at a leisurely gait displaying an ear-to-ear smile.

"I'm so happy you could come. I have missed you so," was her cheerful greeting. She kissed him lightly on the cheek.

Unimpressed, he said, "I've seen you every day for the past two weeks, but your eyes have been blind to me again."

"Oh, Robert, let's not quarrel. It is a lovely night, cold for New Orleans this time of year, but lovely just the same," she said, adding, "You look well and so handsome tonight in that jacket of yours." Her eyes scanned down. "Are those new pants? Do I see...yes I do, you are wearing Western boots?"

Robert had saved seventy-five dollars over the past month or so and the week before he purchased a pair of straight legged, boot cut western pants, dark brown in color, with mother of pearl button snaps at the center of the "v"-shaped back pocket flaps. The leg pockets were cut in a slight curvature configuration to taper across his upper thighs just below the waistline. His hands fit perfectly in the deep front pockets. On his shopping excursion he opted to buy a money clip over a western belt and that night he had thirty dollars in various denominations folded and safely secured by the clip tucked down deeply inside the right hand pocket. When he dressed for the evening he regretted his decision about the belt and wished he had splurged on the leather hand tooled one hanging from the rack with the longhorn steer head and the tiny turquoise stones for eyes accenting the buckle. He decided he'd go back the following week to buy it, but tonight he was forced to go belt less.

His boots were *Tony Lama*, the best the store clerk said he could buy. They were dark brown like his pants and made of lizard skin. Robert didn't know what kind of lizard had been sacrificed for the manufacture of his boots, but lizard "will wear like iron," the clerk assured him, so his decision was an easy one. To help correct his limp the clerk threw in a make- shift, inside-the-boot lift, which seemed to elevate his right foot just enough for easier and less painful strides. The lizard skin was soft and supple to Robert's delight, and tonight was the first justifiable occasion he found to wear them. He felt grand; truly American. A southern gentleman indeed.

Deborah looked like a sailor who had just stepped off one of the merchant ships docked at the New Orleans pier. She had on a seaman's navy blue pea coat, buttoned tightly to her chin, a black stocking hat pulled over her ears, but below the waist, a pair of shapely slacks of dark color, too dark for Robert to distinguish the shade covering her figure. Her only other feminine display was on her feet. A lovely pair of red patent leather pumps with three inch heals. The shoes may have been enough. To Robert in a strange way she had overcome her manly persona to become incredibly evocative.

She took his arm and steered him in the direction she wanted him to go. After a fifteen-minute walk and conversation devoid of substance other than a meaningless description of her friends he was about to meet having "kind hearts and deep convictions", they arrived at their destination. The building's solid stone façade practically abutted the sidewalk. There was no yard. A steep stairway separated the two wings of the structure and nearly required a vertical climb to the entrance to the first level off the street. Robert counted four stories in all. Huge matching plate glass windows ornamented the first floors on either side and faced the street. Above them were smaller windows, normal size, signifying residential units. There were curtains on the smaller, upper floor windows and a few were lighted and visible. Some shades were drawn, others not. None of the windows appeared open. It was too cold outside. The first floor to the left side of the building was dark. The right side was brilliantly lit. Robert could see backs of heads and shoulders and profiles of people milling about inside.

"This is it," she said, and they ascended the stairway.

A main double door appeared at the top step. Deborah reached for the handle but Robert got there first, twisting and pushing it open for her to enter before him. He admired the lead framed pop bottle thick stained glass at the door's eye level center. After a few steps into the dimly lighted corridor she turned to her right and tapped lightly on the first interior door they came to. It was not numbered or marked. Robert stood at her right shoulder and then noticed he was still somewhat shorter than her as the heels of his boots were two inches high instead of her three. The door swung open a few seconds later. A man, middle aged, burly in stature, wavy grey hair, combed straight back and wearing a red checked lumberjack wool shirt answered.

"Deborah," he said, "Welcome. Is this the young man you've told us about?"

"Yes, Clay, this is Robert. Robert, this is Clay." She stepped aside and he reached out his beefy hand for Robert to take.

"Pleased to meet you," the man said and quickly added, "Robert we use only first names here. It is our custom. You will meet many wonderful folks here tonight but kindly refrain from asking them their last names."

Somewhat taken aback and looking over at a smiling and nodding Deborah for confirmation, he said, "Certainly, Sir, I have no problem with that."

"Great," Clay responded, "then please step ahead."

Robert found himself inside what he thought might have been a dance studio, but no one was dancing. No music was playing. Balance Barres apparently for practicing ballerinas ran horizontally along the lengths of all four walls. Mirrors hung behind the balance Barres, nearly floor to ceiling in height giving the sensation that the room was twice as large and filled with twice as many people. In truth, there were around twenty individuals chatting in low voices in small clusters around the room. Metal folding chairs were bunched together at one end of the room. A small, stand up podium was placed before the uneven rows of seats. An aisle separated the rows. Robert met and shook hands with everyone there including Alexander, Larry, Tom, Linda, Hilda, Hillary and David. George, Gloria, Gladys and Grady. No last names. All friendly, but not overwhelmingly so. Robert still felt like a stranger even after the pleasantries were exchanged with each one. He noticed a few southern accents, some twangs, some brogues and some flat nasal consonants. Generally, not an unwelcoming atmosphere. Perhaps cautious or leery might better describe his reception.

Clay called the meeting to order about a half hour after Robert and Deborah arrived.

"Before we begin, I want to make sure all of you have met Robert, Deborah's friend," Clay said. "If you haven't please raise your hand."

No one did.

"Good," Clay continued, "it is rare for us to welcome guests, as all of you know, but for our movement to grow and for our voices to be heard we must open our doors and our minds to new people, people willing to hear our message and perhaps join our cause. Is that not right, my friends?" he asked.

"Yes," was the unanimous response from Clay's small but enthusiastic gathering.

Robert had recently frequented a local theatre in the French Quarter to watch Saturday matinee movies. He thought this practice would be another good way for him to "Americanize" himself, plus it was entertaining all at the same time. The films also were excellent resources for advancing his English language skills. This night he would put his emerging abilities to use by focusing on the various accents and dialects vocalized by attendees at Deborah's first name only, dance studio meeting. One of many screen gems that recently stuck in his mind was *The Lost Weekend,* the Academy Award winning, post war rendition of a struggling chronic alcoholic played by brooding actor Ray Milland. Robert was disturbed by the film, realizing early in its showing how Milland's character reminded him of so many twisting and wrenching characteristics of his father Fodor. He empathized with Milland but throughout the film hated his character all the same. He left before it was over.

Up the street from the theatre was another meeting hall, similar to the one he was in now, but instead, this one was off the sidewalk, down a short flight of steps and into a subbasement that was once but now an abandoned restaurant. Robert was glad he had left before the ending of Milland's masterful performance. That day Robert strolled along the sidewalk and after a short distance, noticed a sign, "All Are Welcome. Please Join Us." He had nothing else to do that afternoon, so he descended the steps and quietly entered the dusty, dingy forgotten dining room through the front door. The meeting was already in progress and like his current setting people were seated in folding chairs in irregular rows with a podium at the front and an aisle running down the middle.

When Robert arrived a man was speaking from the podium at the opposite end of the bare, poorly lighted room. His voice echoed through the cloistered chamber. The air inside was stale and stifling hot. At the speaker's back was the long abandoned bar. Its mirror behind was cracked through the middle. Not one bottle or glass was on display. His audience appeared in rapture, with some nodding their appreciation of his words, while others were mumbling scattered, "Yeses," and "You're so right, brother."

At first Robert thought he had stumbled into another revival meeting like the one he had done so one night a month before when his curiosity got the best of him while walking past the Holy Jesus AME Church of New Orleans, located about a mile west of Harmony Street. That was a memorable experience as well. Robert soon realized he stood out in that crowd of worshipers. He sat in the back, loved the music and revelry, didn't understand much of what was being said by the profusely sweating plentifully gigantic black preacher, but was greeted with kindness and hospitality when the service ended and the parishioners walked past him to disperse. Robert thought Clarence might be in the congregation but he wasn't.

So on that day Robert speculated that again he had accidentally discovered another strange place of religious celebration, but when the man at the podium shouted, "I am an alcoholic!" followed spontaneously by a chorus from the audience, screaming, "Yes, you are an alcoholic and so am I!" Robert realized the theme of that afternoon's festivities was undoubtedly quite different from his experience with the assemblage of Holy Jesus AME Church of New Orleans.

He didn't linger long at that Saturday afternoon gathering quickly discovering that he had accidentally intruded in on a session of the Thalia Street Chapter of Alcoholics Anonymous. Robert's attempt at an early departure prompted a hearty greeting from the self-proclaimed drunkard who from his podium noticed Robert's presence after his self-cleansing confession and that of his audience. As graciously as he could Robert declined the invitation to address the gathering with his own admission, and even with his bad leg bolted out the door from which he just passed through. Loud boos and catcalls chased him away. On his way home that evening he thought about Ray Milland, Fodor, the boos, the booze, and the boozers, vowing never to touch the stuff again even if it meant declining Deborah's invitation to stop for a "little refreshment."

As Clay began, Robert cringed, thinking Deborah had coerced him into attending the Saturday night meeting of the Felicity Street Chapter of Alcoholics Anonymous. He was just about ready to stand up and leave when Clay declared, "My friends, our very lives are at stake here. Our way of life. Our heritage. Our Constitutional rights are being threatened by those who claim to be our leaders, but secretively they have infiltrated our society to eat away at its core."

Robert sat back down in his seat. At his side Deborah circled her arm through his to make sure he stayed right where he was.

The meeting adjourned two hours later. The time was filled with fierce, fiery rhetoric on topics far reaching yet consistently encircling a central theme. Speaker after speaker, all white, some almost as frenzied as Holy Jesus' perspiring preacher, covered every imaginable subject Robert, in his short time in his chosen country, could fathom having any importance. They yelled about the Russians, the Communists, the Democrats, the Republicans, the corrupt unions, the corrupt businessmen, and a world coming to an end unless something was done to stop it. They hated Roosevelt, Truman, Eisenhower, Dulles, Nixon, Stevenson, and Johnson. All of them were crooks. At times during the speeches Robert sincerely believed he was dreaming. At times they sounded so much like his father; alluring, yet frightening, mesmerizing yet repugnant. In the end they were all exhausted, including Robert.

It was the second to last speaker that brought Robert to the edge of his seat. A middle aged, rail thin woman with long straight grey hair, dressed in a three button, two sizes too big cardigan sweater and a skirt that drug the floor. She spoke with sheer impassioned eloquence about the Hungarian Uprising of the very recent past. To Robert she was a messiah. She spoke as if she had been in the middle of it all with a stark clarity only Roman and Fodor could appreciate. She described Soviet brutality; of their inhumanity and contrasted that with the bravery and sacrifice of those dedicated to freedom who fought with rusty handguns, pitchforks and knives against the frothing beasts equipped with fleets of armored tanks, artillery and newly minted jet aircraft. She cried over the rapes and humiliation, the suppression and slaughter akin to nothing the world had witnessed since the Holocaust. She winced over America's idleness while it all went on. Why was her country unwilling to help and why did it turn its back on the Freedom Fighters in the crucial hours of their dire plight? She was disheartened, disgraced over her country's selfishness, claiming it cared more about appeasing the Russian bear than standing tall for democratic justice. She was ashamed. We are cowards. She made Robert cry.

Deborah comforted him as he sobbed. After the meeting adjourned and after gaining his composure he found and gently embraced the lady juggernaut in her giant sweater. He asked her name again so he could remember. "Why, it's Sally," she responded in a high-pitched southern drawl.

"Your speech moved me," Robert said. "How, or should I say, why have you taken interest in the Hungarian Uprising?" he asked.

"Well, Sir, it has become my obsession," she responded with a bold intensity. "I believe our country has literally shunned its principles. Abandoning those people in their hour of need was an abomination and in my own way, with this not so husky voice of mine, I intend to remind all who will listen of America's shameful transgression."

"My I ask you, Sir, why are you touched, if I might say, by my remarks tonight?"

"Because I was there," Robert said.

"Oh my," Sally gasped.

Midnight came and went with Robert, Deborah and Sally still huddled together in a corner booth of Billy Joe's Beer & Barbeque which was located about five blocks from the meeting hall. Robert asked Sally to join him and Deborah for a treat at Billy Joe's whose specialty of pork ribs and chicken, plus just enough Dixie Beer to wash it down, were renowned throughout the Quarter. At first Sally politely refused but both were persistent, finally persuading her to accompany them and continue on the subject that had wrenched at Robert's gut and brought him to tears.

When they finally separated they promised to meet again either as part of the twice-monthly gatherings hosted by Clay or simply by themselves. It didn't matter to Robert. What was important was that he had found Sally and through her he could begin to mine a mountain of emotion and perhaps begin to heal. She listened, hanging on the words he spoke of his time, his experiences, his horror, and the tragedy of it all. She was fascinated at his telling, seeming to have finally found a living flesh and bone participant who could validate all that she suspected to have occurred at the hands of the savage Soviet oppressors sent by the Kremlin to tramp down the righteous and just Hungarian rebellion. Deborah was silent for most of the evening, although when the opportunity arose she was quick to remind Robert of Sally's claim of America's complacency which, "simply affirms how smug and self centered our country has become."

"What's happened to our quest for world democracy?" was the question Deborah asked over and over.

At the two a.m. hour they watched Sally speed away in a taxi which Robert had hailed for her. He prepaid Sally's fare and waved down another for their ride to the boarding house. A soft rain was falling. They decided not to walk. Mrs. Dionne would again be furious with her boarders who blatantly ignore her rules. Fraternizing. In all hours of the morning. Intolerable, she would harangue. Neither cared. In the back seat of the taxi he hesitantly placed his arm around her shoulder. She responded and moved closer. She turned up her face to him and he bent to kiss her lips. Gently at first and then with rising passion. Too soon the taxi stopped and they were home. Deborah pulled away and slid across the seat. She reached in her purse to retrieve the two-dollar fare the driver had requested. Robert tried to protest but she insisted on paying. Together they walked up the sidewalk and climbed the stairs to the porch. The door was shut but not locked. This time Mrs. Dionne's shadow did not cover the doorway. They ascended to the second floor in silence and stopped at Robert's door. She only brushed his lips with hers and then whispered in his ear. "Soon you will be in my bed, and soon my cause will be yours."

He let go of her hand as she stepped into the darkened hallway. Her footsteps faded but were soon replaced by a hushed echo of voices in the distance. Two women were exchanging harsh words. Robert could hear a distant mumbling. Soon, after a creak and the door closing, silence fell. Stepping inside, he found the room and his soul empty. He slept in fits and spurts but did not dream. For that he was thankful. Fodor was lost to the night.

26

Sally took a deep breath, inched up on her toes to come level with the microphone. She began.

"The ragtag squad inched its way along the twelve meter high wall that supported the magnificent archway leading to the eastern entrance of the Bazillika. Their journey to this strategic position had been long and bloody. Their ranks depleted by deadly accurate gunfire. Two were killed on Basa Utca. Three died as they crossed Szent Tamas Utca to join forces in the center square of Esztergom. Their mission was to guard the sacred church at all costs. Roman was among them. There he is." She pointed to the man in the front row aisle seat. "He is with us tonight. God spared him.

"Then on that fateful day his back was pinned against the limestone edifice as he and his fellows moved in single file into position. An ancient American M-1 rifle was slung over his shoulder. Only three bullets remained in the clip. Between them, all they had left was one antitank rocket. Opposite them, on the west wide of the cathedral, were fifteen other Freedom Fighters equally determined to repel the attack.

"In Budapest three days before, as fighting raged all around him, word spread through Roman's ranks that the Soviet invaders were planning to raze Hungary's most sacred religious temple in an act of cruel denunciation of the nation's Christian principles. Roman asked for permission from his commander to return to his hometown to help protect this national treasure. Permission granted. He set out with fifty volunteers. Now they were reduced to twenty-one.

"Roman first arrived in his capital city of Budapest twelve short hours after a group of defiant students who on October 23,1956 stormed the Communist controlled Hungarian Parliament demanding a return to democracy with full restoration of fundamental human rights.

"Their act of defiance touched off a rebellion of monumental proportions. In less than two days of fighting a disorganized, poorly equipped, ill-trained army of common citizens seized back their country. They had defeated the State Security Police and repulsed thousands of Soviet troops, sending many fleeing into the countryside. They installed a new ruling party, the Hungarian Working People's Party, and literally threw the Communists out with orders never to return. Stalin's two-ton head had been severed from his massive thirty-foot bronze body and lay in desecration in Budapest's central plaza. Freedom had been declared for the first time since the end of World War II and the creation of the Soviet bloc. The madmen in the Kremlin were in denial at first, disarray second, but when it became clear that their entire Communist empire was threatened, a determination to destroy their enemies overwhelmed them."

Sally's calf muscles were burning as she stretched higher on her toes to rise above the lectern. She adjusted the microphone only to hear it squeal in protest through the auditorium speakers. Her throat was dry. Her voice cracked. She needed water. None was nearby. Nevertheless she would carry on. This was too important. People had to know this story. Robert's story. Roman's story. She had to tell them. She was the only one who could make them understand.

"The Politburo, while declaring to the world a willingness to negotiate with the new, fledgling Hungarian government, began to form an insurgency that rivaled any thrown against the Nazi regime some twelve years earlier. On November 4, just eleven days after the rebellion began, a huge Soviet invasion force stormed across the border to ransack the country. Their foremost task was to retake Budapest and restore Communist order. Hungarian resistance was resilient. Their leaders cried out for international aid, especially from America. There was only silence.

"Meanwhile Roman and his brothers watched in horror from the shadows of the Bazillika archway entrance as two Soviet tanks moved into position. It was clear to them the gunners were taking aim at the cathedral's front, intending to crumble the eight twenty-two meter high columns that support the tympana which spans above the main entrance. A panoramic photograph of the Bazillika flashed on the lecture hall screen behind Sally, dwarfing her presence on the stage even more.

"If they could bring down the columns the tympana would collapse, followed by the destruction of the fabulous Bakocz Italian red marble chapel housed inside directly beneath the cathedral dome. The sacred chapel came into view. Sally's audience let out an audible "whoa".

"At that moment Roman and his friends stepped from their hiding place. Exposing themselves to intense gunfire. The antitank rifleman took front position. Roman aimed and fired his last three rounds, thinking he might have hit one of the invaders trying to shield himself behind the steel body of the maneuvering tank. From the west archway the small resistance force also moved forward. Better armed than Roman's men, they laid down heavy fire dropping several Soviet soldiers. They too had an antitank rifleman who took aim at the behemoth from their position on the right.

Both fired simultaneously. Only one, the one on the right, found its mark, piercing the armored shield, sending smoke and flame belching out of the top hatch of the disabled monster. Terrible screams of burning, dying soldiers could be heard from inside their armored coffin.

"The tank on the left was not hit. The rocket had harmlessly slammed into the concrete pavement near the tank's steel tread. The rebel rifleman lay dead where he had crouched to fire his wayward rocket. A lethal shot fired by a Soviet marksman had, an instant before, taken him off his target. Seconds later Roman watched as the tank's turret began to rotate like the head of a hungry tom cat tracking a fat mouse scampering across its path.

"Roman ran for cover, heading straight back toward the cathedral wall seeking momentary refuge. Three others followed close behind. The wall and his sanctuary evaporated just steps before his arrival. The blast sent him flying. His pain immediate. He landed meters away and looked through the dust at the gaping hole in his childhood place of worship. Two of his fellows lay among the debris not moving. Blood overtaking life.

"Then, perhaps after moments of unconsciousness, he realized his body being hoisted on the broad shoulders of a stranger. His battered right leg was wet and throbbing. He felt dizzy and sick. The man began to run, carrying him in fireman's fashion. The jarring foot falls of his rescuer sent loud cries of agony from Roman's twisted teeth clinched mouth.

"'Quiet, Son. Be brave," the big man sternly instructed.

At that point Sally stopped to catch her breath again. She nearly disappeared behind the podium ledge as she relaxed to stand flat footed. Only the top of her silver streaked head could then be seen from the audience. The cramps in her legs were almost unbearable. From the side came a hand grasping a glass of water. Gratefully she took it from the professor who stepped back to take his seat beside the podium.

"Thank you for your patience," she said after finishing the water and launching herself up on tip toes again. "I shall continue."

"Roman thought he recognized the voice. Then the man stumbled once, then twice and then he fell; instinctively breaking his pitch, but in doing so unconsciously slinging Roman over his shoulder to send him sprawling on his back in the dirt. Roman hit the ground with a thud. Stunned he rolled over in search of his savior. The man was on his knees was crawling towards him. Roman looked up to gaze through a fog of suffering into the eyes of his father.

"Fodor was still alive when Roman reached him. They had somehow plunged together into a crevasse beside the bomb cratered pot marked road leading away from the cathedral and out of sight of the throngs of storm troopers all around.

"Roman cradled the head of his father in his arms. Fodor's mouth seeped blood from its corners.

"'Why, father?' his son asked. 'Why are you fighting? Fighting to save the Bazillika?'

"Fodor choked on his blood when he tried to speak. His tunic from his days as commander of the fascist Iron Cross unit was soaked crimson and sticky. *I am shot through the chest. I will die as I have lived. Fighting the Communist menace,* his father muttered.

You will not die, father. You have saved me. I cannot let you die. I will run for help, Roman cried, tears now streaming down his mud caked cheeks.

"By then Fodor was gasping for air. His chest heaving and lungs wheezing badly from the open wounds, which had punctured both.

No, son. You must hide now. You have done your duty. You must recover to fight on, his father pleaded

Father, our crusade is over. We have lost. The enemy is too strong. Too powerful. We are being crushed, Roman cried.

"Roman's words seemed to awaken his father just as he began to slip away. *Do not speak of defeat. Never, ever.* His voice trailed off. Again blood bubbled in his mouth. Roman knew the end was near. He gently kissed his father's dirt crushed forehead.

Good bye, my son, Fodor whispered, *Fight on.* His body went limp.

"Roman removed his outer jacket, folded and placed it beneath his father's head. A hot sharp arrow of pain shot through is mangled leg. He looked down to see his own torn flesh. Tourniquet, he thought; I must slow the bleeding. From his dead body he removed his father's prized tunic, shredded the cloth and tied it tightly around his upper thigh. Then he covered them both with branches from a fallen tree nearby; laid down beside his father's corpse and fell asleep.

"Roman's next memory was awakening days later in a makeshift basement infirmary a kilometer or so from where, miraculously, a retreating platoon of Freedom Fighters had stumbled upon them as they ran for their lives through the deep crevasse where Roman and the body of Fodor were hidden.

I am almost through, Sally thought, as she paused to turn the page of her text. She had been so absorbed in her own words; her telling of Robert's marvelous story, that she had forgotten the cramping of her muscles and dryness of her throat. She carried on to the end.

"By then, by the time Roman woke, the fighting was over. It was November 10. The Red scoundrels had won. As Robert so poignantly predicted in the last words his father ever heard; they have crushed us. Indeed they had.

"In the end the death toll was horrendous. More than 2,500 Hungarians, men, women and children were slaughtered, but with them they took out seven hundred Soviet brutes. Two hundred thousand Hungarians fled their homeland as refugees. Our Roman, who we now call Robert, was among them. We are so glad he came to America. I must remind you that he chose to escape to the place that cruelly denounced him. Denounced his people. Left them; abandoned them in their finest hour."

Sally's squeaky voice crested to a shrill. At the sound the Tulane University political science professor sitting stoically on the stage to Sally's right suddenly raised his dozing head to stare up at his guest lecturer in shock and amazement. He could not believe what he had just heard come out of the mouth of this timid, diffident little creature. Now paying strict attention he straightened his posture in his seat.

Sally glanced over at him with a look of pure foreboding. An unspoken warning; an ominous threat expressed in her blazing emerald green eyes. The professor eased his rigidity and peered over his shoulder half expecting to be assaulted by thugs rushing from the auditorium wings.

Sally continued.

"America, for what it did, will never truly be Robert's homeland. It is only his way station. He is here to help us reveal to the world how this country, this alleged bastion of freedom, has been stripped of its cloak of compassion and concern for humanity. It is no longer offers salvation for the world. It is a self-righteous dry hole of hypocrisy. Its leaders, regardless of political party are there in their towers of wealth feathering their own beds and thumbing their noses at the true freedom loving crusaders. America should be ashamed! God help us! God forgive us!"

The professor's knees were weak and shaking but he managed to rise to his feet and move catlike to the podium. He grasped the microphone from her hand as it continued blasting Sally's tirade across the expanse of his two hundred seat, filled to capacity classroom. He cautiously elbowed her aside.

"My, that was quite a moving presentation," he said, looking down at the snarl on the lips of her upturned face.

"Your facts surrounding this historical event are indisputable, Miss, but I am afraid your critical treatise of our country has no place in my classroom," he scolded.

"Let her speak!" A voice shouted from the darkened rear of the lecture hall.

"Our time is up," the professor commanded, "class is dismissed."

27

Robert was not happy with the spectacle Sally created with her rousing speech. He had strongly resisted Sally's invitation to attend the afternoon classroom session at all, but Deborah persuaded him to accompany the demure radical to, as she put it, "Test the waters to see how young people react to an overt indictment over their government's refusal to come to the aid of the Hungarian resistance."

After her performance he stood with Sally outside the entrance to the auditorium. Robert's anxiety grew each time one of the professor's students bolted up to him to grasp his hand and nearly genuflect in reverence at just being in his presence. He was embarrassed to begin with and progressively grew ashamed. On the other hand Sally basked in the attention and adulation.

After nearly a half hour of this unruly demonstration enough of the young throng had dispersed and dashed off to their next class that Robert and Sally were free to move to the exit.

"Good God, Sally, I had no idea you planned to go that far. You were so strong in your remarks. Do you think it necessary? I mean the professor was so angry he was shaking," Robert said as they descended the steps of the main campus building.

"Oh, my dear, it was wonderful. I couldn't have hoped for more. The reaction of that old, stale slouch of a teacher and the warm embrace of his students afterward…I am thrilled. We must continue on our mission. We know our message is penetrating. It reverberates through their hearts and minds. These young people are the seed we must nourish to sprout our movement," Sally responded, seemingly ignoring if not even hearing Robert's attempt at a gentle admonition.

Robert gazed down at her, knowing his words had bounced off her balding grey head with no effect. They fell silent as they made their way to the visitor parking lot to retrieve Robert's car. It was a neat little baby blue 1953 Chevrolet coupe that once belonged to Isaac Robinski but sat untouched behind the shop since his death until one day

Roman offered his boss four hundred dollars to take it off his hands. Sigmund took a month to conclude that Roman's price was fair, and whether this, his dead son's prized possession, next only to his workbench, was worthy of Roman's taking. Finally he decided to relinquish the car at a fifty dollar per week deduction from Roman's paycheck until the final sum was reached and title turned over.

While Roman paid off his debt he spent several nights and long weekends repairing torn seats and headliner, replacing tires, spark plugs, rotors and filters in preparation for its maiden voyage through the French Quarter. He flunked the driver's test on his first try when his directional signals didn't work and he mistakenly made a right hand signal before he turned left. However he passed the test a week later and that night took Deborah to a drive-in movie where they kissed and groped each other until lips and limbs were chaffed and sore, but did no more.

"Will you be at the meeting this week, my dear," Sally asked, as Robert steered through the light traffic toward her apartment house near Canal Street.

"Yes, Sally, I will attend. But you listen to me. I not sure I want to be used like this, like puppet with you pulling strings to promote the anti-American idea. Do you know what I mean? I love where I am. What I am doing with my life. If we, if you, continue your speeches about me they might kick me out of country," he responded with growing trepidation.

"Don't be ridiculous, Robert. Nothing is going to happen to you. Whether you know it or not, there are many powerful people in our group. They will protect you. You have nothing to fear, my dear. Your story is the perfect vehicle, a funnel for our message to the outside world," she said, her final words mouthed in a deliberate poetic rhythm.

When her poem ended, her mood turned dark and ominous. She turned to Robert and said, "Robert, you must accept your fate. Providence rests on your shoulders. You have a responsibility, like it or not, to help us in our crusade. You must not fail us. There is no turning back now. Believe that, acknowledge that, and you will be content. There will be consequences if you shy away from your responsibilities."

Robert was stunned by the vehemence of her remarks. He turned away to watch the road. Sally said nothing more and began to softly hum an unrecognizable tune.

As he drove Sally to her house, Robert reflected on his recent history with Deborah's mysterious no-last name club. Over the past six months he had become a faithful attendee at the weekly gatherings. He missed only one meeting when inflicted with a bad cold to which Mrs. Dionne made a feeble attempt to treat with a concoction of black tea, ginger, and Vick's Vapor-Rub left on a tray at his doorstep.

First names only continued as the cardinal rule at each of the sessions, but as Robert grew to become a regular fixture, his acceptance and perhaps evolving trustworthiness allowed him to gain some insight into those seated about him each Saturday night. He determined that Alexander was an accountant; Larry was a plumber; Tom, a bartender; Linda, a nurse; Hilda and Hillary were bank tellers and David was a pilot. George, Gloria and Gladys were all in the Air Force at one time but Robert was not sure what they did now. Grady owns a trucking company. All Robert could discover about Clay was that he claimed to be a successful businessman. They became friendly over time but friends only in the confines of the converted dance studio. Clay had made it clear that outside contact or communication among club members was strongly discouraged. The only exception was Robert and Deborah and now Sally who were recognized from the first meeting they attended together as the only acceptable trio to openly venture beyond the dance studio doors.

Hour after hour, speech after speech, group members ranted singularly or collectively over the ills affecting America. Ills brought on by corrupt politicians, all scoundrels out for the single purpose of unraveling the moral fiber that had bound the country together since its founding. At first, President Eisenhower had restored their faith and healed the wounds of a postwar nation, but as his second term ended, in their minds he had fallen into a stench-laden pit of decadence. His domestic and foreign policies now leaned horribly to the left. Eisenhower had become a pacifist in his old age, more interested in perfecting his golf game than crushing the bearded, cigar-chopping dictator who had just captured Cuba in a bloody, repressive revolt.

Ike's anointed successor was no better. Nixon, the opportunist, was a closet liberal who chased Communists only for splashy headlines, and lacked the true conviction to root them out. Then there was Kennedy. A spoiled blue blood, born into unparalleled wealth gained through the importation of illegal spirits. He was a papist and an unmistakable Marxist wrapped into one. The members of the group felt no true distinction between the two presidential candidates taking center stage in 1959. The group concluded both Nixon and Kennedy were unworthy. Wholly unworthy.

One of these men, they raved, will be our next leader! How can that be?

Robert never spoke at the gatherings. He just sat with Deborah and listened. Occasionally Deborah would ask questions of the speakers, usually a question with some depth or perception Robert found impressive to borderline ingenuous.

He learned a tremendous amount during the meetings. Often he discovered while reading the *Times Picayune* that he could scan the article instead of reading it word for word knowing that he had already gained sufficient knowledge of the subject from a first-name club member's speech the night before.

Robert struggled through these times, however. His search for answers to questions drilled so deeply into his subconscious by his father while alive, and subsequently in the dreams of his father, placed him on a winding road of sharp curves and narrow switchbacks. One minute he too believed Eisenhower would hand over the keys to the nation to the newest Soviet dictator Nikita Khrushchev. The next minute after reading a profile in *Life* Magazine summarizing Ike's years in office he would silently agree that the President would forever be renowned as one of the free world's greatest leaders.

Robert wavered from a love for his new country to an overwhelming hatred. From a sense of total belonging to abandonment and complete betrayal. Confusion and contradiction dominated his mental state. In his pursuit of objectivity Deborah was no help at all. She could not counterbalance the rhetoric of Sally and the others. Her mind was made up. She had long past lost all objectivity and during their moments alone when not acting like teenagers at a drive-in theatre, she would pound away at him with unrelenting propaganda, mimicking words and themes derived from recent Saturday night sessions. Often Robert grew weary of it all, yet he was always drawn back.

Robert's equal frustration was with Deborah, the woman for which he ached. It was her yo-yo effect on him which set deep in the crevices of his mind. She plays her game to perfection. First, she can spin him up, clinching him tightly, comfortably in her fist, then an instant later she can send him down, plunging, dangling, spinning out of control at the bottom of the twirling string. With a flick of her finger she can wind him back up, clutching him, to rest again, to be caressed. Not unlike the way his father treated him. Yet with Deborah it is the allure of promised sex, not a threatened beating if he did not comply with Fodor's wishes. Was it his weakness or his strength that drew him back? Was it his carnal desire or simply his willingness to capitulate to a superior mind? To one with wisdom and foresight? Or to one frothing with pure intimidation? Robert could not find the distinction. He could be manipulated by those of stronger will pushing him to the precipice of a bottomless pit. Would he fall? Should he stand firm and turn back?

As the weeks passed, first tentatively, cautiously and then with blossoming self-assurance Robert stepped over that threshold of insecurity onto the stage of the abandoned ballet studio, and as he did he shed many things for which he became grateful and truly happy. For one, the dreams of his father on the stage in the vast empty theatre in full regalia, prancing, preaching and pontificating his poison stopped. Ever since Sally exposed Roman's final moments with Fodor dying in his arms in the shadow of the Basillika his anguished nighttime journeys into purgatory were no more. For all the torment Sally caused that day in her telling of Roman's exploits, she somehow helped him wipe the fearsome memories away. Reliving Fodor's death among the Tulane student body ironically, at least for the time, freed Roman from his father's brutal grasp.

Robert did miss his trancelike times with his brother. Painfully seated on the hard unforgiving wooden nail head protruding seat in row 7, Robert at times wished he could trade a few more nights in Fodor's dreamy death grip for the embrace of his brother even if he and Roman were forced to endure another manic harangue. To Robert's dismay, Rudolph failed to return to him as well. The curtain on those pitiful performances may have been finally and unmistakably drawn tight forever. Or so he hoped. For that to happen Robert would sacrifice Rudolph willingly.

Roman also was immersed in his new position managing Roblinski's Appliance and Radio Repair Shop. He was particularly pleased when Sigmund ordered a sign painter to place Roman's name and new title in the bottom right hand corner of a new placard to hang above the front entrance door. Roman was now beginning his third year with the proud Romanian proprietor. Over time Sigmund gradually, perhaps unconsciously, delegated ever-greater responsibility to Roman. Roman took charge of all parts buying, customer relations, major repairs, showroom sales and nearly all financial matters. Each night however, after Roman filled out the bank deposit slips, Sigmund still made his trek to the bank to stash away that day's receipts. The business was growing under Roman's hands-on control. His workdays were long and tedious, but he relished in the measured success of the shop and its growing profits.

Sigmund agreed to Roman's plan to become an exclusive dealer of a new line of Emerson televisions. He also made room in the shop for a few middle line frost-free Westinghouse refrigerators. They sold one of each during the second week in which the products were in stock for a tidy seventy-five dollar net profit per item after they chipped in shipping costs for a first time customer.

After much debate Roman also persuaded Sigmund to hire an apprentice repairman. Work was stacking up in the back room and it was quite clear that Sigmund no longer was adept at the new and ever advancing electronic gadgetry. He was baffled when their first color television, an RCA model manufactured in 1956, was brought into the shop with a blown picture tube.

When Roman took off the back panel Sigmund shook his head, bewildered at the sight of the glass guts of the mammoth console. It was at that point that Sigmund agreed to Roman's recommendation for additional newly trained help. Roman repaired the big box color set after a week's hard study of the product manual, but when he finished he was not satisfied with the picture quality. What he didn't realize at the time was the manufacturer was neglectful in telling its dealers of flaws in the replacement parts, which were producing distorted shades of purple and yellow and awful red-tinted flesh tones on humans grinning through the cathode ray tube. That problem wouldn't be solved by RCA for Roman and millions of other anxious viewers until 1961 when Walt Disney aired the first Sunday night broadcast of the *Wonderful World of Disney.* After that showing a demanding public clamored for a clear, bright, undistorted color view of Tinker Bell waving her magic wand to bring the NBC peacock to life.

28

On an unusually cold and blustery October night Robert and Deborah sipped after dinner anisette laced coffee as they sat in silence in a booth in Katzenjammer's Bar and Grill on Camp Street. They were paying little attention to each other. As were all the saloon's patrons that night, Robert and Deborah were focused on one of the two black and white Philco television sets mounted on the wall above each end of the ornate, slightly curved and elaborately carved mahogany water stained bar. Pictured on the grainy, sometimes snowy and mostly flickering television screens, which Robert knew he could fix if given the chance, stood two familiar figures. Each was speaking alternatively from behind their respective podiums. Richard M. Nixon, Vice President of the United States and his opponent, the esteemed Senator from Massachusetts, John F. Kennedy, were politely but forcefully making their points about the unfortunate occurrences happening just ninety miles south of the Florida coastline.

It was the fourth and last of a spectacular political spectacle being played out in the 1960 Presidential race. The first ever televised debates between the two major party candidates captivated the American electorate and would prove to be the turning point in the November balloting. That night many believed, including Robert and Deborah, that Nixon won two of the first three verbal contests. On this occasion, they speculated, if he could muster a profound final tongue lashing on the general topic of foreign policy, he just might squeak out a victory two weeks hence. However, as the minutes ticked by, Nixon and Kennedy soon found themselves deeply embroiled in heated jousting over Cuba and its Communist, Soviet aligned leader Fidel Castro. Neither candidate was eager to reveal their plans to counter the close encounter with the young dictator but both were determined to convince the public they would take whatever measures necessary to contain the awful spread of Fidel's Red Rule.

Deborah was the first to break the silence with a huff of disgust at Nixon's attempt at saber rattling followed by Kennedy's halfhearted challenge at one-up-man-ship. No longer able to contain herself she whispered to Robert, "Neither one of these bastards has a clue. Neither one has the guts to do anything but talk. They're both disgusting."

With her words Robert turned away from the screen and instantly recalled very similar remarks he heard at last Saturday's gathering. He believed Deborah was parroting nearly the same lines as Clay had spouted during his rousing speech to the tiny conclave of obedient followers.

Robert didn't want his concentration interrupted, but Deborah insisted on doing just that with her next declaration.

"If Nixon had any balls as Vice President he would have demanded that Eisenhower send in the Marines to stop Castro's guerrillas right there on the beach. Hell no! He sat on his hands. If Kennedy was a true military man like he claims, he would have been in the well of the Senate until our troops had recaptured Havana and made Cuba our fifty-first state."

Now totally distracted, having missed Nixon's deer in the headlights look at his opponent after another condescending rebuttal, Robert reluctantly nodded his head in mock approval of Deborah's diatribe, although he had heard only snippets of her hushed reproach.

By then both candidates were summarizing their respective positions, declaring their humility at being their Party's nominees and urging all voters to exercise their sacred democratic rights by casting ballots. At that Robert wedged away his attentiveness to swing in Deborah's favor.

"You're right Deborah. I'm not convinced either man should be President. One of them will be just that. No other choices we have. You are lucky, you know. You can vote. I cannot. My citizenship papers are out there somewhere. It makes me angry to think I am deprived of that right," Robert declared.

"I understand Robert. I must admit I take that right for granted. However, in this case, because of who these guys are and what they stand for, my vote will be no vote," she responded.

"What do you mean?" he asked, now genuinely curious about what she was saying.

"I won't be voting at all. That's my way of protesting. My right as an American not to exercise my right. Most of the people in our group won't be voting either," she proudly declared.

"That would be ridiculous," Robert chastised. "What good will that do? Here I am wishing I could vote and you can, but you won't because Clay and the rest are so full their hatred they are---what's the word---boycotting the election. What are you? Some kind of sheep following in the flock?" Robert's anger rising.

"Don't you dare accuse me of having no mind of my own? I happen to believe Clay and the others are right. They know right from wrong and they see through the veil of hypocrisy these politicians wrap themselves in. I'm leaving. I've had enough of your patronizing. Who do you think you are? You come here three years ago and already you think you're the second coming of Thomas Jefferson. I thought our message was getting through to you and you were coming to your senses," her voice rising above the post debate background noise reverberating through the tavern.

She jumped off the bar stool and reached for her purse. Robert's hand grasped hers before she could pull away.

"Wait a minute, please," he pleaded. "I am coming around. It is taking me longer than you. Many things said at our meetings now ring true. I try to sort out others; like this business with Cuba and the Communists."

Deborah allowed her hand to be held but remained standing, her threat to leave still apparent.

"I just can't decide," Robert continued, "whether the Communists who helped destroy everything my father believed in, the Nazis, his precious Iron Cross, all fascists, should be given some credit, or are they all demons as you, Clay and the others tell me."

Deborah leaned into Robert's face with a questioning look and asked, "How could you, of all people, who saw your country destroyed by those Red scoundrels, ever believe them? Robert, you must realize these people are as bad, if not worse than your father and all of his fascist followers. They killed your brother and given a chance they will kill you and all of us. All our group is saying is we need leaders who recognize this and will strike first, not last."

With that, she slowly pulled her hand away, now holding her purse. Her threat to leave was all too real.

"Please don't go," Robert said, seeming to beg. "I am learning. I get better. Don't give up on me."

She bent and kissed him on the cheek, drew back and quietly but sternly said, "Prove it to me. Make me believe in you. To trust you. I can't do that yet. You must understand."

She turned and walked briskly down the length of the bar and out the door. Robert was alone. Alone again with this thoughts. His confusion. His beliefs torn and tattered. Yet somehow he knew he would be back at his seat among Clay's dutiful crowd. Awaiting a clear message. Awaiting instructions. Proving himself to her and them. What was to be his reward? Greater perplexity? Her further withholding the love he craved? Could he withstand that much longer? What did he have to do to earn it? How long before she understood?

Thirty minutes or so passed before Robert left the dingy place of his misery and took a cab home having left his car at the shop under a weather proof canvass cover. He didn't like driving it when it was cold and threatening a wintry rain.

Just as he inserted the key in his door at Mrs. Dionne's boarding house, he heard muffled voices down the darkened hallway. Turning, he recognized even in the dim light the shadowy figure of Deborah standing at a doorway. Deborah's was not the only shadow in the darkness he had seen it before. The light from the bathroom crossed the threshold to where she stood. It cast enough brightness for Robert to see Mrs. Claire emerge to greet her. She placed both hands on Deborah's shoulders, drawing her close and kissing her, open mouthed. The moments Robert stood staring at the scene seemed like hours. When the couple finally separated to step inside Mrs. Claire's room they pivoted in Robert's direction, smiling mischievously, knowing he had been watching them all along.

29

Robert's mechanical skills were born from his ability to concentrate on a single, often minute flaw in the labyrinth inter workings of the electronic marvels that had flooded the market to satiate his customer's hunger for convenience and entertainment.

Robert had uncanny ability in detecting defects and following them to their source, at which time he would miraculously find the remedy and cure. A misfiring circuit. A hairline crack in a tube or transistor. A tooth missing from a quarter inch gear causing vibrations reverberating just enough to imbalance a record- skipping turntable. Or when others failed finding that elusive loose speaker wire which for weeks prevented its owner from the joyful soulful sounds of masterful jazz. Robert's talent lay deeply in his subconscious not learned from a book or perfected by a mentor. He simply had a knack.

In the weeks that followed many of Robert's waking hours were spent examining the failings of the society he had adopted as his own. Or at least what he surmised as its missteps. He put aside the scene of Deborah and Mrs. Claire's spotlighted embrace, concluding it was of little consequence since he had no influence on her actions, so she became unworthy of further concern. He was happy with those feelings. He couldn't sway her one way or the other, so he decided no longer to try. Instead he turned his attention inward.

His approach to playing a part in fixing America's ills was the same as if he were probing the cause of a malfunctioning flipper on a pinball machine. He struggled to sort out the barrage of information penetrating his skull as he attempted to trace the origin of his mind's eye malcontent to its source. He was given many options to consider, from mass media reports to his Saturday ballet studio meetings, and the circuits he scanned formed a maze of interconnecting strands as complex as a black widow's web. He knew instinctively that accepting a role in uncovering and repairing America's problems was the most important job he would ever undertake.

His discovery of the root cause of his new country's plunge into the quagmire came not from a sudden, startling epiphany such as electric impulses speeding through wires, but it evolved gradually and consistently as filaments heat and glow to bring life to a dormant table top radio. His remedy was as simple as plugging a cord into a wall socket. America had run out of juice. It was unplugged. It needed a jolt to bring it back to life.

Robert began to doubt, even scorn the newspapers, magazines, radio and television broadcasts all of which seemed to revere and glorify America's leaders, especially the Kennedy's. He seldom read a news account without suspecting it was full of distortion if not outright lies. He grew more skeptical, untrusting and suspected cover-ups of misdeeds too numerous to count. He shared his thoughts with Deborah. She was ecstatic. He was secure in knowing he wasn't speaking out for her favor, rather his own. To belong again, free of Fodor, yet still tethered to him in some ways. His father's ideological snare would forever trap him but Robert had broken through Fodor's dark dominating cloud to emerge into his personal sunshine. Robert was thinking clearly now with roots migrating through his soul to anchor him firmly to new ideals. He had found the flaw in America and would help fix it, whatever they said he had to do.

To learn even more Robert immersed himself in the caustic rhetoric rattling the ballet studio walls every Saturday night. Soon he saw himself up there, banging the podium, hammering away with words of venom. It felt good. He felt good. He was part of something bigger than himself. He was back with his troops at the Bazillika. Fighting a just cause.

Then a new, at first, joyful event came about.

30

Sophia Chekhov was late for work at the home office of Louisiana Power and Light a second time in two weeks because her Admiral clock radio failed to sound its alarm at the appointed 6 a.m. hour. If she was late a third time she knew she would be fired from her $2.75 per hour clerk typist post in the billing department. On Monday while riding the bus home from work she noticed the sign hanging from the awning above the entrance of Roblinski's Appliance and Radio Repair Shop and she vowed at the first opportunity to bring her unreliable appliance there for repair. However, she forgot to do so on Tuesday and this was Wednesday, her second time being late, so she had the damn thing in a shopping bag determined to address her problem when her shift ended for the day.

Sophia, a plain looking girl in her early twenties, captured little attention from the other passengers on the Rampart Street bus line. This day as in most winter days she wore a mid-calf length, aging, light grey worsted wool coat over a faded blue cotton dress. Her straight brown hair, parted in the middle, hung past her shoulders. It was covered with a faded blue scarf that didn't quite match her dress. A silver cross attached to a thin gold chain hung from her neck. Her open toe mid-height block heels were brown and scuffed. She needed fresh polish on her toes and her fingernails. Just a dash of eye shadow and pink lipstick decorated her face. Her eyes however were striking, electrifying for those who were lucky to gaze into them, which is seldom because she generally cast them down wherever she went.

Sophia is Russian. She was born in Stalingrad and came to America with her mother who was widowed during the German siege of Stalingrad during World War II. Her mother, Monique, now a marginally successful seamstress, owns a small tailor shop in the lower Garden District with her new husband, Peter. She speaks little of their travels from their war torn native land to their settlement in New Orleans. Sophia seldom sees her mother these days and that's acceptable to her since she is not the least bit fond of her new stepfather. Since being in America, Sophia's aura of shyness persists. Behind her beguiling eyes there is a woman yet to gain adequate self-esteem and confidence. She struggles with her shortcomings knowing a margin of conceit could serve her well.

Sophia decided she would drop off her livelihood threatening radio at Roblinski's shop after the end of her work day shift. She was not due at her evening business class at the Louisiana State University extension center until six p.m. She knew she would have just enough time to do both. But just in case the Admiral couldn't be fixed and her next day and many to follow being unemployed she protected herself against the risk of over sleeping by purchasing two wind-up alarm clocks placed on night stands positioned on either side of her bed.

As usual that afternoon Roman was in the back room; this time deeply pondering the intricacies of a malfunctioning Motorola stereo hi-fi console system when the bell over the front door announced a customer's arrival. He scampered to his feet to greet the late in the day patron since Sigmund had already left for his stroll to the bank with the night deposit. Wiping his hands on his work apron and moving from behind the counter he took in the picture of this less than immediately appealing female as she placed her shopping bag on the counter. With eyes pitched downward to the floor, she asked whether he might be able to fix it.

Still not looking up in response to Roman's request to, "let me see it and I let you know," Sophia placed the unreliable device on the counter and stepped back to allow him to inspect it. When she did she glanced up to catch his eye. Roman heard himself gasp. In just that instant before she looked away Roman was awestruck. He had never seen anything more enchanting. They were equal if not more captivating than the blueness of the still Mediterranean harbor at Marseille at midday, a sight Roman would swear was none more beautiful. Here they were. Her eyes. Equal in splendor.

Roman stammered with an assurance that he would have the radio repaired, "In no time."

She shyly thanked him and turned to leave. Desperate for a reason to delay her departure, he said, "Usually I collect a deposit fee, but since I am very confident that I can fix your radio quickly I'm willing to waive the deposit. If you will give me your telephone number I will call you when I am finished, and if you live close by to where I live I would be most happy to personally deliver it, as early as this evening."

"Oh, that won't be necessary," Sophia said, stopping and turning back to face him; her eyes, this time, flashing like lighthouse beacons to homebound sailors on a stormy night.

"It won't be a problem," Roman responded with a toothy smile of boyish exuberance. "Here's a pencil and paper. Just write it down and I will call you before you know it."

She did as he requested.

In the months that followed and the romance that ensued Roman often spoke of her magnificent eyes and how he swam in them luxuriously every time she glanced his way. She would blush openly and giggle with delight at his compliment.

Within an hour after Sophia left for business class on that first evening of their courtship Roman had the Admiral clock radio working perfectly. She answered his call at around eight o'clock and he was on her doorstep by eight-thirty. She declined his tender offer to go out for "coffee and apple pie" and she even refused him entrance into her apartment for a demonstration of the fully functional apparatus. Instead she took the radio from him, paying the seven dollar discounted service charge. He failed to mention the normal two-dollar delivery fee. But before she turned him away utterly disappointed, she promised to meet him after work that coming Friday.

From that point on, Roman and Sophia were inseparable. That is, except for Saturday nights and despite Deborah mounting rancorous opposition. After Robert's third date with Sophia he told Deborah about her. His announcement came as they ambled along to the converted ballet studio for another weekly meeting. Deborah was stunned by the news. She questioned him harshly about his intentions, "She's unknown to us. We can't trust her. I am sure she's against our cause. Clearly a female protagonist."

By the time they reached their destination Deborah's grilling had grown in intensity.

"What about us?" Deborah shouted. "We were just beginning to find each other. I was growing more comfortable with you by the minute. All that was missing from our relationship was the sex, and I promised you it was coming soon. Now you go out and find some stupid, skanky Russian Commie bitch that will probably pay you to bang her.

"Here," Deborah cried, pulling up her skirt above her waist, "if this is all you want you can have it; right here. Right here and now. We'll go into the alley and you can have all you want."

Robert stepped to her, pushing down her skirt and held her in his arms. She sobbed uncontrollably.

"Deborah," he said soothingly, "Hold on there. What do you want from me? We've been seeing each other off and on now for over two years. It's not going anywhere at least that I can tell. You treat me more like a brother than a boyfriend. You make promises you never keep and when I disagree with you, only a little, you stomp off and go back to Mrs. Claire."

She tore away from him. "How dare you!" she screamed, and slapped him hard across the face.

He grabbed her wrist before she could hit him again, and said to her in the fiercest tone he'd ever used. "Look, Deborah. What you take me for? You push your lover in my face the other night. You think I don't know what's going on? I knew a long time ago, for your information. I just keep thinking I might change you. I am tired of trying and tired of waiting. We can be friends. I come to meetings with you. We talk politics and you take credit with Clay and others for converting me. With that much, you've done a good job. The other; you're lousy at."

When he finished, he let go of her and she dropped her arms to her side. Her whimpering began again as she choked out her defense. "I'm confused, Robert, don't you see. She took me in. She helped me get a job and lent me the money to go to paralegal school. She bought me new clothes. Everything. It was the least I could do. I even cut my hair for her! I can't say I don't enjoy it sometimes, and yes, I admit that I was angry with you the other night and I used her to get back at you, but I'll try to stop. I'll come to you. I promise. Don't push me away. Don't let that Russian whore sweep you up."

It was his turn to shout. "She no whore, goddamn it! I won't stand for you talking that way about her!" With that he looked up and saw several members of Clay's group gawking down at them from the windows of the studio just above the sidewalk where they stood.

"I'm going in. Stay out here all night, if you want. I don't care," he said.

Clay brought the meeting to order a few minutes later than normal, apparently in deference to the lively sidewalk entertainment most in the assembly had enjoyed. No one said a word about the incident to either Robert or Deborah; their attention quickly drawn from an alluring firsthand domestic disturbance to what was now being labeled by the press as the Bay of Pigs fiasco.

That night it was David's turn to howl about President Kennedy's unforgivable blunder. "Never in our history has a man in that office deliberately sent our brave men on a scurrilous suicide mission. He is a disgrace. In the dead of night with promises of support from the mightiest military machine on earth, Kennedy orders our boys ashore only to be slaughtered by those greasy Cuban fucks who are waiting behind the palm trees with every Soviet weapon imaginable," David wailed to his attentive crowd.

"When it became apparent that an ambush awaited our trapped soldiers, Kennedy, the coward that he is, orders our marines, who are standing idle offshore eager to attack in a second wave, to disengage. To leave," he exclaimed. "High tail it and run like scared chickenshit rabbits!

"I am sickened by it all. Hundreds of Americans – we will never know how many – are left alone on the beach to fend for themselves. Ammunition quickly ran out. Their rescue boats full of fight-ready reserves steamed back to Florida in shameful retreat.

"The Cubans, Castro's rebels, the scum of the earth, the Communist fiends, patiently wait the inevitable. When their bullets are gone, they descend on our defenseless troops. Murdering with their sharp machetes. Scalping like savages. Disemboweling with abandon. Blood runs cold, carving rivers of red into the soft golden sand of the island shore," David waxed poetic. His audience was enthralled by his prose and he knew it. He had them. It was time.

"All the while Kennedy sits in his rocking chair in the White House entertaining his corrupt Massachusetts sidekicks. They plot, they scheme how best to appease the Russian bear. They look for a new world order. A world as one. A world where democracy dies just like our boys on the beach, to be replaced by a common cause, a universal system, run by the elite, an oligarchy controlling all aspects of our lives.

"They must be stopped. He must be stopped. Because if we don't stop him, his brother will come along behind, followed by a second brother, and for the next quarter century or more our nation will be Kennedy's kingdom, and the new world order will be theirs!"

By then David was drenched in sweat. His hands shook. In the excitement of his rhetoric he nearly toppled head first over the podium behind which he raved. His listeners never moved and did not notice his shirt had turned a darker shade. They hardly breathed while he ranted. In rousing applause, lead by Robert, quickly joined by Deborah, there was collective agreement that no one had ever acknowledged a speech of such magnitude at the ballet studio before that night.

31

That next Monday Deborah was at her desk at the prestigious law firm of Walker, Walker & Schmidt reviewing the latest pretrial motion filed by the prosecution in District Court in a felony theft case in which her boss Perry Randolph was defending the accused. She was impressed with the artful drafting of the brief. Its author, the locally renowned flamboyant assistant district attorney, Earling Carothers "Jim" Garrison, had all the evidence she concluded, and soon she predicted the court would render a directed verdict of guilty.

She liked her boss, Mr. Randolph, but she liked Jim Garrison better. She liked Garrison so much that she planned to personally deliver her resume to him that afternoon. He hadn't answered her first letter of inquiry about potential employment so this time she would make sure he got it, placing it in his hand herself. Deborah was an early fan of Garrison after he took office and began his crusade against crime and corruption along Bourbon Street. Garrison wasn't afraid to rock the boat, taking on the establishment with his relentless pursuit of pimps and prostitutes, scam artists, gamblers and thieves who ruled the famous New Orleans street scene. She knew he was soon to launch his campaign for district attorney and she wanted to be recognized as an early, ardent supporter, hoping to land a permanent job if he won.

Deborah felt that Garrison's anticrime mentality fit perfectly with the philosophy of those in Clay and David's group. Many times she wished she could offer a bold invitation to the assistant DA to attend one of their sessions, and once she asked Clay's permission to do so. To her surprise, he flatly rejected her notion with a finger waving admonishment and sneering reproach.

Nevertheless she remained a huge proponent and would often slip Garrison's name into conversations at their meetings when the subject turned to the need for better law enforcement in the local community. She convinced Robert of Garrison's acumen and urged him to follow Garrison's achievements often chronicled on local television news programs and in the *Times Picayune*.

Particularly after David's performance the weekend before and Robert's uninhibited applause she was convinced that her friend and possible lover also would become a strong advocate of her choice for New Orleans District Attorney.

Deborah finished her review of the pleadings, rose from her desk and walked into Mr. Randolph's office, tapping on the doorframe to announce her entrance.

"We might as well throw in the towel," she said to her boss as she placed the Garrison motion on his desk.

"Yes, I suppose you're right," responded Randolph. "I'll call the client and tell him to prepare for a plea and some jail time."

That afternoon Deborah's mission to find Garrison and make him aware of her admiration and credentials failed yet again so she left her material with his secretary and went home to Mrs. Dionne's, dejected and depressed. Two days later however, she took a call from his office, thinking she would soon be on the receiving end of another masterful motion for directed verdict when to her delight Garrison came on the line with a warm greeting. She could tell who was speaking from hearing him talk before the television cameras many times before. During their brief conversation Garrison offered her a job on his campaign staff at pay less than half of what she was making but she accepted the proposal on the spot and resigned from Walker, Walker & Schmidt that day.

Among a field of several candidates Garrison won the Democratic primary by a decent six thousand vote margin. A Democratic victory in New Orleans was tantamount to automatic ascension into office. Garrison was sworn in two months later in January 1962. Deborah edged out several other loyal campaign workers to become his personal assistant, close confidante and keeper of the gate to his office. He made sure that her pay topped the permitted government scales. Soon she became the person to see, the person to convince, and the person to wine and dine if you wanted the ear of the new District Attorney.

During the campaign at Deborah's urging Robert occasionally helped out at Garrison's headquarters stuffing envelopes, making get-out-the-vote telephone calls and placing posters in storefront windows, including one at Roblinski's repair shop. Robert did so over the protests of Sigmund who hated politics and vowed never to become involved in local elections particularly when they were between candidates whose offices directly affected the operations of businesses like his. His logic was simple, he told Roman, "If the guy you choose looses, you're stuck. He gets off Scot-free but his backers have to put up with the guy who wins. The guy who wins likes noting better than taking out his anger on the other guy's supporters. It's especially bad when the guy is the District Attorney who has control over the cops."

Despite Sigmund's opposition Roman, for the first time, defied the old man. The Garrison poster went up firmly affixed to the main display window. Sigmund was furious but said nothing more. He was shocked at Roman's disobedience. He also noticed a creeping cavalier contemptuousness in their day-to-day work routines. Roman was making an ever increasing number of decisions affecting the business on his own without consulting Sigmund. He almost single handedly assisted customers. He set repair schedules, and determined prices. He administered and oversaw work agendas for the two apprentices he hired to help shoulder the workload and he was slowly turning Roblinski's shop into a new television, radio and appliance distributorship rather than a repair outlet. About all Sigmund did was traffic cash back and forth between the bank located just across the street.

The shop was bringing in good sums and Sigmund saw his own personal account balances rise steadily. Yet he was uneasy, admittedly afraid to challenge his protégé. He often thought about retiring altogether, but on his days off he was lonely with little to do and no place to go. His business was his life and if he gave it up to Roman all that was left for him to do was count his money.

Roman appeared insensitive to Sigmund's plight. That too was a disturbing realization for the proprietor. Before, with just the slightest hint of bruised feelings, Roman would jump quickly to sooth, sympathize and cajole the owner. No more. If Sigmund complained about anything Roman either ignored him or sometimes even gruffly dismissed him with a wave of his arm indicating his desire for the old man to return to his workspace behind the counter.

Roman's independence and compounding arrogance were bolstered by Sophia in one respect and Deborah in another. Sophia gladly become his lover, accepting, even enthusiastically soliciting his advances. On many nights he never returned to Mrs. Dionne's boarding house. Some of his clothes and personal belongings were finding their way to Sophia's apartment. As his sexual encounters increased so did his self-confidence and haughtiness. Deborah's overtures were different but no less tantalizing. She still dangled tempting prospects of sex, but it was her other recurring petitions that led to his growing aggression. Deborah promised power and prestige. Deborah pushed Robert forward among those in Clay's sanctum. Since his resounding approval of David's diatribe against the Kennedy clan, Robert's star rose steadily at each meeting that followed. Deborah was his strongest supporter and she was not shy in her advocacy.

Robert again went back to the books and newspapers to bone up on the day's events even studying transcripts of Congressional hearings that followed the Cuban Bay of Pigs debacle. He saw the civil rights movement and Kennedy's clamoring for improved race relations as a threat equal to, if not more ominous than the Soviet menace. He began to see the President through a narrowing prism of deepening radicalism and intolerance, reinforced by the words Clay and David belched out each Saturday evening. Except for Deborah, Robert shunned the others at Mrs. Dionne's, skipping most meals, keeping to himself and when a friendly greeting came his way, he often responded with rudeness. He became particularly spiteful of Clarence and grew intolerant of his folksy brand of backwoods wisdom and intellect.

Finding pleasure only in Sophia's bed and in Clay's consortium, Robert's shell grew thicker and sprouted sharp spikes. Then his moment came. Finally Robert was asked to speak to a gathering. He was stunned at Clay's invitation. As he sat there with Deborah at his side, her grinning ear to ear and pushing at his elbow to rise to his feet, something overtook him. Something or someone possessed him. He later realized it was no one in that room. Later, in his dream that night, the first in more than two years, he knew it was Fodor.

Before he dreamed, Robert first stepped to the hallowed place behind Clay's podium.

"Ladies and gentlemen," he began, "I am humbled by Clay's request of me to speak this evening. I am humbled to stand before you and tell you of my fears. As an immigrant, as one who knew little of this country but for its greatness, and one who despite the hardships I overcame to get here, I fear that America's greatness is slowly dying..." He rambled and stumbled forward and made little sense from that point on, but no one seemed to care. Most of his vitriol echoed that of David and Clay, but in the end Robert took it one step further when he huffed and puffed with the hateful, threatening observation that, "We cannot let Kennedy run roughshod over this country for four years. We are the ones to stop him dead in his tracks!"

When he was finished it was Sally who first leaped to her feet to permanently welcome him to the exalted elite. With his performance she shed any doubt about Robert and now, she cried, "We have a triumphant trio of leaders to march us to our destiny!"

Clay winked and smiled at David and both politely applauded with the rest of the crowd. At Sally's urging, the clamor intensified to a roar of approval at Robert's coronation.

When the heavy curtains parted that night to begin Robert's dream the nocturnal scene had changed. In his subconscious state Robert was serene. His slumber was deep and satisfying, unlike those torturous times before. On this occasion Robert watched as Roman, not Fodor, pranced on stage. This time Fodor sat in the audience; his seat in row 7, soft, comfortable, cushioned and encased in red velvet like all the rest. On this occasion Fodor was not alone. The theatre was full. Not a vacant seat to be found. Wait! Who is out there with Fodor? The faces are all the same. The dresses are all white. She is there with him. In the audience surrounding her husband. Hundreds of her, all the same. There to judge him; her son, to warn him, plead with him to come to her. To turn away.

Come to Mass with me. Your father will not know. The Bazillika awaits. Its doors are open. The priest stands at the top of the stairs beckoning in earnest.

Yet Roman turns away. He ignores his mother's calling. Rudolph is there. He is old now. Older than Roman. He displays frizzled grey hair, a torn shirt. There is blood on his cheek. He doesn't touch his milk, but Roman guzzles the port. He paces. His strides rigid and wide. His rage begins. He vomits evil. Terror. A call to action. Not a time to love. A time to hate. A time to kill. Rid our planet of the scourge. Roman is venomous beyond that of his father.

At the height of Roman's wrath, Rudolph looks up from the table to stare in the face of his brother. He is bewildered. Saddened. Then he rises from his chair. A cane is hooked to the back as he slides the seat away. He grabs the cane and limps off stage. Roman is not deterred. He continues to no one, except to himself. He doesn't care that he is alone. He doesn't care what the audience thinks. More port. Now he has grown tired. His throat is dry again. He stops and pivots to stare into the crowd. Fodor slowly comes to his feet with a steady, rhythmic applause.

Fodor is alone now. She, they are all gone. The theatre is empty. All the seats except Fodor's in row 7 are barren, exposed wooden slats, nails protruding, ready to puncture. To cause pain.

Fodor's applause fades. He is tired but heartened by what he saw. Robert awakes. He is content.

32

In the days that followed Robert's caustic hyperbole intensified. He had it ready for delivery. At every opportunity. Offered in abundance without prompting. He was a rare attendee at Mrs. Dionne's dinner table, but on his next visit he lectured her boardinghouse tenants on every topic from the price of sugar to the nuclear arms race. Her guests responded by wolfing down their meals and excusing themselves early to escape his incessant banter. Even Deborah grew tired of his exaggerated claims and joined Clarence and Boudreaux on the porch for a smoke. Miss Hattie was the only one who remained behind as Robert's audience, interrupting him in midsentence to ask if he thought FDR might run for another term.

Robert stormed off to his room after that and immediately wished he had accepted Sophia's invitation for another stimulating night between her newly obtained satin sheets. He fell asleep with acute disgust after reading the latest glowing account in *Time* Magazine of President Kennedy's tax cut legislation. He awoke much later by a light rapping at his door. Groggy, he toppled out of bed and staggered to the muffled sound. On the other side he heard her whisper.

"Be quiet and let me in."

The door handle clicked and Deborah stepped through. Robert moved aside to let her pass. The moon rays shimmering through the open blind at his window pierced her sheer nightgown to reveal a luscious naked body beneath. She tiptoed to his bed and sat down softly. She whispered again.

"Come over here, will you. We need to talk."

"Talk," he responded with indignation. "You came here to talk?"

"Please keep your voice down," Deborah rasped. "Just come here and sit beside me."

Finally, Robert did as he was told. She grabbed his hand as he rested at her side but he playfully began bouncing on the mattress just enough to make the bedsprings squeak.

"Stop it you fool," she said a little too loudly.

"Robert. This is serious. I know you have grown to accept, to fully embrace our cause, but you have to tone down your manner. Your statements are so ferocious. I'm afraid someone's going to report you to the police, to the FBI, or somebody. Our cause can only be won if we remain hidden, silent to the world and vocal only to ourselves. You can't go around declaring war on everyone from President Kennedy on down and not eventually attract the wrong kind of attention. Please. All I ask is for you to tell me and the others of your feelings, not the whole world," Deborah pleaded.

Robert listened intently and finally nodded his head. "You're right. I do get carried away. These imbeciles here tonight. They don't understand. They're either too old and senile or too stupid to care."

"Robert. Don't be so sure. You can't; we can't take chances. Our time is nearing. Clay and David have begun the planning," she said.

"Planning what?" Robert's attention piquing.

"You will soon find out. Meanwhile, we need to raise some money and I expect you will be hearing from either Clay or David about how you can help," she said.

"Wow. Really? They are going to let me help in a bigger way. I'll be ready. I hope you know that," he said assuredly.

"Yes, I know that dear Robert. Now my lovely friend we are going to make love. You are going to do it gently and quietly. If we like it, we will do it again and maybe again after that. If we don't like it we will not try again," she declared.

"I have Sophia," he offered weakly, "and you have Mrs. Claire."

"Don't ever mention that Russian bitch's name to me again," she snarled, "and about her, it's none of your business."

Their lovemaking that night was robotic. She spun her web and he crawled helplessly into it. Their lovemaking seemed everyday, commonplace, borderline lackluster. Uneventful and unsatisfying. She went through the motions as did he, both surprised that the months of flirtatious teasing and rising temptations fizzled so dramatically during the long anticipated act itself. Neither wanted to admit it and neither spoke about it, but both expected it was not to happen again.

She left him with a smile clearly reflecting comradeship as opposed to passionate fulfillment.

33

Roman worked late that next day reviewing catalogues for the new models of Zenith's entertainment centers, which were being introduced in single walnut veneer cabinets containing both a thirty-six inch color television and a stereo high fidelity radio and record changer. Dual speakers rounded out the latest in American electronic ingenuity. He had room on his showroom floor for two sets and since the holidays were approaching he was giving serious thought to taking them into inventory as a Christmas special. Sigmund would never know the difference. He would tell him they were in the shop for repair. He would never understand the book entry of seven hundred dollars put at risk if they didn't sell. Sigmund paid little attention to those details these days. The calendar read Monday, October 22, 1962.

As Roman worked through his chores in the background the *CBS Evening News* came on one of the old Curtis Mathis sets he had just finished repairing. The announcer's voice was different from the deep baritone of the new mustached anchorman Walter Cronkite. Roman still paid little attention until the voice declared a News Bulletin from the White House. Roman turned to the set and stared at the man he despised the most.

"Good evening my fellow Americans," John F. Kennedy said.

A clearly shaken President went on to describe the potential for war and a nuclear holocaust. The Soviets had positioned land-based missiles equipped with atomic warheads on Cuban soil just 90 miles south of the U.S. border. The rockets were aimed directly at major American population centers. Castro welcomed his Soviet benefactors ashore. He welcomed their presence. An overt act of aggression, Kennedy said, that would not go unanswered. Confrontation might be inevitable. Our military is on high alert. The U.S. will weigh all of its options. The President is demanding the missile sites be dismantled immediately. A grim, frightful speech. Marking the beginning for America of ten October days in perilous hell.

Roman watched and listened intently. He was transfixed. His first thought was to rally around the man on the screen. Forget his transgressions for now. Roman's adopted homeland was plummeting into unspeakable peril. We should stand together against this unprovoked threat and not waver in our determination. Then Roman had another thought.

Would the Soviets have come banging on our door with loaded guns if our President had been strong? If he had been courageous, willful and steadfast in his first summit with the dictator Khrushchev? Did Kennedy bring this crisis on himself? On his country? Was it his fault that our nation was squarely in the Russian crosshairs? All the more reason that he should be removed, Roman finally concluded.

Roman was anxious to talk with Clay or David or anyone in the group about the potential catastrophe at hand, but he knew he could not. With the exception of Deborah and Sally they were prohibited from speaking to anyone outside the ballet studio walls. He had to find Deborah. She would help him put things in perspective. Sally would only bellow platitudes. On the off chance that Deborah would still be at work, he called her office. No answer.

Discouraged and frustrated Roman paced the shop floor. His anger rising with each step. He turned back to the television set but by then Kennedy's terrifying speech was over and the evening comedy shows had already begun. "Just like nothing happened," Roman barked at the screen, his voice booming over the canned laughter blaring through the speakers.

"Our country is on the brink of war and you stupid bastards are more concerned with who wrecked Ozzie's car!" he screamed as if he expected Ozzie, Harriet, David or Ricky to answer.

Then the telephone rang. Surprised by the sound, at first Roman thought it was coming from the Nelson family sitcom home but he quickly realized it was the shop phone beckoning. It never rings this late, Roman thought as he ran to pick it up.

"Robert?" The deep gruff voice on the other end of the line inquired. Roman knew immediately who it was. He was stunned and failed to respond immediately.

"Robert, are you there?" Clay searched for an answer.

"Ah, yes, I'm here. This is Roman…err, I mean Robert."

"Robert. You answered, Roman. Do I have the correct number?"

"Yes, oh yes, you have the correct number, Clay. This is Robert. I'm here. You have me. I'm the one," Roman stammered nervously.

"Yes, now I recognize your voice," Clay responded. "Can you talk? Are you alone?"

"Yes, Clay. I am alone. I am working late. I just heard Kennedy's speech. I was hoping I could talk with someone about it. I am so angry at what I heard. How could that man get us into this mess? How could..." Clay cut him off.

"Robert, we can talk about it later. I am angry too. All of us are angry. All of us now know that the time has come. We cannot talk further over the telephone. Can you meet me in a half hour at the Club Cherie? I will be alone at the table in the rear to the right when you enter."

"It's not Saturday. It's only Monday. I thought we could not meet on any other night. Away from our place," Roman replied.

"Don't worry. We're making an exception. This is an important meeting. A lot has to be done in a short amount of time and I want you to play a big part," Clay said almost as if he were talking to a child.

"I will be there in a half hour," Roman promised.

The first shipment arrived at Roblinski's shop two weeks after Robert and Clay met that Monday at the Club Cherie. By then the Soviets had blinked first. Kennedy's blockade had worked and the Russian warheads were on their way back to the motherland with a full armada of U.S. Navy surface and subsurface ships providing escort all the way home. Kennedy was triumphant, erasing his shame over the Bay of Pigs incident and immediately gaining enormous political strength worldwide for his steel spine stare down of the shoe-pounding Red Premier.

Sigmund asked Roman whether the fifty cases of new clock radios might be an overstock but when they were gone the next day he took Roman's word that he had moved the lot wholesale to another dealer who could use the inventory. Three days later, seventy-five toasters came and went. Then twenty-five RCA color televisions. Then thirty-five Kirby vacuum cleaners, all in and out of the shop in twenty-four hours. Just to be safe Roman noted in the daily account register a single sale of each item. This movement of hijacked merchandise continued unabated for six solid weeks. Roman had no idea from where the money was coming or going and he didn't ask.

The Saturday nights that followed were the highlight of his week. The meetings were lively and stimulating but when Robert attempted to bring up the subject of "Kennedy's latest antics," Clay would abruptly change the topic, usually directing the gathering's attention to the most recent civil rights demonstration and the more ominous frolicking of "that renegade colored preacher from Atlanta, Martin Luther King."

Robert accepted Clay's stewardship of the meeting topics without protest but remained deeply curious about the shift away from the demon in the White House to some lowly black villain preacher who was raising only a minor ruckus mostly among ultra liberals in the north where it didn't count.

Robert remained a frequent visitor to Sophia's lustful lair, but he was growing weary of her less than clever hints at permanent cohabitation and possibly even an engagement. He tolerated her gambits and set them aside with the excuse that he needed to save up for the day when he could properly make her an "honest" woman.

He remained close to Deborah, closer in mind than Sophia, but not in body. After they experimented, only to realize the incompatibility of their carnal familiarity, they relaxed and enjoyed the company of one another even more. Their conversations were vibrant, sometimes heated, but always ended in general agreement, reinforcing the radical views which both increasingly held dear.

It was another unexpected telephone call at the shop on a late dreary December afternoon that brought the reality of Roman and Robert's fanaticism into razor sharp focus.

"Robert. It's Deborah. Don't say a word. Just listen, and do exactly as I say."

Roman's heart pounded and his throat went dry as he listened to her frightening monologue. "I've just seen a police report that crossed my desk. Robert, you have to leave town immediately. The cops have been investigating a series of truck hijackings in Mississippi and Alabama and they may have traced some of the stolen goods to New Orleans. The missing cargo is mostly televisions, radios and appliances, and they think, or at least they say, they have a snitch who's telling them some of the stuff may be passing through your shop." Her voice was low and raspy. She stuttered with fright.

Roman took the phone away from his ear. He nearly dropped the receiver. His hand shook uncontrollably.

"Robert, are you there?" Deborah screeched under her breath.

"Yes, I'm here. Deborah, what do I do?" He tried to regain his composure.

"Gather up everything you have. Take all the money you can get your hands on but don't leave a trail. Just go."

"Go where, Deborah, where should I go?" She had to help him. He was lost.

"Denver. You need to go to Denver. There are friends there. People like us. People who believe as we do. They will help you. Clay has arranged everything," she said.

"Denver. I have no idea where that is. How do I get there? Who do I see? I don't have that much money to live on. I will need a job. Deborah, will you come with me? I'm frightened." His voice cracking.

"Robert, I can't come with you. You know that. I hate to say it, but take that Russian girlfriend of yours. She'll go with you. Get in your car tonight and drive. Get a map and find your way to Denver. You will be safe there. I'll make sure the cops are confused enough to get off your tail. Now go. You don't have much time," she commanded.

Deborah put down the phone and took a deep, calming breath. She knew what to do. Since her boss had begun his crime sweep across the city he ordered the beat cops and detectives to file all potential felony reports with his office before making arrests. Garrison's tactic was to review each case for sufficient prosecutorial evidence that, in his estimation, would virtually assure a conviction. This way he kept the cops on their toes and what is more important he would keep guilty verdicts or plea bargains at their maximum peak to ideally guarantee his reelection. It was Deborah's job to screen these reports more for their potential media affect than for legal credibility and provide the District Attorney an ongoing series of fodder for interesting news worthy press conferences.

On this particular evening she had two fairly thick files from the bunko/robbery division, which caught her attention. The first involved two relatively minor jewelry store heists in which hit-and-run thieves smashed glass display cases and snatched a handful of cheap low-grade diamond bracelets before dashing to an awaiting getaway car. The cops had a lead on the name of one of the culprits and were hoping to raid his apartment in the next day or two pending the blessing of the DA and the issuance of a search warrant. What made Garrison's plan somewhat popular with the men in blue was if their cases warranted maximum media exposure the DA would allow the arresting officers to join him on the press room stage. Occasionally some officers were even permitted to say a few words to the horde of scribbling reporters.

After reading the file Deborah didn't think the diamond bandits deserved her boss's personal attention so she put the report in the pile that went directly to the sitting District Criminal Court judge for consideration of the search warrant request.

Then she opened the truck hijacking file and had nearly fainted. In a panic she scanned through it. She called Clay before calling Robert to make sure the Denver connection was available. Now she studied the file in greater detail. Luckily she was alone in the office that evening. Often Garrison would work late with her sifting through reports and planning for future political events. Tonight he was making a speech to the Kiwanis Club annual Christmas dinner and most of his assistants and staff were in attendance as well. Deborah declined to go, saying truthfully that she felt one of her migraine headaches coming on and planned to go home early. As she opened the hijacking file for further review she looked to the ceiling and whispered a thanks be to God for keeping her at work even though her head was pulsating in pain.

Methodically, she combed through the documents and carefully began editing the words. In doing so she began to modify the string of evidence that lead the cops to prematurely finger Roblinski's shop as a fencing way station for the pilfered items. To her dismay the cops authoring the reports had excellent typing skills, so their reports were all neatly aligned and spaced thanks to a standard judicial system-wide supply of Smith Corona's. Luckily there was an identical typewriter at the desk next to hers. Soon the reports had flaws. She broke the chain of evidence, separating the links with made-up names and addresses, times, dates, and descriptions of transporting vehicles that were struck in the robberies. Even the manufacturer of some of the stolen merchandise was changed. Robert talked with her enough about his favorite makes and models of radios and televisions and appliances so she knew higher grades from lower ones and that made it easy for her to doctor the reports with greater precision.

Eventually the papers were drastically modified to the point that when Garrison and his deputies scrutinized them, she knew they would hastily order the befuddled investigators back into the field to clean up their cases. Confusion and distortion were Deborah's goals, and it took her two solid hours to retype the reports in the way she wanted them to read.

A hijacking ring is meaty material for the press and Garrison would want it pursued diligently by the department. It was too risky for Deborah to relegate the case to the inconsequential file. There would be too much pressure from the detectives if Garrison sat on it, so Deborah made sure the doctored documents would be on his desk in the morning. By then Robert would be well on his way north to Colorado; maybe in the company of that Russian pig he was screwing. She had to put her jealousy aside, perhaps permanently, to think and work so no cop, no matter how skillful, would ever have justification to go near Roblinski's shop hunting for the contraband.

Within twenty minutes after Deborah's frantic call Roman was locking up Roblinski's beloved establishment likely for the last time. Roman gathered all of his personal items, including his tools and loaded them in his car parked in the back. He took nothing of Sigmund's and was careful not to leave a single item that belonged to the cache of merchandise that had recently swept through the shop on its way to anxious illicit middlemen. Today was payday. Roman took what was owed him from the small stash of cash locked in Sigmund's desk drawer. He then sat down to write the old man a letter. To his surprise his writing stirred some emotion.

Dear Sigmund,

You will be surprised when you arrive at the shop in the morning and find that I am not here. I am leaving your employment to strike out on my own in search for better things. I am not unhappy with being your assistant. It is just my desire to be my own boss. You have been very good to me. You took a chance on me when I needed it most and helped me understand how business works in America. For that I will always be grateful. All the money remains in the drawer locked in your desk except for my pay for this week. All the items in the shop for repair have been fixed and are ready to be picked up.

You will need to instruct the apprentices from now on. They are good boys but a little lazy so make sure they earn their money and learn from you as I did. I will probably be leaving New Orleans but I do not know where I will end up. When I do I will try to write you. You have become a good friend and I wish you continued good health and prosperity.

Roman

Without folding it Roman taped the letter to the middle of Sigmund's empty desktop, collected his jacket, shut off the lights and left. The process of making sure he departed Roblinski's with as little evidence as possible of him ever being there served to settle Robert's nerves. He had himself under control by the time he pulled to a stop in front of Sophia's apartment building. He knew she was home since they had already planned on being together that evening. Despite his efforts to remain nonchalant Sophia detected apprehension when she opened the door and greeted her lover with a warm, lingering kiss.

Before she could speak he pulled away from her clutch to grasp her shoulders gently and with a wry smile said, "I have a proposal for you."

Sophia wept with joy as she packed her belongings. They decided to spend the night together at her apartment and leave New Orleans first thing in the morning. Just in case Deborah's assurance that she would take care of everything didn't pan out, Robert decided it was best for him to stay as far away from Mrs. Dionne's boarding house as possible. Sophia's rent was paid through the end of the month as was Robert's. It was very important, Robert said, for them to leave New Orleans without owing anyone anything, so they went through all of their bills and accounts and made out checks to mail in the morning. Sophia had no problem quitting her thankless job but leaving without notice meant she would sacrifice a week's pay. It didn't matter. She had never been happier in her life.

It was a restless night for both of them. Robert's anxiety. Sophia's pure bliss.

By ten o'clock the next morning, with the trunk and back seat of Robert's car full, their bank accounts closed, three thousand dollars tucked away in an envelope and locked in the glove compartment, and with Ray Charles crooning "*Hit the Road Jack,*" on the radio they were on Interstate 10 heading west, eventually turning north toward a strange new land.

Part V

Denver, CO
March 1961

34

Bud tried but he simply could not remain in Colorado Springs after his daughters were abducted and ripped from his heart in broad daylight on an order from an idiotic judge, sympathetic to a sociopathic mother and her hermaphrodite looking boy toy. He saw it that way. Nothing could change his mind. He couldn't remain in the city any longer and relive that day or the days preceding. To him without Christina and Tanya his cozy little cottage was now the cruel confines of a razor wire prison cell. He couldn't walk on the same streets as they once did together. He couldn't drive by their school or shop at any of the stores where he bought their school clothes and supplies. It was too hard.

Bud heard his precious daughters were somewhere in Florida with those adult misfits. Living under the same roof. He hated the thought of that man or whatever he was touching them. Bossing them around. Fixing their ham and cheese sandwiches. Being responsible for Christina's insulin. The girls' mother was another matter altogether. That crazy, selfish, uncaring bitch. What a poor excuse for a human being.

God, why didn't I keep running with them? Why did I stop here, stay here; think for a moment they wouldn't find me? Christ, my sister lives here. It was obvious. How stupid I was? How careless.

Night after night he tortured himself. He was in agony. He had to leave. Escape from his self-created demons.

Bud had a friend from high school whose name was Marshall Goodpastor. Marshall was like Bud in many ways but he was more cautious when it came to business ventures. Marshall was one of those acquaintances who appeared on the short list of likely investors in the once robust but now defunct Carlson commodities trading enterprise.

However, Marshall turned down Bud's offer to invest, explaining he only put his money in things he could touch and smell and above all personally control. Marshall said he had no clue what a bushel of corn or a hundred weight of hog meat was worth so he politely told Bud to find someone on his list "who understands all that stuff." Bud wished liked hell he had been more like his friend Marshall.

Marshall had prospered in the rough and tumble business world of product vending. Marshall lived in Denver. That's where he made his money. He was the majority stockholder and chief executive officer of Rocky Mountain Vending, a thriving company that dispensed through a machine every imaginable item for the price of a few lousy coins. By far his biggest and most profitable product was cigarettes even though at the time they cost only twenty-five cents a pack. Marshall had cigarette machines vending thousands of packs of cigarettes a week in four hundred bars, restaurants and gas stations throughout the city. He also had machines in hospitals, drug stores and medical clinics. You could even find Marshall's cigarette dispensaries in a few church basements around town. That made it easy for priests, preachers and rabbis to help stuff their offering plates from their puffing, God fearing congregations.

Next to the top radio stations in the market Marshall's juke boxes played more music for people than from any other single source. A quarter for four songs. In some places where he had cigarette machines he also had pinball machines, candy machines and coin slot pool tables. A dime for a candy bar. A quarter for a game of eight ball. Candy machines placed close to cigarette machines was a good business strategy since most people who were trying to stop smoking ate tons of candy bars. Pool players usually drank and smoked and played music all at the same time so Marshall had those customers coming and going. Marshall wasn't big into dispensing soda pop however. The machines were too big and bulky and the glass bottles often broke. At the time, the best soda pop dispenser was rustic in design. It was the same for coffee machines. Marshall didn't like them either. They often broke down and repairs were expensive. Despite numerous offers from Pepsi, Nesbitt and Coca Cola bottlers to vend their products Marshall consistently declined. He liked smokers, music lovers, pool sharks and sugarholics the best and besides, Marshall was not one to bet on anything but a sure thing.

In Marshall Goodpastor's mind, Bud Carlson was a sure thing. When Bud called him asking for a job Marshall didn't hesitate. Sure,

Marshall knew Bud bet the pot on the commodities business and lost, but that didn't make him stupid, just a little foolhardy and unlucky.

How could anyone control the weather or the mating habits of pigs, Marshall rationalized. Marshall knew Bud was a super salesman and by a fortunate twist of fate, this time in Bud's favor, Marshall was looking for someone with Bud's skills to expand his vending territory east into the rapidly growing suburb of Aurora, and west into the Flatirons region around Boulder. It was good for Marshall that Bud needed a complete and total change of scenery and beside the fact that Colorado Springs was only sixty miles south, Denver was a completely different world. Marshall was more than happy to rest Bud right down in the middle of town.

Bud packed his things and headed north the day after a very lonely and sometimes tearful Christmas Day spent absent his daughters. Marshall's main office and largest equipment storage facility was located at Logan and Eighth Street. On New Year's Eve, Bud rented an apartment on Pearl Street, which was in walking distance of the office. He started work for Marshall on the following Monday.

Bud was particularly glad his new office was as close as it was to his apartment. He could walk to work and get there quickly. Just past midnight that Monday, Denver was hit with a fierce January snowstorm that blanketed the region with twenty-two inches and temperatures plummeting to minus twelve degrees. Despite the weather and being chilled to the bone, Bud was at work on time. Marshall had a private office waiting for him. The coffee was hot and good and his reception from Marshall's staff was genuinely warm and friendly.

While Wendell H. "Bud" Carlson sipped coffee and got acquainted with his surroundings and new staff, Robert Kaye sat shivering and stranded in a massive traffic jam. Three tractor-trailer trucks had jackknifed in the middle of the new four-lane Interstate Highway 25 on which he was traveling. Robert Kaye, aka Roman Sokolowski, aka Roman Klonowski, sat with Sophia Chekhov, known by no other name, stopped dead still, their feet tingling from the cold, their breaths fogging the windshield. The heater in Robert's vintage Chevrolet was producing enough heat to barely protect them against frostbite. Robert hadn't been this cold since his days in Esztergom. His teeth were chattering and every few moments he let his woman know how miserable he was. On the other hand Sophia wasn't complaining. She was as uncomfortable as he was but she wasn't saying a word about her condition. Even though both of them had their origins in the frigid parts of Eastern Europe their days in balmy New Orleans had "thinned their blood," a phrase Robert over heard Clay say at one of the recent Saturday night gatherings. He repeated it to Sophia who looked at him curiously and said, "I don't know what that means."

"Forget it," Robert responded harshly. He coughed and added, "I'm going to catch pneumonia. I'm sure of it."

Sophia paid no attention to his latest assertion. At that moment the most important subject on her mind was marriage. The kind of ceremony didn't matter to her. What mattered was that it happened quickly. She estimated the baby, Robert's baby, had been growing in her belly for at least three months. Their formal union, before God, in the presence of man whomever that may be, had to happen very soon. Her swelling was not apparent to anyone but herself, but Robert had commented on her weight gain and larger breast size recently. Her bigger breasts, he said, made him happy. He made no motherly connection to their growth.

So there they sat in the cold, traffic barely inching forward. The heater in Chevy coupe choked and sputtered, clanging loudly and trying its best to keep the couple from freezing to death. Finally two tow trucks arrived and twenty long minutes later traffic started moving. Three hours after that they were on the outskirts of the capital city. Like they often do in Colorado, the storm, roaring down off the eastern slope of the Rockies, blew through in less than twelve hours so by the time Robert and Sophia were motoring north on Colorado Boulevard looking for Ogden Street, a bright, eye squinting sun was shining, presenting a glimmering crystal array of spectacular white beauty bouncing off the three foot drifts prominent on each side of the newly plowed road. Both of them were awestruck by the grandeur of the wintry scene.

Before Roman locked up Roblinski's shop for the last time Deborah had called back. In their last conversation she gave Robert the name of Clay's Denver contact and the address of a house at which he and "that bitch of yours" can stay. It was a house on Ogden Street. The man's name was Preston Oxnard. Robert should go directly to the house, she said, and under the welcome mat he would find a key to the front door. They were obliged to stay the night and required to call the number she gave him the following morning. Mr. Oxnard would do what he could to help, but Robert needed to find work immediately and start paying rent. No one had the money to support him and his Russian whore, she bitterly added.

As Robert drove in circles searching for Ogden Street and house number eleven hundred, he was starkly reminded of his hunt for

Mrs. Dionne's boarding house on that blistering August afternoon not that long ago. In his mind the similarities were uncanny. Actually he found himself thinking back fondly on his early days in New Orleans. Of Clarence, of Bourdeaux, of Miss Henley, Anton, even Mrs. Dionne. His days before Deborah. His first days with Sigmund. Those were easier times, less complicated, much less to think about, even to fear. He couldn't go back there, to that place or to those simpler times. They were gone forever. Deborah made sure of that. He wanted the blame to rest squarely on her shoulders, but he knew better. He brought this mad dash escape to the dreadful frozen tundra of Colorado all on himself. He wanted to be a part of something important; an event that might reshape the world and make it a better place. He had no idea what that event might be or what role he might play.

I should quit feeling sorry for myself and face the future head on, with courage and commitment. Like Roman; like Fodor.

Sophia brought him out of his nighttime daydream with a sharp squeal announcing, "There it is, eleven hundred Ogden. We found it!"

As promised, the key was where Deborah said it would be. The front door opened to a small foyer, leading straight back to a tiny galley kitchen. It was nearly as cold inside the house as it was outside. However, the lights worked with a flick of the switch. A living room, sparsely but adequately furnished was off to the right. There were two bedrooms in the back and a single bathroom. Twin beds were located in one of the rooms. A double bed, matching nightstands and a single bedside lamp were in the other bedroom. Robert found the thermostat and to their delight when he twisted it they heard the furnace kick on and felt warm air rising through one of the floor registers. A hand written note was on the Formica topped kitchen table. It simply read:

Park your car in the rear.
Access through the alley.
Call this number in the morning.
392-7030

Thirty minutes later the Chevy was parked in back as instructed, the house was warm, and not caring their clothes and meager belongings were strewn about the rooms. Robert and Sophia climbed in between the icy sheets covering the double bed, pulled the wool blanket over them and quickly became entangled in warmth and comfort. They were hungry but bone tired, wanting sleep above all. It had been a grueling journey.

As he drifted off to a much needed rest, he thought he heard Sophia softly whisper, "Darling, I'm pregnant. I hope you will be as happy as I am."

I must be dreaming, he thought, as sleep overtook him.

35

Bud was reviewing cigarette inventory sheets and reading *Billboard* Magazine to make sure the restaurant in Boulder's new luxury hotel, the Saint Michael, had enough smokes for the weekend and this week's top twenty songs were on its restaurant's jukebox when his secretary Mary Lou Jordan told him he had an unannounced visitor.

Bud glanced up from his reading after hearing Mary Lou rap gently at his door. "He doesn't have an appointment. I think he's looking for a job. Seems like a nice fellow. Says he's a mechanic," Mary Lou said. Bud eyed Mary Lou leaning on the doorframe, hand on her hip, head tilted slightly sideways offering a somewhat provocative smile before responding with, "Marshall and I agreed the other day that we could use another mechanic. At last count we've placed twenty machines, five pool tables and we need to wire speaker systems in three locations all in Aurora and Boulder, so maybe the guy, if he's any good, just might get lucky."

Mary Lou, moving toward Bud's desk in a pronounced runway model walk, said, "You're right. Since you've been here…what, just about a month…we've picked up those spots and…what, two others… all in towns we've never been in before? That's fantastic!"

"Three others to be exact," Bud corrected her as she arrived at her destination, leaned forward and placed her hands on the desktop to make sure her boss fully appreciated the low-cut white ruffled blouse she was wearing. The two top buttons were purposefully disengaged to expose the pink trim of her lacy bra.

Bud knew eventually he would have to make a decision about Mary Lou. Either take her home and deal with the complexity and heavy consequences of an office affair or sternly inform her that he's off limits and then have to handle potential anger and bitterness over an overt rejection of her awfully tempting offer. He wasn't going to make that choice today. He had too much work to do, and yes, he was now more interested in talking with the fellow waiting outside.

"Have him come in, Mary Lou, and oh, by the way, I don't like pink."

Startled, Mary Lou's grin was wiped away instantly. She huffed at his remark, spun like a top on her black spike heels, and hurriedly wiggled through Bud's door.

A few moments later she was back to announce, with no hint of friendliness this time, the arrival of Mr. Robert Kaye. Bud stood up to greet the stranger immediately noticing his pronounced limp. He tried not to stare, yet he did instantly appreciate the deep brown, spit shined Tony Lama boots gleaming on his visitor's feet. They look genuine alligator, Bud thought.

Robert's hand shake was firm for a little man, Bud thought, as he offered him a seat in the chair placed next to where Mary Lou stood only moments before. As Robert sat, the door to Bud's office slammed shut and the glass in its frame rattled on impact as a result of Mary Lou's forceful swing.

Forty-five minutes later Robert and Bud were shaking hands again. This time, the clasp was to cement Robert's temporary position, on a trial basis, as a vending machine mechanic starting at sixty-five dollars a week. Later Bud acknowledged to Marshall that he was impressed with the man's verbal knowledge of the electronics world, often times talking well over Bud's head on subjects such as the intricacies of new circuit panels and how the industry could expect better juke box sound quality due to a more direct impulse path through smaller but more efficient amplifiers.

Robert explained to Bud that he preferred Seeburgs over Wurlitzers for that very reason. Bud didn't admit this to Marshall but, frankly, he could care less about either one of the manufacturers. Bud was much more interested in a machine's durability, the number of record plays and the direct correlation to dollar volume each machine could produce before breaking down. Bud said he would start Robert in the repair shop and for the first two weeks he would work under Maurice Hilton, the chief mechanic. If he proved himself and could back up his talk with performance he would be given a five dollar a week raise and the chance to go on repair calls.

Bud didn't ask and Robert didn't volunteer much about his past. What he did reveal during their conversation Robert lied about. Everything important, spanning his life in Hungary, France, New Orleans and all points in between was completely shrouded. Robert said he was born in Chicago to Polish parents; grew up and went to high school there. He never traveled much, he said. Both of his parents were dead. He volunteered that he hurt his leg in an industrial accident, but didn't elaborate on the details. He assured Bud that his injury would not affect his work. He said he learned electronics as an apprentice, working for a man named Mr. Dionne, but he too was dead. It was the only job he'd ever had. He had come to Denver straight from Chicago looking for a new start since Mr. Dionne was like a father to him. His wife's name was Silvia and they were expecting a baby. He needed the job real bad.

Bud concluded that he really didn't have the time or the inclination to check Robert's references. He liked the guy. He seemed smart and confident. Carried himself well, despite the handicap. What could he say about those boots? I'll bet he's flat broke and those boots are his prize possession, but with a baby on the way, I'll get ten times the work out of him.

"Hey, I like those boots, man," Bud offered as Robert hobbled toward his door. "Looks like real alligator."

"Yes, thanks," Robert answered, turning back to acknowledge his new boss. "They're lizard. Don't know what kind, though. Got 'them in New Orleans a few months ago."

"Beautiful," Bud complimented.

"Thanks, again. Thanks for everything, Mr. Carlson. I'll do right by you," Robert promised.

"Call me Bud."

"Bud, then. See you Monday."

Robert exited opening and closing the door quietly and gently. Strange. New Orleans? He didn't say anything about New Orleans. Said he'd never been outside of Chicago before coming here. Huh. Oh well, Bud thought, nice guy, smart. He'll work hard.

36

Robert went home to the Ogden Street hideaway and to his now obviously pregnant wife elated over the events of the afternoon. For nearly four weeks since arriving in what he often described as "this horrendous blizzard prone hellhole," Robert pounded the icy streets of Denver day after day, hour after hour, traipsing to interview after interview producing one rejection after another. He started with the top electronics firms in town and worked his way down the list to the smallest repair shops; some so small they made Roblinski's look like a modern day appliance and television display floor at Sears and Roebuck. He hadn't thought about the vending machine business until one day he stopped for gas at the Standard station on Downing Street. After pumping two dollars worth of regular into his grimy, mud-caked Chevy he satisfied a craving for a Snickers Bar from the candy machine. The gas station also had a pinball machine to which he contributed a quarter for three plays but didn't win a replay. After losing his quarter and while chomping on his candy Robert walked back to his car with a new strategy for gainful employment.

Rocky Mountain Vending was the first company of its kind that he targeted, mostly because it appeared to be one of the largest he guessed by the size of its ad in the *Yellow Pages*. Further, the prospects for employment there were attractive because the main office and distribution center were located within eight or ten blocks of where he and Sophia were living.

Robert and Sophia had married in a civil ceremony at Denver City Hall Annex One before a tired, old, distracted and obviously disinterested juvenile court judge only a week before Robert found Bud and left his office with hopes for a rewarding future.

On purpose, Sophia's wedding dress was chosen two sizes too big to effectively hide her expanding waistline. Nonetheless, it was a sweet pale purple dress, sporting a designer label that the woman at the consignment store assured her had cost at least three hundred dollars new. She bought it for twenty dollars and the smile on her face never went away all day. Robert signed his name to the marriage certificate as Robert J. Kaye thinking it had a better sound to it, plus when written out, his signature had a more distinguished look. He never gave a second thought to what his conjured up middle name would mean if he were ever asked.

After the ceremony, Robert and Sophia splurged on two steak dinners at the Buffalo Bar and Grill on Lincoln Street, which was two blocks from the government complex. They were down to their last five hundred dollars when they celebrated that night and for a few fleeting moments during their dinner Robert found himself marginally happy.

Their money had gone for rent and basic necessities including two visits to the baby doctor who, after his first examination, told Sophia that her timing was slightly off. She was closer to six months pregnant, rather than three, and the reason she didn't look it was the baby was "riding low and down" not "high and out." With the news of just three months left to term, Robert finally scheduled an afternoon off from job hunting to legalize their relationship.

During their first month in residence Robert spoke twice to the illusive Mr. Oxnard on the telephone. Both times, before those conversations, Robert found a note lying on the floor of the foyer apparently having been slipped through the mail slot in the front door. Like the first note they found upon their arrival these two also were identically cryptic and terse.

Immediately go to the telephone booth at corner of Ogden and 13th Street. Await my call the first note said.

Robert did so as commanded, and each time he heard the telephone ringing as he approached the glass cubicle. The voice on the line came across gruff and abrupt. First his caller insisted on rent payments every two weeks instead of every month; then came repeated demands to find work. "In whatever capacity you must find employment. In doing so don't go out of your way to make friends," and finally, "await further instructions," were the instructions of Mr. Oxnard.

Instead of sensing concern as most people would, Robert was thrilled with the mysterious calls. He even looked forward to the next one, basking somewhat in the attention and savoring a sense of participation in the cause, whatever cause that might be. It was obvious that he was being watched. His activities were certainly being monitored. The atmosphere in which he found himself brought him back to his days in Hungary. As a Freedom Fighter. Part of the

Movement. A Revolutionary. His life on the line. The drama was intoxicating. Robert was living that life again. He loved it and he would do anything to make it continue.

Robert didn't share any of these strange events or his escalating fantasies with Sophia. She went about her days mostly oblivious to it all, he believed, content with scrubbing and polishing until their home was spotless. Robert was glad and he gave her credit for stretching their meager resources to the maximum. She became a regular customer at the Goodwill outlet. In the end she applied her appreciable decorating skills to add just a touch of color and beauty to the interior furnishings of the little row house. Robert would arrive home each evening, tired and irritable from his day's futile job search but he would always find his wife cheerful and full of optimism that tomorrow will be the day.

When that day finally came and Robert shared the news about Rocky Mountain Vending Sophia broke down in deep, gulping sobs. Her raging emotions, her fear and anxiety internalized for so long now erupted as she fell into Robert's arms and her baby kicked hard to remind her of its presence. She had been brave, she told him, but terror had recently overtaken her. She was afraid. Afraid that he would leave her. Leave her alone with the baby. With no money, and no place to live. Why are we here? Why Denver?

"We came here to make our fortune," she cried. "But there were no jobs. It took you so long. Why were there no jobs?"

Could she trust him? Did he truly love her? "You're so quiet sometimes. Living inside yourself. Will things be different now? God, I hope so. Please tell me they will."

Robert held her close as her questions and tears gushed in a torrent. He waited for her to stop. To calm herself. He gently wiped the moisture from her cheeks. She sighed heavily. Her tension eased. He patted her belly softly.

"Of course, I love you Sophia and the baby. I am sorry if I've been in my shell. I promise, it's all over now. I am a new man. Things will be better. You'll see," he said, trying to comfort her.

"This is a good job. A good company. I work for a good man. You'll see. I will do good work and he will appreciate that. Mr. Carlson is his name. After a week or two, at most, I will get a raise. I will fix everything they have and make a lot of money. You'll see," he continued, his voice raising as he turned his attention from her to congratulate himself and introspectively boast of his accomplishments.

Bud stopped for a drink at the Branding Iron Lounge on his way home that evening. As he drank his scotch and soda he thought about the little man from Chicago with the bad leg and lizard skin boots. He found him strange, of course, but intelligent, intriguing, perhaps mystifying. He could not pinpoint it, but as he ordered a second round, Bud sensed a deeper, more complex makeup to the man than just a simple, run-of-the-mill mechanic in search of a regular paycheck. For some reason Bud thought he may have encountered a man unlike any other in his life. He had no real reason to doubt Robert's story, yet he remained curious, teetering on suspicion of his accounts of his past. Something about that accent was so distinctive. He thought to himself that he'd never forget it. Just a hint of Scandinavian or Polish, maybe German.

Well, hell, I'm no expert, and why do I care? As long as he does his job. Hold on. There also was that air of confidence, almost arrogance at his own abilities. Staring into his empty glass Bud determined he would put this Robert Kaye fellow to the test at the first opportunity and maybe spend a little time poking around to see what made the guy tick. Maurice will work his fingers to the bone, Bud chucked to himself as he ordered round number three, and *I'll make a point to find out more.*

37

No matter how hard Maurice Hilton tried to stump Robert J. Kaye with the most complex of all problems involving the electronic gadgetry that powered the machines that dispatched goods and games to Rocky Mountain Vending customers, the odd little man breezed through them with ease. It almost seemed to Maurice, a towering former Marine whose arms were covered with exotic tattoos and with a weathered face scorched from decades in the sun, that all Robert had to do was look at a malfunctioning device and it would fix itself.

"The little bastard can tear apart a pin ball machine and have it working perfectly in about the same time most of my mechanics take to change a blown light bulb," Maurice said to Bud at the end of Robert's first week on the job.

"He's the best I've ever had, bar none," Maurice added.

"Good to hear," Bud responded. "I had a good feeling about that guy when he first came limping through that door. Then he inquired, "I don't suppose he's any good movin' equipment around though."

"He's strong as an ox, but his bum leg makes it awkward for him to lift too much weight and carry his part of the load. That makes it dangerous for the boys on the other end, so I've told him all he has to lug around is his tool box," Maurice explained.

"Good. Well, for once we've got someone we can rely on who will carry their own weight sort of speak," Bud replied. "Tell him his raise will be in his next paycheck."

At closing time about three weeks later Bud was in his office inspecting a new coin counting machine. It had been left there for testing earlier in the day by a salesman who claimed it would spit out three ten dollar stacks of quarters in fifteen-seconds, all ready to wrap and take to the bank.

In a week's time on average well over twenty-thousand dollars in nickels, dimes and quarters passed through the fingertips of nicotine starved, music hungry, pool sharks and pinball wizards into the coin slots of Bud's machines and it took three good totally trustworthy secretaries six solid hours to sort out the slugs and count and wrap the real money. Banks of course would not take loose piles of coins. No matter how honest a depositor claimed a particular sack, weighing nearly fifty pounds, truly represented three hundred dollars in slightly used dimes, the bank teller always said, "Go wrap them." They all had to be in ten-dollar paper wrappers for quarters, five-dollar wrappers for dimes and two-dollar wrappers for nickels.

A royal pain in the ass to get that done, Bud heard one of his secretaries complain one day. He couldn't agree more. So, Bud was cautiously optimistic that this particular gadget would drastically lessen the tedious burden of coin counting allowing his secretarial pool to concentrate on more productive chores. More importantly, it allowed him to produce an accurate accounting of funds to reconcile against his inventory and machine play. If he decided to accept the salesman's pitch he would buy three and place all of them in his office, running morning, noon and night and taking a secretary, probably Mary Lou, only an hour by herself to wrap all the stacks.

"Looks like a real good one," Robert offered. "The only thing you need to worry about are the coil trigger springs. After a while they begin to stretch out a little and you might see two coins, mostly dimes because they're thin, slip through, with the machine counting only one. These counters have to be maintained regularly. If they are, they can be a life saver."

Robert was standing in Bud's doorway, hesitating before stepping through, hoping to be invited in. At the unexpected sound of his voice Bud looked up, paused to see who it was and said, "I suppose you know how to fix these things as well."

"Never have, but I've heard about them. I suppose I could figure them out if I had to," Robert replied.

"I suppose you could," Bud said, and then he asked, "What can I do for you?"

Robert remained in the doorway. His leg hurt and he wished he could enter and take a seat. "I just wanted to thank you for the raise. I've been trying real hard and was glad that you recognized my efforts. Like I said, I won't let you down."

"Well, you deserved it, Robert, and I am thinking as the days go by that you won't...let me down that is," Bud came back. "Oh, come on in and take a seat. Is there anything else?" He asked as an afterthought.

Robert was thankful for the invitation. He limped forward to take a seat opposite Bud who had moved the coin counter from his desktop to the credenza placed along the wall behind him. He sat waiting, sensing his master mechanic had something else on his mind. Just then Mary Lou buzzed Bud on the intercom to announce that she was leaving for the day and not realizing that he had company added, "I'll be home waiting for your call."

Bud's hand shot out to switch off the annoying squawk box before Mary Lou could say another embarrassing word. Robert pretended to ignore her announcement and was successful in stifling a smile at the thought of the boss apparently banging his secretary.

Bud had succumbed to the temptation and his decision had been gnawing at him ever since. Mary Lou proved to be as good in actual performance as she appeared in Bud's imagination but he was already paying a high price for her affection with two expensive meal tabs, a Saturday outing to Estes Park and an invitation to the Denver Symphony's performance of Mozart's Requiem, K. 626, the latter he promptly turned down despite her fervent protests. He ended up buying the extra ticket so she could take a girlfriend.

I'll be damn if I'll call her tonight, he pledged to himself in protest. Robert leaned forward in his chair, his pain subsiding and in a manner of seconds stunned Bud a second time by remarking, "I've gotten to know nearly everyone here at the shop so far and it seems to me that you're the smartest one of the whole bunch by far. You seem to be aware of things that go on, I mean, inside and outside the office. Sometimes I overhear you talking about things, like the economy, taxes and politics. I'd like to learn more about those subjects and was wondering if you would mind if I asked you questions from time to time or if I hear you talking about those things to other folks around here and my work is done, that I could also listen. If you don't mind."

Bud was surprised at Robert's humble request but he couldn't help from being mildly flattered at the compliment. He declared his modesty with, "Oh, come on, I really don't know those subjects very well. I do like to read and study and it is good to try to understand how the world around us operates, and who in this world is worthy of our respect; especially the politicians."

Bud watched as Robert seemed to take in his remarks as if they were as poignant as the Sermon on the Mount. His next thought was *is this character pulling my leg?*

After a few moments of silence Robert said, "I would really appreciate that. I've always been fascinated with, you know, current events but since I haven't had much of a formal education and since coming to America, I've tried to find someone, wherever I go, who will take the time to teach me, or at least let me hang around them so some of their intelligence might rub off."

"I thought you were from Chicago," Bud said somewhat taken aback by Robert's reference to heralding from outside the country.

Robert's instant reaction was to deflect the remark. He came back with what he hoped was a clever response. "Oh, you know what I mean. Chicago's south side. That's like coming from a foreign country. It's all full of ethnic groups, all sticking to themselves, speaking their own language, practicing their own religions, eating their own food, marrying each other. They all think they never left Poland or Italy or wherever they came from. It's just how I think. Until I left Chicago, I never really came to America. Know what I mean?"

"Yea, I guess so," was all Bud could say at first, but then he added, "I'm from Nebraska and if that ain't America I don't know what is."

They both chuckled and Robert stood to leave. Bud sensed with his abruptness in standing he was uneasy in continuing the conversation.

"Well, Mr. Carlson, err, Bud, thanks again. I'll be going now," Robert said as he turned toward the door.

"You bet, Robert, and if I feel the urge to stand up on my soapbox in the middle of the office I'll let you know," Bud replied.

With that as he got to the door Robert turned back to face Bud and with genuine look of curiosity. He asked, "Soapbox, what is a soapbox?"

"Oh, that's when someone gets up and rattles and rages on about some issue, or some person, usually another politician who they don't like and they hope to defeat in the next election. By standing there long enough – on that soapbox – they hope they can change the world somehow," Bud said.

"I got it," Robert declared, "Soapbox. I like that. Standing on a soapbox. Well, if I see you on one, I'll come running."

"You do that," Bud smiled. Robert was gone, hobbling through the doorway.

Chicago? Now I really doubt that. Slip of the tongue? Don't think so. Something tells me this guy's got some deep dark secrets, Bud thought. Just as long as he does his job, why should I care, Bud again concluded as he retrieved the coin counter from the credenza, placed it back on his desk and ran through another stack of quarters to test its precision.

Robert slammed his fist on the steering wheel of the old Chevy after climbing inside.

"How could I be so goddamn stupid?" he snarled out loud and this time he punched the hard metal dashboard, "To say something like that, something that could make him suspicious about me, when things were going so well. I can't believe it!"

Robert's hand now ached almost as much as his leg. He tried to calm himself, taking deep breaths and closing his eyes. When he opened them he saw Bud emerge from the shop front door. His overcoat was wrapped tightly around him. Robert watched him turn right and head up the Pearl Street sidewalk walking directly into a strong, frigid freak spring westerly head wind plummeting off the mountains and barreling through the cityscape canyons. Bud arched his back and lowered his head to take on the icy blast. Robert wasn't cold seated in the front seat of his Chevy. Oddly, he was sweating and still shaking in self-loathing. It took him ten minutes to relax sufficiently to turn the key in the ignition, shift into gear and steer for home.

His drive to Ogden Street took only about twelve minutes unless there was heavy traffic on Fourteenth Street and then it took him maybe five minutes longer. This night when Robert stopped at the traffic light at Logan and Fourteenth, he unconsciously glanced to his left and spotted Baby Doe's Lounge, a quaint looking little neighborhood bar Robert recalled that he and Sophia had walked past several times but had never entered. There was a tempting empty parking place right in front of Baby Doe's. On impulse, before the light turned green, he swung the little car in a tight U-turn to take the vacant spot before someone else did.

Robert was not a heavy drinker. Moderate to light was a good description of his habit. He abhorred being sick on alcohol and enduring the hangovers. He knew his limit and he seldom, except with Deborah, consumed more than he could easily withstand. He liked beer, especially the local favorite, Coors, and occasionally he would tolerate a glass of wine, usually a cheap sweet Zinfandel, which seemed to be Sophia's favorite. He hated port. It immediately gave him a headache for some reason. Robert didn't like drinking alone. If he drank he liked to socialize and he was especially fond of doing both with Deborah. He missed her terribly. They had not talked since her instructions to leave New Orleans, delivered with such urgency on that night that now seemed so long ago.

Robert also wasn't one who prowled around at night after work, lying to his wife about his whereabouts. He hadn't found a worthy drinking buddy friend so far, so it was easy to avoid the temptation of a long detour from his normal route home. This night was different. He needed a temporary refuge, time by himself to clear his head, and Baby Doe's seemed like the perfect place to do so, at least for a short while.

When he took his seat at the bar he yearned for her to be there beside him. Unconsciously, three times before he drained his foam headed beer glass, he glanced at the door childishly hopeful that Deborah might come walking through. He ordered a second glass from the cold tap and thought back again to his blunder with Bud, desperate that his cobbled explanation about Chicago's unique ethnicity had been sufficient to pacify him.

Midway through Robert's second round a man took the seat beside him. There were three empty seats at the bar on either side but the man still took the one next to him. Robert looked over at the man and was about to say that he preferred to drink alone but before he could, while waving at the bartender for attention, the man politely asked him…"Mind if I sit here?"

Robert gasped, nearly aspirating his beer. Oxnard. It was Oxnard. The man on the telephone.

In appearance the man was not at all what Robert had expected. His voice on the telephone echoed a vision of a huge individual, tall, muscular, broad shouldered with gigantic hands and feet. A ruddy face, scared and pock marked. Slick backed hair. Intense with a perpetually furrowed brow. Yellow teeth. A snarl on his lips.

This man, the real Mr. Oxnard, clandestine, mysterious and often rude, from the neck up looked like a kindly old Irish priest, or maybe an English literature professor. He was small in stature. Robert could tell that even though he was seated he was about the size of Mr. Roblinski. He had a round, smooth, gentle face with thick grey eyebrows that had almost grown together across the middle of his forehead. He wore round wire rimmed glasses and displayed a wisp of white hair, now nearly gone. From the neck down he looked different from a man of the cloth, however. Impeccably dressed in grey tweed. A three-piece suit with a plain silk vest and white shirt accented by a muted Harmony bowtie. Robert was too stunned to speak.

When the bartender arrived Mr. Oxnard ordered a scotch and soda tall. For a long time he didn't speak. Robert took deep breaths to calm himself again. Mr. Oxnard gulped down half his drink before turning to address the shaken and stirred person beside him.

"Robert, I'm so very glad to finally meet you," Oxnard proclaimed as if he had been told very little about Robert and had somehow forgotten that he had been watching him for the past two months like a hawk hovering over a scampering rabbit. "I must admit that I have been observing you from afar for a while and this is the first opportunity I realized that we might have a few peaceful moments together to get better acquainted," Oxnard added.

Robert was still somewhat in shock. Oxnard's voice was now curiously two if not three octaves higher than his speech over the telephone and when he first sat down. Now it was almost soprano in scale, even feminine it seemed. His newly adopted polite, almost demur demeanor wasn't helping Robert gain any insight into what was happening at that moment or what might happen in the next second. All he knew was this fellow was mighty able at abruptly altering his means and methods of communicating with other human beings, especially his barroom seatmate.

"I hope you like your new home," Oxnard offered. "I see that your lovely wife has decorated it quite nicely, using her unique skills to apply fabrics and color schemes that brighten the interior even in these dark and dreary winter days. Doing so on such a miniscule budget. I declare. I especially like the rose motif she selected for the bathroom."

It took a moment for Robert to realize that, *Christ; he's been inside the house! He's been in our bathroom!* Trying to shake the chill of visualizing this odd creature sneaking around like a burglar or perverted peeping tom, Robert next heard another proclamation that further unnerved him.

"That child of yours, Oxnard swooned, "I can just imagine how beautiful it will be. What wonderful parents you two will make. Do you prefer a boy or a girl, or does it matter?"

"I'd like a boy," Robert eked out while clearing his throat. "Excuse me, Mr. Oxnard," he now continued more clearly, "I am somewhat surprised to meet you this way. I have been eager to do so, as you might imagine. You just surprised me. I guess I didn't expect you, err, you know, to be like you are."

"Oh, my dear boy, I understand. I use my telephone voice sometimes when it's appropriate to, well let's say, establish a relationship with someone at the beginning. When I get to know that person better, and I believe I have gotten to know you well enough, I tend to exhibit my true self. I become comfortable in using my natural articulation," Oxnard said.

By this time Robert had collected his thoughts. He finished his second beer, which gave him a slight boost of confidence to try to redirect the conversation.

"Well, I'm glad you feel comfortable with me. I do appreciate your kind hospitality in renting us your house. Sophia has made it a home for now, but we realize, or at least I do, that it is temporary. I assume my time here in Denver is short and events, or perhaps opportunities, await that may require me to move on. I am prepared for that, Mr. Oxnard. I want you to know that. I am prepared for my assignment, whatever that may be."

At first, Oxnard did not respond to Robert's overture. He looked away as if Robert had disappeared or never been there at all. A strained silence fell between them for the longest time. The only noise was Oxnard chewing hungrily on the melting ice from his tumbler of scotch. Robert couldn't grasp the man's behavior. His anxiety returned. The silence was deafening. Frightening. Robert sensed he should remain quiet, or run for the door.

Finally, after as much as ten minutes passed, Oxnard turned back to Robert. His glass was dry. Not a sliver of ice remained. His expression was harrowing. Fierce. Intense. All outward signs of affability gone. His steel blue eyes bore into Robert's. He did not blink.

The coarse gravel voice returned when at last he uttered his cold harsh words. "You will never speak to me or anyone ever again about a task, an assignment you await, as you called it. Do you understand? You are to keep your mouth shut. You are to trust no one. Never bring up that subject again. To anyone. You will be told what to do and when to do it. You are to work; go home and fuck your pregnant wife and that's it. Do not try to reach me. I will contact you when the time is right. Meanwhile do as you're told or that little unborn offspring of yours may never taste the sweetness of his or her mother's tit. Have a pleasant evening, Robert."

Oxnard slid off the bar stool and in a slow, deliberate gait, walked toward Baby Doe's exit.

38

They named her Victoria. She was born on a Sunday morning. The sun was shining that day for the first time in weeks. Maybe that was a good sign, Robert thought. Robert liked the name. It was Sophia's choice. It had been her grandmother's name. Robert didn't think much more about it or his child or his wife for that matter. He had other things on his mind. It was hard in the early days and especially during the nights after bringing the child home. Robert needed his sleep. He was working long hours. Maurice had released him from shop duty and put him on the road as a roving repairman, hustling from a jammed cigarette machine at a downtown bar, across town to a record skipping juke box and back across the city to an out of whack pinball machine giving undeserved free plays. He was exhausted. At home, the baby never shut up. Sophia had to tend to her. He just didn't have the energy. To top it all off, Mr. Oxnard never left his mind. Not for a minute.

Each day when he rose from bed after a fitful sleep his dreams were not of Hungary or his father or the rebellion but of children crying and mothers nursing. Robert would stumble to the color coordinated bathroom half expecting, still in his groggy state, to find his be-speckled antagonist landlord lurking behind the shower curtain when he drew it back to twist on the hot water faucet. Each morning after dressing he went to the front door searching for a note slid through the mail slot waiting for him with more dreadful instructions. Not one appeared for the longest time.

Goddamn, what did I get myself into, was the nagging nonstop refrain Robert played through his troubled mind. Yet he got his work done. He got it done well. On Maurice's recommendation Bud gave him a second raise to one hundred dollars a week, plus he got permission to use one of the company repair pickup trucks during his off hours. He now drove it to and from work each day. There was a condition to the free transportation. If an emergency repair call came in, Robert was to respond irrespective of the time or day. Within the first week of having the flashy red Ford 150, Robert was called out twice, both times near midnight. Neither time did he get back to bed before three in the morning.

Robert's one reoccurring pleasure was the growing frequency of his conversations with Bud.

Except for the occasional visit to Mary Lou's cottage on Josephine Street Bud was alone much of the time after work. So rather than going home or risking the onset of alcoholism at one of the dives between his office and his home, Bud usually stayed late addressing paperwork, enjoying light reading for pleasure or testing the newest pinball machine or jukebox. His recent routine was sidetracked by Robert however, who increasingly became a regular after-hours visitor.

At first Bud was slightly irritated by his mechanic's uninvited presence and his endless string of questions. They ranged from the true weight of a bushel of corn, a subject Bud had little knowledge of and less interest in despite growing up on the farm and failing at commodities trading, to President Kennedy's triumphant ratification of the Nuclear Test Ban Treaty with the Soviets, a topic Bud took great pride in having studied in some detail. But as time went on Bud realized that Robert's companionship was not only tolerable, but enjoyable. He liked having Robert around for reasons other than his mechanical skills. He looked forward to their meetings.

Bud concluded that the strange little fellow had a true inquisitive intellect. As their sessions occurred predictably, as often as three or four times a week, Bud soon appreciated Robert's capacity to discuss an array of topics mostly centered on current events. There were times when Bud couldn't match the insight Robert could impart, and what began as occasions for Bud's quasi-lectures soon turned into full blown debates.

When that happened Bud would scramble to regain the professorial upper hand through independent research, which at times took him to a branch of the Denver Public Library. Bud subscribed to all the weekly news magazines and periodicals to fill in the gaps left by the local newspapers. He watched as many network newscasts as possible. He brought a television set to his office and even had the *Wall Street Journal* specially delivered. Embracing what now had become a friendship, Bud shelved his suspicions about Robert for the time being. Bud avoided further questions about Robert's past, accepting his shady descriptions of his childhood and work history as a private matter.

Everyone's got something to hide, Bud rationalized, so he thought no more about it.

The year 1963 was proving to be one that many wanted to forget. An avalanche of events. So Bud and Robert had a lot to talk about. Overseas, there was an uneasy calm. Khrushchev had quieted down after his humiliation over the Cuban Missile Crisis and he and President Kennedy decided it best to communicate more often so the secured telephone Hot Line was set up between the Kremlin and the White House for timely chats, with or without a crisis at hand.

At home domestic occurrences were spiraling out of control. The white heat of the civil rights movement was the main topic on everyone's mind. Whether you were for it or against it you couldn't ignore it. It was in your face. Everyday. Bud was one who accepted the inevitable. Integration was coming. So be it. Blacks and whites were finally making peace. Bud genuinely liked that. Bud cheered not too loudly for too many to hear for Martin Luther King when he dreamed his dream on the Washington Mall and marched in protest throughout the South over segregated schools and lunch counters.

Bud was repulsed by the bombing of the church in Birmingham that killed four black girls and he told Robert he hoped for an execution of the perpetrators, if the authorities ever bothered to pursue them. He hired a black applicant for a stock room position over a white candidate for no reason other than to prove to himself that his sympathy had manifested itself into action. He boasted about his decision in his next after-hours discussion with Robert. Their talk didn't go well. Bud was appalled at his new friend's reaction.

"Bud, you may fire me over this, but hiring that man was wrong. Just because he is a Negro shouldn't give him an advantage. It seems to me he got the job because you may have become one of those liberals like the Kennedys who are hell bent on mixing the races. America is fine just the way it is. Would you want one of your daughters when she gets older screwing some black dude because you and Jack Kennedy thought it was the right thing to force blacks and whites to mingle?" Robert spouted out, his voice quivering with emotion.

"Christ, man, what's got into you?" was Bud's immediate reaction. "Are you really some kind of crazy bigot? Look at you," Bud's anger growing. "Who are you to claim some rightful place in mainstream America just because you're white? I don't know if you are even a citizen. For all I know you're some foreigner who's far less American than Charlie Thompson, the black fellow I just put on the payroll. So don't give me your righteous bullshit like some Klansman coming in here with a white sheet over his head."

Bud was furious by then.

"By the way, don't ever mention my daughters like that ever again."

Taking Bud's wrath full force Robert sunk deep in his chair, trying to disappear. He had gone too far and he grappled in his mind for a placating response. How could he recover without lying about his true feelings? It wasn't worth losing his job over a philosophical stance he'd just recently adopted. Besides his newfound wisdom had been implanted and reinforced by people who selfishly forced him into exile for a cause they refused to reveal. Deborah was to blame. Clay was the villain, the racist, the Kennedy hater, not him. Mr. Oxnard, a demon by any measure. The most diabolical of them all.

Robert knew it was taking him too long to react to Bud's tirade. He was reminded of Fodor when Bud had risen from his desk chair and wagged an accusing finger at him as he raged. Robert's head spun.

"Please, Bud," Robert finally pleaded humbly. "I didn't mean it that way. I apologize about your daughters. That was wrong of me. I do have a problem with what's going on with the blacks. Maybe I'm afraid they are going to rise up in rebellion. You know. Armed conflict. Killing in the streets. Tanks rolling down Broadway. I couldn't stand that. I've seen too much of it."

Bud recoiled at Robert's remarks. "What the hell are you talking about? Who was killed? Killed by tanks? What have you seen? Where did you really come from?"

After a long pause Robert plunged ahead. He had nothing to lose at this point. If he told the truth it might help provide this man, someone he had grown to admire, a clearer perspective on his true makeup.

Two spellbinding hours later Bud knew it all. Nearly every detail. Roman's life from its beginning. His mother. Her plight and her early devastating death. His father. The dreams. Rudolph and the Uprising. The tank shell that shattered his leg and launched his destiny to be sealed by Fodor dragging him into the ditch. Then New Orleans, and Mrs. Dionne. Her eclectic assemblage of boarders. Their prejudices and odd couplings. Clarence and Bourdreaux. Deborah and Mrs. Claire. Miss Hattie and her dearly departed drunk and debased husband.

Of course, Roman and Robert both spent a lot of time on Deborah and the web she spun for them in and out of the abandoned ballet studio. Then there was Clay and the other first-name-only club members. The speeches that mesmerized him and changed his way of thinking. Expanded his mind. Made him whole. Mr. Roblinski played a minor role in Roman's tale for no other reason than perhaps Robert's need to protect the kind old man who gave him a chance and remained innocent and oblivious to it all. Just like he decided he would protect Bud if there ever were a need. He left out all there was to know about his real reason for leaving the Crescent City saying only he needed "a fresh start."

"Had run my course there, you understand, and now with Sophia it was time for us to leave all that behind and find our way together in some other place," Robert said, signaling the conclusion to his dramatic revelation.

Bud alternately laughed and choked back tears as Robert's epic was laid before him. Bud marveled how Robert told much of it with such verve. A passion that unmasked a deep scar that had mostly healed but still occasionally seeped puss when a new infection invaded his pores. Yet as both men fell silent to contemplate what had been said, Bud still sensed there was something more. A piece missing. A spoke removed from the wheel. Bud was sure there was another reason for Robert's departure from New Orleans and his embarkation in Colorado. Coming here was not by chance. There was more to it. Much more. What was it?

Another thing disturbed Bud about Robert's unveiling. Always when Robert told of Sophia and their journey to Colorado, he lost the ardor so clear in his rendition of other events. In his talk of Sophia, regardless of the context, Robert's voice would become slow, deliberate and monotone, losing its vibrancy. Long before this eventful night, Bud speculated that Robert lacked feelings for his wife, and their child was an afterthought. After tonight, he was sure.

"Well, Robert, that was amazing. Question is why didn't you tell me the truth in the first place? If what you now say is true I would have admired you more and suspected less about you from the beginning," Bud offered, expressing just enough consternation so Robert knew he still had some ground to make up.

"I don't know, boss. One minute I'm proud of what I've done and the next minute I'm ashamed. I guess when we first met I decided to hide it in hopes you'd never find out," was Robert's feeble comeback.

"You're the one with the loose tongue, slipping in those comments like you wanted me to question the bullshit story of Chicago. I must say this is strange. Hey, no harm no foul. I like you, Robert. You're a damn good employee. You may be a little off your rocker about politics and such, but all of us are welcome to our own beliefs. You just carry yours out there like you're a drum major leading a marching band. That's okay too. Just keep your prejudices to yourself. I don't want any beefs with Charlie or anyone else. If you've got a problem, bring it to me. If something's on your mind, whatever it is, bitch about it to me. I don't care whether its Kennedy's tax cuts or Denver's garbage collectors, leave it at the door, but if you can't, lay your political commentary on me and no one else. Got it?" Bud lectured.

"Got it, boss," Robert shot back with sincerity.

It was close to nine o'clock by the time their extraordinary evening ended. Bud went home shaking his head and wondering what might come next from his master mechanic. Whatever it was, he was sure it would be interesting.

Robert found Sophia and the baby Victoria sound asleep when he arrived home. He was glad about that. He didn't want to contend with either one of them tonight. He had his fill of probing conversations to last him a year. He didn't need Sophia quizzing him about everything from remembering to buy milk on his way home (which he forgot) to when he expected another raise. He was in no mood for her, or either one of them for that matter. He poured himself a tall glass of Coors from the can and ambled toward his favorite living room chair. When he switched on the light, there it was. Slipped through the mail slot lying just beyond the threshold. A plain white envelope. It must have landed there after Sophia had gone to bed, just in time for him to find it when he arrived. He stooped to pick it up. His hands shook and his mouth went dry. He gulped down his beer but was still thirsty. He sat and turned the unopened envelope over and over in his hands fearful of the message inside.

Finally he ran his finger under the envelope flap and plucked out the folded paper from inside. In the now familiar neat hand printed script it read:

The time is drawing near. Soon you will be on an important journey. Prepare yourself. You are to meet me tomorrow evening. Ship's Tavern. Brown Palace Hotel. Dress appropriately. I will not be alone. You must be. Seven o'clock.

39

Robert slept little that night, tossing, turning and pacing, obstructed by his thoughts and bothered by Sophia's soft snoring. Sophia was in the kitchen feeding their child when Robert walked in carrying a hanging bag with his only suit zipped up within.

"What are you doing with your business clothes?" She inquired when she glanced up at him, diverting her attention away from guiding a heaping spoon of rice cereal into the gaping mouth of Victoria who bellowed out for more the moment her mother halted the steady stream of mush sliding down her throat.

"I'm taking it to the cleaners," Robert answered unconvincingly.

"I just had it cleaned; maybe two weeks ago. I don't remember you wearing it since then," his wife responded with growing curiosity.

"Well, they didn't do a very good job. There're still spots on it here and there," was his contrived comeback.

"Do you even know where the dry cleaners is?" Sophia asked light heartedly, with the inflection of a friendly tease.

"What do you mean?" Robert exploded. "What are you trying to say? I don't carry my weight around here? Huh? Is that it? Well, let me tell you woman. I'm killing myself out there and all you want is more. More of everything. I can't satisfy you. You make me sick. I'm tired of this!" His voice rising to a screech.

Hesitating at the noise Victoria stopped chewing and burst into a wailing cry. Sophia sat there stunned, staring blankly into Robert's raging red face. His eyes were blood shot wild. He slammed his fist on the kitchen counter top sending the sugar bowl spinning to the floor, shattering and spreading its granular sweetness in a thousand directions. Before she could speak, he pivoted too quickly toward the rear door exit, but staggered with the unexpected shift of his weight onto his hindered right leg. He yelped in pain and almost fell. Instinctively, Sophia reached for him, but he swung his arm free of her grasp and caught her with a blow from his elbow square to the side of her head. She reeled back, seeing stars before her eyes. Robert regained his balance and turned back to see her slumped in her kitchen chair.

"God, I'm sorry Sophia. I didn't mean it. You have to understand that," Robert anxiously pleaded. He stepped toward her but stopped when she held up both hands to fend him off. She was weeping softly. His words meant nothing. He stood before her looking down as she buried her face in her hands. Victoria was in a frenzy by then.

"I'm telling you again, Sophia, I'm sorry," he yelled over the baby's din. "That's all I can say." With that he carefully turned on his painful limb, hoisted his suit bag over his shoulder and limped out through the kitchen door, slamming it loudly.

Robert spent his day in an agitated state. He regretted his morning tirade but justified his actions since they were directly linked to the pressure he was under. She would just have to understand, he said to himself once and then totally dismissed the incident.

Robert's sole purpose that day was to coast through it to its end and prepare for the meeting that night. He had to be mentally fit. Ready for anything. No distractions, particularly from his wife. He avoided contact and conversation with coworkers when possible and was thankful for finally being dispatched south of Denver to suburban Englewood on an afternoon service call. The work normally would have taken him twenty minutes to complete, but he turned it into a two-hour assignment that consumed the remainder of his workday.

To return to downtown he chose Broadway which would take him directly to the parking lot entrance of the famous old Denver landmark hotel, the location for his meeting. He stopped at a service station at the intersection at Alameda, and in the bathroom changed into his suit that was as clean as if it had been brand new. Sophia surprised him with the suit as a present for his thirty-third birthday a few weeks before. He'd never owned a garment like this before and was unsure why he needed one then. Now, however, he was grateful for her unintentional foresight. Tonight, bringing her back to mind while watching himself in the cracked bathroom mirror and struggling to tie his tie, he promised if things went well he would make it up to her. They would have sex when he got home and she would forget all about his kitchen fury.

Man, these boots of mine go real well with this suit, he smiled when he exited the dingy, foul smelling latrine.

The parking lot attendant at the Brown Palace Hotel did a double take at the suit, its occupant, and the well used in need of a wash pickup truck when he handed Robert his parking stub. Robert shot a nasty look back at him but smiled when he found a parking place right next to the elevator that ran from the subterranean level to the lobby floor.

When he stepped off the elevator into the opulent vestibule Robert looked up to gaze star struck at the stained glass dome ceiling that seemed to float above the room suspended by nothing but air. The silk oriental rugs gleamed under the dim light of the heavy brass lamps, their reverse painted glass shades sending a shimmering downward halo of multicolor glow. Heavy mahogany serving tables stood at the arms of luxurious leather couches and high back armchairs strategically placed throughout the expanse. A huge spray of bright blue Colorado columbines mixed with white orchards, their blooms as big a tea saucers, erupted from a four feet tall canary yellow porcelain vase standing majestically on a round tiger maple table adorning the center of the room. Crystal decanters glimmering with all conceivable varieties of liquors were carried gingerly in the hands of tuxedo clad cocktail waitresses serving the afternoon libations to Denver's elite. A quiet hum of conversation was heard, occasionally interrupted by the high-pitched clinking of expensive glass. Robert was immediately terrified. He felt naked, like everyone in the room was staring at his exposed crotch. He was thirty minutes early. It was only six-thirty. He couldn't stay in here, waiting. Looking like a fool.

Christ, I've got to get out of here. Then a sweet melodic voice came from over his shoulder with an unexpected request.

"Sir, please have a seat. What may I get you? We are serving a lovely pink champagne from France this afternoon. The new Tattinger vintage. Perhaps you would like one?"

Robert turned to look into the emerald green eyes of a spectacular Norwegian appearing blonde beauty. He stepped back, startled. He soon recovered and allowed his eyes to scan downward without inhibition to discover her tuxedo jacket unbuttoned seductively and fitting ever so provocatively over the perfect swell of her breasts.

"Please," she said again and in a ballerina motion swung out her arm and pointed to an empty couch. Robert obeyed her instructions without further hesitation. He sunk into the supple sofa and before he knew it she returned with a tall slender vessel filled to the gold-rimmed brim with a sparkling bubbly. He sipped it delicately after watching a woman across the room dressed in the latest Jackie Kennedy-style wool suit with matching pill box hat retrieve her glass and effortlessly bring it to her lips, pinky finger extended fashionably.

Robert almost dropped his glass when he tried the little finger trick. Yet he began to relax.

Yea, I belong here. Sure. I can do this, he reassured himself.

He set back into the leather and chopped on cashews and gulped down his champagne with abandon. He ordered a second glass and checked his Timex wristwatch. Seven zero five. He jumped to his feet and started across the array of Persian silk flooring. His waitress, full flute on her tray meant only for him, stepped into his path. He halted. She clinched her teeth in a not this time friendly smile and extended the delicacy to him to consume. "Not to be wasted, sir," she said sternly.

Robert grabbed the glass and swallowed the nectar in one swig. He placed the empty container on her tray. Her smile was frozen. She handed him his check. Robert immediately eyed the total and his bad leg nearly buckled. Twenty dollars!

All he had in his pocket was twenty-five and he had to save enough to get the battered pick up truck out the parking lot. He snatched the bill from his now nearly empty money clip and handed it to her. He ignored her extended hand, waiting for more. He stepped around her and kept walking, not looking back to see her rigid grin turn into a sneer nor to hear her muffled voice say, "Cheap son-of-a-bitch, I knew it."

Robert hobbled as quickly as he could through the lobby, around to his right toward the red neon script sign flickering over the entrance to the tavern's front door. He stepped into the brightly lit, pine paneled expanse decorated to delight any hearty seafarer, but few real ones ever came in since the place was eighteen hundred miles from the nearest salt water ocean.

The noise from the crowd inside was clearly in contrast to that which Robert had just escaped. It was nearly deafening. It took Robert a few moments to realize that the people around him were the real afternoon after work drinkers. They were loud and boisterous. Beer bottles clinked, raucous laughter and backslapping were rampant and a few stumbled hurriedly toward the men's room. It reminded Robert of a Saturday night on Bourbon Street yet these patrons were all dressed like him to some extent. The difference was most of their suits cost three times as much as his but Robert wasn't qualified to make that distinction. He scanned the room anxiously. He saw no one he recognized. He stood at the end of the bar and surveyed the premises again. Then he saw an arm rise from a man seated in the farthest corner, next to the window. The man motioned for him to approach.

Robert walked slowly in that direction. As he got closer he recognized it was Mr. Oxnard, again in three-piece tweed suit but this time a bright red bow tie accented his impeccable dress. He was leaning forward in his seat, speaking intently, inches apart from the face of a stranger across from him.

Robert stepped to the table. Without looking up Oxnard nearly yelled to be heard, "You're late!" and then rudely resumed his conversation. Oxnard's companion was listening fixedly and speaking infrequently, and like Oxnard did not acknowledge Robert's presence. Robert shifted his weight. His leg hurt. He needed to use the bathroom. Finally, Oxnard momentarily paused, and still not looking up, motioned to Robert to take a seat. Robert carefully sat and folded his hands in his lap. With the background noise, even now seated, Robert could not decipher the words of their conversation.

Robert studied the profile of the man with Oxnard. His face was angular. High cheekbones. Swept-back forehead. Deep set eyes. Small features. Sculptured nose and thin lips. Robert guessed he was about his age. His reddish brown hair looked to be thinning. His shoulders were narrow. His upper torso thin. He was rather unassuming and plain. He could be European. He looked out of place. He wore an open collared shirt under a light blue windbreaker jacket. He was smoking but he didn't appear to be savoring it. Perhaps out of habit. His drink was dark, almost black. Robert suspected it was a stout beer. Bitter. Robert hated that taste. He sat without speaking or being spoken to for a few more uncomfortable moments before his tablemates eventually stopped speaking to one another and leaned back in their chairs. As if he had just arrived, Oxnard first, and then his companion extended their hands to shake Robert's in surprisingly friendly gestures.

"So good to see you Robert," Oxnard said pleasantly. "Let me introduce this gentleman. His name is Lee. As has been our practice we do not use last names, except of course for me. You know I prefer greater formality."

"Ah, come on, Preston," Lee said, "Since we'll all be working together. You tell me you can trust this guy. Why not tell him?"

Oxnard appeared to cringe at the remarks but did not interrupt Lee from continuing. Turning to Robert, Lee said, "Name's Lee. Lee Oswald. Middle initial H. H is for Harvey. Lee Harvey Oswald. Don't like the name Harvey. Sounds like a circus clown name. I just go by Lee. You're Robert Kaye. Pleasure to meet you Robert Kaye. You and I are gonna be good friends."

40

Bud Carlson met Jeannie Holcroft at a dinner party at Marshall Goodpaster's house on a Saturday night in early July of that fateful year. Marshall lived on Josephine Street with his wife Danielle in a wonderful stone façade rambling one story ranch home, typical of the architectural style of the time and place, but the house was much bigger, by far, than any other on the block. When Bud arrived at the party that night he parked at the curb and for five minutes stared in awe at the huge structure before getting out of his car. The house looked as long as a football field.

Bud was amazed at seeing two painted white brick chimney fireplace spires that shot through the middle of the majestic peaked slate roof. A triple car side entrance garage sat at the end of a sweeping driveway. Through the picture window opened curtains exposed a multi-piece French provincial living room set on magnificent brightly lit display. A putting green like manicured lawn dissected by wide flagstone steps led up to the expansive multiple pillar supported porch and the double hand carved light oak with contrasting inlaid rosewood entry doors. The brass doorknocker depicted the head of a longhorn steer. It was so big that Bud could make it out from the street.

Bud was greeted at the door by a maid, apparently of Spanish origin, named Rosa who asked him to join twenty other people taking their seats on Chippendale style mahogany chairs placed around Danielle's exquisite twenty-four foot long black walnut dining room table. Bud realized he was too late for cocktails and had arrived just in time for the formal dinner seating.

An eight-foot round mass of mangled together deer antlers supporting thirty crystal light bulbs hung above the heads of Bud and Danielle's other guests. The chandelier cast a spattering of brightness that exposed every wrinkle in the faces of every heavily made up female and a few male faces as well. Bud was delighted to be seated next to a stunning beauty who introduced herself as Jeannie Holcroft. Miss

Holcroft was seated next to the portly Mr. Goodpaster who presided at the head of the table.

As the first course was served Bud discovered opposite his seat sat the wife of Marshall's stockbroker. Her name was Camilla Jones. Jerry Jeff Jones was her husband. Camilla pointed out that Jerry Jeff was seated far down the table and to the right. In nonstop banter Bud soon learned that through well timed, smart, low commissioned stock trading Jerry Jeff had made Marshall a lot of money over the years. Marshall acknowledged Camilla's account the first time but ignored her thereafter when she repeated Jerry Jeff's accomplishments for the second, third and fourth time to coincide with the serving of each course. Bud also had an extremely difficult time pretending to listen to Camilla's broken record stories through the five-course dinner. Alternatively he was trying to pay much more attention to Jeannie whom he hoped was trying to pay far less attention to Marshall and more to him, but Marshall was persistent to the point of being obtuse.

Bud knew Jeannie was to be in attendance that evening. Marshall had told him a little about her, leaving out a physical description and detailing only the fact that her presence was anticipated to "discuss a little business proposition." Marshall said Jeannie was majority owner of a hot new restaurant and nightclub in town called the Embers Lounge. He arranged for Jeannie to be there as his special guest and to meet Bud who had been designated as the lead salesman in their combined efforts to land "another big, fat flashy location contract."

To satisfy her customer needs Marshall speculated that Jeannie's club needed at least five cigarette machines, three juke boxes, a full sound system, six to eight pool tables and a solid line up of the latest pinball machines which would occupy a basement room that occasionally serves as the exclusive headquarters for a few private high roller poker games. "Friendly games, mind you, with stakes at levels to exclude the riff-raff," Marshall explained.

By the time coffee was served Bud was totally frustrated with Marshall hogging all of Jeannie's attention but he understood Marshall's motives. Jeannie was undeniably gorgeous.

Elizabeth Taylor gorgeous.

How could anyone resist her, Bud wondered, staring too long at her profile while Camilla's voice rose above the others to recount her husband's low commission transactions once again. Long, thick black as night hair, swept up in a fashionable twist, and secured by a platinum looking clasp sprinkled with settings of what Bud swore might be real deep red rubies. Bud estimated that when her hair escaped from the clasp it would cascade well past her shoulders. A slender neck yearning to be kissed. Her full lips covered pearly white straight as an arrow teeth. Her eyes were dynamic and radiantly blue. Her skin, darkened by a summer tan, glowed. Bud was captivated. She spoke in a Texas drawl that sent Bud's heart pounding like it hadn't in many years. Like it hadn't since Connie first took her seat at his drug store counter. She wore a shimmering red spaghetti strap dress. Her hands and fingers were long and slender. There was no wedding ring; instead an oval black onyx encased in a circle of silver. Glitter sparkled from the heaving tops of her breasts and disappeared down the crevice of her cleavage. She had a throaty laugh which was frequently exhibited to respond to the Marshall's torrent of jokes.

Finally Bud realized a gap in their conversation and he leaped in to fill it immediately.

"Texas, you say. Where in Texas?"

"Longview," she said. "Bet you never heard of it."

"Can't say I have. Bet you like Marshall's doorknocker," Bud predicted.

"Sure do. Family raised a few of them bovine beauties. Cut the nuts off some of them bulls myself," she boasted.

To that Marshall roared, Bud snickered and Jeannie swallowed Marshall's head salesman with her smile. Then without missing a beat, she swept her head from side to side to rivet the attention of both men at each elbow and said, "Let's cut the bullshit, gentlemen. I know why I'm here. Marshall, you're not gonna see me out of this dress tonight or ever for that matter. Your wife won't allow it, and neither will I. Bud, you might have that chance someday if you play your cards right. So with that out of the way, I want ten thousand dollars for placement and thirty percent of the take from all the machines. You can put as many of the latest makes and models at the Embers that you think will fit and rake in the most money. I will give you a one year contract, and if we make as much as we should, it goes to fifteen thousand at renewal."

Marshall looked disappointed and began to pout. Bud raised his hand to her chin and gently turned her head to face him.

"That dress will hang nicely in my closet, perhaps tonight, but not more than a week from now, I promise you. We'll give you seven thousand at set up, twenty percent of the cut, and twelve thousand at renewal if our gross take for the year exceeds forty thousand. You'll get the finest equipment in the world, and I'll service the machines myself."

"Deal," she said, "but you have to take the dress to the cleaners if you get too rambunctious."

"It will be my pleasure," Bud assured her.

Thus began Bud Carlson's second in a lifetime pull-out-the-stops raucous romance with a Cinderella beauty that saw her Prince Charming through a prism of practicality and personal fulfillment.

Jeannie Holcroft stood eye level to her new lover in all ways. In fact, in spike heels she was two inches taller than Bud. She matched his wit and wisdom whether it was childlike frivolity or dead serious debate. She could spot him drink for drink and still walk a straight line without faltering even in her three-inch spikes that shaped her long luscious legs like a handsome Tiffany vase. She clearly preferred beef over fish or foul and belched uninhibitedly when she washed it down with a cold glass of Coors. She preferred blue jeans and boots over slinky low cut gowns but was never without her gold beveled crystal faced Rolex and perfectly polished nails. Bud was enchanted to say the least, but this time he was cautious and wary. She picked up the tab as often as he did. He was along for the ride but always kept one hand on the door latch.

They spent countless hours together after that first night at the Goodpaster's, and by week's end as predicted, the red spaghetti strap dress had its special place, wrapped in a dry cleaner's bag, hanging apart from other garments in Bud's walk in closet.

Marshall threw in the towel after her brush off right before dessert and told Bud the next day he was damn proud of him in all respects. Bud and Jeannie gradually evolved into a fine couple. As the weeks went by they also became friends. They shared their pasts, their accomplishments, mistakes and failures, their guilt and regrets and their hopes and dreams to come. Bud told Jeannie just about everything there was to tell, especially his great love for his daughters and the hole in his heart over losing them. That story made her mad. She swore revenge and pledged to help pursue custody when she saw him cry through the tale at his first telling. She was fascinated with the saga recounting the rise and fall of "Bud the Commodities King," and quizzed him endlessly about how the trades are done especially in the cattle futures market.

She liked those things about Bud. She liked the fact that he took risks, but when he failed he paid his debts and scratched and climbed back out of the pit of financial ruin. He was like her father and her father had been the greatest man in her life. Up to that point.

Bud also learned a lot about Jeannie during those first weeks together. She too had been married before. A disheartening, disquieting, destructive event. Two children; one a daughter, beautiful and bright; the other, a son, she would not discuss. At first. Her daughter remained in Texas with her parents. Daddy helped her get out of the marriage and secured her majority ownership stake in the Embers.

"He gave me a clean slate. I won't let him down and I will pay him back every cent," she resolved. "My daughter will come here when I am on my feet."

"What about your son?" Bud pressed gently. "You don't say much about him. Will he come here as well?"

"He is a special person. My son is in a special place." That is all she would say.

When Bud arrived at work on the Monday morning a month after Marshall's dinner party Robert was waiting for him in his office. It had been just about that long since Robert was in to see his boss either on business matters or for their informal after work bull sessions. Bud missed those occasions. He noticed that Robert had recently appeared distant, remote, and even aloof. He was still performing well by all accounts but he was no longer engaging, or even engaged. Detached was a better word for his behavior. So when Bud walked in that morning and saw his prized mechanic seated in his office visitor chair he was pleased, thinking perhaps Robert was there to reconnect.

Before Bud could take his seat and seeming to ignore Bud's hearty "Good morning," Robert said flatly, "Boss, I need some time off."

Bud didn't appreciate either the rudeness of his rebuke of the greeting or Robert's stiff demand, so his response was equally direct. "You get two weeks vacation after you've been here a year."

Robert held Bud's angry gaze for a moment and then spoke with a different tone taking a less caustic approach.

"I'm sorry, Boss. I didn't mean to be impolite. I do wish you a good morning. I have been under a lot of pressure lately and some things are happening that make it necessary for me to travel a little. So I need to be gone for a week or two."

Bud reacted quickly with, "Is this traveling important enough for you to loose your job over?"

Robert responded with little hesitation as if he had been prepared for the threat. "Yes, I am sorry to say, Bud. If you need to fire me, I understand. I do think this opportunity is important enough to me to loose my job."

"Okay. I suppose I understand. What does your wife say about it? Do you have another job lined up?" Bud probed with growing curiosity.

Robert's acerbic demeanor returned with, "Leave my wife out of this. She has nothing to say about it. I need two weeks off beginning Wednesday. If you have to fire me, well, that's just the way it is. If not, I will be back to work two weeks from now. Let me know your decision." Robert rose from his chair.

Bud slammed his fist on his desktop. "Sit your ass down. Who do you think you're talking to? I like you, Robert. You're the best damn mechanic; maybe the best employee I have. I could tell something's gotten into you lately. You keep to yourself almost to a point of being a nasty little prick. That isn't like you. Maybe I shouldn't, and maybe it's none of my business, but I care about you and your family. I won't put up with your attitude but if you tell me this traveling is all that important; well, maybe we can work something out."

"I would like to do that very much. I think I've been a good employee. There are a couple of other guys that can fill in for me while I'm gone. I've tried to train them well," Robert offered, again attempting to ease the tension and present a solution.

"Okay, let me think about it. You have to know you really pissed me off here. Everyone can be replaced, and life can go on here without you, if we have to," Bud reminded him.

"I know that, Boss, but what I have to do only I can do. No replacements where I'm going," Robert said with a resolute look while rising from his chair to leave.

"Shut the door on your way out," Bud ordered.

Part VI

Dallas, Texas
September 1963

41

Two weeks passed. Robert didn't show up for work when he promised on that Thursday. Considering the conversation he had, Bud didn't expect him to. It would be about four weeks, not two, before Bud heard from Robert again. Following Robert's demand for unscheduled leave, Lee Harvey Oswald and Robert Kaye would be in the company of one another almost constantly. It would prove to be an ordeal for both of them, but they had no other choice. They were acting under the orders of Preston Oxnard and many others.

Oswald and Robert's long assembly was necessary for them to learn, rehearse and re-rehearse a host of actions that lead up to a series of events scheduled for an upcoming Friday, a targeted date less than three full months into the future. Their days together were sheltered away interrupted occasionally by Oxnard and two other men who would visit for short periods of time. These people would arrive and leave unannounced, saying little, observing and whispering among themselves but never contributing to the training process. Training was left up to Oswald. Robert was allowed to return home to see his wife and child a mere three nights out of thirty. Sophia stopped asking about his whereabouts after his first week away.

Their meeting place and Robert's home away from home was at the Saddleback Motor Lodge on East Colfax Avenue near the entrance to the massive Stapleton International Airport compound. Robert found this area of Denver dingy, dirty, and depressing. He quickly discovered that it was mainly populated by pimps, prostitutes, and protagonists hustling, begging and bartering for all sustenance of life. Oswald said he viewed the atmosphere amusing and he seemed to Robert to thrive on the wanton debauchery of its inhabitants.

For most of each day Robert and Lee were enshrined in two adjoining one-room units. They worked in one room and slept in the other. The twin but mismatching beds in their work room were dismantled and mattresses lifted upright and pushed aside to make room for the maps, briefing material and other paraphernalia they spread out on the floor and on a makeshift plywood desk top supported by several of the straight-back chairs decorating the space. At night they ate at a local dive called Ruth's. Oxnard prohibited drinking, so their nights out after dinner consisted mainly of short walks up and down the teeming sidewalks of Denver's main East-West corridor. The heat was unbearable. Temperatures regularly rose past one hundred degrees during the day and cooled only into the eighties at night, unusual for a city known for its mild summer days and cool nights. There was no air conditioning in either of the rooms. They bought three rotating fans in a futile attempt to circulate the stifling air.

As Robert became more familiar with the area, he realized that he was in the only section of town that Marshall Goodpaster blacklisted from offering his vending machines. He remembered Maurice telling him one day that East Colfax was off limits and that Marshall and Bud decided some time ago to let their competitors put up with the pried open, pilfered machines which were easy pickings for the junkies who, they agreed, would sell their mothers for a carton of cigarettes and a pocket full of quarters from a smashed up pinball machine. The first time Lee and Robert had dinner at Ruth's Robert noticed the glass broken on the out-of-order juke box and a padlock securing the dented metal frame of an also malfunctioning cigarette machine.

Good decision Bud, Robert thought at the time.

The rent on their rooms was prepaid by Oxnard for a month. At the beginning of their strenuous sabbatical both Lee and Robert were given a thousand dollars each, all in one hundred dollar bills. At the end of the four weeks each of them had plenty of money left, but Robert a little more than Lee because one night Lee paid top dollar to Cherish just to prove to her that he and Robert weren't "mangy little queers" after all. Cherish was a regular at the street corner where the Saddleback stood, and each night before Lee tried to prove her wrong she would yell from her post under the bright street lamp the epithet littered accusation while they were on their way to Ruth's for dinner. Lee also had to pay Robert ten dollars for the use of their sleeping quarters, and to withstand the genuine groans and grunts from Lee and the contrived ones from Cherish during their act, which lasted a little less than fifteen minutes. When she finally left to resume her station

Lee was sound asleep, snoring loudly, but Robert was kept awake again by the sound of aircraft on final approach to Stapleton's runway three-right.

The Saddleback also stood exactly in the flight path of the only East-West landing strip that Denver's premier airport had to offer.

Late at night about thirty-six hours before Oxnard told them they had successfully completed this part of their preparation, the telephone rang causing Robert to bolt upright out of a dead sleep and scramble for the bedside receiver. It was the only time since their fleabag motel encampment that the telephone had rung in either room. Robert's heart was a runaway when he spoke sharply into mouthpiece.

"Who is it?"

"Robert. It's me. Deborah. I'm sorry to wake you. Are you all right?"

Robert was still in a sleepy daze, and right then knew beyond a doubt that he was dreaming. He started to act on that conclusion and moved to hang up the phone when again he heard,

"Robert. It's Deborah. I know you're there. Talk to me. Don't hang up. I need to know that you're okay. Everyone here is so proud of what you're doing."

Robert swung his legs out to perch on the edge of the bed. He stared into the receiver he had pulled away from his ear. Finally he mumbled, groggy and unsure, "Deborah, is that really you?"

"Of course it is you silly man. God, I have missed you Robert. You don't know how much."

Robert shook his head in disbelief and in a clearer voice asked, "How did you find me? How did you know I was here?"

"What the fuck is going on?" snarled Lee stirring in the bed beside his.

"Nothing. Go back to sleep," Robert gently instructed.

"Oxnard didn't tell us anyone would be calling. That better be one of the good guys," he warned, also now in a clearer voice.

"Don't worry," Robert assured him, "This is okay. It's one of us. Now go back to sleep. I'll finish the call in the other room. Hang up the phone when I get there."

Robert walked quickly to the adjoining unit and picked up that receiver. He heard the click as Lee hung up the other phone.

Even though the room was heavy with suffocating heat Robert felt a chill when he closed the door to the sleeping room to shut Lee off from his conversation. Was it fear or anticipation or both? He wasn't sure. He did know he was thrilled to hear her voice again.

"Robert, are you there?" she asked with an uneasy edge.

"Yes, I'm here," he responded controlling the urge to shout with joy. Then with seriousness, he asked. "Deborah, what did you mean by what you just said, that we are so proud? Who's we?"

"Good. Thank God," she said, ignoring his question.

"Deborah, answer me. How did you find me?" Robert was stern this time.

"Robert, I don't have to remind you that you shouldn't be asking me those questions. You know I can't give you the details about our people."

"What I can say is that I am still in New Orleans. I am still working in the District Attorney's Office, and I'm still meeting with Clay and David who also send their best to you, along with the others. They let me know where you were. They trust me with the secret. I am aware of the plan. They trust me with that too," she added after a slight hesitation.

Robert was silent for a moment and then responded with, "Okay, I understand. I am glad to be talking with you. I was afraid I would never be able to again. Somehow it was like you were cut off from me for good. Like you died or something."

"Oh, Robert, I'm so sorry that it had to happen the way it did. The cops were getting close and we couldn't let them get near you. You were chosen. The chosen one for the plan. We couldn't let anything happen to you. Now it's working out, as it should. We made sure your trail was cold. There is no trace. Still, I hate to be away from you. To see you go off like that. With that woman. Now you have a child with her. Do you love her?" The emotion in her voice rising as she spoke.

Again a silence as Deborah's question hung in the air, eventually to penetrate his pores, sending his mind reeling as no one but she could do.

"Answer me Robert, do you love her?" she repeated.

"Leave it, Deborah. Just leave it alone. Look, I've been at this, whatever it is…training…for over a month now. I'm living with this guy in this rundown motel. It's hot. It stinks. The food is crap. He's strange and he thinks he's some kind of super hero soldier, once calling himself a master mercenary," Robert said, paused, and then continued.

"All he likes to talk about is high powered rifles, whores he's had, and living out his days in Guadalajara, Mexico. We work all day, studying maps, names of places, landmarks, buildings, highways and back roads. I've learned to speak some Spanish. I know more about Mexico than most Mexicans, and I can walk the streets of Dallas,

Texas, blindfolded even though I've never been there. I had to quit a job I really liked. I met some good people while working there who've been good to me. Yes, I'm lonely and frustrated, but I am committed to this, whatever it is, whatever our mission is. I'm committed."

"You've answered my question, Robert. I know you are," she responded.

Then, returning to a pure matter-of-fact tone, she said, "Look, they said I had only ten minutes to talk with you, so I have to go. We know you are committed. We believe in you and we believe in him. Lee is dedicated. We are all dedicated. Someday, Robert, someday soon, if all goes well we will be together again. That is the long-term plan. You will be far away with new names and new identities. You will be rich. Comfortable and living in luxury. If you want me I will come to you. Freely. I will be your reward.

"Goodbye Robert. Your time; our time is drawing near." The line went dead. The dial tone humming, overtaking the sensuous, intoxicating message contained in her last few words. Slowly, hesitatingly, he replaced the receiver in its cradle. She had him again. She would never let him go. He would do anything for her. Now his mission had greater purpose.

Three days later in the early morning hours Oxnard tapped lightly on their motel room door to announce his arrival and command their departure.

"You're going to Mexico," he announced, as Lee and Robert were each packing their meager belongings. They were under Oxnard's watchful eye as he stood by the open door to their rundown unit. It was a rare cool, rainy day, the first since they had been holed up in their dank dungeon.

"Finally the weather's broke and it's almost pleasant here and you tell us it's time to go," Lee chided, but pleasantly, for once attempting humor and cheerfulness. Then he began to question Oxnard more seriously.

"Why not Dallas?" Lee asked. "From all the information we have on the place, I thought we'd be going there. Besides, Christ, it must be six weeks, maybe more since I seen my wife. You remember I left her there right after we moved in so she's a stranger to the town much like me. Unless she's spent it all she's got plenty of money right now, but I'll bet she's lonely. I really wouldn't mind seeing her," Lee added as an afterthought.

"You'll see her in plenty of time, but it's too soon for you to go back to Dallas. There are preparations to be made in Mexico. Dallas is a couple of weeks off, maybe more. There are people in Mexico, including in Mexico City, whom you need to meet. They will be there to help you." Then Oxnard added with sneering condescension, "You think she's lonely just because you're not around. Maria's attractive enough. She's probably taking good care of herself. Don't give yourself too much credit."

Robert closely eyed Lee for a reaction to Oxnard's spiteful verbal backhand, but to his surprise, all he heard coming from Oswald was a resolute chuckle and..."You're probably right. She's okay when she fixes herself up which ain't very often. Maybe she's gettin' better at it now that I been gone. Damn, I did do her a favor when I got her out of Russia, but nobody ever said I owed her the rest of my life."

Then Lee turned to Robert who was gathering all the papers strewed around the room and prodded him with.... "What about you, Kaye? You goin' back to your wife when all of this is over? Is your plan to dump her in dirty old Denver and meet up with that hussy who called you the other night to lick in your ear over the telephone?"

Before Robert could utter a word in reproach Oxnard exploded with...."What the fuck are you talking about? Who called here? Who called for you?" His fury showing in his contorted face.

Robert recoiled at the small man's assault, but quickly regained his ground with a bold response to which he even surprised himself. "First, I don't have to answer to you for everything I do or people I talk to. She's one of us, know it all. Deborah from New Orleans. She called with her support and encouragement, representing the people down there who are behind us."

"Oh, I got it," Oxnard responded, trying but failing to keep his rage at its peak. "The blonde Norwegian bitch you were fucking down there before they ran you out of town with your pregnant girlfriend and sent you here for me to look after."

Robert lunged menacingly toward his antagonist. Sensing a breech in the ranks and perhaps even a mutiny Lee wisely leapt into Robert's path just as he bolted toward the door where Oxnard once stood. Lee's quick reaction caused Robert to hesitate momentarily. Pausing slightly before attempting to sidestep Oswald, Robert growled at Oxnard with... "I've had enough of you, you little bastard. I've proven myself to you and the others at every turn. I deserve to be here and I deserve your respect. It's none of your goddamn business about her, my wife or anybody else as long as I do my job."

Clearly outside the room with plenty of optional directions to run if needed, Oxnard was stunned into silence.

"Okay, hold on there friend," Oswald cautioned. "Both of you are right. Robert, these people; the one's we're working with to accomplish our little task do need to know all they can about us. Whenever something like this happens, they're gonna get real nosey. There's a shield around us right now to protect themselves and us. It's there to make sure we get the job done and get out cleanly. Undetected. Home free. Out there, you know, flying like an eagle. So he has a right to know about your lady friend, your wife, your child, everything. That's how they work. So put up with it."

Lee then turned to Oxnard who had cautiously stepped back into the doorframe.

"Preston, you don't have to be such a prick about things," Lee began his gentle lecture. "This guy here is a little more sensitive about things than I am. He don't like everybody knowin' every time he goes waggin' his pecker out there in the wind. This woman, Deborah's her name, right Robert? Well, she's apparently big down there in New Orleans. High up in the organization. Trusted. Respected. Works inside the DA's office. Can keep law enforcement off track if necessary. You know she helped him get out of town when things heated up on him there. She got this guy involved in the first place. So we should be thanking her. You need to trust him, Preston. I do. So should you. Right? About his wife? I get the feeling he's not made up his mind about her so let's just leave it at that. I suspect she'll get some money just like Maria, and that should be enough to keep her quiet. So let's kiss and make up. We got a lot of work to do.

"Mexico awaits! Andale!"

They left their adjoining motel rooms spotless. Every scrap of paper, boxes, cartons, pencils, pens, markers, even tissue and toilet paper were wrapped in bags and burned in the cement incinerator in the rear motel parking lot. They swept the frayed, worn carpets, scrubbed the cracked linoleum floors, polished the chipped furniture with paste wax, and washed the grimy windows. When they were done not a trace of their month long habitation remained. No fingerprints within miles. The next morning when the housemaid arrived to clean she sat on the creaky bedsprings bewildered, thinking she had already cleaned the room but forgot that she had.

Robert called Sophia shortly before they boarded their flight to Houston where their layover would be an hour before going on to Mexico City. He was standing at an airport pay phone next to the Western Union booth. He had just wired a thousand dollars into a new checking account he opened in her name. The money would be credited in the morning.

"Sophia, this is Robert," he said evenly.

"I know who it is," came her gruff response.

He hurried to get it all in. "I am sorry again but I won't be coming home for a while longer. I will be traveling. In the morning in a checking account at the bank in your name only will be a thousand dollars. Pay the rent. Buy yourself and the baby something. How is the baby, by the way? When I get back we will talk. There will be more money for you. I promise. I don't know when that will be but I will call you and we will talk." He ran out of words and purpose.

She was silent for a moment.

"I went to see Mr. Carlson. He is worried about you. You have been irresponsible. A bad employee. He was fair to you. Gave you a job. Helped us when we had no money. Then you walk out on him. He's a good man. You should apologize. You hurt his feelings," she spoke haltingly.

She continued. "I do not care any more, Robert. My baby is fine. She is beautiful. She doesn't know who you are. Neither do I. This is okay. You are a stranger in my house now. A burglar in the night. You steal from me. You take my heart. You violate me. Mr. Carlson will help. He's a good man. He met my daughter. He says she looks like his daughters when they were babies. Goodbye, Robert. Talk is over."

The line went dead, humming in his ear like a time not long ago. He hung up the receiver, checked his receipt for the money wire and walked to the gate where Lee Harvey Oswald waited.

42

Sophia had not told Robert the truth about seeing Mr. Carlson on just a single occasion. She and her child had become regular fixtures in Bud and Jeannie's lives since Robert disappeared. Bud opened his arms and his wallet to the forlorn, desperate woman during her first tearful meeting in his office. From that point on she and the baby Victoria occupied much of Bud and Jeannie's spare time together in a generous attempt on their part to fill the void left by Robert's absence.

Bud was astonished when Sophia arrived unexpectedly at his office to tell him about Robert's call and the cash hitting her bank account.

"He called. How do you say? Out of the blue," Sophia gushed as she rushed into his office. "He sent me a thousand dollars. It's in my bank account. I checked this morning."

Bud shook his head in disbelief as her latest tale sunk in. "A thousand dollars?" he replied. "Now where do you think he got that kind of money?"

"I have no idea, Mr. Bud," she responded. "I don't really care. I need the money. I can stop begging from you. He said there would be more. Maybe he will be true this time. He gives me money to live on. A good sign. Maybe I should take him back when he comes. Maybe he will be good to me this time."

"Sophia, don't worry about asking me for help. What you need to worry about is you and your child. Can you really ever trust him again? Will he hurt you again if you let him come back; if he ever does? I say take all the money you can from him, but don't spend it. Keep it in the bank. Spend the money I'm giving you instead," Bud earnestly instructed.

"Mr. Bud, he said I could spend it. I am ashamed coming to you. As a beggar. A hobo. I would rather sell myself on the street than ask you for more." She began to weep softly.

"Don't be ridiculous. Stop it now, Sophia. Now listen." He was stern with her now. "We don't know where he's getting the money. It may be stolen. He may have fallen in with bad people who are paying him to do bad things. We have to be careful. If he calls again and offers you more money, take it, but don't spend it. Do you understand?"

She wiped the tears, blew her runny nose, and sighed heavily.

A child, just a child, Bud though as he sat watching her seated across from his desk.

Finally she spoke. "Okay, Mr. Bud. "I will do what you tell me. I won't spend the money and I will take from him if he calls again. You say I must be careful. Yes, I will. I promise. I will tell you if he calls again."

"Good. Mary Lou has a check for you. It's enough to last you a couple of weeks. You call me or call Miss Jeannie any time. You know our numbers. When you are ready Miss Jeannie still has a job waiting for you if you want. You can either be a waitress or a hostess to start. Take your pick. We can arrange for someone to take care of the baby while you're working. Just let us know." He rose from his desk chair hoping she would get the hint that it was time to adjourn.

"Thank you, Mr. Bud. Someday I will pay you back. I will. I will call Miss Jeannie today. I am ready to work. It will be good for me. Work will let me think about other things. You'll see. I will be a good worker," she vowed.

"I know you will," he acknowledged.

After she left, Bud called Jeannie to tell her the latest episode in Sophia's continuing plight. For some odd reason he couldn't shake his sense of obligation to the woman and her child. Jeannie questioned him about it, finding it strange that he would commit his time and resources so completely to them.

"I don't know," Bud told her, "she's been abandoned with a child. She's lonely. She's scared. Kind of like I was. You know, kicked in the teeth by someone you trusted; someone you loved; someone you never thought, for a moment, would do that to you. Since I can't help my own kids right now, maybe this is how I can make up for it."

From that point on Jeannie's questions stopped and she was equally supportive of Bud's decisions about Sophia and her baby.

Three weeks passed. During that time Sophia began work at the Embers. She opted for an evening shift hostess slot in the main dining room. She told Jeannie she was not quite ready for the challenges of waitressing. Too many things to remember all at once, she said. However, she hastened to add that she hoped to advance to that position as time went on.

Things were quiet for a time. Days went by for Bud without having to deal with the nagging burden of Sophia, her child and her wayward husband. He concentrated on expanding the business and his devotion to his lover.

Then early one evening came a frantic call from Sophia. Her words were borderline hysterical. "He called me again, Mr. Bud. He called me here at the restaurant while I'm working here. He said he would try to see me soon. It sounded like he is close by. Maybe he is. Do you think he's come back? He asked if I needed money. I said yes. He said we would give me five thousand dollars this time."

Good God, Bud thought, this is getting stranger by the minute.

"Mr. Bud, are you there?" she asked fearfully.

"I'm here, Sophia. How did he say he would get the money to you?" Bud asked.

"He's coming to give it to you to give to me. He said it was cash. He is giving you the cash money," she replied.

Now, I've heard it all, Bud said to himself. Either this is a joke or this guy's stepped into something big.

43

Bud absolutely loved the new 1963 Ford Thunderbird convertible. The sleek lines, the happy face chrome grill, the scoop on the hood, leather seats, swing away steering wheel, wide white wall tires, air conditioning and the Kelsey Hayes 42 spoke chrome wire wheels. Bud couldn't get over the big round taillights, and he preferred the two-seater with the removable vinyl tonneau cover. That engine, that big, bold 340 horsepower, triple carburetor police interceptor engine. He was smitten. He wanted one badly.

So he was awestruck when he arrived at his office on that unusually warm October morning and saw the sparkling, see-your-reflection-in-the-black-paint, brand new, still with the temporary license plate tags, wire wheels and all, classic Ford-made machine parked at the curb outside his front door. He stood and gawked at it for ten minutes, circling it several times, inspecting every inch. The convertible top was down, again a rare occurrence for any driver touring Denver in the early morning hours of most autumn days. No one was around the gleaming beauty. Bud knew whoever owned it must be stark raving mad to leave a chariot like this unattended. Even the windows were down. There was a large duffel bag abandoned on the front passenger seat.

"Like it?" The questioning voice came from over Bud's shoulder as he stooped to gently pass his hand along the right rear fender skirt. He immediately recognized who had spoken. Bud stood and slowly turned to face a grinning Robert Kaye who was leaning in the doorframe of the main office entrance.

"I should whip your ass," Bud angrily snarled.

"Now, now. Come on, Mr. Bud. I come in peace," was Robert's attempt at a soothing response.

Bud started toward him somewhat threatening. Robert instinctively held up his hands to ward him off. Bud stopped a few paces away.

"Look, I'm sorry, Bud. There's no excuse for what I've done. I've treated everyone important to me very bad. I know that. I'm trying to make up for it as best I can with money for Sophia and the baby. She will never understand. All I can do is try to make her comfortable."

Controlling his ire, Bud started in with the questions. "Where have you been? What is this with the money? How could you just up and leave, kicking your wife and baby into the gutter like you did? I thought you were a better man than that. Have you no conscience, or compassion?" Bud paused trying to think of more barbs to hurl.

"Bud, you have to listen to me. I can't; no, I won't tell you anything. Frankly it's none of your damn business. You are my friend. I trust you. That's why I'm here. I know you probably won't do this for me, but maybe you will for Sophia and her daughter."

Bud's rage surged uncontrollably. He grabbed Robert's jacket lapels and jerked him close to within inches of his contorted face. "You son-of-a-bitch. She's your daughter! She's yours! You're responsible for her. How can you deny that?"

"Take your hands off me," Robert warned. His face promising retaliation. "I don't want any trouble from you Bud."

Not out of fear; rather resigning from a fruitless situation, Bud loosened his grip and stepped back. Calmly now, he said, "You're right Robert. It is none of my business. You do what you have to do. I took your wife and child under my wing when you split, and they've become sort of my latest project. Yes, its charity. What's it to you? I had no right to intrude. I think you are a little prick for what you've done, and by the way, I don't care if you're the best damn machine mechanic in the world, you're not getting your job back. You're fired." Bud added with a menacing grin of his own.

Contentious, Robert smiled back. "I don't want my job back." Then turning increasingly serious, he added, "I am leaving town again soon. Before I go I wanted to ask you to do something for me. Really, it's for Sophia, the baby and me."

"Before you do that," Bud interrupted, turning back again to gaze upon the dream machine, "You can't tell me this wonderful thing is yours."

"It sure is. It's mine. Bought it two days ago. Right off the show room floor. A dealer down in Albuquerque. Drove it up here yesterday. Set me back fifty-three hundred bucks with all the options," Robert rattled off with pride.

"Christ, what a beauty," Bud sighed.

"Want to go for a ride?" Robert offered.

"No," Bud responded, shaking off his boyish lust for the Ford. "Okay, Robert, what do you have on your mind? What do you want from me?"

After Robert drove off, squealing the tires for effect and probably a little in-your-face snobbery, Bud moved behind his desk and sat uncomfortably to contemplate Robert's wildly incredible solicitation.

Sitting at the bar at the Ember's one evening a month before, Bud struck up a conversation with a man who called himself Max; Max Nedbalski. Max was a big man, possibly six foot three. His frame was stout and rigid. Hands and feet were enormous. His eyes were steel grey and his face gentle in a relaxed state but one knew fierceness lurked, when needed, behind a disarming smile. Max turned out to be a twenty-year veteran Denver police detective currently assigned to the robbery and burglary squad. Max and Bud had a pleasant two-hour conversation while Bud waited for Jeannie to get off work and for Max to slowly but inevitably become stinking drunk. He was off duty, so it didn't matter, but when Jeannie finally took a bar stool seat beside Bud to rest her aching feet, they soon decided there was no choice but to drive Max home and walk him safely to his door.

His arms slung around both their shoulders, Max staggered up the stairs, onto his porch and into the awaiting arms of his angry but happy he was home wife, Linda. He bid his faithful escorts farewell for the night with a promise to, "Be at your service if you ever need me."

Later during the day of Robert Kaye's unexpected rise from the shadows Bud decided to call Max with a question.

"Could you run a trace on a new car for me to see if it's stolen?" He tentatively inquired.

"Sure, my friend, just give me the details," came Max's friendly response.

"It was supposedly bought in New Mexico," Bud added.

"No problem," Max reassured him. "We've got this fancy new system that helps us communicate with departments out of state damn near as fast as the blink of your eye."

"That would be great," Bud said and then plunged ahead. "Could you also tell me if a guy is wanted for anything; like if there is a warrant out for him, or if he's a suspect on a robbery or something like that?"

"Now that's gonna be a little more complicated and probably take more time, but I'll try; just give me the facts; just the facts man,"

Max chuckled at his feeble attempt to parody the famous line from the ever popular *Dragnet* television series.

Two days passed before Mary Lou told Bud there was a police detective on the phone for him.

"Nothing, Bud," Max began, "there's nothing on this guy at all. We checked all the aliases. He's clean. The car was paid for in cash. One hundred dollar bills, according to the dealer in New Mexico. He even prepaid the license plates and bought insurance for it from a broker who works with the dealer. All paid for in cash. We're still checking with Immigration, like you suggested, to see if he's in the country illegally, but I doubt if those monkeys will come up with anything. They wouldn't know if Khrushchev himself was askin' for asylum," again chuckling at his own stab at humor.

"I'll be damned," Bud said. "I would have bet he was trailing dirty laundry somewhere, but if you say he's legit, who am I to question?"

"I didn't say he was legit. I said there's nothing on him right now. That could change tomorrow. If he's already done something it could be that the good guys haven't caught up with him yet," Max explained.

"Tell you what. If you see him again; if he wants to meet you or tour you around in his fancy car flashin' Ben Franklins, you let me know. I'll show up as a casual guest and we'll see how quick we can shake him down," Max offered.

"That's a deal. I really appreciate this Max. I really do. I'll call you if he comes around again. We'll do a number on him," Bud boldly promised in response to Max's gesture.

They hung up with Bud still debating whether it was wise to leave out the part when, before speeding off, Robert unzipped the duffel bag in the front seat of the black 'Bird to reveal piles of tightly wrapped stacks of one hundred dollar bills.

"There's forty-thousand dollars in here, Bud," Robert said, "I want you to think about how I should invest it. You can be my partner. We could buy this business if you want. This vending machine business. Or something else. I don't care. There's plenty more where this came from. Think about it. I'll be back soon with more. I'll give some to you to take care of Sophia and the baby. I promise. Then it's you and me, Bud. No stoppin' us," he had boasted with a touch of the maniacal.

44

The flies were swarming everywhere. Buzzing in his ears. Landing on his lips, attempting to squeeze between them into his mouth in search of moisture. Fruit flies. Big as moths. Biting if he let them stay on his skin too long. He couldn't sleep. They were worse at night. They were worse than the mosquitoes and the chiggers, but not worse than the water. He was sure his diarrhea was turning into full-blown dysentery. Mexico. He hated it, every square inch of it. The heat in Chihuahua made heat in New Orleans feel like an ice cold shower, which he needed badly. It had been three days. Three long days of utterly hellish misery. Being in Mexico was part of the plan. Lee said so. Mexico will be their second stop after crossing the border at El Paso. Their escape route. Their road to freedom.

"We continue from there to South America where wealth and luxury and women and jewels and fine food and tequila and haciendas bigger than the White House await," Lee gushed exuberantly during their celebratory dinner after arriving at the U.S. border town.

Lee and Robert made the grueling, normally twelve and a half hour trip from Denver to El Paso in a little less than ten hours alternating driving the big black 'Bird in two hour shifts while the other tried to sleep in the cramped passenger seat of the flashy two-seater.

Their cruise never topped safe speeding ticket avoidance seventy miles an hour. As they motored on the newly completed Interstate 25 through the heart of New Mexico, they kept the convertible top down for most of the way. As a result, both were suffering from excruciating sunburns that were now beginning to blister and leak runny fluid down their painful necks and backs. The most pleasant part of their journey was crossing the low lying Las Cruses Mountain range, which gently rises in elevation to touch the outskirts of that lovely hamlet. El Paso is just over the horizon.

Robert and Lee were met in El Paso by two men neither had ever seen before. Their meeting was brief and somewhat cordial and took place in the motel Rio Grande parking lot where they had been told to stay. The names of their welcoming party were Joe and Jack. They reminded Robert of younger versions of Clay with their barrel chests, massive arms, thick necks and close-cropped hair. Both were dressed in dark suits and each wore grey felt hats, each of which was soaked in sweat as they stood in the beastly hot afternoon sun quietly giving instructions. After a brief conversation all four men drove together to another motel on the Mexico side of the border and were told that this is where they were to rendezvous on the night following the day of the event. After that they drove back to the Rio Grande where Robert and Lee got out to watch Joe and Jack drive off without another word.

"They didn't even say goodbye," Lee said in mock offense.

The next morning Lee and Robert crossed into Ciudad Juarez and drove the two hundred odd miles south. To guide them, there were few mostly inaccurate road markers to pinpoint the exact route and distance to Chihuahua. Neither spoke much during the trip as each mulled over detailed instructions given to them by Joe and Jack. They kept the convertible top up this time to shield their peeling skin from the harsh rays. Each had a fresh new pocket full of Yankee dollars and a thirty-eight-caliber handgun holding six shots apiece. Armed, Robert felt strong and purposeful.

Once in the miserable heart of the teeming Mexican town where they soon learned there are twice as many donkeys pulling carts, as there are sputtering, blue smoke belching automobiles Robert and Lee were again met by two strangers. Both of their new companions also wore suits, but theirs were tailored white linen and their hats were Panamas. Yet they were ripe full of further directives regarding actions to be taken on the second day after the day of the event, and on into the days and weeks that followed. Their Mexican hosts were much more friendly to Robert and Lee than their American guides had been. They didn't have any money to offer; rather they took a hundred dollars from Robert to "keep that beautiful car safe from thieves and vandals during your stay, senior." Their hosts let them buy several rounds of warm Mexican beer at a bar where Robert noticed how big and thick the flies were and where one of those donkeys relieved itself on the sidewalk at the front door. No one seemed to notice or care about either the flies or the foaming yellow deposit.

Three long horrific days in Chihuahua passed before Lee got the call sending them back to the States. This time they pushed the convertible upwards of ninety miles an hour risking blown tires and bent axles on the two lane rutted Mexican roads until they reached the border and safe haven. Arriving in El Paso Lee announced they were splitting up. He told Robert to drop him off at the Greyhound bus terminal and to head back to Denver and "take up with your wife, or do whatever you wish, until I call you."

"When you get there Oxnard will contact you. Be ready to move quickly. No questions. Just be ready," were Lee Harvey Oswald's stern orders.

45

When Bud woke from his dream his cloudy sleep soaked mind was in a whirl, processing two stark, conflicting emotions. One was of jubilation. The other was a terrifying panic. This mental clash left him drained, sweating and crying out in joy one-second and bellowing in freight the next. Jeannie shook him hard to bring him around.

"Jesus, Bud, what was that all about?" she quietly inquired after altering his near hysteria to a state of relative calm.

"I don't know," he responded in a hoarse whisper; his mouth dry and parched. His throat raw from the screams.

"I'm lying right here in this bed. You're not here. I'm awake and I look up. From the ceiling one hundred dollar bills start floating down, raining all around me. They are all mine. The bills begin to stack up. It's a gusher of money. I'm ecstatic. I'm rich beyond imagination. Then the falling money begins to turn red. First a little and then the bills drifting down become wet, and then soaked. When they are so saturated in red they begin to drip drops as they fall. The drops fall on me. The drops fall in my mouth. The taste is sweat, yet nauseating. The drops are blood. First a little, then a lot. The blood comes pouring off the bills as they float toward me. Into my mouth. I'm choking. I can't breathe. Blood is everywhere."

"Wow," exclaimed Jeannie, "that's a good one. I wonder what that means."

"I'm not sure if it means anything," Bud responded, "but I have an idea."

Two days later Mary Lou strutted into Bud's office to announce that he had an urgent telephone call. She could have told him about the call over the intercom system but she preferred to deliver her news in person, hoping her tight skirt, sleeveless silk blouse presence would prompt another romp with the boss, but Bud didn't even look up from his paperwork until she had spun on her spike heels to wiggle out the door.

He picked up the receiver after she departed.

"Bud, this is Robert."

"I know who it is."

"The last time I saw you I asked if you would do a favor for me which will end up being good for Sophia and the baby. Remember?" Robert asked.

"Yes, I remember," Bud acknowledged cautiously.

"Well, today I'm asking you to help me; to help them. This needs to happen now."

"I'm listening."

"I would like to meet you this afternoon. Somewhere. I don't care. In the city park maybe, or anywhere. When we meet I'm going to ask you to take forty thousand dollars from me, all in cash. I want you to take the money and put it somewhere safe. Maybe in the safe in your office. It shouldn't go into the bank. That might raise suspicion. In a few days, if things go right, I will call you and ask you to give Sophia half of it – twenty-thousand – and I want you to take the other half and keep it."

No response. Robert hesitated. "You still there?"

"I'm here," Bud replied.

"Okay, if things don't go well, all you will get is the forty thousand. If they do go right you'll get another sixty thousand, say, within a month. Sophia gets half and you get the other half – just for helping me."

Another pause.

Bud waited; then asked. "Why don't you just give it to her yourself?"

"'Cause I don't trust her," he retorted. "She'll just blow it. If you give it to her and advise her how to spend it, or save it or do whatever, maybe invest it, she will be better off. She needs to know it's coming from me, not you. You are her adviser. I'm her benefactor."

"For this you're going to give me half?" Bud asked, his skepticism at its peak.

"I am. I've told you many times how much I respect you. I know how much you care for Sophia and the baby. You're the only one who will look after them when I'm gone for good. That's why I'm asking you to do this," Robert said.

"Last time I saw you, you talked about us buying a business with your money. Has that changed? You don't want to go into business with me now?" Bud asked, provoking and prodding.

"No! I can't! Things have changed. You just have to take the money. I won't be around," was Robert's clearly agitated response.

"Okay, I was just asking," Bud replied calmly.

Then Bud broke the silence. "So, Robert, where are you going? I won't bother asking you where this money is coming from because I'm sure you won't tell me, but let's assume I do this for you, does this mean you are disappearing completely, never to see your wife and child again…just leave them the money to buy their love and secure their happiness?"

Bud heard a deep exhale on the other end of the line. Bud could tell he had hit a raw nerve.

"Bud, I won't explain another thing. Will you do it or not? Will you do it for Sophia?" Robert's tone was harsh and direct.

A few moments passed before…"Denver City Park, by the north entrance to the Denver Museum of Natural History. Two o'clock. Bring the money in a bag easy to carry," Bud instructed.

Detective Max Nedbalski was seated cross-legged leaning against a hundred foot tall oak tree pretending to read *Catcher in the Rye*, which he checked out of the Denver Public Library the afternoon before. One eye was on J.D. Salinger's prose and the other on Bud seated fifty yards away on the marble and stone knee wall that accented the north entrance to the Denver museum. Today it was featuring an exhibit of artifacts pilfered from the Mesa Verde Cliff Dwellings located about four hundred fifty miles south of that exact spot. Max and Bud had been waiting for more than an hour. It was ten minutes after three. A cold breeze stirred through the grove of tall blue spruce pines to Max's right. He zipped his jacket up around his neck. He saw Bud stand from his chiseled perch and look over in his direction.

This little charade is about to end, Max thought, I told him this was all a farce. Max also stood and pocketed the book. He began a slow stride toward his friend.

Then he saw him. The man's limp was pronounced. His foot appearing to drag behind him. Slightly built. Hunched over, bundled up; wearing a heavy blue Navy Pea coat, baseball cap and blue jeans. From that distance Max could still detect evidence of shiny high-heeled cowboy boots on his feet. Made him appear taller. He carried what looked like an Army issue green duffel bag slung over his shoulder. Max abruptly returned to his pre-assigned seat at the base of the tree. The man's eyes, shielded under the cap did not look Max's way; rather they kept staring straight ahead, bobbing slightly because of the limp. The two men met on the sidewalk away from the building's entrance. Max saw the man's hand extend in greeting. Bud took it and shook it tentatively.

Okay, that's okay, you're friendly, Max thought, but wary.

The duffel came off the man's shoulder and he placed it at Bud's feet. An intense conversation, which Max could only see but could not hear, erupted between the two. He opened and glanced down at his book. The pages were upside down.

Then the man turned quickly, and with surprising agility hobbled in the direction from which he came. Bud picked up the duffel and walked in the other direction. Not more than three minutes elapsed from the man's abrupt, unexpected appearance. Max waited a few more minutes before rising again from his cold, hard seat to amble nonchalantly in the direction Bud had gone. By that time his legs were cramped, and for a short time he limped just like the man who left the money.

"Exactly forty-thousand; just like he said," Bud declared.

"Doesn't look counterfeit to me," Max observed.

The two were alone in Bud's office. The bills were stacked in neat one thousand dollar piles, covering the top of Bud's desk.

"Put it all in your safe if you think that's the best place for it. I've taken down a random number of serial numbers from the bills here. Tomorrow I will run them through the FBI's new system that tracks stolen currency based on their serial numbers. It's amazing how they do it, but it works. I should know in a day or two if this dough is hot. If it is we'll have to confiscate it and a manhunt for that character will get underway," Max said.

After a moment he added, "Bud, for some reason, I don't think it's stolen. Something tells me this guy is connected to some big time operation. Maybe it's drugs. But he don't look the part. I don't know. We have no reason to arrest him, or even tail him. We've checked every criminal source file there is and so far, nothing. He's broken no laws as far as we can tell. All he's done is abandon his wife and kid and unfortunately that ain't against the law neither," Max decreed.

46

"Leave tonight. Drive the speed limit. Don't do anything stupid. When you get to Amarillo find a Ford dealer and sell the car, or trade it in, but whatever you do don't show up here in that black hot rod of yours. It'll attract more attention than the opening of a new strip club."

Lee's words were direct but not harsh or condescending. Robert heard them well and was crestfallen.

"Get rid of the Thunderbird?" Robert asked with certain resignation, already knowing what the answer would be, yet he had to make one final try.

"No doubt," Lee came back emphatically, "That damn car, beautiful as it is, can't be inside a hundred miles of us. Get one that's all white. Something that runs good, big engine and fast, but looks like every other clunker on the road."

Robert slept just four hours before settling comfortably in the big bucket seat of his 'Bird and heading south on the Interstate. The four hours he'd spent in bed at the Mountain Motor Court in Castle Rock, south of Denver were restless and wasteful. He now wished he'd left right after talking with Lee instead of trying to sleep.

The smooth, quiet hum of the big Ford engine was hypnotic. His eyelids blinked heavily. He turned up the radio to the throaty howls of disc jockey Wolfman Jack blasting rock and roll and sage teenage advice from his broadcast booth at XERB, the Cuidad Acuna Mexico radio station located right along the mighty Rio Grande. Robert liked the music and hoped he could get the signal when he and Lee headed for Chihuahua in the next few days. He hit the button on the door panel. The driver's side window descended rapidly to unblock a rush of frigid early morning air. He decided to stop in Trinidad, Colorado for coffee and breakfast. He'd make up the time through the wide open stretches of flatland New Mexico before turning south and east toward the Texas panhandle.

He reached Amarillo mid morning but he kept on driving. He would not give up his prized machine. To hell with him, Robert concluded. He had enough money in his pocket to buy another car when he arrived in Dallas, so Lee would never know what he did with the Thunderbird. When he passed through the Texas town on his way south he wistfully waved a middle finger at a Dodge dealership full of used cars. Yep, he'd buy a Dodge when he got there and safely store away his black beauty. A Dodge would bring them good luck he decided. It was Monday morning, November 18, 1963. Suddenly fatigue overtook him. On the outskirts of Amarillo he pulled into a rest stop, quieted the big engine, slid back the driver's seat as far as it would go and slept for an hour.

He rolled into the Dallas at five-forty five that afternoon. As instructed he took the Elm Street exit off the Central Expressway and found the Longhorn Coffee Shop just off the highway ramp on his right. He was hungry and exhausted. His leg was killing him, having sat idle, bent and cramped for the nearly thirteen-hour trip. The parking lot of the tiny dour-appearing eatery was nearly empty but he drove on for another two blocks and found a space along the street. Every fiber in his body seemed to ache. He slowly climbed out of the car to stand on the hard concrete sidewalk surface and stretch his angrily rebelling muscles. He haltingly limped the two-block distance back to the restaurant with pain increasing with nearly every step.

As he drew near, the stench of rancid garbage and discarded cooking grease attacked his nostrils to momentarily dampen his hunger. A chill passed through his upper torso from a short gust of dry, cool Texas air. He realized that all that covered him from waist up was the stained sleeveless tee shirt that he'd worn since leaving Denver. He looked down to grimace at his deeply scuffed prized Tony Lama's. He entered the establishment to find the nauseating odor from the outside diminished only slightly. Two men occupied a square Formica top, chrome legged table placed against the rear, water stained, faded green cinderblock wall. Robert scanned the room for Lee. One of the men motioned for him to come toward their table. As Robert moved closer he recognized one of them as the man whom they met in El Paso, but he couldn't remember if he was either Joe or Jack.

Neither spoke as Robert took an empty seat at the table.

"Where's Lee?" Robert asked.

"Workin'," replied Joe or Jack. "Don't matter."

"He's supposed to meet me," Robert said.

"Won't be happenin'; not tonight at least," Joe or Jack declared.

"You'll be alone for a while. He ain't showin' up for a day or two," one or the other added.

"Wasn't the plan," Robert asserted.

"Plans change," both declared simultaneously.

"I'm starving. I'd like to eat something even at the risk of food poisoning in here," Robert said. He glanced over his shoulder into a grim faced waiter whose tee shirt displayed a stain even larger than that on Robert's.

"Food's good. You eat. Then we'll talk," Joe or Jack promised.

An hour later, his belly full but rebelling from an overcooked said-to-be rib-eye steak, lumpy mashed potatoes, greasy brown gravy and cold peas, Robert left the restaurant with directions to drive east to Haskell Avenue. He was told to look for a red brick ranch-style single level house overlooking Fair Park. The house was fairly easy to find despite the darkness that had overcome the day. Robert's black mood was brightened by his discovery of a single car garage in the rear yard. Again concerned that Lee might be lurking inside or nearby he cautiously drove past the residence and parked at curbside three houses away. If he had to confront Lee over his decision to keep the car, he was prepared with a defiant, unwavering stance.

Screw him, I'm too important to this operation, whatever it is. If he doesn't like it, that's tough. I'll take care of things. They won't mess with me now, Robert reassured himself.

He walked from the car into the yard and circled the house. A single dim light shown from inside. A streetlight further illuminated the scene. He went to the garage. He found the door ajar. Lifting it, he was delighted to find it empty. As quickly as his legs would perform he hurried back to retrieve his beloved automobile. Its long, sleek body fit nicely inside. Under the night sky he lifted his spare Army duffel bag from the Thunderbird's trunk and carried it, full of his clothes instead of money this time, around to the front door. As he was told an hour or so before, the key was under the outdoor welcome mat. He stooped to retrieve it, but before he could, he heard the front door creek open.

A lightning bolt of fear ran through him.

He rose up, fully expecting a snarling Lee Oswald to appear but instead stared with glee into the handsome face of Ms. Deborah Henley.

Robert was sleeping soundly, breathing deeply and peacefully; his naked body face up and spread-eagle on the double bed. Deborah lay on her side, barely clinging to the edge of the bed. She rose quietly and stepped to the window. Smiling into the late fall moonlight which brightly shone through she pulled back the cheap cotton curtains and stared down at the garage.

Damn, that's a beautiful car he's driving. Wonder where he got it. I'll ask him in the morning, she resolved.

The grin returned to her face. She was doing her job well. Performing as expected. As ordered. It was David who made her assignment clear.

Take care of all of his needs from the time he arrives until Friday morning and then leave. Do not hesitate. Come straight back to New Orleans. You know where to find the car. Its tank will be full. There will be money locked inside the glove compartment. You had a fine time at the beach in Miami. Your time there, where you stayed, what you ate, drank and what you bought will be well documented with elaborate forgeries. Deception at its finest.

Since joining New Orleans District Attorney Jim Garrison's staff Deborah worked countless hours of overtime accumulating a fair amount of vacation leave. She was due for some time off. She also collected gigantic heaps of responsibility bestowed upon her by a boss who had the single focus of being reelected and then possibly eyeing either the next vacant U.S. Senate seat or maybe the governor's office. Garrison trusted Deborah explicitly. With her help his budding political career was taking shape quite nicely. She prioritized the prosecutor's case files after deciphering the extent to which high profile public notoriety could be captured, especially when the DA himself entered the courtroom in the quest for justice.

When Deborah asked Garrison for some vacation days around the Thanksgiving holiday week he was happy to comply. She needed a little "beach time," she said to work on her fading tan. He said take two weeks. "You deserve it."

Deborah gently rolled Robert onto his side to muffle the increasing volume of his snoring and gently slipped back into bed. She hoped she could sleep. Yet her silent recounting of the task before her precluded rest for now.

She was not to be seen in public with either Robert or Lee. She was to remain housebound through the week, waiting patiently each day for Robert's return, and then she was to grant his every wish. She worried about everything from a police raid to returning to work without a suntan. Her task was not difficult and she had a fine tuned escape plan, but that did not quell her anxiety. Wistfully, she hoped for bright, warm sunny Dallas days so when Robert was working she could strip down and lie naked and vulnerable in the outdoor heat. But wait. This is November and the temperatures might not rise above sixty degrees. Could she brave the cold for a phony Miami tan? Deborah liked to sunbathe in the nude. Luckily, the little one story track home which she and Robert occupied had a high wooden fence encircling the back yard so she mused in the darkness that, if she purposefully exposed it all, she would remain secluded. She decided she would at least try to sunbathe, but if it became impossible, she would occupy the tanning salons over the weekend after returning to New Orleans on Friday.

DA Garrison will never be the wiser.

No problem, she concluded. This is easy, I've got it all figured out, plus it wasn't so bad with Robert this time. It was certainly better than the first time.

Deborah rose from bed a second time. Again to stare out the open window, her eyes scanning the rear yard, finding it lit surreally by the moon which had just appeared over the treetops. In the moonlight she noticed the outline of a child's swing set placed prominently in the middle of the narrow, sparsely grass covered, mostly weed-infested expanse. The breeze moved the empty swings in a gentle swaying motion. They were childless. Aimless. Waiting to carry precious cargo ascending into the air. In her line of sight the swings suddenly catapulted wildly without purpose, propelled by an unexpected gust of wind, to clang, like an alarm, against the metal triangular support posts. Did they not once deliver thrills and shrills of inspired youth? Now gone. Why did their passengers leave? Were they forced to go? To die? Prematurely. Before their time. Never to regain control for a smooth upward flight. Suddenly a foreboding gripped her. She clutched at her silk gown bought only yesterday for their first night together and tried to shield her body from the cold draft. She failed. A chill ran through her and she shivered from it. Sunbathing is out of the question, she concluded.

What is their mission? She pondered, crawling silently back into bed and pulling the sheet and blanket up tightly around her neck. *When I find out on Friday, if that's the day, will I feel heartened, accomplished, or will I be empty, swinging in the wind purposelessly, having lost something or someone like a vanquished child?*

She fought for sleep but it still wouldn't come just yet.

She lay there quietly, hearing nothing but Robert's labored breathing. Was she at peace or was she at war? Was she content with her decision to be there with Robert, or was her decision to come foolish and reckless? Was she about to take part in a great event or a horrific spectacle? She wasn't sure what was going to happen this coming Friday, but she knew it would be big. Real big. Clay and David said so. Bigger than anything she had ever experienced. She remembered the days leading up to her assignment. Her enthusiasm at the time was wholly stimulated by the recent speeches of her leaders.

They were passionate and spellbinding; euphoric nearly, and when Clay pulled her aside that night to lay out the plan for her trip to Dallas her elation was overwhelming. He was vague on exactly what Robert and this man named Lee were planning to do, but without vacillation Clay assured her that it would be "a monumental incident; a turning point in history; the rebirth of our nation as our forefathers once designed it."

She had never seen him project such exhilaration. She embraced his fervor and then focused on her mission. Mrs. Claire left little doubt that she was very unhappy with Deborah's announcement on Sunday that she would be gone for the entire week and that she would be traveling alone. Deborah dismissed her protests and slept that night in Robert's old room, which Mrs. Dionne had yet to rent. It had been vacant for more than a year.

Deborah tossed and turned. Robert stirred with the disturbance. She caressed his bare back and he sighed and moaned without further motion. She returned to her reflections. She was eager to meet Lee and she was so very proud of Robert for being selected to carry out this undertaking… whatever it was.

Since reuniting this night, Deborah soon realized that a profound change had come over Robert. One instance stood out. She was surprised and disturbed at Robert's reaction to her announcement of Mr. Roblinski's death. He almost seemed to disregard the news and only expressed a seemingly uncaring manner about the cause; instead preferring to know whether his shop had been sold.

"He likely died of a heart attack or stroke," she offered without his prompting. "Alone. He apparently collapsed while working on an old portable radio. They didn't find his body for two weeks. Very bad. His customers stopped coming in after you left. His shop was in shambles. Junk piled everywhere. Sad. I think you broke his heart when you disappeared; not even saying goodbye," Deborah added.

"I'm sorry. That was another life. I'm disappointed he let the place go to hell," was the callous way Robert responded.

When her mind finally went to rest she felt another chill at the prospect of Friday, but this time not from a frigid puff of air.

47

Mary Lou handed Bud his itinerary for his trip to Albuquerque. He decided to drive rather than fly. He didn't like airplanes so he had to leave a day early to allow plenty of time to arrive for a series of meetings with representatives of vending machine manufacturers who were gathering there for their annual convention and trade show.

Bud looked over the neatly typed list of activities Mary Lou had meticulously prepared. He realized he would be extremely busy from Wednesday afternoon through Friday evening with his last meeting with the owners of the new AMI line of jukeboxes. She allowed a full twelve hours of driving time from Denver to the New Mexico City which meant he could take the road trip leisurely. As he scanned down the page he noticed a folded piece of paper clipped to the bottom. He unfolded it and read:

Just say the word and I'll come with you…

He looked up and she stood before him smiling seductively. He shook his head no and waved her away.

◆

Robert awoke rested and refreshed. He hadn't felt better in months. Deborah, her silk nightgown carelessly bunched up over her waist exposed her glorious bare backside. She lay at his side, sleeping soundly. He was in heaven. He could stay there forever. Instead he eased out of bed and in twenty minutes was showered and dressed and on the telephone calling for a taxi.

By late-morning, in plenty of time for his first rendezvous with Lee, Robert bought a white 1961 Dodge Coronet, four-door, showing only twenty thousand miles, new tires, a working radio and an engine the size of a mountain. He roared off the dealer lot at 11:45 am and found Lee Harvey Oswald at the predetermined street corner of Gaston Avenue and North Peak Street.

The main and side streets of Dallas carried light traffic as Robert drove and Lee talked incessantly. It was Tuesday, late afternoon. They had been in the white Dodge since noon; driving, memorizing the streets, the landmarks, the routes, alternative routes...plan A, plan B, plan C. They went down Houston Street, up South Market, down South Lamar, over to Akard Street; up to Commerce Street all the way out to North Hall. Repeatedly. They had burned nearly a full tank of gas when Lee finally said they were through for the day.

"By the way," Lee asked after giving Robert vague directions to a location he had never heard of, "what did you do with the Thunderbird?"

"Sold it, like you told me to, got almost as much as I paid for it. Have quite a bit left over after buying this," was Robert's well thought out lie.

"Good. Glad you did. That damn thing was dangerous," he replied without giving another thought on the subject.

Lee said he had to work that night at his new job so they had to quit their merry-go-round tour around five o'clock. Robert didn't quite catch the name of the place where Lee said he worked. In some building where they store books. A warehouse, he thought. It was four-thirty when Lee told Robert to stop and let him out. They were in an unfamiliar residential neighborhood. Lee got out of the car. Robert offered to drop him off at work instead.

"No way, neither you nor this car will come anywhere close to where I work. You understand?" Lee sternly instructed.

"Sure, no problem," Robert said.

"I'll walk from here. You should be able to find your way back to the house. It's real close, just go over on South Ervay and then turn on Haskell," Lee pointed in that direction. "Tomorrow, same time. Pick me up where you did this morning and we do this all over again, but this time we go out farther, toward the main highways."

Robert groaned in silence. Lee moved away from the car and stepped onto the sidewalk. Robert knew the way. He gunned the Dodge toward South Ervay Street and sped toward the awaiting embrace of his beloved.

Wednesday was the same as Tuesday, just as Lee promised. By four thirty that afternoon with another tank of gasoline consumed, Robert knew the streets of Dallas, its parkways, expressways and main highways as well as he knew the inside of his room at Mrs. Dionne's

Boarding House. Throughout the day Lee grew increasingly sharp and sullen. He simply told Robert where to turn and when, and said not much more. At the end of the day Lee again directed his driver back to the same street curb where he exited the vehicle the day before. This time before climbing out of the car he handed Robert a legal size piece of paper neatly creased down to a perfect square.

"Take this and memorize it tonight," Lee ordered. "It's a map. Tomorrow I want you to know every turn, every stop sign, every stop light, the speed limits, the entrance and exit ramps, two lane, four lane roads, school zones, bus stops...everything. Know it so well that you could drive it blindfolded if you had to. Tomorrow, this is the route we will practice. You will know it by heart and you will know how and when to take detours if necessary. When you are done memorizing it, burn it. Do not show it to that cunt you're with or anyone. Understand?" Lee was emphatic.

"Sure, got it, no problem," Robert said with conviction. He didn't like the word Lee used to label his sweetheart but said nothing about it.

◆

About the same time as Lee's cryptic command resonated in Robert's ears, Bud was cruising south along the new Interstate Highway 25 just passing over the Colorado border and beginning the slight incline up Raton Pass into New Mexico. He was content and comfortable, nestled in the thick, black leather seats of his gunmetal grey Lincoln Continental four-door. His was the sleek luxury sedan with the four doors that opened from the center of the chassis. He pegged the speedometer at a safe, steady seventy miles per hour. This speed gave him plenty of extra time to cover the estimated eight-hour journey to Albuquerque in little less than seven hours, assuming he maintained that average speed. He had been on the road just under three hours.

It was a clear, very crisp fall afternoon. Temperatures were in the mid thirties. Streams of warm air from the big Lincoln's heater nicely blocked any chill entering his domain from the outside. He thought of Jeannie and how she satisfied him completely, yet apprehension remained that he could not meet her needs equally. He wasn't sure he loved her but he was sure he craved what she provided him now. He thought of the work ahead of him through Friday night and dismissed any concern about fulfilling those related responsibilities wholly. He thought of Mary Lou and grinned about what she would probably be doing to him at just that moment if he had allowed her to come along. He quickly dismissed those visions but a tingle in his groin remained for a few seconds more.

He thought of his baby girls, no longer infants, longing for them desperately and weeping inside at their absence. His love turned into an inferno of hate at the next thought of Connie and the demon that now surely claimed his children as his own. He turned up the volume on the radio to draw the curtains on his despair. He decided to stop for dinner at one of the numerous rest areas that had sprung up along his route. He planned to arrive around nine o'clock to assure a long night's rest before the chaos of the convention began that next morning. Tomorrow would Thursday, November 21, 1963.

◆

That Wednesday night Robert dreamed of Fodor. It was the first time since the last time and that was many months ago, longer than he could remember. The dream lasted only minutes. Robert recalled it the next morning while waiting for a luscious breakfast of grits and biscuits, smothered in sausage gravy obediently placed before him by his deep abiding soul mate.

All Deborah had on that morning was a red pinafore apron tied around her neck and waist and white furry slippers. She cooed as she poured his coffee. But this morning Robert was distracted from the lovely sights and sounds that came from her. Fodor had made his brief appearance hours before, invading and conquering him again. His father spoke little during the dream. His few words seared into Robert's consciousness.

They were alone in the concert hall. Both on the stage, facing each other. There was no audience. All the seats displayed their red velvet covers; all except one in row 13, the wooden slats of that one exposed.

Fodor stepped across the stage to his son. He held out his hand. Something dangled from his middle finger. Held aloft by a colored ribbon. It sparkled in the stage lights. The sheen blinded him. He squinted and looked away. Fodor spoke.

"This is yours. You have earned it. Wear it with pride. With honor. You must wait until Friday. Friday will be the day."

Robert reached to grasp the object. It was his father's cherished Iron Cross. They stepped back from each other. Fodor rapped the heels of his polished jackboots together in a loud crack and snapped to attention with a raised stiff armed salute. Instinctively Robert returned the fascist gesture. A faint applause could then be heard coming from the shadows of the hollow auditorium. "Bravo!" Robert looked for the source. His friend Lee stood at Seat 7 Row 13, now clapping loudly. Robert turned back to face his father again but this time he discovered he was alone. Quite alone.

48

"Do you have your .38; the one like mine you got in El Paso?" Lee abruptly asked Robert as both sat in the front seat of the Dodge at the conclusion of another long, grueling day on the road.

"Sure I have it," Robert responded.

"Good. Bullets?" Lee asked.

"Sure, it's loaded. Why would I have it unless it was loaded?" Robert came back indignantly.

"How many rounds?"

"I have a full box. I guess there's fifty." Robert's anger grew.

"Good." Lee said, still not looking over at him, instead, staring blankly ahead through the grimy windshield of the Dodge. It had been raining off and on throughout the day and the windshield wipers were scarred, leaving streaks smearing the entire expanse of the glass. The only occurrence that broke the monotonous routine of the day came at noon with Lee's abrupt order to "stop at that sporting goods store…see it over there? Go in and buy a good pair of binoculars. Not the most expensive ones, just a good pair."

"I have a pair of binoculars. I can give you mine," Robert replied to the order.

"Are they any good?" Lee asked

"Yea, they're good. Army issue, I think; high powered," Robert said, and then asked, "What do you need them for?"

"To see better with. What do you think? I need them today. Where are they?" Lee asked.

"In my duffel bag in the trunk," Robert responded.

"Good, don't let me forget them," Lee instructed.

Like the day before Lee was pensive, but this day to an extreme. He's lost in his head, Robert concluded. Cold and cruel with his sparse condescending comments. Robert accepted the offense, sensing a violent eruption if he protested. Yet Robert was spent with frustration. He decided to press his annoying companion and seek some insight into the plan, assuming there was such a thing.

"Lee," Robert boldly ventured, "you've been sort of tough to get along with since I arrived here in Dallas. You've kept me in the dark about your plans, and that's okay. I've gone along with this chauffeuring routine for longer than what I care to think. I know these neighborhoods and streets and highways better than any cab driver you could ever find. Now you ask me if I have the gun, and then you want binoculars. The last time I checked cab drivers don't usually carry weapons and usually don't need binoculars. Can't you give me some idea what's on your mind? What I can expect over the next day, or week or month?"

Despite Robert's pleas Lee remained stoic, continuing to stare straight out through the filthy windshield. A long silence ensued. Finally.

"Fuck this! Fuck you! I'm bailing out. You're such a asshole. I don't deserve your big shot attitude, like I'm some flunky sitting here kissing your ass. To hell with you," Robert raged and reached for the driver side door handle to let himself out.

"Don't you move," Lee growled. Then his voice softened.

"You're right Robert. I have been a jerk. You'll understand why, soon. You'll come to appreciate this wall I've built up between us. I have to keep you away from the details of the plan. Yes, there is one. An elaborate one. However, for your own protection, mine and the others, I have to do this alone, but you will play an important part. You can't even imagine how important." Lee threw his head back to rest it on the top of the seat. He closed his eyes, sighed heavily and smiled as if in a pleasant dream.

After a moment, he proclaimed, "It all happens tomorrow."

◆

Bud worked the crowd at Thursday's special reception for the "vendors", those company representatives like him who bought or leased the equipment that played the music, dispensed the cigarettes, challenged the pinball players and dispatched the pool balls to fulfill the insatiable cravings and test the skills of their consumers. The latest vending machines on display at the convention hall were dazzling, but not as appealing as the bikini clad models who caressed the gaudy plastic and chrome gadgets or lounged on the green felt tables, or bent low to punch up another selection on the magnificent 1964 Rockola

Deluxe model featuring 150 spinning .45 recordings of America's favorite music, no matter what your taste in tunes might be.

Bud had a good day, a great day. He purchased the equipment he needed for the next year and figured he'd saved at least twenty percent off the wholesale prices. He lined up good, reliable sources for parts that guaranteed overnight airfreight delivery which previously had been impossible. He began direct talks with a competitor which currently dominated the Western Slope towns in Colorado about a potential buyout. In all as the evening began it was time to celebrate just a little, so he kept the bar in close range as he roamed through the display aisles of the convention complex.

He decided to stay through Friday to continue discussions with the Grand Junction-based company executives, beginning with a late breakfast meeting followed by continuing talks through the afternoon. They had an extensive agenda to cover.

Time passed. Circulating through the crowds he began running into the same people he'd seen a few minutes before. He looked at his watch. Nine-thirty. He'd been hard at it since seven that morning. Suddenly fatigue crawled up his back and into his neck. The hall was thick with smoke. His eyes burned. The ice in his glass of Jack Daniels had melted. His stomach growled in protest. Dinner in the room, he concluded, prompting him to look for an exit and the nearest elevator bank.

◆

Robert played back Lee's instructions over and over in his head, mouthing his words so no detail would be misplaced or forgotten. His assignment won't really be that hard to carry out, but the intensity in which Lee voiced his instructions heightened Robert's unease. By nine-thirty that evening he decided he had rewound Lee's missive enough. When and where he was to park the Dodge, when and where he was to drive to his next station if Lee wasn't at the first, and then to his next location if Lee failed to show, and then to the final rendezvous point, and then to drive carefully with his passenger south, preferably taking the Stemmons Freeway. Clothes packed neatly in the trunk. Plenty of food since they would be driving straight through to Chihuahua. Plenty of water. A little beer. Obviously a full tank of gas.

Be at the first station at exactly eleven thirty. That meant he could sleep in late, make love, eat breakfast, and still have time to load the car. He wasn't worried about the Thunderbird. When she inquired about the car on that first morning after their first night together he told Deborah that she could have it to drive back to New Orleans where she would wait for instructions to join him in Mexico. She would drive it there as well so they could continue on together, to South America or wherever their wonderful new life as a couple might take them.

I got it, man. No sweat, Robert silently, sternly affirmed to himself and to Lee. He then turned to Deborah who was seated on the couch next to him reading the newspaper.

Nonchalantly she muttered, “Kennedy’s coming to town tomorrow.”

Robert replied. “Yea, I know. Heard that today.”

He pulled the newspaper from her hands and gently pushed her down on the seat cushions.

“I’ve been ready all day. I never thought you’d ask,” she whispered seductively.

49

At precisely eleven thirty a.m. Dallas, Texas time Robert arrived at the location of his first assigned post, the corner of Field and Elm Street. The streets were packed with cars and people. He drove around the block twice before taking a chance and parking close to a fire hydrant knowing that if a cop came by he would move the car quickly to avoid a confrontation. That was another thing Lee had pounded away at him. Avoid the cops at all costs.

This crowd must be for Kennedy, Robert speculated as we watched the growing throng move in the direction of a confluence of roadways called Dealey Plaza, the location where Robert read in the newspaper he'd taken from Deborah the night before that Kennedy's motorcade would pass through sometime around one o'clock.

I guess I wouldn't mind seeing him. They said Jackie would be along. That might be interesting, Robert assumed while noticing that the hordes were growing larger. Oh, well, it's not worth it. I don't like either one of them. She seems like a snotty, stuck up bitch, Robert decided.

Twelve-thirty. Robert realized he had dozed off for a moment or maybe longer. He was startled awake by a car horn blaring nearby. Damn it, I can't do that. Christ, I was out for almost nearly a half hour! He rolled down the window of the Dodge and gulped in fresh air to clear his head. The breeze was cool, not cold. The sun was shining brightly, heating up the inside of the car and creating a compelling atmosphere for unwanted sleep.

Suddenly a disquieting notion struck him. I wonder if... No it can't be...I wonder...What if he's gonna do something. What if Lee's... No, he's crazy but he's not that crazy...But he thinks like me, or at least he says he does...Kennedy's like all the rest of them, out to steal our rights and give them to the blacks. He wants to create a new world order, bargain away our liberties and power, cave into the Soviet devils; allow Cuba to rot...

More than once I thought we'd all be better off if he was dead... No, Lee might protest or something... Sure I'm here to pick him up and split down to Mexico... But all that because he's gonna protest against the guy? Are there others involved? Are they all gonna protest too? Maybe try to disrupt the big party today. Why the guns? Why the binoculars? Why Deborah? What's Deborah really doing here? Coming all the way from New Orleans just to see me? Was she told to come? How did she know I would be here?

Twelve-forty-five. Goddamn, I wonder. Where did Lee say he worked? Some book storage warehouse. I saw a place that looked like that down there in Dealey Plaza. Where Kennedy's gonna pass through. I'm not stupid. I knew all along they weren't ordering me around and giving me money and telling me to go here and there for my health. I knew I was part of something big. Something important that would make things better. Deborah and I talked a lot about that. Even this week. Is this it? I thought maybe some kind of military operation somewhere. But this? Are these guys; Lee and those goons, Jack and Joe, gonna do something to Kennedy? Today? Am I a part of that? Driving the get away car?

If I were, would that be so bad? As long as we could get away with it. No, that would be okay if they killed him. Is that what Fodor meant? Wait until Friday?

Robert looked down at his hand resting on the seat beside him. It shook uncontrollably. He lifted it and grasped the steering wheel of the Dodge, squeezing it hard until the shaking stopped.

One o'clock... Not many people were left in the streets in front or on either side of him. He could see all the way to Main Street. A motorcycle patrolman cruised past not noticing his too-close proximity to the hydrant. Robert's window was down. A man and two children walked by.

"Aren't you going to see the President?" one of the little boys asked Robert with a quizzical look.

"No, I have to work," Robert replied.

"Too bad," the child said and ran quickly to catch up with the man and the other boy.

One-ten. In every direction Robert looked, the streets were empty of people. Only cars were parked along each side of the neighborhood thoroughfare jammed bumper to bumper.

It was eerily quiet. A squirrel scampered after another up a tall oak tree in the yard next to the Dodge. Then Robert heard the faint sound of sirens off into the distance.

One more time, Robert reminded himself. If Lee comes by and doesn't come to the car I am to move to the second stop at Harwood Street and Commerce. I am to wait 10 minutes and if he doesn't show up I am to move again, this time to, Elm and... and... oh, yea, Elm and Murphy. Then if we still don't connect I'm to go to the bus depot and wait. Surely by then we will be together and on our way to Mexico.

One twenty. The sirens grew louder. Robert opened the driver's side door, got out of the car and looked ahead toward Main Street. People were standing along the street, three, four, maybe ten deep. He couldn't see a thing except for the long line of clustered heads and backs.

One twenty-five. The sirens were getting even louder. He heard cheering in the distance.

One twenty-eight. The cheering intensified. Hand held flags began waving above their heads.

One twenty-nine. He heard the roar of motorcycle engines passing down Main Street through the intersection with Elm. Robert was a short block away. The mob was hollering and clapping.

One thirty. The crowd already began dispersing. Some turning to walk back in Robert's direction. They were quiet now. The thrill was gone. The outpouring of adulation was over. Robert would have liked to have seen him in his limousine. He noticed the little boy, now being carried on the shoulders of the man. Certainly his father. The other little boy was walking alongside, holding tightly to the man's hand. They all carried tiny American flags clinched in their fists.

Then the sirens were heard again. That's strange. Robert got back into the Dodge to wait. One, then two, then four motorcycles sped past him, sirens at a pitch. Then a police cruiser. Lights flashing, tires squealing.

One thirty-three. Robert looked closely through the strolling pedestrians for Lee. He didn't spot him. He would be patient. He was calm then. His hand no longer shook.

One-forty three. Robert spotted Lee walking briskly on the sidewalk toward him. His head was down. At the intersection was a taxi. Lee lifted is hand to signal the driver. What the hell? Lee climbed into the cab. They drove away. What the hell?

Okay, not a problem. I'll move on to Harwood and Commerce. Surely he'll jump out of the cab and we'll get going. Must be a reason for him taking the cab. Robert steered the Dodge down Commerce Street, driving slowly. He reached the intersection in four minutes and easily found a parking place. He scanned the area looking for Lee. No sign of him. Ten minutes passed. Okay not a problem. Onto the bus depot. That's it. He took the cab all the way to the depot. That's probably smart. Maybe somebody other than me is looking for him.

One-fifty seven. Then another strange occurrence. On the street corner Robert saw two women crying. One nearly hysterically. He inched the Dodge along slowly, pulling up closely to where they were standing. A man was next to them with a transistor radio in his hand held up to his ear. Robert heard him say to no one in particular...."Kennedy's been shot."

Good Christ, he did it!

This time Robert drove a little faster toward the bus depot, hoping he wasn't late and Lee would be waiting. He arrived in about seven minutes. As he approached the building Robert saw Lee enter another taxi and drive off. This is crazy. Robert decided to follow the cab at a safe distance since it appeared to be traveling in the same direction he was supposed to be going.

The Oak Cliff area of Dallas was a plain, somewhat barren patch of landscape dotted by tiny frame houses, few with garages and still fewer with well-kept lawns. Lee told Robert that he lived in a boardinghouse in the neighborhood near North Beckley and Neely streets and that in the event they were unable to join up by then, Robert was to park at that intersection and wait for him indefinitely.

Robert slammed his fist on the Dodge's dashboard. He lost the taxi in traffic. Mostly because there were more cops swarming all around him than he could count, running red lights and stop signs and adding immeasurably to the turmoil. Robert decided to head toward Lee's neighborhood to find the boardinghouse and wait for his friend. It only took him five or six minutes to motor into the vicinity, fully expecting to easily find Lee's home. He visualized a place like Mrs. Dionne's palatial dwelling. He smiled at the thought of Dallas's own version of Clarence, Boudreaux and Miss Hattie offering unfriendly greetings to prospective residents from their front porch sentry posts. Instead, all Robert found was row after row of decrepit quarters accented by an abundance of unruly knee high weeds and sunflowers. He stopped and parked at the intersection of Beckley and Neely. He was nervous, agitated, not really fearful, just on-edge. He couldn't sit there. *I'll drive around a bit; maybe I'll spot him.* Ten minutes later he did. Near the intersection of East Tenth Street and Patton Avenue he pulled to the curb and stopped. *"I'll wait here, make sure he's not being followed.*

Shutting off the engine Robert noticed a man in the yard down the street struggling to mow his enormous patch of weeds with an old push mower. He wasn't having much luck. Otherwise, the area was deserted much like an Old West ghost town. Up the block from the man hard at work Robert spotted Lee in mid-block, heading toward him. He hasn't seen me yet. His head's still down, shoulders hunched. At that moment a black and white police cruiser pulled to the curb beside him. Lee froze. Momentarily, so did Robert.

Two ten. Never knowing why, Robert reached into the Dodge's glove compartment to retrieve the revolver. Five live rounds. He switched on the car's big motor. It rumbled to life. The Dodge rolled forward toward the patrol car. Lee had not moved. The patrolman swung open the driver side door and stepped out onto the sidewalk. He was at least a head taller than Lee and must have out weighed him by fifty pounds. He'll take Lee down easily, Robert concluded. He moved the Dodge closer. Robert cut the engine. The Dodge coasted. Robert swung the wheel to the right, to the wrong side of the street. He stopped the car nose to nose with the cruiser. The policeman still had his back to Robert. He must not have heard him approach. The police radio was squawking out nonstop messages at a fever pitch obscuring all other sound. The patrolman was saying something to Lee. Lee was nodding his head. Robert opened his car door and stepped out. Revolver in hand. He went around the rear of the Dodge and took a short step onto the sidewalk. His right leg nearly buckled. Lee noticed Robert approaching. Curious, the patrolman turned to look. Robert raised the revolver, pointing at the officer's chest.

Two fifteen. "Shoot him!" Lee yelled.

The policeman struggled to retrieve his holstered pistol. It was too late.

Robert fired. Never knowing why. Officer J.D. Tippit clutched his chest and fell, already dying. Four rounds had pierced his heart.

Lee stepped around the mortally wounded officer now lying face down on the sidewalk. He heard him moan. A gurgling sound came from his throat. Lee's stride caught the edge of a rapidly expanding pool of blood. His partial footprint stained the concrete. Surprisingly calm, Lee came face to face with Robert.

"You did good," Lee said with little emotion. "Now let's get out of here."

Lee grabbed Robert's shirt and spun him around. Robert's leg gave way to a staggering bolt of pain. He went to his knees as if beginning to pray. Already at the driver's side door, Lee turned and barked. "Get up, you bastard!" Lee's eyes frantically scanned the area. The man with the push mower had abandoned his task. The machine was left standing idle in the middle of the weed patch. No one was in sight.

"I'll drive," Lee shouted as Robert finally climbed into the car. He remained in a daze, not thinking, only reacting. Lee slammed the Dodge in reverse and when clear of the dying patrolman's cruiser, sped forward, spraying loose gravel and dust into a high cloud. The car's rear end fishtailed to the right as Lee steered around the corner and sped away. The man who left his mowing emerged from his house and stood on his front stoop. He squinted at the blurry scene down his block. Moments before he thought he heard a car backfire. That's what caught his attention. It was odd. Four times? Four bangs? He could make out a car parked midway down the block. Something obstructed the sidewalk. He decided to investigate. Where the hell are my glasses? Unknowingly by the time he was walking slowly toward the fallen patrolman the getaway car and its killers vanished from view.

Lee hit the brakes of the Dodge hard and slid to a stop in front of one of the dilapidated houses which Robert, still in somewhat of a stupor, thought may have been less than a mile away from his killing. My killing. I did it. God in heaven I murdered him!

"I forgot something," Robert heard Lee declare as Lee leaped from the vehicle, leaving the engine idling and ran up the short cracked and crumbling walk to #1026 North Beckley.

Instinctively Robert slunk down in the passenger seat. No, the old man mowing his lawn didn't see anything. He didn't even look up when I first parked. We're okay. Nobody saw anything. We're clear. Come on Lee; let's move.

Minutes passed. Again the sirens. Threatening, close by.

Ten, then fifteen, then twenty minutes. Past two thirty. The engine was still running. Robert's head was clear by now. What is he doing for God's sake?

Robert slid across the seat to the driver's side. At the instant he placed his hand on the gearshift knob a police cruiser with lights flashing turned the corner and slowly came toward the Dodge. Robert gasped. Robert knew his revolver was on the floor on the passenger side where he dropped it after leaping inside. He started to reach for it but the pistol had slid under the seat during the wild ride from the murder scene and was out of sight.

One bullet left anyway. Wouldn't do much good.

Two officers were in the cruiser when it pulled up alongside the Dodge. The uniformed men clearly looked agitated.

"Is there a problem, officer?" Robert asked, surprising himself at the control in his voice.

"Where have you been, mister?" The officer riding as passenger responded. "We got a President who's probably dead by now and a murdered police officer several blocks away, and you ask if we've got a problem. Damn right we got a problem. Many problems. What are you up to? You live in this neighborhood? We're lookin' for a car, probably two men inside. Don't know the make or model or even the color, just a car. Big help that old man was; blind as a bat. What about it?" The officer was gruff; his rapid fire questions too numerous to answer all at once so Robert waited.

"I'm here to pick up a friend for work. I did hear about the shooting. Jesus, that's awful. Any news about his condition? What about the officer? My God, what's going on? No, I haven't seen anything. I don't live around here. My friend is inside. He's sick and won't be going to work so I was just leaving. I'll probably be late now." Robert smiled inwardly at his spontaneous performance, but kept a solemn face.

"They say it's probably fatal. The President that is. We're lookin' for his killer and now some other son-of-a-bitch that's murdered Tippit. Probably turn out both of 'em is colored. Let me see your driver's license," the officer commanded.

Robert did as he was told, retrieving the laminated card from his wallet and handing it over.

"From Colorado, hey? You better get a Texas license if you plan on stayin' here. We need the tax money. Costs ten dollars. Get on your way," he ordered.

Again, Robert did as he was told; driving slowly, checking his rear view mirror every few seconds in case the officers changed their minds. They didn't.

The man mowing his lawn didn't see a thing. I am free.

He drove a few blocks before determining the best route back to his temporary home and his lovely Deborah. He headed in that direction. He drove past a movie theatre but couldn't catch the feature displayed on the marquee. He'd persuade her to go with him.

Same plan but better, this one without Lee.

She'll do it. Why not? *She's undoubtedly in love with me. Probably always has been.*

As he drove along, the radio broadcast broke his daydream. The President is dead. A white male suspect is being sought. Police are investigating the shooting of a patrolman. The two incidents are not related.

"The hell they're not related. I'm one of only two people in the whole world right who knows who did it." Robert said out loud to no one but himself.

Twenty minutes later he was in front of his love nest. He locked the doors on the Dodge before bounding up the walk for her embrace. Can't be too careful. Car's full of valuable merchandise. There's a crime spree underway, you know, Robert chuckled to himself.

He stood in the middle of the living room. His calls to her unanswered. Echoing now. The house was empty. Deborah was gone. All her clothes. Everything. Robert collapsed and wept on the same couch used the night before for their lovemaking. She was all that mattered.

◆

The horrific news of Jack Kennedy's shooting was delivered by a waiter who brought lunch into the private meeting room where Bud and his counterpart company executives were discussing the firm's most recent financial report and their projections for net profits for the end of the year. All four sat in stunned silence as the thought of the wounded, perhaps dying President sunk in. One man said, "Do you think someone's trying to overthrow the government?"

There was a television set in the room. Bud got up to turn it on. For the next hour or so they sat and watched and listened in suspense as conflicting news reports were sorted out in a desperate attempt to make the event tragically clear.

Shortly after Chet Huntley at NBC News removed his black, horn rimmed glasses to deliver the somber death notice to the world, Bud and his contemporaries decided to suspend their discussions until further notice. Bud went back to his room, switched on his television set, laid on his bed where he remained transfixed for the long agonizing hours that ensued.

Part VII

Denver, CO
November 1963

50

Robert woke from a deep slumber. He did not dream. The love couch on which he had wailed like a child over the disappearance of his lost lady proved to be a comfortable, soothing place of repose. It was pitch black outside. The sun long set. He never made a habit of sleeping during the day but this day was different in so many ways. He turned on the table lamp and checked his watch. Eight-thirty. It had been an eternity since those four shots rang out - four shots that punctured that man's chest and heart, immediately rendering him lifeless.

Four shots fired, not by a killer, but by a servant; a patriot, a man of honor who could not have stood by to watch others act. Not a man who would murder without just cause. Robert began to cry again. Not for his innocent victim, but for his own stupidity. His willingness to relinquish control over his own acts. Lee didn't pull the trigger. Robert did. Lee made it happen. Lee told him to shoot just like Lee told him to turn right or left at the next corner, maybe a hundred times or more during those endless, useless driving rehearsals.

Robert, the servant, did it every time. Without question. He took those orders like a good soldier should. Just like Fodor instructed.

Don't question your superiors. It is your duty. It is your destiny. His sobbing ceased as abruptly as it began. It was time to run.

◆

Bud too had fallen asleep in his room in this town he decided he didn't much care for. It will always be the place and time when he heard the sad news. He knew he would hate the memory. Bud voted for Jack Kennedy. He didn't much care for Nixon, but he hadn't paid much attention to politics until Robert Kaye challenged his intellect on the subject during their frequent after work hours discussions.

I wonder what little Robert Kaye is thinking right now, Bud pondered while standing under a piping hot shower in preparation for dressing and heading toward the hotel dining room for dinner.

I wonder what he's doing with all that money.

Bud decided he didn't want to be alone that night of all nights. He wanted to share his grief with others, even with strangers. It would be easier that way. He had spoken with Jeannie who told him she was shutting down the restaurant and lounge for the night and maybe the entire weekend to join in the mourning. He told her he planned to leave early the next morning and would try to be in Denver by mid afternoon. They would meet and find comfort with each other. While buttoning his shirt and slipping on his pants, the announcer on the television set told him about the arrest of Lee Harvey Oswald.

◆

Robert didn't hear about Lee's capture until he was nearly sixty miles south of Dallas traveling at a modest speed on the Stemmons Freeway, a route he knew by heart would eventually take him to El Paso and Mexico and freedom. He was cruising leisurely in his big, black beautiful Thunderbird. When Robert awoke earlier and regained his senses, again fear gripped him. Not a fear of being caught. Absent fear of a regiment of cops swooping down to carry him away to the Texas electric chair. No, Robert was afraid Deborah had taken his car. At the thought, he ran out the back door but seconds later yelped with joy when he saw it there, locked in the garage, safe, untouched, gleaming in his flashlight beam. His chariot was standing by. Waiting to carry him away. Switching cars had been easy. The Dodge now sat quietly in the garage, having done its job; besides what better way to elude suspicion than to be wheeling down the highway in this machine. No one would ever look for a murderer driving a get-away car like this.

Robert twisted the Thunderbird's radio dial to peak volume. He had the convertible's top down. The wind was whipping through his hair, carrying occasional chills. He didn't care. He sucked in the crisp air. Frustrated though, he was seeking lively, upbeat music, looking for Wolfman Jack, but instead all he got were funeral marches and choked up disc jockeys recapping the day's events. When he heard Lee's name blaring through the car's speakers, Robert nearly lost control of the vehicle. He swung the wheel abruptly to the right and slid to a stop on the shoulder.

"Captured in a movie theatre," the newscaster said.

What the hell were you doing watching a goddamn movie? Robert questioned only the shadows. "Being interrogated not only in the death of the President but the cold blooded murder of Dallas Police Officer J. D. Tippit," the announcer continued.

They think he did it!

Again convulsive sobs sprang from Robert's throat. His bellowing drowned out the rest of the newsman's broadcast. He decided instead they were tears of joy, of relief, not terror or guilt.

Oswald's going to take the fall. As well he should. He made me do it. He's the killer, not me.

Robert drove through the night arriving in El Paso well past midnight. He splurged and checked into an upscale fifty dollar a night Holiday Inn and slept luxuriously long into Saturday afternoon. He had nothing better to do.

◆

The screeching peal of the bedside telephone sent Bud bolting upright in bed, scrambling to find the source of the din to quiet it. He bumped his elbow on the nightstand and screamed in pain before finally locating the cussed receiver and rudely shouting into it.

"Hello. Carlson here."

"Bud. Oh my God. I'm so glad I found you. You can't even imagine. Are you all right?"

Even though the voice penetrating his ringing eardrums was clearly halting and shaken Bud immediately recognized who it was.

"Mary Lou. What the hell are you doing? What do you mean, am I all right? I was fine until you woke me from a dead sleep. I damn near killed myself finding the phone. This better be good," Bud warned.

"Mr. Carlson, this is Agent Thomas Kincaid of the Denver Office of the Federal Bureau of Investigation. Mr. Carlson, we understand you are currently in room 207 of the Hilton Hotel in downtown Albuquerque, New Mexico. Is that correct sir?"

"Yes," Bud stammered, his eyes wide and his senses acute from the shocking statement he'd just heard.

"Mr. Carlson. Agents of the FBI and United States Secret Service are currently standing outside your hotel room door. They are prepared to take you into custody either peacefully or by force if they need to. Do you understand?"

"Yes," Bud stammered again.

"Are you armed, sir?"

"No," Bud quivered.

"Very well. If you are armed you will be overpowered and likely killed. There is no escape. All exits to the building are covered. There are specially trained sharpshooters on the roofs of buildings surrounding the hotel. Just so you know. Now, please put down the phone. Don't hang it up, and walk to your door, open it, and allow the agents to enter. Please do so within the next fifteen-seconds or the agents will break down the door. Do you understand?"

"Yes," Bud said, choking, this time.

"When you open the door, lie flat on the floor and place your hands on top of your head."

"Okay, that would be fine," Bud responded, speaking like he would to a sophisticated sommelier suggesting a fine bottle of wine; yet his mouth was as dry as a cracked creek bed. His tongue felt swollen. A sudden chill convulsed him.

Bud's knees were trembling to the point that he could hardly take the seven strides to the door. As promised, there they were, waiting with a battering ram if he had not made it within the time allowed.

Fourteen hours later Bud's grueling interrogation was still underway.

◆

The last time Robert was truly drunk was on the occasion of his first real date with Deborah. Eating oysters and drowning each one in Dixie Beer. This time he drank himself into a stupor at the bar at the Holiday Inn and decided to stay that way until Sunday morning. He had plenty of money to support his binge but occasionally needed another fifty or one hundred dollar bill from the duffel bag in the trunk of the Thunderbird parked in the hotel lot. His mission throughout the night and early morning hours was to participate in each round of drinks downed by his fellow patrons who were all soaking up their sorrows and raising their toasts to their fallen leader. Many of those rounds came at his expense. Around noon that Sunday Robert finally bought the last round for his freeloading friends and decided to sober up with the help of a big breakfast at the café next door. As he paid the last tab, he overheard the bartender tell a waiter that the newscaster just announced Oswald was being moved to the Dallas County Jail and that, "They're gonna show that son-of-a-bitch on television."

Robert hoisted himself back up on the barstool to wait as the bartender flicked on the screen of the television set resting on a ledge suspended above the bar. It had a fuzzy picture. Robert knew he could fix it.

Christ, there he is. They must have beaten the crap out of him. He looks like hell.

Flanked by two huge deputies proudly donning their Stetsons for the cameras Robert watched as Lee in shackles stepped toward the camera. His eyes cast down. His expression forlorn.

Look up Lee. Smile for the camera.

Then Robert saw a man suddenly blocking the view on the screen. There were two pops, maybe three and then pandemonium ensued.

"Oswald's been shot! Oswald's been shot!" the announcer screamed.

Hey, the guy in the hat...the black hat...who just shot Lee. I only got a glimpse. Mostly the back of his head. For a second there, he looked like Jack. Jack of Joe and Jack. Our friendly hosts here in El Paso. Those two big pricks in their Fedora hats. No, it can't be. God that looked like him. No, I must still be drunk.

◆

"Okay Mr. Carlson, let's go back through it again. You say this guy Robert; he's an expert mechanic, fixes juke boxes. You like him, he's a good employee, has a wife and child. You help him, you grow fond of him; everything's fine until a few months ago, and then he starts acting weird, starts talking politics, becomes more radical as the months go by and then he disappears for a while; comes back, gives you this money, then disappears again. Wow, what a story. Let's stop there for a minute. Then I want you to go back to the beginning and fill in all the details on everything I just said," the FBI agent commanded.

"I've been over it fifty times already," Bud pleaded.

"I don't care how many times we go over it; a hundred more if necessary. We want every bit of information in that head of yours out here for all of us to hear," the agent responded.

Bud told the story again, trying hard not to miss anything while desperately striving to be consistent in his telling. He already knew, now into the sixteenth hour of his ordeal, that inconsistency would prolong the questioning and heighten further suspicion. Several times he thought about demanding a lawyer to stop the badgering but dismissed that temptation since he was committed to cooperating. Yet he remained terrified that his detention would continue indefinitely. Another hour went by. Another retelling to the point where Robert disappeared a second time.

At the end Bud decided to play his card. "Agent so and so, whatever your name is, I am asking you to contact Detective Max Nedbalski of the Denver Police Department. If you do, I believe he will verify my story and help us make some progress here. I'm not going to say anything further until you speak with him. I need him to help convince you that I had nothing to do with the President's murder. As far as my involvement with Robert Kaye, if he is a suspect, it is as I've tried to describe it. I'm telling the truth. If you don't call Nedbalski I'll stop talking and ask for a lawyer."

The agent, the fifth one to have taken turns grinding away at Bud since his arrest, stopped his pacing around the dungeon-like room, leaned down, looked sharply into Bud's eyes and pounced on him with a shrill.

"Who is this guy? You say he's a Denver cop! Why haven't you mentioned him before? He knows all about this? Knows about the money sitting in your safe? Now you tell us. You protecting him? Is he involved?" the agent yelled.

"Please, just call him," Bud responded calmly, turning his head away from the agent's onslaught, every muscle and fiber in his being exhausted and spent.

◆

Robert went to the duffel bag in the trunk of the Thunderbird and pulled out another small stack of bills. It was Monday morning. The day of the funeral. It was the day after Lee's stomach was ripped to shreds by Jack's close range bullets. Robert thought he remembered hearing the television announcer proclaim Lee's demise but he wasn't sure. He was so drunk by around two o'clock on Sunday; the time they said the surgeons gave up and pulled the sheet over Oswald's face, that the whole incident had become a blur. He forgot to eat breakfast as well, and just drank through the day. Robert drank alone. Terribly alone. Even among the crowds that swarmed around the television sets in the lounge, in the café, in the hotel lobby, everywhere he went, he was alone. He watched in silence as the throngs passed by the coffin in the Capitol Rotunda, Jackie in her black veil. He was part of that but was alone. He felt no joy, even though he should have since he had done his duty and no one would doubt that he played an important part. That is, if he got away and told them so. Told Clay and David and all the rest, especially Deborah. If he were caught, they would never know. All would be forsaken and forgotten. For now he was only caught up in the sadness. Was it sadness over the deaths, or because Deborah was gone? Left alone.

Through the haze one thought kept coming back to him.

How strange. Why did they let Jack; what was his name? The television guy said Ruby, I think, get so close to Lee to hit him point blank? If this guy were Kennedy's killer, wouldn't they protect him better than with just two struttin' for the cameras Dallas dicks on each arm?

Robert limped up to the registration desk at the hotel and paid the clerk in advance for five more night's stay at the going rate.

Robert decided he was not ready to journey south to Mexico. He did not know why. Maybe he was taking a risk remaining in the country. Maybe someone would connect him to Lee, to Jack Ruby, the Jack of Jack and Joe who Robert now knew unmistakably was the man who killed Lee before a worldwide audience. Seeing Ruby's front-page photo in that morning's newspaper seared the image into Robert's brain.

Son-of-a-bitch, it's him all right; Robert said a little too loudly when he pulled the newspaper from the Holiday Inn's newsstand.

With fresh cash in his pocket Robert went back to the bar to join hundreds of millions of people across the globe watching the solemn procession, the rider-less horse, the drums beating methodically to the funeral march down Pennsylvania Avenue, across Memorial Bridge and into Arlington National Cemetery. He watched the little boy salute; Jackie light the Eternal Flame, and thought *I am a victim of this senseless assassination like all of these other people.* I am not the reason. I am not culpable. I am in mourning like all the rest.

Yes, Lee is dead. Jack is in jail. Deborah is likely back in New Orleans. Back with Clay and David at the dance studio.

Were they celebrating? Were they sad, or were they joyful? Were they laughing at me, knowing I'm a fugitive while they are safe; a great distance from the mayhem?

Wait, they don't know about me. No one saw me. No one's looking for me. No one cares.

51

Max Nedbalski sat across from Bud at the long, grey metal table in the interrogation room buried deep beneath the Albuquerque jailhouse. They were alone, but they weren't. A dozen pairs of anxious eyes peered into the room through the one-way glass. The microphone under the table picked up every sound they made. Twenty-three hours and counting since Bud lain prone and handcuffed on the hotel room floor. They let him sleep on the cot in the corner of the room awaiting Max's arrival. His supper was a cold ham sandwich and strong black coffee to keep him awake.

"They're listening; right?" Bud asked his friend.

"Yea, they're listening. I'm not your lawyer, so they can," Max confirmed.

"What's the link, Max? Did they tell you why they came after me? How is Robert connected to all of this? How'd they do it? Why are they doing this to me?"

Max instinctively moved closer to Bud as if to deliver a secret message but he knew his words would never be private. He was telling it so the others could gauge Bud's reaction.

"Binoculars. They found the binoculars in Oswald's room," Max said evenly.

"Binoculars? What binoculars?" Bud's response was a deeply quizzical look at his friend, a look oblivious to the significance of Max's revelation.

On the other side of the mirror the agents glanced at each other. Some skeptical of Bud's reaction; others watching the scene unfold differently.

Maybe he was ignorant of the connection.

"A pair of binoculars ended up in Oswald's room. They think Oswald or a second shooter planned to use them but didn't, or maybe they did. They don't know at this point. Most are saying that Oswald was the only shooter. That he acted alone. While others think Robert may have been the second shooter, or there was another assassin and that Robert was supposed to be the driver of a getaway car. They are looking for a late model Dodge sedan. A gas station clerk thinks he recognized Oswald in a car with another man driving who'd stopped for gas a couple of days before the shooting." Max explained.

"What about the binoculars?" Bud's own curiosity was now apparent; his dread remaining beneath the surface at that moment.

"They were bought in Denver. They had your fingerprints on them," Max proclaimed.

"Oh, my God," Bud moaned. Now it registered. The puzzle suddenly solved.

"I bought them. I gave them to him for his birthday; at least he said it was his birthday. He told me he loved to watch the birds in City Park when he went there with his wife and baby," Bud said, suddenly feeling nauseous but not from the stale ham sandwich.

52

It was Tuesday. The President's funeral was over. People's lives retaking a hint of normalcy. Thinking about Thanksgiving. Robert sat by himself in the near empty hotel café sipping coffee and reading every word of every story about the events of the days before.

They apparently operated on Oswald in the same operating theatre as Kennedy. Amazing. Jackie would stay in the White House as long as she wished. President Johnson, however, was making preparations for a quick move from the Naval Observatory into his new residence. Robert reread some of the same stories. He had nothing else to do and no place to go.

Then he sensed someone hovering over him. It wasn't his pestering waitress who was ending her shift and wanted to clear his tab and collect her tip. Robert looked up from his newspapers. The man standing over him asked rather politely, "May I sit down?"

Without waiting for an invitation Joe of Jack and Joe sat heavily in the booth across from Robert. He removed his fedora and placed it on the table. He was expressionless. He wiped his brow with a clean white handkerchief from the breast pocket of his dark suit. "I'd like some coffee if you don't mind," Joe said.

"I don't want any trouble," Robert said nervously.

"Neither do I," Joe responded.

The restless waitress arrived with a piping hot pot of fresh coffee and poured a cup full for Joe.

"Robert; things didn't go quite as planned," Joe began after stirring four heaping teaspoons of sugar into his cup in what Robert thought was an attempt to turn the brew into syrup.

"You should have enough money with you to get into Mexico and vanish. Why haven't you left? What are you doing here, drinkin' coffee and readin' the newspaper?" Joe probed.

Robert was silent. The threatening tone of Joe's voice seemed to intensify with each of his words.

"You need to go now. Get in that fuckin' car of yours and head across the border. Don't look back. Don't ever come back." Joe was spewing his words by now. His spittle splattered on Robert's cheek.

Robert dabbed himself clean with his paper napkin. "If I go or stay it won't make any difference, will it?" Robert responded defiantly. "You're gonna kill me anyway."

Joe leaned back in his seat, grabbed his cup and gulped down the last drop of his sugary mixture. "Can't say but if I was you I'd take my chances on the run," Joe advised.

With that Joe got up, put a dollar bill on the table and said, "Don't be stupid. You got nothin' to bargain with. All the others are protected. You're the only one exposed. You're the only one they can get to. If you live that long, and they find you and lock you up, there won't be another guy like Jack to put you out of your misery." Joe strolled off smiling and tipping his hat to the waitress when passing her by.

◆

At about that time Bud and Max, with Max driving the big grey Lincoln four-door, crossed back over the New Mexico border into Colorado. Bud exhaled as they exited the Land of his Disenchantment "What was that?" asked the detective who had persuaded the Feds to allow him to take Bud into protective custody.

"I don't know. I guess I'm glad to be home. Away from all of that. I must say I've had better weekends," Bud said with a glimpse of sarcastic humor.

Max chuckled. "Yea, I can imagine. So have I."

"Did they also put you through the wringer?" Bud asked.

"Yes, they did. They were not happy with me not writing a report about you and Robert to begin with, and especially allowing you to put all that money in your safe. They admit there was no crime observed when he gave you the cash but they still took their shots at me. The whole bunch of them, the FBI, Secret Service, Dallas cops, everyone. They're all ducking for cover right now. They're all being blamed for not protecting him so I expect I'll feel the heat for some time to come," Max said.

Then his tone grew even more serious. "You know this is only the beginning. These guys will be relentless with you. You can bet right now they are digging deeper into you than you ever knew possible. Before they're done they'll have counted the hair on your balls."

Bud looked over at his friend and nodded in resignation.

Max continued, "You need to tell your family when we get home. Have them prepared. No doubt the Feds will soon be on their doorsteps, looking for anything that might tie you or them to individuals or groups who might have supported Oswald or Robert. At this point no one knows if there was a conspiracy at all. All they know is that Oswald somehow ended up with those binoculars. They came from you, apparently through Robert Kaye. They're theorizing that Oswald may have intended to use them or a second shooter may have wanted them. It's only a theory. It's a good one. Unfortunately, with your link to Robert you may have given them evidence to expand on that theory."

Bud's attention was riveted on the detective.

"This is the biggest crime of the century," Max went on. "The government will use all of its resources to get to the bottom of it. However, there are politics involved even at this early stage. There are those in the government who hope like hell that Oswald was a single lunatic acting on his own. That, of course, would disprove a widespread conspiracy and keep it all contained. Frankly, that's best for the country. Signs of an unstable government are tempting to our enemies. The Soviets are probably rejoicing now and licking their chops."

"Others may believe Kennedy was killed in an attempt to overthrow the government and that Oswald was part of a vast ring of politically motivated thugs who saw the country controlled by a Kennedy family dynasty for decades to come, and they set out to destroy the first king in the line of succession. Or some believe his killing was revenge over something he did while in office, like pushing civil rights or the Bay of Pigs. Who knows?

"My bet is regardless of the evidence the conclusion will be that Oswald acted alone. Robert Kaye's or Bud Carlson's names may never be made public," Max openly speculated.

"Will we ever know the truth? I doubt it. I do know that they'll turn over every rock as far as you're concerned. They'll know everything there is to know about you and your family. So get used to it and get your family used to it," Max advised.

He paused and then probed, "Is there anything you haven't told me?"

Bud did not hesitate. "No, Max, I swear. You know it all. I've told you and them the truth," Bud responded earnestly.

"I believe you. I'm sorry you have to go through this," Max said sincerely.

They rode along in silence for a while and then Bud asked, "With all of this, do you think they might find my daughters?"

"Count on it," Max answered.

"Then it will all be worth it," was Bud's response with a smile, his first in many days.

◆

Instead of driving due south, Robert headed west not thinking about a destination, just thinking about survival. Somehow his instincts told him a longer lifespan was possible if he remained on this side of the border rather than crossing over, so he steered the Thunderbird toward the next major town, Tucson, Arizona.

Robert was surprisingly calm as he drove along Route 10. Joe's threat, or more likely Joe's promise of his imminent death, had not caused panic or a sense of desperation. Maybe he already knew his fate and he'd take a bullet to the brain real soon and it would all be over. Maybe he was confident that the authorities would chase Robert Kaye's story into one blind alley after another until this whole mess blew over.

Maybe he just didn't care. What did he have to live for anyway? Other people had destroyed his life. Beginning with Fodor, then the Soviets, then Deborah, and then finally Lee Harvey Oswald. At least with Lee, connected to him as he was, Robert Kaye, aka Roman Sokolowski, would die a famous man. A man of mystery and intrigue. A man featured in the history books. A man no one could ever say for certain didn't fire a second shot through John Kennedy's skull.

But why should I take the fall alone, Robert asked himself as the desert stretched endlessly out over the hood of the black beauty.

They've all abandoned me. Why should I protect them?

Two hours later Robert pulled into the parking lot of the Tucson Police Department.

◆

Bud took the day off on Wednesday to call and explain the situation to each of his family members. By the time he got to his parents, who still lived on their Nebraska farm, three FBI agents were already seated in their living room. Jeannie met him at his house but she had a difficult time finding a parking place on the street since most of the spaces were already taken by plain unmarked sedans occupied by men in white shirts and narrow black ties.

When Bud went to work the next day two agents were waiting for him in his office with a search warrant demanding access to all corners of the premises plus complete financial records of the company since its inception. Marshall Goodpaster assured the agents full cooperation. Bud spent the day producing every document in his possession. He provided the agents with their own private office in which to work and he made sure Mary Lou brought them coffee and fresh, not stale, sandwiches for lunch. She wore her skirt too tight and her blouse too loose but the agents hardly took notice.

At day's end they said they would be back on Friday and warned him not to disturb anything in their workspace.

Late Friday afternoon Bud was summonsed to Denver FBI headquarters for further questioning. There was much more to discuss. He was not allowed to leave until early Sunday morning. The forty thousand dollars confiscated from his office safe was now resting in an evidence locker in the basement of their building. The money was a topic that couldn't be put to rest.

◆

"That's a fantastic story there Robert, if I do say so. You've got a real big imagination," the agent grinned with pure disdain.

"So you're sayin' you and Oswald teamed up there in Denver; trained together for weeks; traveled all the way to Mexico to map out your escape; came back to the States...you goin' back to Denver and Oswald goin' off to Dallas. Then you get this call and you meet him in Dallas and you drive around for a week planning how you're gonna get out of town fast sometime on Friday. All along you don't know that Oswald's gonna kill Kennedy and you've been duped into helpin' him? You think he might... just might be plannin' something big. Is that right? Is that what I'm supposed to believe?" The agent's voice was mellow and melodic. Without allowing Robert to answer, he exploded.

"What do you take us for, a bunch of fucking idiots?"

"You come marchin' in here with a platoon of Tucson cops on your heels, all of them thinkin' they've captured the second assassin, and you're tellin' us this cockamamie story because some bad guys out there are gonna kill you because they put Oswald up to it and you're in the way, and maybe, just maybe, there's a vast conspiracy tryin' to topple our government.

"You little piece of shit. I should stomp your head in," the agent exclaimed and slammed his fist on the table on which Robert casually rested his elbows.

"Every word's the truth," Robert said, looking up in his face to respond calmly.

At the sound of a door opening behind him, the burly Fed spun around away from Robert who was seated in a room not too dissimilar to that in which Bud was grilled a few days before. A man handed the agent a folded piece of paper. He opened it and read. A long silence ensued while the Fed paced the room occasionally glancing at the note in his hand. Finally he stopped and sat down across from Robert. His voice returning to conversational tone.

"Okay Mr. Kaye or whatever your name is. Let's just say for a moment that you are telling the truth. Let's just say you knew Oswald and you unwittingly helped him, but all you knew was something big was gonna happen. Let's just say you did all those things with him like goin' to Mexico and drivin' around Dallas like a madman. Let me ask you, did you ever buy anything for him or give him anything?"

Robert sat back in his chair, removing his elbows from the table and crossing his arms to ponder the question for a short time.

"Nothing except for a pair of binoculars," Robert replied.

◆

"I think it might be best if you took some time off," Marshall suggested cautiously to Bud as they sat in his office after another day of endless searches and questions.

"I can't just sit in my house, waiting for these goons to search it again, or to take me downtown to ask me the same questions I've answered a thousand times," Bud replied.

"Bud, I can't blame you for being distracted. I can hardly keep my mind on work. I can imagine how hard it is for you to concentrate," Marshall observed.

"Marshall; look, I can handle it. I need to come to work everyday just to get my mind off it, to think about something else. Don't keep me away. Let me work, it's the only way I'm gonna get through it." Bud was pleading now.

"Okay, I'm behind you. I think you know that," Marshall said with reassurance.

"I do, thanks," Bud said.

"Did you hear that Johnson's ordered a so-called blue ribbon committee to investigate the assassination? To be headed up by Justice Earl Warren," Marshall said.

"The Supreme Court Earl Warren?" Bud asked.

"That's him," Marshall confirmed.

◆

"So now there's this bunch of strange characters who meet every week in some abandoned dance studio and none of them ever reveal their last names. You and this woman who lives with you in this boardinghouse go to these meetings and all they talk about is how disenchanted they are with the government. How they hate all politicians, especially Kennedy. Am I right so far?" Robert's new interrogator, the sixth in succession, asked.

"So far, that's correct," Robert, agreed.

"Okay, and you think these people, or some of them, maybe this Clay or this David fellow, might be involved in a plot with Oswald? You being where you were and going to these meetings and all, and then being contacted while you're in Denver, you think maybe there's a connection. Am I on the right track there as well?"

"Yes, you are," Robert affirmed.

"Great. Now there's this guy in Denver, this Oxnard fellow. He tells you his last name, but he's the only one who does say his last name except of course Oswald, and you think he's connected to the people in New Orleans. Why would he give you his last name?"

"Don't know," Robert said.

"Probably an alias, you think?"

"Could be," Robert acknowledged.

"Okay, but he's the one who introduces you to Oswald who's come to Denver just to meet you. You're some special guy, huh?"

"I don't appreciate your sarcasm, sir," Robert responded sharply.

The agent was momentarily taken aback by Robert's boldness but quickly continued. "So at the end of your training with Oswald in Denver, you drive to El Paso in your fancy Thunderbird. There you meet up with two heavies. You think one of them was Jack Ruby, the guy who killed Oswald."

"I know it was him."

"Goddamn boy, this is a blockbuster if it's all true. But you know what I think? I think you're some crazy little punk who sits in front of the television set all day. Your leg's all busted up, so you can't get any women. You live in a fantasy world. You play make believe. Along comes the story of the century and you decide to put yourself right in the middle of it. Robert in Wonderland. You're gonna become famous. You'll make yourself out as a pure innocent victim of a bunch of radical anti-government zombies who help Oswald pull off the murder, and right now they're hiding out there in the swamps of Louisiana just waiting to plug you just like Oswald did the President. And Ruby did Oswald. How close am I, Robert? Ain't I gettin' close to the truth?"

"Go fuck yourself," Robert responded defiantly.

◆

By about that time nearly thirty multipage teletypes had been transmitted from Tucson, Arizona and Denver, Colorado to FBI headquarters in Washington, DC regarding the potential connection of Robert Kaye to the tragic death of the President. A fairly equal number were transcript summaries of several agents' accounts of their interviews with Robert and Bud. As more of the secret documents flew over the encrypted wire machines, investigators in the Capital City noticed a reoccurring theme to the transcriptions.

Something akin to, "Robert Kaye is nothing more than a poor, frustrated, neurotic misfit who fantasizes about having been a hero in the Hungarian Uprising and coming to America to find his fame and fortune as an inventor of new electronic gadgets. He claims to be a political extremist who dreams of leading a group of fellow malcontents into a new world utopia. He gets caught up with a fringe group of radicals in New Orleans who like to spout off about the ills of American society and talk wildly about revenge and rebellion. Kaye is probably the only one who takes their nonsense seriously.

"He also has delusions about a woman in the group and thinks she is a special messenger assigned just to him to proselytize wisdom and truth. He falls in love, but she rejects him and he marries on the rebound and leaves town in search of a new beginning. He's so important to their cause they cannot let him go so a new guidance counselor finds him and brings him back into the fold. He is given money and goes on exotic trips to further his radical indoctrination. Finally, his big moment arrives. He is introduced to Lee Harvey Oswald. They become fast friends and little by little Kaye is brought into Oswald's inner circle.

"He hears about the planning for a big event. He knows Oswald is the ringleader but not much more. Kaye becomes Oswald's sidekick, but Kaye is kept ignorant of the details of the plot; only that it is to be a major happening. He trains with Oswald, travels with him, carries his bags, and chauffeurs him around.

"They design an elaborate escape plan after this big event, but all Kaye knows is it will happen on Friday, November, 22nd.

"On the big day, disaster strikes. Their plan goes array. Oswald is captured and then killed. Kaye runs for his life. Soon they find him. He is out of favor now, so he thinks they want him dead. He runs again, but this time into the arms of the law.

"The transmissions to Washington about Bud are less mocking and acerbic yet they describe him as shrewd, wily and clever who, while outwardly pledging full cooperation in the investigation, is yet to "come clean" about Kaye and the mysterious binoculars. They dismiss the money in his safe as inconsequential, noting that, "Kaye probably won it gambling somewhere and looked to Carlson to help him invest it."
"Therefore, agents in the field recommend that the Bureau's surveillance of Carlson continue indefinitely and "spontaneous, unannounced detentions take place to accommodate further questioning." The response from Washington was full concurrence. "Keep up the heat," senior officials ordered.

"Meanwhile investigators ironically grow weary and increasing leery of Robert's assertions. Several times his jailors threaten to set him free. Only then would Robert reveal a little more, desperately trying to entice the Bureau into offering him permanent protection and a free ride, supported by the government, into societal oblivion."

"I'll tell you more about Clay, or I'll tell you more about Oxnard. Want to know what Oswald said to me once? Follow the money they gave me, it will lead you back to them," Robert would blabber frantically when he faced unguarded freedom.

The process went on for weeks, then months.

Bureau agents eventually, at their leisure, located Preston Oxnard in Denver. They spent an hour with him over a friendly cup of coffee at a local restaurant, and quickly labeled him a harmless "kook" who they were sure never met Robert Kaye, let alone became his liaison to Lee Harvey Oswald.

As a matter of courtesy, however, a large number of censored reports ultimately found their way to the office of New Orleans District Attorney Jim Garrison.

The documents landed on Deborah Henley's desk on a Tuesday morning in December 1964. They came by regular mail with no special markings, not even a return address. Out of habit she opened the envelope and without noticing the source or the contents placed the stack of papers on the corner of her desk for further review. She was sorting the rest of the mail along with the overnight police blotter when Garrison came out of his office and casually strolled up to Deborah's desk to engage in their normal idle early morning chatter.

Nonchalantly, he lifted the documents from her desk and began to read. Moments later, his voice cracked excitedly as he spoke, "Deborah, my God, did you see this?"

She glanced up at him from her work, surprised by his animated question.

"No, what is it? Those papers came this morning in a blank envelope. I thought it was junk mail," she responded, now very curious.

Garrison walked back toward his office. As he stepped away Deborah heard him murmuring words barely audible. "Holy Christ, this is unbelievable."

Then nearly shouting, "Unbelievable… Holy Christ!"

Deborah scampered into his office and shut the door.

As Garrison read aloud from the pile of memoranda Deborah's heart pounded faster, her whole body grew clammy. She felt faint.

Robert Kaye, one of several aliases, formerly claiming to live in New Orleans, is in protective custody in Arizona, alleged to be associated with Lee Harvey Oswald in plot to kill Kennedy. Kaye claims to be connected with a mysterious, clandestine group in New Orleans. A radical anti-government mob that meets periodically in an abandoned dance studio somewhere in the French Quarter. Befriended by a female who introduced subject to the assembly. Leaders only go by their first names, Clay and David. Both are supposedly prominent businessmen in New Orleans. Name of female consort not revealed or unknown. Other names in the group are Sally and Tom. Subject is of Hungarian descent. Immigration status unknown. Walks with pronounced limp reportedly due to war injury incurred while fighting Soviets in 1956 uprising.

Bureau highly skeptical of subject's claims. Subject appears delusional at times, bordering on irrationality.

"This is fantastic!" Garrison exclaimed, finally looking up from the documents to search for Deborah's whereabouts and her reaction.

She was seated across from him, pale and at first uncommunicative.

"Deborah, what's wrong with you? Don't you see the potential in this?" Garrison railed disappointed, yet intrigued by her lack of shared exuberance.

Finally she recaptured her stoic self-control and said, "You bet, boss. This is fabulous. They seem to be laying it all right in your lap. Leaving it up to you to pursue it or not."

"That's what I find curious. Why haven't the Feds swarmed all over this town? Why would they just send these explosive reports to me without even a Bureau return address? What are they thinking?" he pondered openly.

"Maybe they don't believe this guy," Deborah offered. "Maybe they think he's a fruitcake and he's made it all up. Some of what you read seems to speculate on his mental state; frankly whether he's crazy and just looking for attention to make a name for himself," she added hurriedly in a frantic attempt to cast doubt in Garrison's mind.

Garrison sat in silence for several moments, reading to himself. As she watched him scan the documents Deborah knew, after being intimately but only professionally involved with him for many months, that he was contemplating his next move.

At last he looked up at her and smiled broadly. "I don't give a shit whether the Feds including J. Edgar Hoover himself think Robert Kaye is a moron, we're gonna launch an all out, no holds barred investigation into a potential conspiracy into the assassination of John F. Kennedy. Yes, right here, right in our own backyard.

"This is our ticket, Deborah. International headlines. Every nightly newscast. Forget the next term. On to the Governor's mansion. No! Onto the U.S. Senate. This is every man's dream for someone in my position, with my ambition. We're gonna find ourselves a Mister Clay, and a Mister David, and a Miss Sally. We're gonna find this mystery woman, and who knows, maybe they exist and it's all true, maybe not, but maybe they did help Oswald. Christ, so much the better, but who cares, it's the investigation that's important," Garrison exclaimed.

He walked from behind his desk around to where Deborah sat. She stood and offered a weak smile. He grabbed and hugged her mightily.

◆

It was a Tuesday in December 1964. Bud was seated at his favorite lunch counter in a place called the Summit Café, chomping on a turkey and Swiss on rye when the empty stool beside him was suddenly occupied by a man he knew, but a man devoid of a friendly face.

"We have Robert Kaye, or whatever his name is, in custody in Tucson, Arizona," proclaimed FBI Agent Chester Gold.

"He claims to have obtained the money he gave you from a group he was involved with who plotted with Oswald to kill Kennedy. He says you knew about that and you agreed with it. Is that right?" Agent Gold asked with a menacing sneer.

"Bud finished chewing on his last bite of sandwich, calmly took a sip of lukewarm ice tea, and turned to Agent Gold presenting his own unpleasant grin and said, "That's total bulllshit, Chester and you know it."

"I do; I know that," Agent Gold replied, "I had to ask you anyway; just for the record."

"So how long have you had that little bastard in the slammer," Bud inquired.

"Since last December when he turned himself in," the Agent responded.

"Everyone up and down the line; all the way to Hoover and maybe even the White House seems convinced that he's a pathological liar who is physically crippled and broke and looking for a big splash of notoriety to boost his ego and snag a free ride into witness protection for the rest of his life."

"How's that? What are you saying? How could he ever claim he needs government protection?" Bud asked, now deeply curious.

"He says he's been threatened by his former benefactors, who now want him out of the way because he got too close to Oswald; that he knew Oswald's every move; except the last one… pulling the trigger," Agent Gold said.

"So Robert Kaye says he became Oswald's right hand man, but he didn't know anything about the assassination. He was given money and told what to do by this group, and with that, a larger conspiracy existed, blowing a hole right through the Warren Commission's lone gunman theory. Is that it? Do you think he's crazy, Chester," Bud asked.

Agent Gold folded his hands and placed them on the lunch counter in front of where he sat. He looked around the diner avoiding Bud's piercing gaze. At last he sighed and spoke in a hushed tone.

"I'm probably the only guy in law enforcement on this planet who believes the miserable rat. Well, besides Max Nedbalski. It's because of you. What you've told me and told the other agents. No doubt, Max helped convince me as well. There's tons of solid evidence supporting this guy's story. The binoculars; the money; the black

Thunderbird; his own movements in Dallas. This mysterious woman he keeps referring to. Jack Ruby in El Paso. The people in New Orleans. All of it. There is not a word about him or any of this is in the Commission's report. It's like he doesn't exist," Gold said with complete exasperation.

"I'm the only one who gives his story any credibility. No one else in the Bureau will touch it. I've tried. They all tell me to sit down and shut up. My career's at stake. I'm telling you it won't go anywhere from here. Soon they'll close the books on him, label you nothing more than a greedy swindler who took his money and planned to gamble it away. Then POOF. Case closed. We'll all go back on the same path with the same marching orders… support the sole assassin theory and quickly put this whole goddamn nightmare behind us."

53

"Deborah, you have to calm down. There's no reason to panic. As long as you keep doing what you're doing. There's too much distance between us and where Garrison is going with the investigation," Clay spoke assertively into the telephone receiver.

"I don't know if I can control things," Deborah replied, her voice quivering with strained emotion.

"He's now hoarding all the reports produced by the investigators. Some of them are even bypassing my desk and going straight into his office where he locks them up in his safe. I've only been able to attend two of the last three grand jury sessions because he's got me off doing other things. That really concerns me because that's where he stacks up the evidence and builds his case for indictments. Unless I know what's going on in those sessions, I can't keep steering them away from us."

Clay did not respond for some time.

"Are you there?" Deborah shrieked into the mouthpiece.

"Yes, I'm here," Clay said, concern creeping into his voice.

"Deborah, then you must try harder. You have to be bold. Take some risks. There's too much at stake. If we don't know the contents of those reports, how can we remain proactive in building a stronger shield around all of us, including you? You are the only one who can keep him off-track. Do not fail!" Clay abruptly hung up the telephone and turned to David who was seated comfortably on a long black leather couch placed along the wall in Clay's posh French Quarter office located just off Canal on Poydras Street.

David's relaxed state abruptly changed when his longtime friend had suddenly slammed down the telephone receiver and turned to face him with an uncommon look of anxiety, bordering on abject panic.

"She's cracking, David," Clay said with a guttural rasping voice. He coughed and hacked for several seconds before reaching for the Sterling silver pitcher on the corner of his desk and pouring ice water into a tall crystal glass. He drank it down in giant gulps before speaking again. "She's no longer reliable. We need to penetrate Garrison's office through other means. Perhaps even removing her to avoid exposure."

As Clay spoke he paced the room slowly traversing across the exquisite Persian rugs that cushioned his steps. David watched his friend's movements and mannerisms with an intense gaze.

"It will be done, Clay, I will handle it. You relax. I don't want you dying on me from a heart attack," David smiled at his attempt to lighten the moment while providing words of reassurance.

"Garrison's a buffoon. The whole country has bought into every word in the Warren Commission report. Garrison's riding on total hearsay and third hand information. All impeachable sources, and he knows it. He's a publicity hound. If somehow he manages to come after us we will bury him with credible witnesses and one conflicting story after another. Alibis all around. He'll end up chasing his tail for the next five years. Embarrassing himself immensely. That grand jury will get so sick of him they'll probably indict him as a public nuisance," David added with an additional stab at humor.

Ignoring the levity, Clay said with uncertainty, "You better be right about all of this, David."

"Remember, the best friends we have in this world right now are Chief Justice Earl Warren, the FBI and Lyndon Johnson. To save the country they've all convinced themselves that Oswald was a lone wolf. We just need to keep them thinking that," David added.

"What about Robert Kaye? What do we do about him?" Clay asked, then added, "He's been singing like a canary for months now."

"When the Feds kick him loose... well, it may be unpleasant for him," David responded.

"Fine. I'm glad there is a plan. He could be worse for us than Deborah," Clay said, and then exclaimed at what he saw. "Why do you keep that photograph?"

David was hunched forward in his seat on the couch grasping with both hands and staring intently at a four by five inch black and white, rather grainy print. He chuckled at Clay's outburst but placed the print back into the inside pocket of his suit coat.

"I can't believe you are carrying that around with you. A photograph of you and Oswald with those other air cadet pilots of yours. Are you crazy?" Clay barked.

"Don't you understand, Clay? This is my keepsake. Those were the good old days with the Louisiana Civil Air Patrol; teaching those kids to fly, and to hunt and shoot. Oswald was never too good you know, as a pilot, that is. He often got airsick. I even think he was afraid of heights. He became a good shot after I gave him a few pointers," David proudly proclaimed, then added, "There's no other copy of this, Clay, so don't worry. I keep it because it reminds me of how skillful I was in taking that fine fellow and shaping him into the most hated human being in the world."

54

It took Bud three solid days but he read every word of the eight hundred and eighty-eight page Warren Commission Report once it was released. Chester Gold and Max Nedbalski were right. Not a single word was in there about Robert Kaye, Bud Carlson or anyone ever connected with either one of them.

"Not a word," Bud said to Jeannie, closing the thick hardbound copy and placing it on the coffee table in front of where they sat.

"It almost seems like you wanted your name in there," Jeannie remarked curiously. "Did you?"

Bud considered her question for some time before answering. "Well, after all they've put us through it would have been the right thing for them to say something, like he was a good American; he told the truth. He helped in the investigation. Something positive."

"Don't you see; if you were even mentioned, or if Robert was discussed in any way, it widens the circle around Oswald and points to a conspiracy. They couldn't stand for that," Jeannie reminded him.

"I know. You're right. Will we ever know the truth? After the hundreds of hours they spent interrogating me, you'd think there would be some written documentation. Was all of that hidden away somewhere in a vault under the FBI building or burned in their incinerator?" Bud paused and added.

"What about Robert? Is he alive? I spoke with Sophia the other day. She's never heard a word. She's still in Las Vegas. Her divorce is final. She's dating a black jack dealer she says loves her child and makes them both happy. I'm glad for her," Bud remarked wistfully.

"Bud," Jeannie said sternly, "Listen to me. You just closed that book. See it right there, on our coffee table in our house where you just put it. It's done. It's over. We will never know the truth and that's okay. It will be a wonderful story to tell our grandchildren." She patted her swollen belly and leaned toward him to gently kiss his cheek.

"I hope you're right sweetheart but something tells me there's more to come," Bud replied with an allusion of dread.

◆

When orders finally came down the FBI chain of command from Washington to the Bureau office in Tucson to release Robert Kaye from custody, he had gained twenty-five pounds from the high caloric jailhouse diet, grown a full beard and his hair hung to his shoulders in wavy lengths to emulate the emerging counterculture "hippie" style of the day. Long before his discharge, agents ceased their interviews of him. They had grown tired of his fabricated ranting, as they viewed it, and simply allowed him to huddle in his jail cell and fantasize over his place in history. He claimed he was writing his own Warren Commission-type report on the assassination of John Kennedy and would someday refute all the government's unsubstantiated assertions. His handwritten pages on the subject counted well over three hundred.

Robert wept uncontrollably the night before they escorted him to the front gate of the compound to bid a not-so-friendly farewell. He carried his papers in a satchel a guard gave him and had forty-five dollars in his pocket, the exact amount in his possession when he turned himself in many months before. It was beastly hot that day in Tucson, hotter than normal for early May with the temperature in the mid nineties. As Robert limped along in the direction of the Greyhound bus depot he was reminded of his first day in New Orleans; where and when it all began. He remembered how he struggled carrying his heavy duffel and his burdensome thoughts of the unknown. His anxiety overcome by his determination kept him going until Mrs. Dionne's home for the wayward brought him in. Robert was thankful for that. He was thankful for Sigmund Roblinski and now wished he could tell him so. Yes, he was thankful for Deborah. She had fulfilled him. She gave him purpose. In a twisted way she replaced Fodor. Robert realized that now. She solidified in Robert what his father had shaped but could not quite harden.

No doubt she was to blame for his actions. She led him to conspire and to kill wantonly, spilling innocent blood on that Dallas sidewalk while Lee Oswald watched and nodded his approval. He would never expose her. He talked openly about all the others, but never about Deborah. She was sacred and pure. She made him hate and she made him love. If he went to her now he knew he would die even in disguise. He must find another port of New Orleans at which to disembark and start again. Without her, without it all, only his memories of the truth.

Robert inserted the key into the bus depot storage locker. It opened easily. A bright, piercing sunlight shone straight in to unveil his duffel, the same one he carried up Mrs. Dionne's steps and passed by where Clarence sat and rocked with contempt. He unzipped a section to eye the stacks of bills. The currency was enough to take him anywhere, to provide passage to the new. He closed the bag, slung it over his shoulder and limped toward a nearby parking garage. There Jesus Rodriquez, the senior lot attendant, was on duty as he always was at this time of day, every work day since Robert drove the Thunderbird down the ramp and bought a ticket thirteen months ago. Jesus was glad to see Robert after all this time. He led him to a dark, cool rear corner of the garage's third level to where it rested, awaiting his return, fully sheathed bumper to bumper in canvass wrapping. Once a week during Robert's confinement, Jesus took his call. They would chat amicably yet Robert would remind Jesus to drive it only through the garage's four levels to keep the fine machine well lubricated and the battery charged. Those were the only calls Robert made from his jail cell to anyone in the outside world. Remember, Robert would say, if you get the urge to drive it off, and steal it from me, you will be caught, because every cop in this country is looking for that car. Jesus believed him. He did as instructed patiently awaiting the day of Robert's return and the payment he deserved. Together they removed the Thunderbird's cloak. He tossed his duffel in the truck but not before retrieving twenty-one one hundred dollar bills. He climbed in the driver's seat and turned the key. The power plant roared to life. Robert grinned. Jesus grinned and pocketed the cash. He hitched a ride back up to his tollbooth and watched as Robert steered the automobile up the ramp and into the sunlight. He wondered if the cops were still looking for the car. Not my problem anymore, Jesus grinned again. Chihuahua would be his first stop, just as he and Lee planned, and then on to Mexico City and then beyond.

◆

"Deborah, please join me in my office," New Orleans District Attorney Jim Garrison said as he swept by her desk on his way into his private quarters.

Deborah rose from her desk chair, her knees weak. She grabbed her steno pad and a pencil, which she always kept at the ready for times when orders like these were issued. For weeks the atmosphere in Garrison's office had grown ripe with anticipation. To Deborah, ripe with a stench. A stench of fear. Garrison had cut himself off from all others in the office. Even his closet advisors, Deborah included, were permitted into his sanctum only when asked and only with information he felt pertinent to the case.

Garrison, alone, took charge of the grand jury sessions, not allowing any of his deputies or his investigators inside the heavily guarded courtroom. Rumor was he was carefully and methodically building evidence, shared with no one else, and would soon shock the world with his findings. The theory being he had targeted several New Orleans citizens and intended to bring them to holy justice for their monstrous acts.

Over the preceding weeks Deborah tried many times to reach Clay and David. She was cut off from them as well. They refused to take her calls. To see her, even to speak. She was alone. Isolated. Adrift. Mrs. Claire was concerned. Deborah had her moods, but never to this extreme. Never this desperate. She could not even touch her, let alone make love.

Garrison already was seated behind his desk when Deborah arrived to take her place across from him. He was looking down at a stack of documents and smiling broadly. His grin put Deborah into a state of near panic. An almost maniacal glare dominated his demeanor. He held it for some time. She waited for him to acknowledge her presence.

"My dear, the time has finally come. Our destiny is finally sealed. Tomorrow the eyes of the world will be upon us. We will name the scoundrels who helped kill our beloved President. They will be known to all. We will bring them to justice against all odds, against all who swore there was only one who acted single-handedly," Garrison spoke as if addressing a political rally.

Deborah's hand quaked. She put down her pencil. Garrison did not notice. His eye closed. His chin uplifted like a tent preacher praising his Lord.

Finally she could not hold back another moment. "Who are they, boss? Can you tell me who these people are?"

Garrison lowered his look toward the heavens and came eye level with Deborah. His stare lost its divinity and reassumed its fierceness.

"You don't know them, I'm sure, so I can tell. You are my confidant. Their names are Bertrand, Clay Bertrand, also known as

Clay Shaw, and a mister David Ferrie. I have sufficient evidence to directly link them to Oswald and others as the joint sources for their training, financial support, logistics, and planned escape. I am convinced there was a second gunman and these men, once I am done with them, will tell me who that person or persons was. Like Oswald at the hand of Ruby, I do not expect that second assassin to be alive, but we will know of him just the same. Tomorrow morning at ten I will hold a press conference to announce the indictments. Their crimes will be revealed. Their arrests imminent. Their convictions… certain." Garrison again lifted his head to the sky to revel in his words.

Deborah gagged and swallowed hard to remove the bile from her mouth. She stood and turned away from him to hide the pallor of her appearance. He did not realize her movement. She gained the strength to speak. She had to. If she didn't he would know something was amiss.

"That's fantastic, boss. I am so thrilled. I am so proud of you. You will be a national hero. It is an honor just to be near you."

David was astonished that Deborah had obtained his unlisted home telephone number. Yet he reminded himself of her position with the district attorney's office and its uncanny ability to gain access to private information. Her call hollowed out his insides. He could not move from his overstuffed easy chair. His full glass of expensive Kentucky bourbon formed a puddle on the carpet at his feet having also splattered a quantity on his blue silk slippers. His sockless feet inside the slippers were soaked and felt sticky. He could not cry although he tried.

The drawer to the interior of the gleaming black walnut round top table to his left was open part way. In it were his reading glasses and his revolver. The bourbon filled glass had tipped and fallen when he reached for the pearl handled piece the first time. The fall of the glass to the floor temporarily muddled his intent.

David was no coward. David was a pilot. An Army man. A leader of men. An example of good. He would fight the charges. Garrison had no case. Why did David's heart race so? Why the sudden pain? Why did his vision blur? Why the numbness in his left arm? Was that the cause of his spilled drink? His last thought brought him peace. His heart stopped before cowardly impulses overtook him to gain control. Before he had to pull the trigger.

David was found the next day by his housekeeper coming to clean. His prized pearl handled revolver still rested in the drawer. His Siamese cat licking the sugary substance off his exposed ankles.

◆

Jim Garrison was so overwhelmed by his moment of glory he did not realize that Deborah was absent that following morning. One of his investigators counted one hundred and twenty-three reporters, photographers and cameramen at his news conference. All three television networks covered the event live for their audiences. It was four o'clock in the afternoon following seven private interviews Garrison granted to selected correspondents before he asked an assistant to seek her whereabouts.

The light fixture in the bath down the hall from Robert's old room at Mrs. Dionne's lovely home on Harmony Street was partially yanked from its moorings in the ceiling by her weight. The brown cashmere scarf Mrs. Claire gave her on the anniversary of their first year together held taut when the sudden drop caused by the loosened light fixture snapped her neck easily. Miss Hattie found her dangling and spinning as the scarf twisted and untwisted in haunting revolutions. She was transfixed by the site for several moments before calmly descending the stairs to summon the others who were gathered for their ritual breakfast meal. After seeing the body, Mrs. Claire ran from the house screaming obscenities. Hours later she was admitted to the mental ward at Baptist Medical Center after police found her wandering down the median strip of Highway 10 stripped of all but her bra and panties.

Garrison did not know of Deborah's fate until three days later when her name appeared on the non-suspicious death list routinely compiled by the homicide division. Her death ruled a suicide warranting no further investigation.

◆

Clay sat in a holding cell chatting with two of the guards on duty awaiting the arrival of his attorney who had just secured bail for his impending release from custody. They were joking about the sad state of play of the newest expansion team of the National Football League New Orleans Saints but all in the trio expressed pride in their city for snagging the franchise in anticipation of the creation of their very own professional football powerhouse.

Clay was outwardly at ease, but terrified at his core. Word drifted through the cellblock the night before about David's untimely death and its implications surrounding Garrison's case. Clay would have to stand alone against Garrison's vitriolic assault. His lawyer assured him often that the evidence was shallow at best and even though the district attorney could establish a business and social connection with David there was no corroborating evidence supporting a plot.

The blurred photo of Oswald with David and his Civil Air Patrol squad was leaked to The *Times Picayune* which displayed it on the front page and quoted Garrison in the caption as saying it provided irrefutable proof of the link. That link was with David, not with Clay who stood apart. Nevertheless, Clay cursed his dead friend for his carelessness. Police found the print in a suit coat pocket hanging in David's closet. No one else in the dance studio cadre was charged, or even named as a witness. Garrison's crusade of nearly two years came down to a handful of witnesses with shoddy claims Clay's lawyer promised would be ripped to shreds once he got them under cross examination. All of this was of little comfort to the man who really knew the truth.

Clay's lawyer arrived at last to break up the football chatter and spring his client to begin preparation for trial. Garrison promised a speedy spectacle. Pressure was mounting on him to bring forth what he maintained was rock solid proof.

◆

The sidewalk café where Robert sat on that Sunday morning was basked in bright sunlight and warmth. After months of practice while incarcerated in Tucson and now while in Mexico City Robert's command of the Spanish language was nearly absolute. He was practicing various dialects to gain greater proficiency in his speech. As he did before he was striving to fit in and adapt effortlessly into another new society to gain its acceptance and further his standing.

As the days before his Mexican pilgrimage in his precious Thunderbird began to fade in his memory and cloud his subconscious Robert assumed a more easy posture. He stopped looking over his shoulder. He'd sunk deeply, he felt, into the culture, spending his days driving through the streets and into the country side, arriving back for evening shopping in the markets, to take in the festivals, the Mariachi concerts, and to study in the libraries self teaching reading of the language and the nuances of the syntax.

Since leaving Tucson Robert made only minor refinements to his appearance. His shoulder length hair and beard was now neatly trimmed and coiffed. His clothing remained modest yet always clean and pressed. Money was of little consequence. Plenty remained in the various banks he utilized across the capital city, none ever questioning the large cash deposits. Gringo dollars were always welcome, whatever the source. There was never a question. He enjoyed the company of strangers. Prostitutes came to him once every week, and he would sit alone at the cafes inviting unfamiliar guests to join him for conversation.

So, it was not a surprise, in truth a pleasure that morning to grant the request of the stunning young Mexican maiden in her yellow sundress, raven black hair and sparkling chocolate eyes to ask to occupy the empty seat at his table. She smiled and spoke of her gratitude saying she had just come from Mass and was dying for strong coffee and a place to rest her sandal shod feet. Their exchange soon became animated. The midday crowd grew less dense as the afternoon crept in. Soon they were the only patrons remaining. The square was nearly deserted.

As Robert was attempting to describe his recent acquisition of an ancient Mayan ingot from an antique dealer nearby, his delightful companion could only laugh and say the shop was known for selling fakes. She urged caution in his next purchase. She then said she had something of equal interest in her shopping bag to show him. She reached down into the bag to retrieve the object. She kept it under the table, playfully teasing him into guessing what it was. Robert joined her game willingly, his face jovial in her presence. The revelation came seconds later. Once, twice, then three times in rapid succession, each time the expression on his face gradually faded from enchantment to disappointment to deepening grimace.

The bullets from the silenced twenty-two caliber automatic pistol penetrated Robert's sternum but stopped short of severing his spine. He lay back in his curved back wrought iron seat as if there was a need to stretch from being in one position too long. Blood began to seep from his chest, spreading red to soil his white linen open neck shirt. His killer stood calmly, slipped on her shoes and placed her and Robert's large cotton napkins over the expanding stain. She walked briskly from the café to the next street corner and gracefully slid into an awaiting white Mercedes sedan to speed off.

Gripped with agony, his pain spawning delirium, Robert thought of Oswald.

Those images on television. The shock on his face when Ruby's shots found their mark.

Robert chuckled at the irony and blood spurted from his lips. He struggled to his feet. His chair tipping over when he stood partially erect. He looked around but no one was there. At this, he didn't care. It was siesta time. He stumbled out onto the sidewalk and set out for his final destination. His blood leaving a spotty trail behind. He grew weaker with each labored step. He did not cry out, only moved forward. Then he was there, his place to rest. He struggled up the steps to the top, and he sat and waited. The doors to the Holy Church of Santa Maria stood beyond his reach. A priest will soon come, Robert thought. A priest to welcome him inside. Anoint him in forgiveness. Robert waited until his last breath. No one ever came.

55

Detective Max Nedbalski parked his unmarked vehicle at the curb just out of view from the window to Bud's office that overlooked Pearl Street. Agent Chester Gold sat in the front passenger seat. They were happy men. The gifts they had to deliver would bring joy.

Agent Gold turned to look into the back seat of the car with the childish Christmas morning-like thought of making sure his presents were both still there, still under the tree. He found they were and got out, walking hurriedly to Bud's front door. Max waited nervously. He spoke quietly to his passengers. "He will love you like you've never been loved before."

Soon Chester and Bud emerged, Bud looking for his gifts and finding them staring back in wondrous disbelief. He sprinted to where they were. He could finally hold them.

Christina and Tonya waited patiently for the man they could only faintly remember, but a man they somehow knew would restore their comfort, their protection, and as Max had said, an unconditional love.

During its penetrating probe into every aspect of Bud Carlson's life, the FBI found his girls. Their names had been changed, their lives in constant turmoil as their mother uprooted them constantly in search of a better life for herself in the arms of a man who only became an illusion. Her friend in the Pontiac vanished long ago.

It took the same judge who took them away fifteen minutes to grant Bud custody of his precious offspring and the jury an hour and a half to find Clay Shaw not guilty. Jim Garrison left office in disgrace. His dreams evaporated; his evidence forever discredited.

56

"Sold! To the gentleman in the third row. Ninety-two thousand five hundred dollars, a bargain to say the least," the elegantly dressed silver haired Barrett Jackson auctioneer announced to the throng of antique car enthusiasts gathered for the annual Palm Beach selloff. "You got a gem of a '63 'Bird; that's all I can say," he added as the black beauty rolled off the platform to make room for a gleaming candy-apple red 1967 Corvette split window fastback.

Theodore "Big Ted" Jamison was happy with his purchase but not ecstatic like others seated around him, many of whom were there to fulfill unmet boyhood dreams of owning the car they could never afford but lusted after during their impoverished youths. Big Ted was an accomplished well-heeled collector and dealer and he lacked emotional attachment to his acquisitions. He wanted the Thunderbird to fill an empty parking space in his line up of Ford's classic sports cars, which occupied his garage. With the purchase his goal of owning every model off the assembly line since 1955 through their first ten years of production had been met. Ted didn't care much for the old 'Birds built after 1965. He thought their style and engineering faltered with the 1966 model so he switched to collecting Jaguars.

At first this particular car concerned Ted because it came from Mexico. The story he got was it was discovered in a locked garage behind a small hacienda in a Mexico City suburb by an estate attorney assigned to settle the affairs of a man who died recently leaving no immediate known heirs. The man had a brother who apparently passed on years before. When they were younger and active, the Garcia boys were known for their matching white linen suits, wide-brimmed Panama hats and radical, mostly anti-American political activism. Ted knew nothing and cared even less about the car's prior owners, only that the vehicle was original in every respect. Original engine, transmission, drive train, seats, dashboard instruments and even the radio had to match perfectly in serial number only to that vehicle for

Ted to even consider it. When the Mexican attorney advertised the 'Bird on E-Bay Ted dispatched his mechanic to the capital city for a personal inspection. The reports came back that the car was flawless. Ted tried to buy it on the spot for fifty thousand dollars but the attorney refused, speculating on a higher possible sale price if it went to auction in the States. Besides, his fee was predicated on the total settlement proceeds which were to be collected by the Mexican government.

Ted's mechanic included one strange element to his descriptive report, however. When he removed the canvass cover and opened the trunk he found a few curious objects. They included a first edition copy of William Manchester's *The Death of a President*; John F. Kennedy's *Profiles in Courage*, a .38 caliber Colt revolver with a single live round in the chamber, a pair of worn-out cowboy boots, and an odd looking iron cross suspended from a bright blue ribbon. The attorney said those items would be sold separately. Ted didn't want them. All he wanted was the perfect "Bird."

Epilogue

Six months before my fateful meeting with Bud Carlson and three weeks before he died doctors had sawed open his chest to perform one of the first, and at that time highly experimental and extremely dangerous, open-heart by-pass surgeries ever performed in the world. After it was over outside the operating room the head surgeon told me that the operation had not gone well.

"We successfully harvested the veins from his legs and after much difficulty performed the grafts. Due to the extent of the disease we did not remove the deteriorated arteries; rather looped the harvested veins over them to restore adequate blood flow." The grim-faced surgeon declared. "However, damage to the heart muscle from the coronary episode was catastrophic. When we examined the heart, it appeared almost black in color from the dead and dying tissue. He has very little time to live. I closed his chest. Take him home and make him comfortable."

Even though it was weak and raspy I was glad to hear his voice on the morning I received his unexpected call. Calls at that hour struck fear that his end had come.

"Not yet. I'm still alive," he said. Could I come to his office? Today, if possible. He had something to tell me.

"What are you doing in your office?"

"Felt like being here. Can you come?"

"Yes, I will be there in two hours." I was a hundred miles south of Denver at the time. It would take me that long to get there.

On that day, as the man I adored more than any other rocked slowly in his big leather office chair, sipping strong black coffee, pausing frequently to cough painfully, and gasping for air to keep the organ that failed him from fluttering to a stop, I first heard the incredible story of the man he knew as Robert Kaye.

When he finished Bud was finally relieved and satisfied. Someone else now knew it.

"Do with it what you can. Take it. Run down the leads. Find him, if he's still alive. Find out who he really was. Tell the world; tell anyone who will listen," he instructed.

Then leaning back in his chair he shook his head, sighed and warned, "You know, most people won't believe you. They made up their minds a long time ago. It's been 10 years. It's old news. But tell it anyway. What the hell. And don't ever forget those binoculars. They're the key."

Bud then slowly rose from his chair and allowed me to help him to an awaiting taxi that would drive him home and back to his bed.

Bud passed away about three weeks later. To serve as flower urns, my mother and I had Bud's favorite pair of western boots bronzed and placed at his gravesite to flank his marble gravestone. I think they were lizard skin. Definitely *Tony Lama.*

There the story sat, untold as I pursued and accomplished a few other things. I ask myself today what kept me from re-telling it much sooner? I did try, however, right after he died. I tried to get someone to listen. My managing editor at the *Pueblo Chieftain* at that time said the newspaper would not fund an investigation. Other media outlets were impressed with the story but declined to pursue it as well. Even back then Kennedy assassination checkout-stand tabloids, fabricated yarns, books and movies alleging outlandish conspiracy theories already lined the bookshelves of many world wide homes and libraries.

Was Bud's account just another hack-kneed attempt to exploit the tragedy? No. This was not fodder for another splashy soon to be discredited headline. He was a good man; an honest man who made a death bed revelation. Why would he lie? He didn't. I know it. Even with that knowledge I could not find enough financial support to run down the leads and find Robert Kaye. Such an effort takes time, a lot of money and a relentless commitment. If it were to be done I had to do it on my own. At the time I simply could not devote months, perhaps years of my life chasing the story. So, right or wrong I allowed Bud's memory of the events to be buried along with him. Life went on without him. Children and careers. Years slipped by. Lame excuses, I know. I'm not sure why, but perhaps like the old, fairly decent journalist I used to be, I needed corroboration. Even with Bud, verification was essential. But I never doubted a word.

In recent years the saga of Robert Kaye began again to eerily obsess my dreams. I found relief by retelling Bud's story to family and some close friends at the occasional dinner party, but in the end I always came away feeling anxious and frustrated.

Certainly today as the 50th anniversary of the tragedy approaches opinion polls still consistently suggest that a vast majority of Americans who know their history do not believe that Lee Harvey Oswald acted alone. I have been among that majority since spending that day with my uncle. There is no doubt in my mind that Oswald had help in carrying out the assassination of President John F. Kennedy. There were others involved; make no mistake. Was a man called Robert Kaye one of them? I think so, but I can't prove it. No one can. The Secret Service and FBI might have, but they chose not to try. Never, to my knowledge, has the name Robert Kaye nor any of his many aliases ever been mentioned in the tens of thousands of pages published or in the hundreds of hours of film produced on the subject.

Was there a reason? .

I admit I didn't take a deep plunge into the darkened abyss of the Kennedy murder mystery like hundreds before me and probably hundreds coming after, each of them searching desperately for that hidden shred of evidence to finally debunk the government's lone gunman conclusion. No, I didn't delve into the massive Kennedy killing library because, in Thunderbird Conspiracy, a novel, my motive was not aimed at proving one way or the other if Oswald acted on his own. I do however present some interesting new, tantalizing theories never published before which might spur another in an endless series of conspiratorial pursuits.

Bud Carlson was real. That's a fact. Robert Kaye was real as far as I know, and I firmly believe Bud's recount of him was real. This is a book of historical fiction. It is however based on the facts presented to me by a man I trusted without reservation. From my imagination I filled in the gaps in Robert Kaye's odyssey through life examining Bud's perception of him and speculating in his absence how and why Robert Kaye became what he was....an obscure but perhaps vital figure in the Kennedy calamity. My purpose here is to tell Bud's story before Robert Kaye entered his life, and how after he did, so profoundly impacted it following this horrendous act of violence.

One thing I always wondered, admittedly seeking independent substantiation, was if any of Robert Kaye's many names would ever show up in any official government document. In some file somewhere. I searched off and on for years. And then along came the long-awaited release of the Kennedy Assassination files by the National Archives. By an Act of Congress, nearly 30 years after President John F. Kennedy lost his life to assassin bullets, the National Archives and Records Administration (NARA) in Washington, DC announced that all of the official records on his killing were being released to the public. The implication of the announcement was stunning to someone like me believing that complete documents, uncensored for everyone to see, would be made available for public inspection. Finally, the whole truth would come out. That was 1992. But not so fast. A few months later another announcement was made. Come to find out that the first batch of documents, many redacted, was only a small portion of what actually exists. The public was told to wait a while longer before a clearer glimpse at the truth might be available. In 1994 the record keepers broke their silence again issuing seven press releases, each announcing that the, "NARA (is) to open additional JFK materials." Three more press announcements saying the same thing were issued in 1995; six in 1996, nothing in 1997, five in 1998 and three in 1999.

In 2000 the NARA made a big splash with, "Lab Tests on Kennedy Assassination Evidence Now Complete." Thirty seven years to complete lab tests?

Nothing much has occurred since then except three announcements in 2004 and 2005 about more materials available for inspection, and then the latest....It will be 2017 before *all* of the files will hit the street; 25 years after they were supposed to. And after that I would expect another press release saying once again....*More to come.*

What's there for inspection already fills a warehouse. NARA says if you want to take the time you are welcome to inspect five million pages of records, (many still redacted) photographs, motion pictures, sound recordings and artifacts all occupying two thousand cubic feet of space. What is there left to withhold, censor or hide all together? I still don't know why they won't release all the files, instead leaking them in bits and pieces. Nonetheless with the aid of modern computer technology I began scanning the millions of pages made public at various times over the years. I found nothing, for so long.

Year after year, press release after press release drove me back to search the national records again for Robert Kaye's or Bud Carlson's names. I tried every variation I could think of using all of the nicknames or aliases that Robert Kaye had given Bud over the three years they knew each other. But each time my search came up empty. *No record. A blank page.*

Then on one Sunday afternoon in 2008 after reading that more material had been released I went to the on-line files again, typing in my search prompts. But this time I added "Denver" as a tag to each inquiry. After three or four tries, there they were. Big as life. After forty years; just as Bud had said.

FBI Case File 124-100110-10403
FBI Case File 124-100014-10224
FBI Case File 186-10036-10297
Teletype Urgent 12-13-63 To Director and SAC, Dallas and Washington Field from SAC El Paso
Dozens more.....
Memorandum to Director: 12/27/63 Oswald, Lee; Denver Office, Unsubstantiated Sighting; No Physical Evidence, Denver
Memorandum to Director: 1/09/64 Oswald, Lee, Kaye, Robert, Sighting, Denver
Memorandum to Director: 4/09/64 Oswald, Lee, Kaye, Robert Activities in Denver
Teletype to Director. 12-13-63, Agent in charge, Weisheit, Jr., US Secret Service contacted man named Robert Kaye.

And on they went, dozens of secret communiqué, an extensive file on a man to my knowledge whose name has never appeared in any official public record before or since. Not one word about him appears in the Warren Commission report or any official publication I can find anywhere, any time.

So what did this exhaustive investigation conclude about Robert Kaye?

*"Kaye has told a wild story of having met a man he believes to be Oswald in early 1963 who hired him to go to Mexico City...*One agent wrote.

Another reported on January 9, 1964 that he interviewed Kaye in Tucson, Arizona, who said, *"Lee gave Kaye $300 in $50 and $20 bills as traveling expenses to go to Mexico City and obtain a package from an unknown man. Kaye was to return this package to Lee in Amarillo, Texas, when Lee would then give Kaye $3,000. Lee alleged to have given Kaye (a) small calendar on which dates were marked. Lee also gave Kaye (a) small slip of paper on which was drawn a map which Kaye was to follow to meet unknown man in Mexico City.*

*"For the information of the Bureau, during the course of a searching interview with Robert Kaye it was determined that he is at times vague beyond belief and when pressed to be more specific he becomes obviously annoyed and arrogant. He is a man of under average stature; gives all the appearances of having an inferiority complex and strives vainly to make up for his insufficiencies by an overactive imagination...*Wrote another.

"Kaye's only explanation for the differences in the stories which he told to the Secret Service Agent in El Paso and the interviewing agents in

Tucson, Arizona, was that he had a very poor memory and had great difficult (sic) in recalling details. He was unable to explain why he considered his memory to be accurate in this instance...... Still another maintained.

"Kaye has told (a) wild story of being approached by a man he believes (to be) Oswald in Denver in early October with proposition that he traveled (sic) to Mexico City to meet unidentified male from whom he was to receive papers which he was to deliver to Amarillo, Texas. Secret Service report did not make any mention of the calendar or map supposedly given to Kaye by Oswald and it is likely this is (a) new figment of his imagination... A particularly skeptical investigator said.

"Despite (the) fact that Kaye's claims as to his activities both before and after assassination have been largely discredited"... Seemed to sum it up.

It doesn't take a reader long to conclude that Federal authorities at that time eventually labeled Robert Kaye, alias Roman Sokolowski, Robert Klonowski, among others, as stark raving mad. Just by the tone of the reports investigators took great pains to disembowel Robert's story, finding him simple minded, nearly illiterate, bizarre, and disoriented. Yet they kept talking to him for months, asking the same questions over and over. The records are clear about that. They wouldn't leave him alone.

Publicly, Lee Harvey Oswald wasn't supposed to have any friends. He was a lone wolf; remember?

There are other things in the file that are equally baffling. Here's the question that will never escape me. If Robert Kaye was a fraud, a scam artist, and glory seeker, as the Feds describe him, why did Federal agents nearly drive my uncle mad for two years after the killing, terrifying him and his family almost daily with threats of imprisonment and ruin? Their harassment almost forced Bud Carlson into bankruptcy. It strained his second marriage to the point of near collapse and probably contributed to his early death. All for what?

Despite only passing references to him in several reports, why was Bud, his wife Jeannie and step-daughter put under twenty-four hour surveillance for months after the assassination? And why was Bud repeatedly hauled down to Denver FBI headquarters to be interrogated incessantly? Perhaps it was just thorough police work; perhaps not. Bud most certainly didn't think so. Bud always thought that the Feds branded Robert a lunatic because they didn't like what he was saying. It didn't quite fit into their rush to judgment about who killed the President and why. But they weren't absolutely sure so they kept up with the investigation and harassment.

There was an agent, very likely a lonely and ostracized man working deep in the official ranks, who was of the same mind as Bud. Bud would never tell anyone who he was. Not even me. He promised this man, who Bud eventually came to know and trust, that he would never reveal his identity. He took that secret to his grave. I respected and admired his steadfastness in that regard. Bud was unsure exactly when the Feds lifted their around the clock watch over him and his family. But shortly before they did, Bud's friend, this agent, pierced the shroud of silence and secrecy that had suffocated them for years.

Bud said he kept asking his unlikely confidant the simple question…Why?

"Why are you still hounding me and my family? Why the harassment? I've told you everything; so many times. The story never changes. It never will."

Finally, perhaps in a moment of weakness or an act of compassion borne from sheer human decency, the agent said, (and Bud remembered this part as if it happened the instant before he said it to me), "The binoculars, man. It was the binoculars. The binoculars we found in Oswald's apartment the night of his capture. That's the link to Kaye and the link to you. You bought them and gave them to Kaye, and Kaye must have given them to Oswald."

Bud Carlson said he knew Robert Kaye would sink into oblivion just as rapidly as he had briefly risen from obscurity. Not because my uncle was a great prognosticator; rather he was told as much in no uncertain terms by the one man in this episode whom he would eventually come to trust and respect. Bud believed this Federal officer was telling him the truth. And he believed the agent believed him as well. Bud Carlson gave the binoculars to Robert Kaye and Robert Kaye gave them to Lee Harvey Oswald, and on that terrible November Friday in Dallas when law enforcement stormed the tiny hovel in which Oswald lived with Marina, they found those binoculars. Right there in the closet. Bud's fingerprints on them, Robert's as well, and of course, there were Oswald's. That's why they hunted Bud down in Albuquerque and slammed him to the hotel room floor shoving a gun in his face, just like they would an assassin or his accomplice. An enormous mountain of weight was lifted from Bud's shoulders when that agent spoke, yet he said he shuttered in terror to think his gift to an employee, and at that time, a friend, might have been used in some fashion to commit murder. Murder of the President. Kaye said he liked bird watching. Strange, Bud thought at the time, but Robert was a strange guy, so he bought him binoculars for his first year anniversary on the job.

"After all of this, most of us don't think you had anything to do with it. Most of us; not all. There are some who will never give it up; some in the Bureau; some outside," Bud quoted the agent as saying. "But remember," Bud said he added, "Take comfort in this. Officially we got our man. We got our killer and he acted alone. There is no Robert Kaye, officially. He does not exist. If he ever surfaces, he will be discredited. Labeled a kook. Irrelevant. There are no binoculars. There never were." But then he added dejectedly, "They may never clear you completely."

So what was I supposed to do with all of this? How was I to tell Bud's story in such a way as to bring him, all the others, and all the events and circumstances surrounding that tragic period in our history to life without it all becoming waste paper, tossed aside, soon forgotten along with all the other trashy conspiracy tales?

The leads are cold, stone cold. I let them drift away. Who's left alive to talk to now that I've finally gotten around to writing about it? How can I do Bud and his story proper justice? Robert Kaye, whomever or whatever he was, may still be alive. That's possible. Who knows? He disappeared, remember? He was never heard from again by anyone Bud knew including Robert's wife whom I called Sophia in the book, although it is not her real name. She moved to Las Vegas the last time Bud heard, and she later vanished from there as well. Bud kept his promise about the trusted agent so I can't talk to him. Who else is left? The only thing I can do is write this book as historical fiction. Fictionalizing Bud's story as a novel but basing it on many hard facts isn't so bad, is it? I tried to fill in the blanks by describing people and things Bud wasn't so sure about. For instance he didn't know details about Robert's life in Hungary, only what he told him about the Hungarian Uprising and his wounds, which by the way, he didn't describe that way to the FBI at least in their written accounts. They got a different story. Their declassified reports say Robert Kaye grew up in Chicago and was Irish and injured in an industrial accident. I think Bud knew better.

So I made up Fodor, Rudolph and his mother. We don't know if he ever lived in Esztergom, Hungary, or exactly how he was wounded. Bud said Robert knew a lot about the Hungarian revolt and he despised the Soviets with an extreme passion. In their very own declassified documents the FBI says Robert was once called Roman and that he developed extreme right wing leanings coupled with genuine fascist beliefs toward the end of his time with Bud. Embracing that bizarre philosophy had to be prompted by someone. Why not from someone like Fodor?

We're not sure how he made it to New Orleans or how long he lived there. We do know that Robert told Bud he visited there often and met some people but we don't know exactly who they were. Maybe there were characters in his life like Mrs. Dionne, Mrs. Claire, Clarence, Bourdeaux, Miss Hattie and the lovely Miss Deborah. We know he was shy and reserved at first but could become hardened, bold and threatening. He was an expert mechanic, and electrician. We know that for a fact. That's why Bud hired him in the first place.

But we don't know where he worked in New Orleans or for whom he worked, so Sigmund Roblinski provides that link. We're not sure if he ever met Clay Shaw or David Ferrie, who the real, and eventually disgraced New Orleans District Attorney Jim Garrison was convinced were the masterminds behind the assassination. That's not me imagining that part of the story.

We do know that Garrison at one time had a strong case against those men, but something happened to destroy the chain of evidence. Garrison's indictment against Shaw and Ferrie came easy. David Ferrie died shortly after the indictments came down from mysterious causes, so he never went to trial but Clay Shaw did. However Shaw never saw the inside of a jail cell. He was acquitted on the jury's first ballot. Garrison became a laughing stock until Oliver Stone tried to resurrect his image in his movie *"JFK"*.

Was there a conspiring snitch in Garrison's office that steered the DA off course? We will never know for sure, so why not make her Deborah? And why not Deborah and Robert? Someone had to lure him into the snake pit.

Based on what he was told by the agent who befriended him Bud strongly believed that Robert was in Dallas on November 22, 1963. We don't know what he did that day for sure but there always has been evidence that Oswald had an escape plan that somehow went array after he walked out the front door of the Texas School Book Depository moments before the police cordoned off the building. Someone was waiting somewhere to help him flee. It could have been Robert. Bud thought it was. Maybe he was right. And now there are many who believe there was a second shooter of Patrolman Tippit. That's explosive. Did Robert pull that deadly trigger instead of Oswald? No one will ever know for sure.

And all those tales about Bud, the tortured man who God snatched from us so soon, were mostly point of fact. He was proud to have sprang from Hank's loins. Vera gave him his short life and Dorothy and Genevieve idolized and pampered him as his sisters. He couldn't wait to leave the farm in Nebraska, but before he did he drank a little too much one night; wrecked his new car and broke his neck. That's what kept him out of the military during the war. Bud was one hell of a salesman and most of the time he made a decent living at it. Much to his initial delight he met Connie. She gave him two gorgeous daughters but took them away and turned that part of his life into a living hell. The divorce was ugly but the child custody case was even uglier until he had to give up the fight and let them go after paying the last legal bill he could afford. In their teenage years he finally got them back. Then Connie came home begging for forgiveness. Thank God he rejected her pitiful pleas. Too bad he didn't live long enough to walk either of his daughters down the aisle. Neither did the coward in the Pontiac, by the way.

My Uncle was never a commodities trader with his father, but Agricultural ventures did go sour for both of them with the slump in farm prices and lack of good jobs in and around Grand Island, Nebraska. Both had to leave town for better opportunities elsewhere. Hank and Bud paid off everyone before they left.

Bud ended up in Denver just like I wrote, and that's where Robert Kaye came looking for work. While he was becoming radicalized and running off to Mexico with a guy he claimed was Oswald, my uncle was building a successful vending machine business and running head long into the stunning Miss Jeannie. He did eventually marry her and despite their trauma at the hands of a suspecting law enforcement community they kept the marriage together through it all. She never wavered in the toughest of times even when the Feds would follow her to the grocery store or watch her through the kitchen window doing dishes. His favorite car was that big black '63 Thunderbird convertible, the one he said Robert was driving when he came to see him that day, but for some reason Bud never bought one. I could never figure that out. Perhaps he grew to hate even the sight of that car. There never was a Max Nedbalski. I made him up for the book but today he's real. He's Bud's great, great nephew, and my grandson. He's five years old.

Bud, you'd love him as much as I do. So, I hope you approve of the way I finally handled all of this.

One last thing, I still watch the National Archives website for new releases of Kennedy Assassination documents, waiting for the day when someone gets around to mentioning those binoculars. Think they ever will? I doubt it, don't you?

With all due respect, and love
The son of Dorothy, Bud's sister

RIP Bud Carlson

Made in the USA
San Bernardino, CA
22 February 2013